Harriet's Favorite

Franklin's Choice

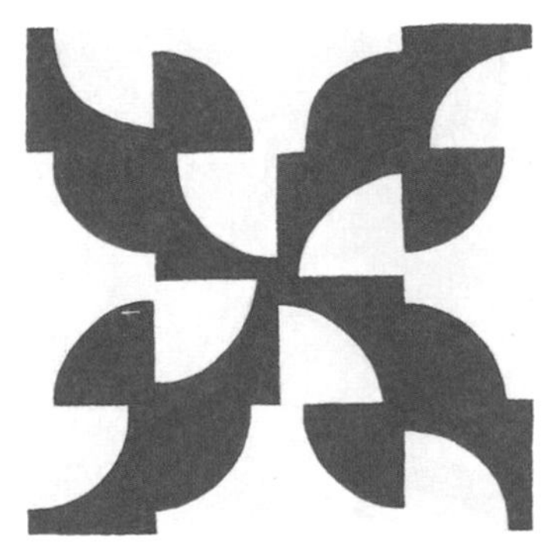
Oregon Trail

Rose of Sharon

Courtyard Quilters

Rocky Road to Salem

ALSO BY JENNIFER CHIAVERINI

The Christmas Quilt

The Sugar Camp Quilt

The Master Quilter

The Quilter's Legacy

The Runaway Quilt

The Cross-Country Quilters

Round Robin

The Quilter's Apprentice

Elm Creek Quilts:
Quilt Projects Inspired by the Elm Creek Quilts Novels

Return to Elm Creek:
More Quilt Projects Inspired by the Elm Creek Quilts Novels

Circle of Quilters

An Elm Creek Quilts Novel

JENNIFER CHIAVERINI

SIMON & SCHUSTER
New York London Toronto Sydney

SIMON & SCHUSTER
Rockefeller Center
1230 Avenue of the Americas
New York, NY 10020

This book is a work of fiction. Names, characters, places, and incidents either are products of the author's imagination or are used fictitiously. Any resemblance to actual events or locales or persons, living or dead, is entirely coincidental.

For information about special discounts for bulk purchases,
please contact Simon & Schuster Special Sales: 1-800-456-6798
or business@simonandschuster.com.

Endpaper illustrations by Melanie Marder Parks

Designed by Lauren Simonetti

Manufactured in the Unites States of America

10 9 8 7 6 5 4 3 2

Library of Congress Cataloging-in-Publication Data
Chiaverini, Jennifer.
Circle of quilters : an elm creek quilts novel / Jennifer Chiaverini.
p. cm.
1. Compson, Sylvia (Fictitious character)—Fiction. 2. Female friendship—
Fiction. 3. Quiltmakers—Fiction. 4. Quilting—Fiction. 5. Quilts—Fiction.
6. Women—Fiction. I. Title.
PS3553. H473C7 2006
813'.54—dc22
2005054092

ISBN-13: 978-0-7432-6020-6
ISBN-10: 0-7432-6020-1

To Nicholas and Michael Chiaverini.
I love you a million billion.
I love you infinity.

Acknowledgments

I am more thankful for the friendship, dedication, and expertise of Denise Roy, Maria Massie, and Rebecca Davis than I could ever adequately express. I am also grateful for Annie Orr's tireless efforts behind the scenes and the beautiful artistry of Honi Werner and Melanie Marder Parks. How fortunate I am to work with such brilliant, talented women!

Hugs and thanks to Lisa Cass and Jody Gomez, who cared for my boys and gave me time to write, and to Anne Spurgeon, who laughs with me, commiserates with me, and answers obscure historical questions with remarkable speed and accuracy.

Many thanks to Brenda Papadakis and Ami Simms for inspiring me with their quilts, creativity, and contributions to the quilting world. Thanks also to Lee Keyser for her suggestions for the romantic date in Seattle that appears in this book, and to Joelle Reeder of Moxie Design Studios, who created my fabulous new website.

Thank you to the friends and family who have supported and encouraged me through the years, especially Geraldine Neidenbach, Heather Neidenbach, Nic Neidenbach, Virginia and Edward Riechman, and Leonard and Marlene Chiaverini.

Above all else, I am grateful to my husband, Marty, and my sons, Nicholas and Michael. Whenever the frustrations, disappointments, and loneliness of the writing life get me down, you remind me that I already have everything I ever wanted.

Circle of Quilters

Are You an Accomplished Quilter Seeking a New Adventure?

Seeking qualified applicants to join the circle of quilters at the country's finest and most popular quilters' getaway, located in beautiful rural central Pennsylvania. Applicants should demonstrate mastery of two or more of the following subjects: hand piecing, machine piecing, machine quilting, pattern drafting, computer-aided design, quilt history, quilted garments, hand dyeing, or other notable quilting technique. Seasonal work, flexible schedule, and/or live-in arrangement available if desired. Teaching experience and sense of humor required. Ability to tolerate quirky coworkers, emotional turmoil, and the occasional minor disaster highly recommended. If that didn't scare you off, send résumé and portfolio, including sample lesson plans for two courses, photos of completed quilts, and letters of recommendation from at least three students to

Elm Creek Quilt Camp
Attention: Sarah McClure
Elm Creek Manor
Waterford, Pennsylvania
16807

ADA EOE

Chapter One
Maggie

Every morning after breakfast, the Courtyard Quilters gathered in the recreation room of Ocean View Hills Retirement Community and Convalescent Center to quilt, swap stories about their grandchildren, and gossip about the other residents. Nothing escaped their notice or judgment, and woe be it to the new resident or visitor who pulled up a chair to their circle uninvited. No one made that mistake twice, not if they coveted the friendship of seventy-year-old Helen Stonebridge, the leader of the circle of quilters and the most popular woman in the facility.

Within days of coming to work at Ocean View Hills—a name she had trouble saying with a straight face considering they were in Sacramento—Maggie Flynn joined the ranks of Mrs. Stonebridge's admirers. Maggie had heard other members of the staff mention the woman as a sort of unofficial leader of the residents, but it wasn't until she witnessed Mrs. Stonebridge in action that Maggie understood how influential she truly was. On that day, Maggie was sorting art supplies in the recreation room not far from where the quilters gathered every morning after breakfast.

Their conversation turned to an altercation in the cafeteria the previous day in which a certain Mrs. Lenore Hicks had knocked over another resident in her haste to be first in line.

"She plowed right into Rita Talmadge's walker," tsked one of the quilters. "Rita tumbled head over heels, and Lenore didn't even stop to help her up."

"Lenore must have seen the banana cream pie on the dessert tray," another quilter explained. "Never get between that woman and pie."

"Rita could hardly dodge out of the way," said the first quilter indignantly. "She's had three hip replacements."

Maggie was puzzling out how someone with only two hips could have three hip replacements when the youngest of the group, Mrs. Blum, piped up, "This isn't the first time Lenore's bumped into a lady with a walker. Remember Mary Haas and the Mother's Day brunch? Margaret Hoover and the reflecting pool? Velma Tate and the Christmas tree?"

The quilters considered and agreed that Lenore did appear to have a habit of barreling into the less agile residents of Ocean View Hills. So far none of her victims had suffered more than bumps and bruises—and in Margaret Hoover's case, an unexpected al fresco bath—but if the pattern continued, it was only a matter of time before someone broke a bone.

"I would be less concerned if these incidents didn't happen so frequently," mused Mrs. Stonebridge. "It's also troubling that Lenore didn't help Rita to her feet. No pie is worth adding insult to injury."

The other ladies waited expectantly while Mrs. Stonebridge deliberated, her needle darting through two small squares of fabric with small, even stitches. Maggie found that she, too, had stopped sorting out watercolor paints in anticipation of the verdict.

After a few moments, Mrs. Stonebridge spoke again. "Dottie,

would you please tell Lenore that I would enjoy chatting with her whenever she has a spare moment?"

Mrs. Blum, the spriest of the group, nodded and hurried off. Maggie suspected that Mrs. Stonebridge expected an immediate response despite the casual wording of the request, and sure enough, Mrs. Blum returned several minutes later with a tall, solidly built woman with a slight stoop to her shoulders and a look of puzzled wariness in her eye.

Mrs. Stonebridge greeted her with a warm smile. "Oh, hello, Lenore. Won't you sit down?"

Mrs. Hicks nodded and seated herself in the chair Mrs. Blum had vacated. Mrs. Blum frowned and glanced about for another chair to drag over into the circle, but the only empty seats were heavy armchairs near the fireplace. She folded her arms and stood instead.

"You wanted to speak to me?" asked Mrs. Hicks, anxious.

"Yes, dear," said Mrs. Stonebridge. "You see, I'm worried about you."

Mrs. Hicks, who had clearly expected to be reprimanded for some forgotten offense, relaxed slightly. "Worried? About me? Why?"

"I'm concerned that you might have an inner ear disorder. You seem to have some balance problems. I'm referring, of course, to your unfortunate collision with Rita in the cafeteria yesterday. Anyone can have an accident, but you must have been feeling especially unsteady on your feet to be unable to help Rita up after you had knocked her down."

"Oh," said Mrs. Hicks, uneasy. "Well, I was in a hurry, you see, and her friends were there to help her, so I thought she was all right."

"It turns out she was," Mrs. Stonebridge reassured her. "But I'm sure you saw that for yourself when you went back later to apologize."

Mrs. Hicks said nothing, a guilty, pained expression on her face.

"Oh. I see," said Mrs. Stonebridge, sorrowful. "Well, I'm sure your balance troubles are nothing to worry about, but you should get yourself checked out just in case."

"I'll see the doctor today," said Mrs. Hicks in a small voice.

"And—this is just a thought—since poor Rita is still bruised from her fall, perhaps you could bring her meals to her until she recovers."

"The busboys can do that, can't they?"

"It will mean so much more coming from you, don't you agree?" Mrs. Stonebridge smiled. "Should we say . . . a month? Do you think that would do?"

Mrs. Hicks agreed, and for the next month, three times a day, Rita Talmadge waited at her favorite lunch table while a repentant Mrs. Hicks brought her meals to her on a tray. Mrs. Talmadge was satisfied, and Mrs. Hicks, who received a clean bill of health from the staff physician, learned to be more courteous of her fellow residents.

Maggie marveled at the simple elegance of Mrs. Stonebridge's solution and how well it restored harmony to Ocean View Hills—and at how willingly Mrs. Hicks and Mrs. Talmadge had complied. Over time Maggie learned that conflicts were often resolved with Mrs. Stonebridge's guidance and she found herself thinking that it was a shame the former professor of anthropology could not lend her services to heads of state in troubled regions of the world. Mrs. Stonebridge read the *Sacramento Bee* daily and the *New York Times* on Sunday, and her opinions on world events were always thoughtful and well reasoned. At least Maggie thought so. She had no doubt Mrs. Stonebridge could offer brilliant and graceful solutions to conflicts around the globe if only political leaders knew where to find her—and if those same leaders could be persuaded to submit to her decisions with the same humility and desire for harmony as the residents of Ocean View Hills.

Since Mrs. Stonebridge kept herself apprised of events in the lives of the staff members with the same thoughtful diligence she applied to her fellow residents and to world events, when Maggie's personal life took an unexpected turn, she decided to tell Mrs. Stonebridge right away. She would ferret out the truth eventually anyway, and Maggie would not want to hurt her feelings by having her hear it secondhand.

On the morning after her twenty-fifth birthday, Maggie came into work early so she would have time to deliver the news before her shift started. She found the Courtyard Quilters gathered in the recreation room, their chairs arranged in a circle in front of the windows with the view of the garden, just like always. Mrs. Stonebridge looked up from her sewing to smile at her. "Well, there's the birthday girl. How was your party last night?"

"It was all right," said Maggie. After work, she had met her two best friends for happy hour at La Hacienda, where they filled up on free nachos, sipped margaritas, and discussed the men at the bar—at least her friends did. Maggie merely played along, pretending to admire the cute guy in the tan suit who had smiled at her. She had little interest in meeting someone new a mere four hours after breaking Brian's heart.

"Well?" inquired Mrs. Blum, trying to get a good look at Maggie's left hand, which she quickly concealed in her pocket. "Did he pop the question or didn't he? Don't leave us in suspense."

"He didn't," Maggie said. "We broke up."

The Courtyard Quilters' exclamations of astonishment and dismay brought an orderly running from another room. Mrs. Stonebridge waved him away with a shake of her head and a reassuring word.

"That louse," said one of the quilters. "I always knew he was no good."

"He's a good man," Maggie defended him. "He's just not the right man."

"How can you call him a good man after he broke your heart?"

said Mrs. Blum, tears in her eyes. "And I've already started your wedding quilt!"

"I warned you not to," said another quilter. "That's bad luck. Never start a wedding quilt until you've seen the engagement ring on the bride-to-be's finger."

"He didn't break up with me," explained Maggie. "I broke up with him."

This time, the quilters responded with exclamations of incredulity. "It's not because of that sense of humor thing, is it?" demanded one. "Because that's a lot of malarkey. Who cares if a man laughs at your jokes?"

"That's not it." At least, that wasn't the only reason, although Maggie had always been troubled by how out of sync their senses of humor were. She could not remember a single time in three years that any of her small witticisms or amusing anecdotes had made Brian laugh. Smile politely, perhaps, but not laugh out loud in pleasure or joy. If he had no sense of humor at all, she could have excused it, but he laughed loudly enough at movies—even dramas—and at his friends' corny jokes. What made a person laugh spoke volumes about one's way of looking at the world. Brian's stoic response to things that amused Maggie made her feel as if they were gazing upon the same landscape but facing opposite directions.

She understood the Courtyard Quilters' astonishment. In their three years together, she and Brian had occasionally discussed marriage, but Maggie had assumed their discussions were purely hypothetical. They had attended friends' weddings and confided how they intended to do things differently when their time came—but neither of them explicitly said that they were talking about marrying the other. Then came the day Brian's mother invited Maggie to try on her late mother-in-law's emerald engagement ring, a treasured family heirloom. "You'll need to get it sized," she had advised her son as the ring slipped too easily past Maggie's knuckle.

Inexplicably, Maggie had been seized by panic. She quickly removed the ring and replaced it in the jewelry box, managing a fleeting smile for Brian's mother. Had everything been decided without her? Brian's family seemed to assume that he would propose and that when he did, that she would accept. The thought filled her with dread. She liked Brian; she liked him very much. He was friendly and cute and loyal and easy to please—"All qualities one would look for in a golden retriever," Mrs. Stonebridge had remarked only weeks ago, when Maggie confided in her after the engagement ring incident. "But do you love him?"

Maggie wasn't sure. She enjoyed spending time with him and believed they could have a decent, steady life together. But she had to believe there was something more, something greater, in store for her. It was unbearable to think that she had nothing more to look forward to but a good old reliable ordinary life.

She had hoped for more time to sort things out, but as her birthday approached, Brian hinted that he had a very special evening planned. He reserved a table at the finest restaurant in Sacramento two weeks in advance, and she found a bottle of expensive champagne hidden in the back of his refrigerator. Alarmed, Maggie began making excuses not to see him, but he knew her shifts, her haunts, her home so well that he merely showed up wherever he knew she would be, forlorn and determined to put things right. He was so hurt and bewildered by her sudden, inexplicable coolness that she knew she would never have the courage to turn down his proposal. So she broke up with him before he had a chance to ask. Worse yet, she broke up with him by email, which was so cowardly of her that she couldn't admit it to the quilters.

"What was it, then?" asked Mrs. Blum, bewildered. "Brian seemed like such a nice young man."

"He was. He is," said Maggie. "But he's not the one."

"Maybe he's not the one but he's good enough," retorted one of the quilters, whom Maggie knew had never married.

"Hester, you won't change her mind," said Mrs. Stonebridge. "Maggie's holding out for true love."

"As you should," said another quilter, wistful. She was famous among the residents for her five marriages and four divorces. "I didn't, and look where it got me."

"I did," said Mrs. Blum. "I was blessed that I met my true love when I was only seventeen. He's out there, Maggie dear. You'll know him when you meet him."

"In the meantime, you'll always have us," said Mrs. Stonebridge. And since Mrs. Stonebridge seemed to think Maggie had made the right decision, everyone else thought so, too, and she never heard another word of dismay or disapproval on the subject.

Two days later, Maggie walked home from the bus stop after work, dreading the thought of spending the rest of the evening alone packing up Brian's scattered belongings. He had already returned a carton of her own things—books and CDs, an old toothbrush anyone else would have thrown out. She would have to return the faded green sweater she had borrowed from him so long ago that he had probably forgotten it had ever been his. It had been her favorite, but she could not bear to put it on anymore.

Maggie reached her own street and passed a middle-aged couple cleaning up after a garage sale. More to procrastinate than to hunt for bargains, she browsed through some books and old vinyl albums stacked in boxes on a card table. She found a copy of Brian's favorite Moody Blues album and had to turn away. At the next table were several folded baby blankets in pink and yellow gingham. She moved on down the aisle and had nearly summoned up enough fortitude to go home when a glimpse of faded patchwork brought her to a stop.

It was an old quilt draped indifferently over a table. Intrigued, Maggie studied the patterns as best as she could without moving the tagged glassware displayed upon it. The two quilts she had made in her lifetime—one a Girl Scout badge requirement, the other a gift for her sister's firstborn—by no means made her an expert on quilts, but she knew at once that this quilt was unique, a sampler of many rows of different, unfamiliar blocks. The Courtyard Quilters would probably be able to identify each pattern easily—if they could see the pieces clearly enough through the layers of dirt.

"How much is this?" she called to the woman running the garage sale.

"That?" The woman dusted off her hands and drew closer. "You mean the quilt?"

"Yes, please. Is it for sale?"

The woman looked dubious. "We were just using it to hide an ugly table. I guess I'll take five bucks for it."

Maggie reached into her purse. "Are you sure?"

"Are you?" the woman countered. "Don't you want to take a better look at it first? It's not in very good shape."

Maggie agreed, though she had already decided to take the quilt home. They carefully moved the glassware and lifted the quilt from the table. The woman held it up so that Maggie could examine it. It was filthy; a good shake flung up a cloud of dust but left the surface as grimy as before. The woman apologized for its condition and explained that it had been kept in the garage since they moved to the neighborhood twenty-six years earlier. Her mother-in-law had bought it at an estate auction, and when she tired of it, she gave it to her son to keep dog hair off the car seats when he took his German shepherds to the park. Still, it was free of holes, tears, and stains, and the geometric patterns of the blocks were striking.

Maggie paid the woman, folded the quilt gently, and carried it home. There she moved the coffee table aside, spread the quilt on the living room carpet, and studied it. All one hundred of the two-color blocks were unique, and each had been pieced or appliquéd from a different print fabric and a plain background fabric that might have been white once, but had discolored with age and neglect. Along one edge, embroidered in thread that had faded to pale brown barely distinguishable from the background cloth, were the words "Harriet Findley Birch. Lowell, Mass. to Salem, Ore. 1854."

The discovery astounded her. How had a beautiful 133-year-old quilt ended up as a tablecloth at a garage sale?

The next morning she took the quilt to Ocean View Hills, and on her first break, she hurried to the recreation room to show it to the Courtyard Quilters. They were as excited and amazed as she had anticipated. "This is a remarkable find," said Mrs. Stonebridge, bending over to examine a block composed of sixteen tiny triangles. "What an impressive assortment of fabrics, and what care she must have given to every stitch for the quilt to have held up so well through the years."

"This is a genuine treasure," exclaimed Mrs. Blum. "Here's a LeMoyne Star block, here's a Chimney Sweep. . . . Hmm. Here's one I've never seen."

The other Courtyard Quilters drew closer for a better look, but no one recognized the pattern.

"I wonder who Harriet Findley Birch was," said Mrs. Stonebridge. "She had an excellent sense of proportion and contrast."

The other quilters agreed, and one added, "Maybe if you found out more about the quilt, you could find out more about her. Or vice versa."

"And of course you must find out how to care for such a precious antique," said Mrs. Stonebridge. "Well, my dear, it seems you have yourself a research project, just in time for the weekend."

On Saturday Maggie went to the Cal State Sacramento library to search for books on preserving antique quilts. She found a few books of patterns and others with old black-and-white photos of traditional quilts, but none with the information she sought. A librarian suggested she contact a professor in the art department, so she made an appointment the next day during her lunch hour. After viewing the quilt, the professor put her in touch with a friend, a museum curator in San Francisco named Grace Daniels. Maggie had to take a day off work to meet with her, but the ninety-mile drive from Sacramento was well worth it. The curator confirmed that the quilt was indeed a rare and unusual find. Grace offered to clean it properly for Maggie in exchange for permission to allow the museum's photographer to take a photo for their archives and for information about the quilt's provenance.

Maggie agreed, and the next day she returned to the home where the garage sale had taken place. The woman was surprised to see her again, but invited her inside to talk about the quilt. She called her mother-in-law, but all she remembered was that she had bought it at an estate sale run by an auction house in Bend, Oregon, about 130 miles southeast of Salem.

Maggie returned to the library and searched microfiche versions of all the phone books for the state of Oregon. She listed every Findley and Birch she could find, beginning with the Salem area, then Bend, and then working outward. It was slow, painstaking work that consumed several weekends while she waited for Grace Daniels to finish tending to the quilt.

Starting at the top of her list, she phoned the Findleys and Birches and asked if they knew of a Harriet Findley Birch, a quilter originally from Lowell, Massachusetts. Most said they had never heard of her; a few mentioned other Harriets much too young to be the one Maggie sought. One man said he did not know any Harriets, but he knew several Harrys she could call.

"Why would anyone think information about a Harry Birch would be useful?" Maggie asked the Courtyard Quilters one day when she found time to run down to the recreation room to update them on her progress—or lack thereof. "This is impossible. I should have known I wouldn't turn up anything."

"You can't give up now," protested Mrs. Blum. "Not after piquing our curiosity. Our old hearts can't take it."

"Don't play the 'We're so fragile, have pity on us' card on me," Maggie teased. "I saw you doing the polka in the library with Mr. Maniceaux not two weeks ago."

"Oh." A faint pink flush rose in Mrs. Blum's cheeks. "You saw that, did you?"

"Don't abandon your project so soon," urged Mrs. Stonebridge. "Someone on that list might be a descendant of Harriet Findley Birch. You'll never know if you don't call."

Maggie feared that it would be a waste of time, but she promised the Courtyard Quilters she would consider it.

A week later, curiosity and a sense of obligation to the Courtyard Quilters as well as the museum curator compelled her to resume her calls. Two-thirds of the way through the names and numbers she had collected, she reached a man who said that his great-grandmother's name was Harriet Findley Birch. "When I was a kid," he said, "my grandmother took me to see Harriet Findley Birch's grave, not far from our original family homestead in Salem. It's a tradition in our family, a pilgrimage we make when we're old enough to appreciate her."

Thrilled, Maggie told the man about the quilt she had found and asked him to send whatever information she could about his great-grandmother. He agreed, but the information Maggie received in the mail a week later was disappointingly scanty. Harriet Findley was born in 1830 or 1831 in rural Massachusetts. She married Franklin Birch in 1850 and traveled west along the Oregon Trail sometime after that. She had six children, only two of whom survived to adulthood.

The next week Maggie returned to the museum. The quilt had been so beautifully restored she almost did not recognize it. Her information about the quilt's provenance seemed hopelessly inadequate compensation for Grace Daniels's work, but the curator brushed off Maggie's apologies. She had made a few discoveries of her own after contacting a colleague at the New England Quilt Museum in Lowell, Massachusetts.

The Lowell curator had not heard of the Harriet Findley Birch quilt, but she had posed an interesting theory. The more than one hundred unique fabrics in the quilt suggested that Harriet had ready access to a wide variety of cottons. Though she could have saved scraps for years or traded with friends, it was also possible that she had worked in one of Lowell's cotton mills before her marriage. A mill girl could have collected scraps off the floor that otherwise would have been swept up and discarded, and before long acquired more than enough for a quilt. Grace's colleague was not convinced that Harriet had been a mill girl, however, because existing diaries of mill girls from Harriet's era rarely mentioned quilting as a pleasurable pastime. Instead these young women new to the excitement of the city spent their precious off hours enjoying lectures, exhibitions, and other cultural events outside of the boardinghouses where they lived.

"I don't suppose we'll ever know for certain," said Grace.

Maggie reluctantly agreed they were unlikely to learn more.

She took the precious quilt home and draped it over her bed. She sat in a chair nearby and gazed at it lovingly, but with an ache of regret. The more she learned how rare and precious the quilt was, the more she realized she had no right to keep it.

But the extra print the museum's photographer had made for her was not enough.

She bought colored pencils, graph paper, and a ruler and began drafting the beloved little blocks, imagining Harriet Findley Birch sketching the originals so long ago. Had she worked on her quilt on the front porch of her boardinghouse, enjoying the fresh air after a fourteen-hour shift in the stifling mill? Had she sewn in her parents' front parlor, envying the confident, independent mill girls who passed by her window on their way to work?

One Saturday morning after she had drawn ten blocks, Maggie visited a quilt store the Courtyard Quilters had recommended, the Goose Tracks Quilt Shop, to purchase fabric and sewing tools. She felt too shy to ask any of the busy customers or saleswomen for help, so she wandered through the aisles scanning the bolts for fabrics that looked like Harriet's. She chose ten, carried them awkwardly to the cutting table, and asked the shop owner to cut her enough of each one to make a six-inch quilt block.

"Okay," the woman said carefully, clearly recognizing her as a novice but not wishing to discourage her. "Do you think a quarter of a yard will do? An eighth?"

Maggie had no idea, but just in case, she asked for quarter-yard cuts.

"We have fat quarters over there if you're interested," the woman said, gesturing with her scissors toward stacked rows of baskets full of rolled bundles of fabric. "What are you making?"

"A sampler."

"Bring some of your finished blocks along next time. I'd love to see them."

Flattered, Maggie agreed, but her quilting skills were so rusty she wasn't sure she wanted to show her handiwork to anyone. Fortunately, when she told the Courtyard Quilters about her project, they eagerly offered her a refresher course in the art of quilting by hand. With their assistance, she relearned how to make a precise running stitch, how to appliqué, how to sew perfectly smooth curves, and how to set pieces into an angle. Breaks and lunch hours she usually passed on her own she now spent in the company of the Courtyard Quilters. By the time she finished making her eighth block, she had earned a chair of her own among the circle of quilters.

A few weeks after her first visit to the Goose Tracks Quilt Shop, when Maggie had completed ten blocks and had sketched the second row of ten, she returned for more fabric. This time she knew exactly what she needed and chose from the baskets of fat quarters with confidence. The shop owner recognized her and asked how her sampler was progressing. Maggie placed the ten little blocks on the counter, her pride in her work abruptly vanishing as other customers gathered around to look. "I'm just a beginner," she apologized, fighting the urge to sweep the blocks back into her purse. To her surprise, the other quilters admired her work and insisted they never would have guessed she was a beginner.

"What do you call this pattern?" asked one of the women, indicating a five-pointed star.

"I don't know," said Maggie. "I'm copying blocks I found in an antique quilt."

With prompting from the quilters, the whole story of Harriet Findley Birch's quilt came out. The women marveled at Maggie's lucky find and begged to be allowed to see Harriet's quilt for themselves, so Maggie agreed to meet them at the shop the following Saturday.

In the interim, she completed five more blocks and sketched a dozen more in anticipation of her return to the quilt shop. The women she had spoken to the previous week must have told their friends, because more than twice the number of people she had expected were there, eager to admire Harriet Findley Birch's masterpiece. After seeing the original version, several of the quilters told Maggie that they respected her courage for taking on such a daunting project, which would surely take years to complete. Until that moment, Maggie had not thought of how much time she would need to invest in her replica. She simply wanted one she could keep.

Harriet's quilt began to consume more and more of Maggie's life. She sketched blocks in the morning before leaving for Ocean View Hills. She sewed by hand with the Courtyard Quilters on her lunch hour. After work she made templates, or read books about the mill girls of Lowell, or tracked down leads at the library, longing to know more of Harriet Findley Birch's story. Her work friends complained that they never saw her anymore, so she made time for them when she could. They did not understand her new fascination and tentatively suggested she start dating again. "I don't have time," she told them.

And then came a day she had long dreaded: the day she finished sketching the one hundredth sampler block.

She called the woman from the garage sale and arranged to meet her. She carefully typed up everything she had learned about the quilt, including her unconfirmed theories about the life of Harriet Findley Birch. The woman's eyes lit up when she saw the folded bundle in Maggie's arms. "I was hoping you would bring it by to show me after you restored it," she exclaimed, holding her front door open and ushering Maggie inside.

"I didn't bring it just to show you," said Maggie. "It's worth much more than I paid for it and I think in all fairness I should return it to you. Or, if you're willing, I would be very grateful if you would allow me to keep the quilt and pay you the difference."

"Don't be silly," said the woman. "It sat in my garage for all those years and I did nothing with it. Thank goodness you rescued it before it was nothing more than a rag."

"But . . ." Maggie hesitated. "You could probably sell it for much more than what I paid you."

"Well, certainly, *now*. Thanks to you. You're a sweet girl, but you don't owe me anything for this quilt. You bought it fair and square, and if you decide to sell it for a profit, then more power to you."

Grateful, Maggie told the woman everything she had learned about the quilt and felt herself at ease for the first time in months. But the feeling did not last. The next day she phoned Jason Birch and offered the quilt to him, the only descendant of Harriet Findley Birch she had been able to locate.

"That would be awesome," Jason Birch replied. "I'd love to have that quilt."

"Okay," said Maggie, heart sinking. "Should I send it to you, or would you prefer to pick it up? I would hate to risk losing it in the mail—my heart nearly stops just thinking about it. But if the drive is too inconvenient, I could insure the package for a lot of money to encourage them to keep track of it."

"When you put it like that . . ." Jason hesitated. "I should at least reimburse you for your expenses."

"I bought it for five dollars at a garage sale."

"What? Five bucks? In that case, keep it."

Maggie was tempted to thank him and hang up, but she couldn't. She could not let him turn down her offer because he believed the quilt was an old rag. "I had the quilt cleaned by an expert and I know it's worth much more than what I paid for it. I could have it appraised if you like."

"No. You know what? It's not like my family *lost* Harriet's quilt. One of us chose to sell it, and that choice has consequences. You should keep it. It's obviously important to you. I'll make you a deal: You keep the quilt, but let me know anything you learn about my great-grandmother."

"I'll do that," Maggie promised, grateful.

Now that Harriet Findley Birch's quilt was truly hers, the original impetus for sewing her replica was gone, but Maggie enjoyed her project too much to abandon it. Every week she stitched a few more blocks; every Saturday she met with the regulars at the quilt shop to show off her progress. A few of them asked whether she'd mind if they tried their hand at a few of the patterns. Flattered, Maggie agreed to share her drawings with them. She had completed eighty-four of the blocks and had already begun sewing them into rows.

A year and a half after discovering Harriet's quilt at the garage sale, Maggie completed her quilt top. During her next lunch hour, she layered and basted it on the Ping-Pong table in the Ocean View Hills recreation room. Many of the residents gathered around to admire her work while the Courtyard Quilters threaded needles and helped her baste the top, batting, and backing together. Their enjoyment salvaged what had otherwise been an unpleasant day. At the morning staff meeting, the director informed them that their parent company had sold them off to an HMO, one with a reputation for slashing budgets and cutting staff. Maggie had an excellent record and the faith of her supervisors, but those accomplishments suddenly seemed inconsequential.

When new management took over a few months later, Maggie kept her job, but ten of her coworkers, including her direct supervisor, were laid off. Maggie was shaken enough to consider canceling her long-anticipated vacation to Lowell, Massachusetts, to research Harriet Findley Birch's life, but she had already purchased her airline tickets and people were expecting her. Postponing her trip might help prove her commitment to her job at a critical hour, but with Ocean View Hills in such disarray, the ideal time for a vacation might never come.

"Go," Mrs. Stonebridge commanded. "You've been wanting to do this for so long. You'll regret it later if you cancel your plans."

"We won't let them fire you while you're gone," promised Mrs. Blum. When the other quilters looked at her in exasperation, she quickly added, "Not that you're in any danger. That's just silly."

It didn't seem silly to Maggie, but finally she realized she could not cancel a trip that had been so many months in the planning. In Massachusetts, she spent a week admiring the fall foliage, exploring the local quilt shops, and sharing Harriet's quilt with the curator of the New England Quilt Museum. The curator in turn introduced Maggie to local historians and a professor who had extensively researched the history of the cotton mills. He was able to identify more than twenty of the cotton prints in Harriet's quilt as fabrics made in the early nineteenth century by the Merrimack Manufacturing Company, and he promised to see what else he could find in his university's extensive historical archives.

The visit was over far too soon, but Maggie returned home determined to complete her own quilt. The Courtyard Quilters had identified many of the traditional patterns for her, but there were many others none of them had ever seen, nor could find in any quilt pattern reference book. Maggie invented names of her own, inspired by Harriet's imagined life—Oregon Trail, Rocky Road to Salem, Mill Girls, Lowell Crossroads, Franklin's Choice.

On the same day Maggie finished sewing the binding on her quilt, the staff of Ocean View Hills were offered the opportunity to accept a ten percent pay cut or a pink slip. With great misgivings, Maggie chose the pay cut. She loved her job but wondered how much longer she would be able to keep it.

She forgot her worries for a time on Saturday, when she displayed her completed quilt at the Goose Tracks Quilt Shop. Her new friends were there, as well as many other quilters who had heard through the grapevine that she might bring the finished quilt that day. They admired and praised her work, and took photos—not only of the quilt, but of Maggie posed beside the quilt, and of themselves with Maggie in front of the quilt. Several encouraged her to enter it in a quilt show, but Maggie thought of how far her quilting skills had come since she began the quilt and shuddered to think what a judge might say about her first blocks.

After the group broke up, Lois, the quilt shop owner, came over for a closer look. "It's lovely," she said. "What are you going to call it?"

"My Journey with Harriet," said Maggie. "Do you think that's all right?"

"I think it's perfect, but it doesn't matter what I think. It's your quilt." Lois bent forward to study one of the blocks more closely. "I was wondering if you would be interested in teaching a class here in the shop. So many of my customers have admired your quilt. I'm sure they'd want you to show them how you did it."

"I've never taught quilting," said Maggie. "I'm not even a very experienced quilter. I'm just a motivated beginner."

Lois shrugged. "I don't care if you just started quilting last week. If you can make a quilt like this, you have something to share. I'll pay you, of course."

Maggie thought of her recent pay cut, summoned up her courage, and agreed.

Almost immediately, she wished she had not. What if no one signed up for the class? What if the students mocked her graph paper sketches and cardstock templates? But she needed the extra money, and she understood completely the desire other quilters might have to re-create Harriet's quilt for themselves. If they wanted her help, she couldn't ignore them.

In the month leading up to her first class, Maggie redrafted some of the blocks and designed templates. She wrote lesson plans and made new versions of the first five blocks she planned to teach, this time using popular jewel tones that she thought would appeal more to her students. If she had any. Lois said that the classroom held a maximum of twenty students, but a typical class at the shop enrolled half that number. Maggie fervently hoped for at least five. She would not break even, but at least the classroom would not be completely empty.

On the evening of her first class, Maggie drove to the Goose Tracks Quilt Shop and found the parking lot full. Lois met her at the door, shaking her head. "I warned people to sign up early, but no one ever believes me. The waiting list is already twelve deep, so if someone doesn't show up, let me know right away, okay?"

Struck speechless, Maggie nodded and made her way through the store with her box of quilts, blocks, and handouts. Twenty students awaited her in the classroom. They murmured with expectation as she went to the front and unpacked her box of supplies. She started class by displaying Harriet Findley Birch's quilt and was stunned when the students burst into applause. As she explained the general structure of the course and took in their eager nods, a glow of warmth began to melt away her fears. She was not alone in her admiration for Harriet Findley Birch's magnificent creation. Just like the Courtyard Quilters, the women gathered here felt the same way.

With each week, she felt more assured and confident in front of the classroom. Each week she demonstrated several blocks, which her students began in class and completed at home. When the course ended, her students begged Lois to create an advanced class especially for them, so Maggie agreed to teach them some of Harriet's more difficult patterns while repeating her first course for beginners. After those courses concluded, she added Harriet's Journey III to her schedule. The local quilt guild invited her to speak about the quilt, and she did so, not realizing until they handed her a check afterward that they had intended to pay her. The guild must have enjoyed her presentation, because they recommended her to another guild, who recommend her to another, until it seemed that every quilt guild within two hundred miles of Sacramento had sent her an eager invitation.

Not long after her first class of students began bringing their own completed Harriet's Journey quilts to show-and-tell for her newest students, Maggie received a letter from the history professor she had met during her visit to Lowell two years before. His search to find a record of Harriet Findley Birch's employment at the Merrimack Manufacturing Company had failed, but he had discovered convincing evidence in the *Lowell Offering,* a literary journal for the mill workers. In 1849, a mill girl had contributed a story about a young woman torn between the independence she enjoyed as a mill worker and her love for a handsome suitor. The professor had enclosed a copy.

The story told of a young woman, probably a thinly disguised version of the author, who lamented, "Though earning her own living was reckoned as a suitable accomplishment for a young maid, few would consider it appropriate for a wife to spend her hours thus employed. Indeed, Hannah's own dear William had often declared that no bride of his should weave or spin in the mills when she could be better occupied cooking his breakfast. And yet Hannah loved him, and would cleave to his side, though he would summon her from the friends and life that had become so dear and bid her go with him to distant lands far from home and family."

The author was Harriet Findley.

At last, Maggie filled in the missing pieces of Harriet's story. She had worked as a mill girl until marrying Franklin. When her husband decided to move west, Harriet, the obedient wife, had agreed, though her heart broke to part from her dear friends, many of whom still worked at the mills. Knowing she would no longer be able to trade patterns with her acquaintances, she stitched her masterwork as a record of all the blocks they knew, so that no matter how far west she traveled, she would have a wonderful variety of patterns to choose from when making quilts for her growing family. Scraps she had saved from her own days in the mill intermingled with pieces shared by beloved friends and relatives. She could not have sewn on the seat of a jolting wagon as they crossed the country on the Oregon Trail, so she had likely pieced the blocks in Lowell and quilted the top in Salem. Into the quilt she had stitched her grief, her hopes, her faithfulness, and her memories.

That was the story Maggie told in her classes and lectures, admitting that it was only one possible version of Harriet's life. Her students did not seem to mind the ambiguity, but they often spoke of finding Harriet's home in Lowell and of seeking out the indisputable truth. Wouldn't it be wonderful, they sighed, if they could find an old, sepia-toned photograph of Harriet? A diary in which she had confided her reasons for making the quilt? Letters she had written home to Lowell from the Oregon Trail?

Maggie, too, longed to know the truth, but she was grateful for every cherished scrap of information she had collected over the years and would not demand more.

When Maggie had saved enough money, she bought a new car, choosing a sensible model with a large trunk and excellent gas mileage because of her expanding schedule of speaking engagements. Her first road trip took her north to Salem, Oregon, to

Harriet's final resting place. She planted flowers by the headstone, and on the soft green grass nearby, she spread out Harriet's quilt and the four duplicates she had made. She spoke at a nearby quilt guild that evening, spent the night in a bed-and-breakfast run by the guild treasurer, and drove home in the morning after meeting Jason Birch for breakfast. She wished she could have stayed longer, but Ocean View Hills had cut her vacation from two weeks a year to three days, a reduction that would have been considered unfair and damaging to employee morale when she had first begun working there.

Maggie taught nearly every evening at the quilt shop and twice on Saturdays. She was more grateful than ever for the extra income after a second round of budget cuts trimmed the staff at Ocean View Hills by another four employees and a promised cost of living increase fell through. One evening, Maggie tentatively approached Lois about increasing the fee for her classes to cover printing expenses. "We could do that," said Lois, "but surely you don't plan to give away your patterns forever."

The day her pattern book, *My Journey with Harriet: The 1854 Harriet Findley Birch Quilt,* was published, Lois threw a party in Maggie's honor at the quilt shop. Her sister, brother-in-law, and two nieces flew in from Phoenix, and the curator of the New England Quilt Museum sent her flowers. The most able of the Courtyard Quilters attended, and Maggie was finally able to reveal the secret she had been keeping since the day she had begun her manuscript: The dedication of her book read, "To the Courtyard Quilters, who welcomed me into their circle, offered me their guidance, and shared my journey with Harriet from the very first step."

Lois had sold out of copies that night, and the book's brisk sales at Goose Tracks were mirrored in quilt shops across the country. Second and third printings swiftly followed. Maggie taught workshops at quilt guild meetings and lectured at national quilt shows. She moved across town to a larger house with a spacious formal dining room she converted to a quilt studio. Childhood friends with whom she had fallen out of touch contacted her after reading articles about her in their local newspapers. A former teacher phoned after spotting *My Journey with Harriet* featured in a book club supplement of his Sunday newspaper.

But her success was tempered with sorrow. Her beloved circle of quilters, whose numbers and composition had always fluctuated over time according to what Mrs. Stonebridge euphemistically called "natural attrition," began to lose members faster than they could welcome newcomers as concerned family members responded to staffing cuts by transferring their mothers and grandmothers to other facilities. Mrs. Stonebridge's son wanted to move her closer to his home, but she told him she would never leave Ocean View Hills as long as at least one friend remained. Maggie wanted to believe that would be a very long time, but each day her hopes diminished.

When *My Journey with Harriet* went into its twelfth printing seven years later, Harriet wanted to create a revised and updated edition, but all her editor wanted to know was when she intended to write something new. "When I find another quilt like Harriet's," replied Maggie, hoping that would end the discussion.

"How hard have you looked?"

"Not very," Maggie admitted, but she promised to try harder if her editor would agree to consider a new edition. It was an unsatisfactory compromise, so Maggie hung up with the excuse that she had to get to her day job.

She arrived at Ocean View Hills to find the staff fairly roiling with uneasiness. Rumors had circulated for weeks that their HMO was going to consolidate with another health care corporation, and no one in management knew what that would mean for their jobs and their residents. Though Maggie could not help feeling as unsettled as the rest of her colleagues, she reassured herself that her thirteen years of exemplary employment had to count for something.

The blow came at an emergency meeting of all senior management. Ocean View Hills was not going to merge with anyone. The other health care corporation was going to buy them out and shut them down.

Maggie did not understand the reasoning behind their decision. The director, visibly shaken by his own pending unemployment, provided a lengthy explanation about profitability and tax liabilities, but Maggie was too upset to follow the corporate finance intricacies. She struggled to absorb the truth that in six months, her beloved residents would be scattered around northern California wherever their families could find appropriate care for them, and she would be out of a job.

"At least you have your quilt book and your teaching," a coworker grumbled to Maggie in the lounge where the senior staff had gathered to collect their wits before returning to work. They had been sworn to secrecy until a letter could be drafted to the other employees and the residents' families, although Maggie doubted any of them could keep silent for long. The other employees knew about the meeting, and as far as Maggie was concerned, it would be cruel to mislead them.

"I can't live off that income," said Maggie. Worse, she had received only vague assurances from the director that their pensions would be protected. She also had a modest 401(K), but although she was only thirty-eight, she had hoped to take early retirement in ten years and devote herself to quilting and writing full time. That dream, she knew, was over.

In a move that received criticism from some of the residents, the director informed their families first and allowed the family members to tell their parents and grandparents as they deemed best. Some of the Courtyard Quilters felt that Maggie had betrayed them by not telling them about the closure as soon as she knew. "I wanted to tell you, but I couldn't," Maggie said. "The director forbade it."

"What do you care what he says?" glowered one of the quilters. "What's he going to do, fire you?"

"Don't blame Maggie," said Mrs. Stonebridge, kindly but in a manner that demanded cooperation. "She has professional responsibilities that take priority over ties of friendship. What if one of the patients from C Wing overheard us talking before their children had an opportunity to prepare them? Consider how that might upset the poor dears."

C Wing was where the patients with dementia and other serious chronic medical conditions resided. Thinking of them, the quilters relented. Some even murmured apologies, which Maggie accepted although she did not think she deserved them. She had wanted to warn them of what was coming, but she could not afford to give the director any reason to fire her.

"I can't bear to think our circle of quilters will be split up," lamented Mrs. Blum.

"We can try to stay together," said another. "Maybe our children could find a place with room for all of us."

One quilter shook her head. "Not me. My daughter has already decided that I'm moving in with them. The girls will share a bedroom and I'll get the extra." She paused. "It will be wonderful to see more of the kids, but I'll miss my girlfriends."

"We will have to keep in touch as best we can," said Mrs. Stonebridge. "With any luck, two or three of us will end up in the same place."

The Courtyard Quilters nodded, believing their longtime leader by force of habit, or, Maggie thought, as an act of faith.

That evening at the quilt shop, she taught her class so woodenly that Lois thought she was ill and offered to take over. Maggie briefly told her what the real problem was and forced herself to shake off her worries and get through the evening. She could not afford to lose this job, too.

As she packed up her teaching materials, Lois entered the classroom with a magazine in her hand. "I'm tempted not to show you this," she said, opening the magazine as she passed it to Maggie. "I would hate to lose you."

Maggie read the ad Lois had circled in red pen. "A quilt camp," she said. "That sounds like heaven. But it's all the way across the country."

"You could come back to visit. And teach for me."

"Don't worry," said Maggie, hugging her friend. "I couldn't leave California."

"When you see Elm Creek Manor, you'll change your mind."

Maggie doubted it, but she tossed the magazine in the box with her class samples and took it home.

The next morning, she scanned the Help Wanted ads over breakfast. There were several listings for jobs in geriatric care, but none comparable to her current position in either authority or compensation. After a tense day at work, where she comforted more than one tearful junior colleague in the staff lounge and promised to write letters of recommendation for several more, she found Lois's magazine in her quilt studio and gave the ad for the quilt camp teaching position a second look. After supper, she went online and Googled Elm Creek Quilts. She perused the camp's own website thoroughly, but also read evaluations and reviews former campers had posted on quilting bulletin boards and blogs. The comments were unanimous in their praise. Elm Creek Quilt Camp sounded like a wonderful place, though Maggie was not sure how she would fare in winter weather after spending her entire life in California.

With nothing to lose, Maggie put together the portfolio the Elm Creek Quilters had requested and sent it off, hoping for the best.

She also sent out résumés to every retirement community within a hundred miles, but received only three requests for interviews. As the weeks passed, the residents of Ocean View Hills began to disperse as children and grandchildren found them new homes. Going to work became lonelier and more dispiriting as one by one the Courtyard Quilters departed and her closest friends among the staff left for new jobs or retired at a fraction of their pensions.

A month after Maggie submitted her portfolio, Sarah McClure from Elm Creek Quilt Camp called with an invitation to come to Pennsylvania for an interview. As a test of her skills and creativity, Maggie was also instructed to design an original quilt block that could be used as a logo for Elm Creek Quilts. She was so thrilled to have an interview that she would have agreed to anything. She adapted two of Harriet Findley Birch's patterns, a leaf design and a star, and overlaid them to create a new block. Imitating Harriet's flowing script, in one corner of the block she embroidered "Elm Creek Quilts" and in another, "Waterford, Penn."

Throughout the years, Harriet had often felt like a guardian spirit to Maggie, lingering just beyond her vision, offering wisdom, encouragement, sympathy, understanding. Maggie wondered what Harriet would make of her pinning all her hopes on a job on the other side of the country. Perhaps more than anyone else, she would have understood.

The plane touched down at the Pittsburgh airport after a bumpy descent above meandering rivers. Maggie rented a car and drove the rest of the way to Waterford on a winding journey through the Appalachians, whose lush, forested hills cradled patchwork farms in valleys below.

From the highway, the town of Waterford appeared to be everything Lois had warned—remote, rural, and overpopulated by college students. Beyond the outskirts of town, Maggie drove down a rough gravel road through a leafy wood, taking the left fork that led to the rear parking lot as Lois had recommended.

The narrow road wound through the trees and emerged into a sunlit apple orchard through which several women strolled. The car passed a red barn, climbed a low hill, and crossed a bridge over a creek. Then the manor came into view—three stories of gray stone and dark wood, its unexpected elegance enhanced by the rambling, natural beauty of its surroundings.

She parked the car, leaving her messenger bag in the trunk with her suitcase. She considered going around to the front entrance, but when three other women entered through the rear door without knocking, she followed them inside. She peered through the first open doorway she passed and found herself in the kitchen. Two women bustled from stove to countertop to refrigerator, too intent on their work to look up. "Summer, would you help me with this?" one of the women asked as she opened the oven to reveal a large roasting pan.

"You're on your own," replied the younger, auburn-haired woman. "I don't eat anything with a face, and I don't help cook it, either. I could have put together a very plausible tofu chicken if you had let me."

The first woman made retching sounds, and Maggie left, reluctant to disturb them. She continued down the hall until she arrived at a foyer with a black marble floor, tall double doors on the far wall, and a ceiling open to the third story. Women of all ages climbed a grand oak staircase that led to balconies on the second and third floor, or passed through a doorway opposite the front entrance. Maggie asked one of the women where she might find Sarah McClure, and was told to try the library on the second floor. At the library, an older woman wearing glasses on a silver chain told her to try the kitchen. Perplexed, Maggie said, "I was just there, and I didn't see anyone but the two cooks."

The woman laughed. "Two cooks? Oh, that's rich. Well, rather than send you on a mission to find Sarah, may I help you instead?"

"My name is Maggie Flynn. I'm here for a job interview, but

it's not until tomorrow. Sarah McClure said I should spend the night here."

"Maggie, of course. I should have recognized you from the photo in your book." The older woman shook Maggie's hand briskly. "I'm Sylvia Compson. Have you had a chance to look around?"

Except for getting lost on her way to the library, Maggie had not, so Sylvia proposed a tour. She showed Maggie what seemed like the entire estate, from the library where most of the camp business was conducted to the hallways lined with bedrooms for the campers. Back on the first floor, Sylvia led Maggie into a grand ballroom that had been separated into several classrooms by tall, movable partitions. Voices and sewing machines created a happy buzz, and when Maggie remarked that she wondered how the students avoided being distracted by the sounds from adjacent classrooms, Sylvia said, "Distracted? Oh, they enjoy eavesdropping on one another. We consider it part of the entertainment."

From the converted ballroom they went to the banquet hall, where four young men, three of them surely no more than teenagers, were setting ten round tables for supper. "Michael, don't forget the soup bowls," Sylvia called out. "And close the curtains partway so it's more difficult to see the food."

The eldest looked up from his work and nodded solemnly. "Don't worry. I'll take care of it." Another boy, blond and handsome, snorted and shook his head.

"They're brothers. The younger one has trouble accepting that the elder is in charge," Sylvia confided as she led Maggie from the room. "The other two are new this summer. One is the son of the neighbor of one of our instructors, and the other is the son of one of our instructor's colleagues. They're working off a rather large debt to another Elm Creek Quilter. They're quite a pair of juvenile delinquents, or so I've been told, but Michael and Todd will keep them in line."

Maggie nodded, trying to sort out the tangled relationships. She wondered how much she would be expected to remember for the interview the next day. And why would Sylvia not want the campers to see the food on their plates? Lois, who had attended the camp twice, had praised the cooking. Her only complaint was that she had gained two pounds from the rich desserts.

The tour turned to the grounds of the manor, which Sylvia seemed to believe were just as essential to the camp as the classrooms and dining facilities. They passed several quilt campers who recognized Maggie, and a few of them asked if she had come to Elm Creek Manor to teach a class. Grateful for the perfect timing of their praise, Maggie told them she had come for an interview, but she would be thrilled to become an Elm Creek Quilter.

By the end of the day, she realized that was true—and not only because she desperately needed the work. She longed to be a part of the world these amazing, inspiring women had created. It was a haven in the central Pennsylvania countryside, a place of respite and healing. If they offered her a job—whether as teacher or office clerk or scullery maid—she would gratefully sign up for a lifetime term.

Sylvia left her to explore the estate on her own until supper, when she joined the staff and campers in the banquet hall for a delicious meal of roast chicken, sautéed vegetables, and an amazing spicy chickpea soup served with warm flatbread. Five women introduced themselves as the other Elm Creek Quilters and made her feel as welcome as if they had known her for years. After supper, she toured the north gardens with Sarah McClure, the woman she had mistaken for the head chef earlier that day. Sarah told her about the manor's history, from its founding in 1858 by Sylvia's great-grandparents and its role as a station on the Underground Railroad to its rebirth as a retreat for quilters. When Sarah mentioned that Sylvia's ancestors had left behind quilts and a journal from the manor's earliest days, Maggie thought of how long she had yearned to discover a similar record of Harriet Findley Birch's life. She hoped that Sylvia treasured these gifts and wished she could be invited to see them.

As twilight approached, Sarah escorted her back to the manor for the evening program, a fashion show of the campers' quilted clothing. Afterward, Sarah showed her to a charming room on the third floor with a private sitting area and a sampler quilt on the bed, and bade her good night.

Weary from travel and the extended effort to impress, Maggie slept soundly.

The next morning after breakfast, she repacked her suitcase and dressed in her new tan slacks, a crisp white blouse, and a blue blazer, hoping that they would mark her down for not wearing a suit. Her only suit, a black, somber ensemble she wore to funerals and board meetings, summoned forth too many memories of unhappy occasions to be worn on a day when she needed every ounce of confidence.

Carrying her small suitcase and messenger bag, she went downstairs to the first floor to find the parlor where she was supposed to officially meet the Elm Creek Quilters. On her way across the foyer, she heard a frustrated sigh drift down to her from somewhere above. She looked up and spotted a white-haired woman seated in an armchair on the second-floor balcony.

"Are you okay?" called Maggie. "What's wrong?"

"Oh, it's nothing. I just can't appliqué a smooth curve to save my life, that's all."

Maggie glanced at her watch and saw that she had a few minutes to spare. "Want me to take a look?"

When the older woman gratefully agreed, Maggie returned upstairs and demonstrated her variation of the needle-turned appliqué technique. The older woman took a few awkward stitches and shook her head in frustration. "I still don't understand."

Maggie showed her again, but more quickly this time, mindful of the waiting Elm Creek Quilters. Then she apologized and explained that she was late for an appointment.

"That's all right, dear." Behind her pink-tinted glasses, the older woman's blue eyes beamed with satisfaction. "I think I've learned all I need to know."

Maggie hurried back downstairs to the parlor and knocked on the door. Sarah McClure invited her inside, where some of the other Elm Creek Quilters were seated on the far side of a coffee table, across from a single armchair.

"Gwen couldn't make it," said Sarah as Maggie seated herself. "She has a class. But this is really more of a formality, since you've already met everyone."

"Almost everyone," said a pretty blonde Maggie did not recognize. "I had to go home and feed my family last night, so I missed the supper party. I'm Diane."

"Maggie Flynn." Maggie rose to shake Diane's hand, which felt smooth and cool, though Diane squeezed a fraction harder than necessary.

Sarah began with a few perfunctory questions about Maggie's employment history. When Sylvia asked her to tell how she came to publish a book, Maggie told the story of discovering Harriet Findley Birch's quilt and how that one chance encounter had changed her life. At another Elm Creek Quilter's request, Maggie showed them the block she had designed. Everyone complimented her pattern and handiwork—everyone except Diane, who took a page from a folder on her lap and frowned at it. Giving it a surreptitious glance, Maggie recognized the paper as a color copy of a photograph of her original My Journey with Harriet quilt. With a quaking heart she thought of her first few blocks, those first stumbling efforts that had eventually launched her career, and wondered if Diane was marking her mistakes. Surely a missed stitch or two would not be evident in a picture of that resolution.

Then Diane set down the photocopy and tapped two squares with her pen. "I thought your original block looked familiar."

Maggie did not like the emphasis Diane placed on "original block," but she nodded. "I adapted two of Harriet Findley Birch's patterns to create my own. Since I'm best known for documenting her quilt, I thought that would be appropriate. Was I wrong?"

"Your block is fine," the youngest Elm Creek Quilter assured her.

Diane did not look as if she agreed. "I was wondering, too, why you didn't send us any pictures of your other quilts."

Maggie hesitated. "I sent twelve photos."

"Yes, but all twelve are of the same quilt. You haven't made twelve different quilts; you've made twelve versions of the same quilt."

"They aren't exactly the same," said Maggie. "I've used different fabrics, color palettes, and techniques with each variation. Each version was made for a specific purpose." She reached into her messenger bag and pulled out copies of the same photos she had included in her portfolio. "This one, my third Harriet's Journey, was an exercise in contrast and value. The blue and white version I made entirely by machine just to prove to some of my reluctant students that it could be done. I personally prefer hand piecing."

"You do seem capable of adequate handwork," said Diane, "which makes it all the more disappointing that you sold out to the machine mafia."

"I don't understand."

Diane gestured to the photo. "You said it yourself. You prefer one technique, but you pandered to lazy advocates of an easier method to reel in more students, to sell more books."

Taken aback, Maggie replied, "I don't consider it selling out to encourage a quilter to try a project that is more challenging than what she's previously attempted."

"Of course not," said Sylvia briskly. "Does anyone else have a question for our guest?"

Summer glanced at her notes and looked up with a smile for Maggie. "How do you account for your continuing interest in this one quilt? It's not just about the patterns, is it?"

"No," said Maggie. "Although I'm awed by Harriet's sense of geometry, balance, and proportion as well as her technical skills, my fascination has always been with the quilter more than with her creation. Who was she? Why did she make this quilt? Did anyone help her? What did she think about as she sewed? Did she have a good marriage? Was she happy? Was she lonely? Did she regret leaving Massachusetts for the West? There's so much I'll never know about her, but working on this quilt makes me feel closer to her."

Some of the Elm Creek Quilters nodded, encouraging her to continue. "Over the years, I've made several visits to Lowell to try to retrace Harriet's steps. I've found tantalizing clues to her past—a baptismal record, a bill of sale for a plot of land that her father owned, a few other facts relating to her ordinary daily life. But a collection of facts isn't the truth. I think Harriet's truth lies in the story her quilt tells, and that's the story of a woman who was creative, resourceful, and steadfast. I'll never know for certain, and that mystery compels me to make sure she is remembered, not only for her sake, but for all those other women whose sacrifices built this country but whose names never made it into the history books."

Sylvia smiled. "If only we had more time, I have some quilts in my attic I would love to show you. I think you would appreciate them."

Sarah took that as her cue to wrap up the interview, and Maggie was surprised that she was no longer eager for it to end. For all that she had promised Lois she could never leave California, she had seen enough of Elm Creek Quilt Camp to know that she would feel at home there. Aside from Diane, the Elm Creek Quilters had been kind and welcoming. She knew she would enjoy working with them and becoming their friend.

Now she could only hope that the impression she had made over the previous twenty-four hours would be enough to dispel any concerns Diane might raise after she left.

Sarah rose to show her to the door. Maggie shook their hands, even Diane's, and told them she hoped to hear from them soon. She collected her bags and left the parlor to find that someone had arranged a row of folding chairs along the wall just outside the door.

The white-haired woman she had tried to help earlier was in the hallway leading to the west wing. She brightened and seemed about to speak, but Maggie was spent from the interview and did not want to talk. She turned quickly and hurried to the tall double doors that marked the front entrance, though her car was parked around back.

As she stepped out onto the veranda, she saw a younger woman dressed in an interview suit struggling up the stairs with an oversized stroller and two little boys in tow. Maggie could only imagine how Diane would react at the sight of the children, and although this woman was the competition, she was moved to sympathy, knowing what was in store for her.

"Watch out for the blonde," Maggie warned as they passed on the stairs. The young mother paused, but Maggie had a long drive to Pittsburgh ahead of her and a flight to catch, so she hurried on her way.

Chapter Two
Karen

If Nate had not been too busy to go to the grocery store as he had promised, Karen would not have been forced to load the boys into the car and drive to the store in the rain. If she had not had to endure the boys' nonstop begging for sugar-frosted junk marketed by cartoon characters, she would not have felt entitled to a reward. If she had not been so annoyed at Nate, she would not have tossed the *Modern Quilter* magazine into the shopping cart on her way to the checkout line, and if she had not bought the magazine, she never would have seen the ad. So, in a way, everything that resulted, all the embarrassment and stress and frustration, was Nate's fault.

If she had not felt guilty about the purchase, she would have learned about the job that same day, but as she unpacked the groceries she imagined her husband's lament at the sight of the magazine. "Think of all the trees that died for those pages," Nate would say. "Don't they have an online version you could read instead?" Nate had cancelled his last newspaper subscription while still in graduate school, and Karen had allowed hers to lapse after they had dated for six months and she realized his anti-newsprint stance was not a passing phase. They had not had a magazine in the house since the subscription to *Parents* they had received as a baby shower gift ran out four months after Ethan was born. If Nate came home and found a magazine in her hands, he might keel over in shock. She could not do that to him, so she hid the magazine in her fabric stash, taking it out only when Nate was at work and the boys were asleep. Those two events coincided only rarely, so it was not until two weeks after purchasing the magazine that she discovered Elm Creek Quilt Camp was hiring.

She postponed telling Nate about the job not only because she would have to admit how she had heard about it, but also because she was not sure she ought to apply. It was not as if she had an abundance of free time. Even with Ethan in nursery school three mornings a week, she still had plenty to do tending to his increasingly active little brother. Her house looked like the before photo in a redecorating makeover, and come to think of it, so did she. She didn't need more work; she needed a month alone at a tropical spa with daily massages and handsome cabana boys to bring her fruity drinks with little paper umbrellas in them while she relaxed on the beach.

But to work at Elm Creek Manor . . . She wistfully remembered the week she had spent at quilt camp a few months before Ethan was born, a time when she had naively considered herself accomplished and capable because her children had not yet taught her otherwise. The week's stay had been a gift from Nate, who had secretly made all the arrangements after she had mentioned that she had been seized by an irresistible urge to make a quilt for her firstborn. Maybe she had been under the influence of the breathtakingly adorable pictures in the clandestine stash of baby magazines she had secreted in her underwear drawer, because none of her friends or family quilted, and she had not grown up with quilts around the house. She had no one to teach her, and she was afraid what would result if she tried on her own. Then she happened across an arts program on cable featuring an interview with a male quilter from the Pacific Northwest whose work was exhibited in galleries across the country. The baby quilt Karen envisioned was nothing like his wild, abstract creations, but she figured that if a man could quilt, so could she.

As she and Nate shopped for the nursery, Karen told him she wished she knew how to quilt without expecting anything more than sympathy. But Nate's understanding of quilting was that it involved reusing scraps of worn fabric that would otherwise end up in a landfill, so he was all for it. He found Elm Creek Quilt Camp on the Internet and surprised her with a week's stay, no doubt pleased to foster her budding environmentalist frugality. Soon after she returned home, however, he learned that quilters need new fabric just as painters need paint and sculptors need clay, and he regarded her steadily increasing stash with concern and resignation as it threatened to outgrow the linen closet and spill into the hallway.

If Karen were more experienced, she might have put her application in the mail immediately, but she had quilted for only five years. She had tried to teach quilting only once, to her best friend, who had eagerly chosen a pattern and purchased fabric but had never actually cut out any pieces. It was a less than exemplary record, one she was certain the other applicants would far surpass. She pictured the Elm Creek Quilters passing her application around a long table, marveling at her hubris before tossing her file into a paper shredder.

That image made her wish she had never seen the ad. If she ever returned to the manor, it would be as a camper, not as an Elm Creek Quilter.

Monday night blurred into Tuesday morning. Lucas woke twice to nurse, and Karen dozed uncomfortably in the rocking chair until he drifted off to sleep. She returned him to his crib and stumbled back to bed, but on the second return trip, she stepped on a Tickle Me Elmo doll, which promptly burst into giggles, waking Ethan. She told him to go back to sleep, but not long after she lay down and pulled the quilt up to her chin, she felt the mattress shake as Ethan crawled into bed between her and Nate. Twice before sunrise Karen was jolted awake by her son's feet in her ribcage, a sensation oddly reminiscent of her pregnancy, though far less entrancing than when he had been on the inside.

In the morning, Nate shut off the alarm clock and muttered something about sleeping in—a lovely idea in theory, but impracticable for the parents of young children. Lucas rose at his regular hour, calling out for milk. Half asleep, Karen brought him into the master bed to nurse as she lay curled protectively around him. She drifted back to sleep stroking his downy blond hair, his sweet baby softness warming her heart, the fragrance of baby shampoo soothing her into slumber. Later she woke to the sound of the shower running. The sliver of the bed Nate had occupied was empty, Ethan was snoring, and Lucas was sitting up in bed, smiling at her. "Poo poo," he announced, and held up his hands. While she slept, he had removed his diaper and fingerpainted the sheets with the contents.

In the summer, the boys' playgroup met at the park every Tuesday and Thursday morning, but on Tuesdays Ethan had a swimming lesson first. "Did you feed the boys?" Karen asked Nate as she raced into the kitchen after a quick shower and a scramble through the unfolded clothes in the laundry basket for something to wear.

"Lucas had cereal and toast."

"What about Ethan?"

"He said he wasn't hungry."

"If he doesn't eat now, he'll want something five minutes before his swimming lesson starts."

Nate shrugged. "I can't force him to eat."

"Did you pack the swim bag?"

"I thought you did it."

Silently, Karen counted to five. Every Monday night she asked him to pack the bag, and every Monday night he agreed. Every Tuesday morning, he assumed she had already taken care of it. Did he think she had squeezed it in between Lucas's midnight and predawn feedings? "Could you please pack the bag so I can grab some breakfast?"

"Sure, honey." He rose and kissed her, coffee mug in hand, and went upstairs. She tracked his footsteps from Ethan's room to the main bath to their room, hastily spooning down a bowl of muesli while standing at the sink. She had just finished when Nate returned with the blue nylon bag and put it on the kitchen table between his plate of toast crusts and Ethan's cereal bowl.

"Did you remember everything?" asked Karen, clearing away the dishes.

"Yep." He gave her a quick kiss. "I have to go. I have student conferences."

"Did you remember the swim cap?"

"Uh huh." Nate took his lunch from the refrigerator and stuffed it into his backpack.

"Towel?"

"Yes."

"Coffee cup?"

He paused. "What?"

"Coffee cup. When you went upstairs, you were carrying a coffee cup."

"Oh. I think I left it on the dresser." He glanced at his watch. "Do you want me to go get it?"

"That's all right. I'll get it."

"Okay. I'll see you later." He went into the living room to say good-bye to the boys, then hurried off with a cheerful wave.

After the door to the garage closed behind him, she tried not to open the bag to make sure he had remembered everything. She hated feeling like she always needed to check his work, but the urge was insistent. Towel, swim cap, and goggles were tucked inside the bag just as Nate had promised, but the swim trunks were old, faded from chlorine, and size 3T. Karen had no idea where Nate had found them, since they should have been packed away in the basement with the other clothes Ethan had outgrown and Lucas could not yet wear. If Ethan managed to squeeze into them at all, the waistband could quite possibly cut off his circulation.

Can't he read a tag? Karen wondered as she hurried upstairs to Ethan's room. *Does he not know his son's size? Didn't he recognize the right pair from last week?*

She took a deep breath and tried to let it go. Nate was in a hurry, students were waiting for him, and how many dads knew anything about their kids' sizes? He had tried to help, and that was what mattered.

She retrieved the coffee cup from the bathroom counter on her way back downstairs, finished packing the swim bag and the diaper bag and the lunch bag for the park later, and called for the boys to come and get ready to leave. Ethan came at once, but Lucas ran away, laughing, and hid by climbing behind the armchair and covering his eyes with his hands.

"We can still see you," his older brother said.

"No see," Lucas insisted.

"And we can hear you. Mom, tell him he's not hiding right."

"Time to go." Karen reached behind the chair and lifted Lucas to his feet. He promptly went limp, forcing her to haul him out into the open. She wrestled the boys from their pajamas into their clothes and cajoled them into holding still while she slathered them in PABA-free sunblock. She had barely finished one of Lucas's arms when he grabbed the pink bottle and flung it behind the piano.

"No pool," said Lucas. "No pool, please?"

"Honey, we have to go to the pool." Karen dropped to her hands and knees and strained to reach the sunblock. "Your brother has a swim lesson."

"No pool. No swim!"

"You don't have to swim," said Ethan reasonably. "Just me."

"I swim. I swim!" Lucas tugged at Karen's T-shirt. "I swim, please?"

"When you're a big boy, you can take lessons, too."

Lucas sent up such a wail of dismay that she had to promise him a treat from the club's vending machines just to get him to calm down. When Ethan protested, she had to assure him that he could buy something, too.

"Treat," said Lucas happily as she buckled him into his carseat.

"I'm going to get Cheetos," said Ethan.

"Cheetos," shouted Lucas. "Cheetos, too!"

Karen muffled a groan. Nate would have a fit. She would have to scour the boys' fingernails clean of all traces of blaze orange cheese residue before he came home from work. What did it say about her that she so quickly resorted to bribing her sons and hiding the evidence from her husband?

"Mom," said Ethan as they pulled into the parking lot of the swim club. "I'm hungry. Can I have my treat now?"

"Treat," echoed Lucas.

"No, honey, we don't have time."

"But I'm starving."

"You should have eaten breakfast."

"Daddy didn't give me anything."

"I'm sorry, sweetie." They were already five minutes late. "You'll have to wait until after your lesson."

Ethan grumbled as she rushed them into the locker room and threw him into his swim gear. To her dismay, the exchange had given Lucas the impression that snack time was imminent. "Cheetos," he cried plaintively as Karen carried him while she led Ethan from the locker room to the pool. The room smelled of chlorine and wet cement, and Lucas's every wail echoed off the walls. Karen left Ethan with his instructor and hurried Lucas into the waiting room. Catching sight of the vending machine, Lucas struggled in her arms until she had to set him down. He ran across the room and flung himself at the Plexiglas. "Cheetos! Cheetos! Cheetos!"

Three mothers sitting near the tinted glass overlooking the pool broke off their conversation and stared at him, then looked daggers at Karen. Smiling weakly, Karen hurried over and wedged herself between her son and the vending machine. "Lucas, honey. After your brother's lesson. Remember?"

"No! No! Now!"

Bewildered, she picked him up and winced as she avoided his flailing limbs. This was so unlike him, the mellow kid, the one who made her and Nate realize just how challenging Ethan had been. "Honey, calm down. It's okay." She held him close and patted his back as he squirmed in protest. "We talked about this. Remember? We'll have a treat after your brother's lesson—if you're a good boy."

"Cheetos, Mama," he wept. "Please."

It was pitiful to watch. "All right. Okay." She set him down, a howling mass of fury and tears and despair on the blue industrial pile carpet. She dug around in her back pocket for change and came up with a quarter and two dimes. With a sigh of relief she slipped the change into the slot, pressed the buttons, and waited for the snack to dispense—cheerfully narrating each action in a vain attempt to assure Lucas his precious Cheetos were on the way. His misery abated only after she placed the open bag in his hands.

"There." She straightened and rested her hands on her hips. "All better?"

He smiled wanly up at her. Only then did she become aware of the conversation by the window. The other mothers were not trying to keep their voices low, and although they did not look at her, she suddenly had the impression that they wanted her to overhear.

"I can't believe she rewarded that tantrum—"

"I pity that child's teachers in a few years—"

"—that's what a diet of junk food does to children—"

"—someone needs a parenting class—"

"—yes, a lesson on how to redirect negative impulses—"

After the moment Karen needed to realize the women were talking about her, she scooped up Lucas, yanked open the door to the locker room, and ducked inside. The door closed too slowly to block out the derisive laugher she had left behind. "Stupid, gossipy bi—" Just in time, she remembered Lucas's rapidly developing vocabulary and clamped her mouth shut around the word.

This was not the first time she had earned outright disdain from mothers like these, women who managed to handle, apparently effortlessly, the tasks of motherhood and look good doing it. They made their own baby food from organically grown fruits and vegetables. They wore white cashmere twinsets knowing their children would never dream of spitting up on them. They had shiny hair and manicures and wore their prepregnancy clothes within six weeks of their deliveries. They found time to iron. Their children had never tasted a trans-fatty acid. They read all the current books and articles on the latest trends in child development. Having stepped off the fast track for the noble art of motherhood, they pursued their new profession the way they had once pursued advanced degrees and corner offices. They scorned and pitied mothers who stuck their kids in day care and regarded with bewilderment mothers such as Karen's best friend Janice, mother of four with one on the way, who seemed not to know when to say when, and Karen, scattered and disorganized and unable to pull herself together. When Karen had resigned from her job within a week of returning from her eight-week maternity leave, she had tried to befriend such women at Kindermusik and library story hour, but they smelled her desperation and gave her polite but chilly rebuffs. They did not know that she had once been as successful and confident as they. What was it about motherhood that made her doubt everything she had once admired about herself?

"One, Mama?" offered Lucas, holding a gnarled orange twig of Cheeto to her mouth.

"No, thank you." She redirected the offering and looked up at a sudden movement in the mirror. On the other side of the locker room, a smiling, slender woman in a perfectly tailored suit turned away from a locker, a gym bag slung jauntily over her shoulder. Karen nearly choked. With Lucas balanced on her hip, she swiftly turned toward the nearest locker, ducked her head, and spun the dial as if she knew the combination.

The click of black pumps on concrete paused beside her. "Karen?"

Reluctantly, Karen turned around. "Oh, hi, Lucy."

"Karen! I can't believe it's you." Lucy's makeup was flawless, and she looked well rested and refreshed. Karen dimly remembered feeling like that once, long, long ago. "You're looking—" Lucy sized up Karen in a swift glance. "Wow! How long has it been?"

Karen rose and instinctively tucked loose strands of hair behind her ears. "Um . . . almost five years now. Four and a half."

"It's hard to believe it's been so long." Lucy smiled at Lucas. "He's gotten so big! Is something wrong, little guy? You look sad."

Karen took in his tear-streaked face and runny nose and cringed. "This is actually my youngest, Lucas. You met my older son, Ethan."

"You had another one! How great is that? Two boys. He is just so cute." Lucy pressed a hand to her chest, as if it ached from adoration. "You know, every time I see all the precious little girl clothes at Neiman Marcus, I think I should have a baby, too."

Karen nodded, her face straining from the effort of maintaining a pleasant expression. Why couldn't she have taken five more minutes before leaving the house to fix her hair and put on makeup? "So, how have you been? Are you still seeing Eric?"

"Eric?" Lucy laughed. "You *have* been gone a while. I haven't seen him in years."

"Is that right?" For some reason Karen found this enormously depressing. They had seemed so in love. "What's new at work? How is everyone?"

"Don't get me started. Last year we moved into the new building—you probably heard that—but hardly anyone's happy with the office assignments. Riegert retired last fall, Donnie got married—" Lucy waved her hand. "You know. The usual."

Karen nodded, though she did not know and desperately wanted to. For years she had spent most of her waking hours with these people, but four and a half years ago, they had abruptly vanished from her life.

"But what about you?" said Lucy, concerned. "How do you like the whole stuck-at-home-mom thing?"

What could Karen say? "It's everything I hoped it would be, and so much more," she enthused, forcing a grin. "It was definitely the right choice for me. And . . . we usually go by stay-at-home mom, not stuck-at-home. It feels more voluntary that way."

"That's wonderful," said Lucy, relieved. "I really admire you. I could never give up everything I've worked so hard for."

"You'd be surprised what you can do when you believe it's right for your family."

"I suppose so. I admit sometimes I envy you. It must be so nice not to have to work."

Karen kept her smile fixed in place and nodded.

Despite the swim lesson, Karen and her boys were not the last of the playgroup to reach the park. Janice and her four children did not arrive until more than twenty minutes after Karen parallel parked her compact car between the minivans already lined up along the curb.

Janice's three eldest children ran for the playground as Janice followed, carrying the oversized tote bag with their lunches and balancing her one-year-old on her hip. Though she was only five months into her pregnancy, she could easily pass for eight, a fact that had panicked her until an ultrasound confirmed that she was not carrying twins. Janice had said that whenever she took all of the kids to the grocery store, other shoppers regarded her with either profound sympathy or alarm. Once, a well-meaning elderly woman had taken her aside and kindly encouraged her to discuss birth control options with her physician, secretly if she had to, if her husband disapproved. At her last prenatal appointment, a pregnant woman struggling to amuse her bored two-year-old in the waiting room remarked that Janice was either very brave or very insane. Janice laughed as she recounted the stories, but Karen knew she had begged her husband to get a vasectomy two children ago. Whenever she was especially annoyed with him, she threatened to perform the operation herself.

"Sorry I'm late," said Janice, panting, as she spread out her blanket and settled herself and the baby upon it. "I got trapped in a phone call with the food police."

"What was it this time?" asked one of the other mothers, who was changing her three-year-old's pull-up pants on a nearby blanket. "Peanut butter?"

"No! God forbid. Even I know enough not to bring peanut butter. Peanuts can kill."

"You forgot to cut the grapes in half," guessed Karen, who had committed that same infraction on her first turn to provide the morning snack for Ethan's nursery school class, earning herself a lecture on hidden choking hazards from the room parent.

"Your school is strict," remarked Connor, the only stay-at-home father in the playgroup. "We can bring anything except candy and soda."

"The food police aren't official representatives of the school," said Janice. "The peanut rule is a school policy, and understandably so, but the others have been tacked on by a few overzealous parents with too much time on their hands."

"So what did you do?" said the oldest mother in the group. She and her husband had been surprised by a late-in-life third child, and she regarded with bemused skepticism the innumerable new parenting rules that had sprung up since her first two children passed through the preschool years.

"I brought the wrong kind of milk."

"Buttermilk?" asked one of the mothers. She was an uncertain parent who often described her child's development in terms of the dog obedience classes she had put her standard poodle through a few years before. "Chocolate?"

"Spoiled?" said Karen.

"No! Honestly, do you really think I'm that bad? I brought milk. Fresh milk, regular nonchocolate milk. However, I failed to select organic, BGH-free milk."

"What's that?" asked the oldest mother.

"One more thing to worry about," said Connor, who regularly regaled them with magazine articles on subjects such as pesticide residues in applesauce.

Janice smote her brow in mock dismay. "I thought I brought those children something healthy, but apparently it was not quite healthy enough. Tell me, where am I supposed to find organic, bovine growth hormone–free milk? And how much more than regular milk does it cost?"

They all laughed, except for Connor, who looked ready to defend the food police, and Karen, who knew exactly how much that kind of milk cost and where to find it because it was the only kind Nate allowed in the house other than soy.

"Some kids are allergic to dairy," one of the mothers warned, then excused herself to chase down her youngest daughter, happily wandering from the playground.

"I promise I'll take soy next time," Janice called after her. Then, all at once, every child seemed to need something: a push on the swing, a snack, a referee, a cuddle. The conversation broke up in a scramble of caregiving, as most of their conversations did. Few of their chats were as long in duration as this one had been. They had learned to converse in bits and snatches.

Later, as Karen and Janice pushed their youngest ones on the swings, Karen told her about her morning with the coven of mean swim moms and her former coworker. Janice interrupted with incredulous laughter when Karen repeated Lucy's statement that Karen did not work. "Oh, of course we don't work," said Janice. "We just sit around and let our feral children scavenge for food and clothing in the streets."

"When working mothers imagine our days—if they imagine them at all—they think of playdates at the park, hugs and kisses and peaceful naptime on spotless cotton crib sheets. Hours of maternal bliss and fully requited love. They have no idea what it's really like."

Janice nodded emphatically and Karen did not bother to continue. Janice, mother of four and a half, already knew very well what life as a stay-at-home mother was like. That was one of the reasons they got along so well. Each admired the other for simply managing to shower, dress, and get out of the house once a day. Sometimes Karen felt as if Janice was the only person she knew who demanded nothing more of her.

Karen adored her children. She loved them beyond measure. However, if pressed, if forced to admit the truth, she would confess that she structured her entire day around coordinating the boys' naps so that she could have a half hour to collapse in a chair and catch her breath. Some days she could almost weep just thinking of the mind-numbingly repetitious nature of her daily routine. And while she claimed the playgroup was for the boys, it was really for her, because if she did not have a conversation with someone above the age of four at least once during the day, she sincerely believed she would go stark raving mad.

Worst of all was the knowledge that someday she would have to give it all up.

"Motherhood is the only job in the world where your every decision is questioned and doubted and criticized," said Janice. "No matter what you do, no matter what choice you make, someone somewhere is convinced that you are doing irreparable harm to your children. And she probably has a vocal, militant group of like-minded mommies on the Internet backing her up."

"Maybe not the only job," said Karen. "What about President?"

"Okay, maybe President. But he's well compensated for it."

"And we all know that if you don't get paid for it, it isn't work." Karen had been guilty of that assumption before she had children, and now, thinking of the millions of working women who still operated under that misconception, she could not feel angry, or indignant, or even frustrated. She simply felt tired, much too tired to try to enlighten them.

Janice pushed her son's swing for a moment in silence. "Speaking of paid work . . ." She paused. "There's no delicate way to phrase this. I'm getting a nanny."

Karen stared at her, forgetting to push the swing or move out of the way. Lucas bumped into her. "Mama, Mama, no no no," he complained as he twisted in the swing.

She straightened out the chains and gave Lucas another push. "You're serious," she managed to say. "Why do you need a nanny?"

Stupid question. Who needed a nanny more than Janice?

"Don't hate me," said Janice. "I'm going back to work. In a manner of speaking, since I'll work out of the home. Remember the birthday parties I ran for Elise's and Jayne's girls?"

Karen nodded. Janice, a former producer of children's public television programs, threw legendary birthday parties complete with themes, costumes, and games that could only be described as enchanting. When her eldest daughter turned five, Janice arranged a fairy tea party like something out of a movie, with cute little girls dancing around the backyard in ballerina skirts and delicate wings made from wire and tulle. Even Ethan, the only boy, wore a pair of emerald green wings and ran around calling himself a dinosaur dragonfly. The photos would surely mortify him in years to come, although he had enjoyed the party as much as the girls.

"I've helped so many other moms with their parties that I finally decided to make it official," Janice explained. "I can do something I enjoy, still be with my kids, and make a little money, too."

"I'm sure you'll make tons," said Karen, forcing a smile. "Enough for a Mercedes with built-in car seats. Congratulations."

She asked for more details, reminding herself that Janice was her closest friend, the only friend who understood her anymore, and she ought to be delighted and encouraging for her sake. Instead, she was so stunned and envious that she soon gave up responding with anything more than wordless murmurs. *I am a bitter, mean, little person,* she thought. *I nag my husband and I can't be happy for my best friend.*

It seemed a long time before Janice finished explaining the specifics of her new job and discussed her family's need for extra income with the new baby coming and five college tuitions to plan for, as well as her own ache for some kind of life of her own apart from bottles and diapers and nursery rhymes.

"You never needed a life before," said Karen lightly, watching the older children running and climbing and tumbling over the playground like a pack of happy puppies. "You were as committed to the calling of maternal drudgery as the rest of us."

Janice laughed, but as her eyes followed Connor as he raced to stop his youngest from pouring a bucketful of pebbles down the front of her sundress, her smile faded. "I want my own income. There's no such thing as job security anymore. Or marital security."

"What?" exclaimed Karen. "Is something going on with Sean? His job, or . . . you two?"

"No. Not yet. But sometimes you never see it coming."

"Janice, no." Karen shook her head. "Sean would never leave you. He adores you. He would never be interested in someone else. He can hardly keep his hands off you."

Janice gestured to her round belly. "That much, at least, is true."

"Please don't tell me you're taking this job as an insurance policy in case Sean leaves you. I've never seen a man so in love with his wife, and that includes my own husband, as much as I hate to admit it."

"What are you talking about? Nate worships the ground you walk on."

"You're half right. He worships the *ground.* I know he loves me and he loves the boys, but the reason he'll never leave me is that he knows he'll never find anyone else who will agree to wash and reuse aluminum foil."

"I don't think Sean will leave me for another woman, either," Janice acknowledged. "But it's not just about the money. I need this. Don't get me wrong. I love being a mom. You of all people know I do. But I need something else. Something that's just for me. Sometimes . . ." Janice gestured to the playground, where Connor had all but disappeared beneath a shrieking, laughing pile of children. "Sometimes I feel that the woman I was before I became a mother is drowning, and if I don't reach in and hold her above the waves long enough for her to take a breath, she won't make it."

Karen did not know what to say. In silence they watched the older children play until their two toddlers kicked their dangling legs and fussed, indignant at being forgotten in the swings.

They ate lunch at the park and played for an hour more before a chain reaction of toddler meltdowns set in, signaling the end of the play date. Karen drove around for a half hour before Ethan and Lucas fell asleep in their car seats. Then she turned the car toward home, torn between guilt for the waste of precious fossil fuels and giddiness at the thought of perhaps as much as an hour to spend as she pleased. Miraculously, she was able to carry Lucas to his crib and Ethan to the living room sofa without waking either boy.

After checking the answering machine and the mail, she hurried downstairs to the basement. If they ever saved enough money for a larger house, Karen would insist upon a home with an extra, above-ground room she could claim as her own, a quilting room that could double as a guest room. For now, a desk salvaged from a garage sale, a second-hand sewing machine, and two stacks of milk crates for storage served as her quilt studio.

She switched on the baby monitor and pulled out the magazine, settling herself down on a metal folding chair in front of the desk. She had read the ad so often that the magazine fell open at the proper page, and she read the requirements again although she had nearly memorized them. The Elm Creek Quilters wanted someone accomplished, but they were not asking for the impossible. Karen knew how to piece and quilt by hand as well as by machine, and she considered herself especially adept at foundation paper piecing, which ought to qualify as a "notable quilting technique." She met the requirements. Other applicants would probably far exceed them, but Karen could not let the potential competition discourage her from applying.

The logistics of returning to work would make the competition for the job seem like a breeze. Ethan would need to be transported to and from nursery school three mornings a week. Lucas was still nursing, and she didn't relish the thought of hauling a breast pump to Elm Creek Manor. She would just have to wean him. If she'd had any backbone at all, she would have stopped nursing him months ago, but it was less exhausting to simply give in to his demands. Eighteen months was definitely old enough for her to wean him without guilt, and it would be easier once she had a strong motivation to stick to it.

But who would care for the boys in her absence? She had heard too many alarming reports of day care centers to contemplate one for her children, but Nate's job was secure—and would become more so, once he had tenure—and they could afford a nanny. Her heart quaked at the thought of peeling her sobbing babies from her legs and handing them over to a grandmotherly woman with a crisp British accent and her hair in a bun, but she quickly turned her thoughts to the beautiful estate where the quilt camp was held, the friendly, encouraging faculty, the joy of creativity and camaraderie she longed for in her daily life but had not truly felt since quilt camp. At the time, in the middle of her first pregnancy, she had laughingly described her week at Elm Creek Quilt Camp as one last opportunity for fun before the demands of motherhood took hold. A few months after Ethan was born, she finally understood why the other mothers at the Candlelight welcoming ceremony had nodded knowingly instead of smiling at her joke.

She would hire the best nanny in the world, she told herself. A Penn State student majoring in elementary education or premed with a concentration in pediatrics. Mary Poppins. The nanny would be so nurturing and affectionate that the children would not even realize Karen had left the house until she returned home in the evening. They would run to meet her at the door as they ran to meet Nate, and they would beg cuddles and kisses as they told her about their fun, educational, and enriching day. They would probably cry when Nanny said good-bye. They would probably cling to her and beg her to stay for supper. On weekends, they would ask why Nanny had not come, and if they fell and scraped a knee, they would sob for Nanny rather than their mother.

She had not even mailed in her application yet, and already guilt and jealousy had set in.

She brushed the thoughts aside and plugged in her laptop. She had nearly finished updating her résumé—she had very little to add—when Lucas's cry pealed over the baby monitor. After scrambling to conceal all evidence of her activity, she ran upstairs to her younger son, vowing that she would tell Nate her intentions that evening as soon as he came home from work.

She procrastinated by waiting until after supper, for that brief period of relative calm after the boys finished eating and ran off to the living room to play and before they returned to ask for popsicles. Karen insisted on clearing the table while Nate finished his water, realizing too late that this was a sure sign she wanted something from him. They never waited on each other except on birthdays, after arguments, or when one was feeling amorous and was hoping to overcome the other's desperate need for sleep.

Until Karen quit her job, they had always divided their expenses equally. Even on their first date, she had insisted on paying half of the check. Nate had put up a modest fight, but eventually his desire to convince her he was a modern, sensitive, egalitarian male overcame his instinct for chivalry. They were students, with students' modest incomes. Frequent dating would quickly bankrupt him if they didn't split the costs, and neither wanted anything to stand in the way of seeing each other again.

Karen had never expected a simple blind date for lunch to turn out so well, even though her roommate and her roommate's boyfriend had been trying to set them up all semester. For months, heavy course loads and a general reluctance to find out exactly why their mutual friends considered them an ideal match prevented them from arranging to meet. Eventually they ran out of excuses and agreed to meet between classes for a quick bite to eat. Karen skipped her favorite seminar to stay for a dessert she really didn't need and more amazing discoveries of all she and Nate had in common—a fervent belief in the musical genius of Paul Simon, an inability to care about professional sports, an almost embarrassing depth of knowledge of *Buffy the Vampire Slayer* lore. Nate's earnest charm and warm sense of humor had quickly erased Karen's doubts about their four-year age difference and the gap between Nate's graduate student status and her own as an undergraduate junior. He had already confessed his environmentalist leanings, and after he walked her to her car and saw a late model, low-emission, fuel-efficient Volvo at the curb, he seized her hand and kissed it. Karen was suddenly very glad her parents had insisted she take her mother's car instead of her father's Cadillac to college, and forever after wondered what Nate would have done had she come on bicycle.

"What's on your mind?" asked Nate as she filled the sink and squeezed dish soap into the stream from the faucet. They had a dishwasher, but Nate disputed the manufacturer's claim that it used less water and energy than hand washing. So they used it to store the trashcan and the recyclables bin instead.

"Nothing," said Karen quickly. "Well, okay. Something. Sit down," she added, as he began to rise. She retrieved the magazine from the diaper bag on the counter, where she had placed it in anticipation of this moment. She returned to her seat and set the magazine on the table before her. "Please don't panic."

"Panic?" He looked warier than she had ever seen him. "Why should I panic?"

She gestured to the magazine. "Because I allowed one of these into the house."

"What?" He glanced at the magazine. "This? That's what all this is about?"

She nodded.

He strangled out a laugh. "You nearly gave me a heart attack. I thought you were going to tell me you were pregnant again."

He of all people ought to know there was little chance of that. Karen flipped the magazine open and placed it before him. "I think I'd like to apply for this job," she said after giving him a moment to skim the ad. "It's not my traditional line of work, but I think I'd enjoy it more than any other part-time work I could—"

She broke off at the sound of a thud from the living room. She paused, but when neither of the boys howled in pain or outrage, she returned her attention to Nate. "So. What do you think?"

"Sounded like something hit the wall."

"No, honey. About the job. Look." Karen pointed to a line of type. "It says seasonal work and flexible hours are available."

"But it's all the way in Waterford."

"That's an hour drive at most."

"What about the kids? Won't you miss them?"

"Of course I'll miss them, just like you miss them when you go off to work in the morning." She had expected objections to the magazine, but she had not prepared any counterarguments to concerns about the job itself. "Elm Creek Quilt Camp is open only March through October, so I would be working less than if I tried to get a teaching job someplace. We always said I would go back to work when the kids were old enough—"

Another thud sounded from the living room, followed by an ominous crash.

Nate twisted in his chair. "Ethan, what are you boys doing in there?"

"Nothing!" Ethan shouted. "Lucas threw his sippy cup at the lamp again."

"Why?"

"He needs a reason?" asked Karen.

"Because the first time he missed," called Ethan. "It fell off the table and rolled under the sofa. I can't reach it."

"Just leave it alone. I'll get it."

As he rose, Karen placed a hand on his arm. "May we finish this conversation later?"

"Sure." He pushed back his chair. "First chance we get."

Karen watched him go, muffling a sigh. She waited, but when she realized he was not returning anytime soon, she got up and finished cleaning the kitchen.

Later that evening, she bathed the boys while Nate checked his email and graded exams. He shut down his computer long enough to read the boys a story and tuck them into bed, but soon after she kissed the boys goodnight and turned off their lights, the phone rang. She snatched it up, praying that the boys would sleep through the noise. It was one of Nate's undergraduate students, frustrated with a particularly difficult section of code he was trying to write for a class project. While Nate patiently talked him through it, Karen returned to the basement and finished her résumé. She printed out a copy and took it upstairs to seek Nate's advice, but found him in the recliner, feet propped up, computer on his lap, eyes riveted on the screen.

Rather than interrupt him, she returned to the basement and put in a load of laundry. She switched on the baby monitor and worked on a foundation paper–pieced Pickle Dish quilt in between shifting loads to the drier and folding the clothes. By the time she carried the basket of warm, crisp, neatly folded laundry upstairs, Nate had fallen asleep. She made sure to save all of his documents before shutting down the computer and carefully setting it on the table beside him. It was a warm night, but she drew a light quilt over him and shut the windows before turning off the lamp and going upstairs to bed, laundry basket balanced on her hip.

"Karen?"

She left the laundry basket on the landing and returned to the living room. "I thought you were asleep."

Nate turned on the lamp and reached for something on the

floor beside his chair. It was the *Modern Quilter* magazine, and when he placed it on his lap, it fell open to the ad. "Do you want to talk about this job now?"

Karen was so tired that all she wanted to do was close her eyes and crawl into bed, but she had laundry to put away, bills to pay, and three unanswered emails from her mother waiting on the computer. She needed eight uninterrupted hours of sleep, not a lengthy, overdue conversation, but she got down the laundry basket and nodded.

"Do you really want to work at a quilt camp?" asked Nate. "Would you— I mean, I thought your quilting was just a hobby. When you said you wanted to teach, I thought you meant—"

"You thought I meant teaching undergrad business courses at Penn State," Karen finished. "I know this isn't what I went to graduate school for, but I loved quilt camp and I think I'd enjoy working there. It would be fun."

He studied the magazine for a moment before closing it with a sigh. "I guess life hasn't been much fun for you for the past four and a half years."

"No, honey, that's not true." She loved her life with Nate and the boys. She had never laughed so much or thought herself so utterly necessary to another human being. "But I do want something more. Something . . . separate. Something where I can be just me again and not someone else's mom. You know, almost everyone I've met since Ethan was born knows me not as Karen Wise but as 'Ethan's Mom' or 'Lucas's Mom.' Isn't that sad? Even other mothers don't bother to learn mothers' names."

"So you want to get a job to prove there's more to you than motherhood?"

"That's part of it, but not everything." She hesitated, wondering how to explain without hurting his feelings. It wasn't because her best friend had found a job and she resented being left behind. She had earned her own money ever since accepting her first baby-sitting job at thirteen, and she hated depending upon someone else's income. She hated that guilty feeling of spending Nate's salary, even though she knew he considered his earnings to be hers as much as they were his own. In theory she agreed; he would not be able to be both a father and a tenure-track university professor if someone else were not willing to care for his children during the day. Karen agreed with that philosophy, and yet, she still wished she had a little part-time income to spend as she pleased, guilt-free.

"I'm sure I'll want something full-time when the boys are in school," she told Nate. "But in the meantime, a part-time job like this one would help support my quilting habit."

"Then you should apply."

"What about the kids? We'll have to get a nanny or day care or something, and we'll have to work out a schedule to cart them around to their activities."

"We'll figure something out." He lowered the footrest of the recliner and beckoned her to curl up on his lap. "If other families can manage, we can. First, get the job. We can work out the other details later."

Karen had never taught quilting, but in her previous life, she had taught introductory marketing courses as an MBA student at the University of Nebraska. Before the boys woke the next morning, she searched the basement for the carton holding her old graduate school papers and books, still taped tightly shut from their move to Pennsylvania eight years before, when Nate accepted an assistant professorship in Penn State's School of Information Sciences and Technology. She hoped some of her undergraduates' teaching evaluations would qualify as letters of recommendation from former students. Her students had graduated long ago and she had no way to track them down before her application package was due.

She drafted sample lesson plans after taking Ethan to nursery school, typing with one hand while cradling a nursing, dozing Lucas on a pillow on her lap. She doubted she had the sort of employment history the management of Elm Creek Quilt Camp expected of their applicants. What would they think of her four years as an associate director in Penn State's Office of University Development? Would they have any idea what that meant, or should she work into her cover letter pertinent details such as the size of her office in Old Main or the fact that she had been the youngest associate director in the history of the university?

How would she reply when they asked her why she had abandoned such a promising career?

The truth was that she had fallen passionately in love with Ethan the moment she held him in her arms in her hospital bed. She stayed awake throughout the night holding him, marveling at him, rather than miss a single moment of his first hours in the world. The nurse scolded her and threatened to whisk him off to the nursery, telling her she would be sorry later that she had not taken advantage of the chance to get some rest. She would have ample opportunity to admire her baby later, every day until he left for college if she so desired. Karen refused to hand over her son and compromised by sleeping with Ethan in the bed beside her. The nurse did not approve, but fortunately her shift ended at six in the morning, and the nurse who replaced her believed that a newborn could never be held too much.

As her last trimester drew to a close, Karen had written detailed notes for her colleagues and assistant so they could carry on smoothly in her absence, and she had reassured her superiors that she would be back on the job eight weeks to the day after she gave birth. She and Nate managed to obtain a place for Ethan in the most sought-after day-care program in town, the Child Development Laboratory operated by the College of Health and Human Development right on the Penn State campus. Karen knew Ethan would be well cared for, but as the eight weeks of her maternity leave raced by in a blur of wonder and exhaustion, she grew less certain she would be capable of leaving him. She spent every evening of the last week crying in the glider rocker as she nursed Ethan to sleep, as Nate sat on the edge of the bed worriedly watching her and assuring her that everything would be fine.

On her first day back to work, she put on the least obvious of her maternity ensembles, having not yet managed to fit into her prepregnancy suits. She kissed Nate good-bye and offered him a ride as she had hundreds of times before, but this time she loaded a breast pump in the car along with her briefcase. She left her precious baby sleeping in the arms of a competent-looking caregiver and made it all the way back to her desk in her beloved office in Old Main before racing back to the Child Development Lab with a hasty excuse for the first colleague she passed on her rush out the door. Remorseful and relieved, she buckled Ethan in his car seat and drove home.

During Ethan's afternoon nap, she phoned her most understanding supervisor, apologized, and promised to return in the morning. This time she did not even manage to leave the Child Development Lab before hurrying back for her baby. The following day she turned the car around before reaching College Avenue. That day, after meeting Nate in his campus office for a tearful discussion, she phoned her supervisor and told him that the next time she returned to Old Main would be to submit her letter of resignation. He replied—rather cheerfully and not at all surprised, or so it had struck her then—that he had assumed as much. They had already cleared out her desk and would interview her potential replacement the following morning.

Unfortunately, every embarrassing, graceless misstep was part of her employment record and fodder for a job interview. Given her history, the Elm Creek Quilters might be justifiably wary of hiring a woman who had intended to return to a job she loved but found, at the very last possible moment, that she could not bring herself to leave her baby. They might also be concerned that she would quit Elm Creek Quilt Camp if she became pregnant again. But what could she do? She could not retract her choices, and despite the hassles and the loss of income, she never regretted stepping off the career track to stay at home with her boys. She could not help it if the Elm Creek Quilters held her indecisive wavering against her, but she would tell them the truth and hope for the best.

Nate had given her a digital camera for her birthday, so it should have been an easy matter to photograph her quilts for her portfolio. It would have been if the boys had not been so eager to help. Ethan insisted on holding up the quilts for her, but although he stretched his arms high above his head and stood on tiptoe, even the smallest crib quilts dragged on the ground. When reasoning with him failed, she pretended to take pictures his way, but suggested they also hang the quilts in case they needed extras. Ethan agreed that this sounded like a good idea, but then he insisted on posing in front of each quilt and smiling brightly while she took the picture. Bribes or threats were powerless to persuade him to step out of the shot. Meanwhile, Lucas flung her other quilts into the air and danced upon them where they landed on the floor, apparently mistaking them for the parachute at Gymboree.

When she finally gave up, she had wasted an hour and squandered the last bit of her carefully conserved patience. She stuck Lucas in his playpen, handed out Veggie Booty, and put on a Dragon Tales DVD before locking herself in the bathroom with the quilt magazine. Ten minutes of deep breathing and art quilt inspiration later, she emerged with a renewed sense of resolve and purpose—only to find Lucas asleep on one of her quilts with his little diaper-clad rump sticking in the air and Ethan engrossed in the adventures of Zak and Wheezie. Karen abandoned her project for the rest of the afternoon rather than jeopardize the miraculous calm. After supper, she prevailed upon Nate to distract the boys while she quickly hung the quilts and snapped pictures during fifteen precious, uninterrupted minutes.

The lesson plans took her two weeks to complete, since she could work only when the boys were asleep and after Nate came home from work. Second-guessing every decision, she edited and revised her portfolio repeatedly and might have continued to do so except she ran out of time. Though not completely satisfied, she made an eleventh-hour sprint to the post office and sent the portfolio next-day express, return receipt requested. If she never heard back from Elm Creek Quilters, she did not want it to be because her portfolio had been lost in the mail.

Nate told her that, having done her best, she should now put the application out of her thoughts. Pacing and worrying would not hasten their response. Karen grit her teeth and promised him she would try. It was so easy for him. He left every morning for a job he enjoyed in a department that seemed eager to grant him tenure. At the end of an interesting day, he returned to the boys' joyous welcome, their favorite playmate grown even dearer in his absence. He could tell her not to worry because if the Elm Creek Quilters never contacted her, his life would clip jauntily along as it always had, unaffected by her disappointment.

Two weeks passed with no reply except for the postal service's confirmation that her portfolio had indeed reached the mailroom of Elm Creek Manor. She wished she could vent to Janice about the excruciating wait, but something held her back, even as Janice waxed enthusiastic about how she and her husband were converting the living room into a home office. Karen was unsure why she concealed her own tentative step back into the working world, except, perhaps, because it was so tentative. She had applied for the job at Elm Creek Manor and that job only. She did not peruse the want ads in the *Centre Daily Times* or submit her newly updated résumé to online services. A foray into the safe, nurturing world of quilting was just about all she could handle, and she wasn't completely confident she could manage that.

On a Friday morning more than a month after she submitted her portfolio, Karen was trying to coax some oatmeal and bananas into Lucas when the phone rang. "Hello?" she asked, pressing the receiver tightly to one ear. Nate had already left for work or she would have asked him to take the call upstairs.

She could not make out the reply over her children's clamor. Lucas was cheerfully banging his spoon on the table and exhorting her in language he alone understood, and Ethan was running around the house shouting, "Efan to the rescue!" As he sprinted past, she saw that he wore nothing but the cape to his Superman pajamas and a pair of socks.

"Hello?" she said again, prying the spoon from Lucas's hand. "I'm sorry, I didn't catch that."

"May I speak with Karen Wise, please?" asked a woman who sounded close to her own age.

"I'm Karen. Sorry for the noise."

"Don't worry about it. This is Sarah McClure from Elm Creek Quilt Camp."

"Oh, hi!" Karen made a frantic gesture for Ethan to quiet down.

He stopped running and strained to reach the phone. "Who is it, Mommy? Can I talk to him?"

"No, sweetie. It's for Mommy."

The woman on the other end laughed. "It sounds like you have company. Is this a bad time?"

"No! No, this is great." Karen desperately did not want her to hang up. "I'm glad you called."

"Can I talk?" pleaded Ethan. "I'll use my good manners."

"My colleagues and I were very impressed with your portfolio," said Sarah.

"Thank you." Karen turned her back on Ethan and covered the mouthpiece with her hand. "Honey, please. I can't hear."

"Mommy! Mommy!" Ethan punctuated each shout with a leap for the phone. "Please, Mommy! Let me talk, too!"

"We haven't taught many classes in paper piecing, so your experience would complement us nicely." Sarah paused. "Would it help if I talked to your son?"

Karen was mortified. "Oh, no. That isn't necessary. He's all right."

"Really. I'd be happy to."

"Well—" Karen thought quickly. "Okay. Here he is."

Thrilled, Ethan held the phone to his ear. "Hello? Who's this?" A pause. "Oh, I thought you were Daddy." He looked up at Karen. "Efan." A slight pause. "No, not Efan. E-Fan," he said, emphasizing each syllable. "My baby brother's name is Lucas. I use the big boy potty but Lucas still goes in his diaper. Once after his bath Mommy couldn't get his diaper on fast enough and he peed on the rug."

"Okay, honey, thank you, that's enough." Karen snatched back the phone and took a quick, deep breath before putting it to her ear. "Hi. Sorry about that."

"That's all right. Sometimes it's easier to just give them what they want, so long as it won't hurt them."

"That's the truth. Do you have kids?"

"No, but I know many childish adults. Back to the job—if you're still interested, we'd like to invite you to Elm Creek Manor for an interview."

"I'm definitely still interested." Karen ducked as a blob of oatmeal sailed past her ear. Lucas crowed for joy as she scrambled for a pen and paper to take down the date and time of the interview.

"One more thing," said Sarah after Karen assured her she knew the way to the manor. "We're asking all of the applicants to create an original block design and bring it to the interview."

"What sort of design?" Karen's heart sank a little. Somehow Sarah made "all of the applicants" sound as if there were hundreds.

"A new logo for Elm Creek Quilts. Use whatever techniques showcase your talents best."

"Any particular size or colors?"

"You know, you're the first person to ask. Let's make it a twelve-inch block, and use whatever colors you prefer. I suppose I should call everyone else back and let them know."

Or not, Karen thought. Then the other two hundred applicants might get it wrong and be disqualified.

After they hung up, Karen gripped the counter, exultant and yet slightly queasy. She had an interview. Even Ethan's interruption and potty talk had not scared away Sarah McClure from Elm Creek Quilts. She had an interview. Not only that, she had but one week, two days, and four hours from the time she hung up the phone in which to design and make an original quilt block.

Karen knew this quilt block would be the most important pattern she ever designed. She had never taught quilting, published a pattern, or won a ribbon in a national quilt show. It was something of a miracle that Sarah McClure had requested the interview at all, considering how many expert quilters would give their entire fabric stashes for an opportunity to become an Elm Creek Quilter.

Still, Karen knew from her stay at Elm Creek Quilt Camp that the women who worked there were more than close friends. They were a family, and selecting someone to join a family was a far more complex and difficult matter than selecting an employee. They surely had any number of qualified instructors from which to choose, but they would be seeking something more, someone who understood what Elm Creek Quilt Camp meant to quilters worldwide, someone who would cherish Elm Creek Quilts as much as they did.

Karen knew this single quilt block could be her best opportunity to prove she was that person.

She chose bright, cheerful cottons from her fabric stash and stacked them on the kitchen counter for inspiration, hoping a passing glance as she cooked or hauled laundry upstairs from the basement would encourage an idea to spring forth from her subconscious. As she took the children through their daily routine, a part of her thoughts were elsewhere, sketching, considering, revising. With two days to go, she stayed up late into the night armed with a pencil, a ruler, graph paper, and a pot of coffee. The kitchen table was covered in eraser crumbs by the time she finally went upstairs to bed, but her pattern was finished and, unlike her portfolio, she thought it was well done.

The next morning, she dragged herself from bed for Lucas's second feeding, deeply regretting her decision to forego sleep the night before. Lucas dozed as he nursed but became suddenly alert as soon as she tried to return him to his crib, so she put on her slippers and carried him downstairs to the kitchen, where Nate was reading a Dr. Seuss book to Ethan over breakfast.

She asked Nate to hold Lucas so she could shower, and as she handed him off, she glanced at the kitchen counter. "Where's my block?"

"Your what?" asked Nate, settling Lucas on his lap.

"My quilt block." Karen searched through the pile of mail, glanced at the floor, and opened the dishwasher to check the trashcan. "I left the pattern right here last night."

"Daddy spilled coffee," volunteered Ethan, spooning cereal into his mouth.

Karen turned an inquiring look upon Nate, who shook his head. "There weren't any quilt blocks there, just some papers and junk mail." His mouth twisted into a sour frown around the last two words. A forest of credit card applications filled their mailbox every week despite Nate's attempts to remove their address from mailing lists.

"Those papers were my quilt patterns." Karen checked the trashcan a second time and noticed that a new white plastic bag lined it. "Did you take out the trash?"

"It's at the curb," he said, but, having guessed the answer, she was already hurrying past him to the front door. Grass clippings stuck to her bare feet as she padded down the driveway and lifted the lid of the nearest garbage can, recoiling at the stench. Grimacing, Karen pulled out one bag, unfastened the tie, and peered inside. A man passed walking a pair of black labs, who sniffed the trash and then Karen before continuing on. The man deliberately averted his eyes, and Karen suddenly remembered she wore nothing but panties and Nate's extra-large Cornhuskers T-shirt, shrunken and faded from many washings. She tugged the shirt down as far as it would stretch and continued digging through the bag with her free hand. After a while she abandoned the first bag and tried the second, then frantically reached for the third when she heard the garbage truck shifting gears down the block. She had almost given up hope when she spotted a few pieces of paper, now wadded into a ball and soaked through with coffee. She shook off an orange peel and a few soggy Annie's Cheddar Bunnies only to discover that she held a crumpled piece of waxed paper. Her drawings were nowhere to be found.

She returned the trash bags to the can just as the garbage truck came into view. A low whistle followed her as she scurried up the driveway back to the house. It occurred to her that, aside from Sarah's praise for her portfolio, it was the first compliment she had received in months.

Nate was feeding Lucas in his highchair when Karen entered, trailing grass clippings and coffee grounds. "I couldn't find them, and now the garbage truck has come and gone, so that's that."

Nate looked as if he knew that whatever he said next was bound to get him in trouble, but he had no choice. "Did you check the recycling bin?"

"The recycling bin?"

"It was paper," he explained carefully. "I always recycle paper."

She knew that, but somehow coffee-soaked paper did not seem

to qualify for recycling. "Why didn't you tell me that before I dug through the trash on the curb?"

"I thought you were going upstairs to shower. I didn't think you'd go outside dressed like that."

Karen yanked open the dishwasher and found her drawings buried under bottles and cans in the recycling bin. "Great," she said, as the pages dripped coffee.

"I'm sorry," said Nate. "I thought they were your rough drafts or I wouldn't have thrown them away."

Karen spread paper towels on the counter and lay the ruined pages upon them. She would have to do them over, but at least she could refer to her original drawings rather than working from memory. Sighing, she went to the sink and scrubbed her arms from fingertips to biceps using hot water and antibacterial soap. "I suppose once they absorbed all that coffee, they probably did look like rough drafts."

"I really am sorry."

"He's sorry, Mommy," said Ethan, and Lucas babbled out a few earnest syllables in agreement.

"Okay. Fine. He's sorry." Relenting, Karen added, "I'll just do them over after supper. You're still planning to take the boys to the park, right?"

Nate took a sip of coffee and shook his head. "I can't. I have a meeting at five-thirty."

"But you said you'd be home at five so we could eat early and I could have the evening to sew my quilt block."

"I'm sorry, honey. The department chair dropped a curriculum review on us at the last minute."

Karen shut off the water and snatched up a towel. "But I was counting on you. I need the time more than ever now that I also have to redo my drawings."

"Can you wait until Saturday? I'm sorry, Karen, but I can't come home early. I don't have a choice. You remember what it's like to work."

Karen stiffened. "Yes, actually, I do."

"Mommy's mad at Daddy," observed Ethan to no one in particular.

"I'm not mad," said Karen, though she was.

"I'll redo the drawings for you this weekend," offered Nate.

"No, you can't." Karen flung the towel onto the counter, but picked it up, folded it, and hung it on its usual wall hook when she remembered Ethan watching her. "It's a test for the job interview. I have to do it myself."

Just like everything else around here, she thought.

On the morning of her interview, Karen showered and tried on some of her suits from her Office of University Development days. With some effort, she managed to fit into her loosest, most forgiving suit. The skirt was a bit too snug around the hips and thighs and the jacket was surprisingly snug at the bosom, thanks to Lucas's sustained nursing. If she got the job and convinced Lucas to wean, she would shrink back to B cups in a matter of days. She studied her transiently ample profile in the mirror and decided the suit fit well enough for the interview. It had to, since her only other options were yoga pants or maternity jeans.

She hung up the suit, making a mental note to iron it later, pulled on her sweats, and went downstairs to have breakfast and kiss Nate before he bicycled off to work. "I have to leave by two," she reminded him, following him out to the garage with Lucas riding her hip.

"I'll leave campus no later than twelve-thirty," he promised, strapping on his helmet.

"Can you make it noon, so you can watch the boys while I get ready?"

"Sorry, I can't. I have a meeting. I'll leave as soon as it's over."

"Twelve-fifteen?"

"The second the meeting's over, I'll be on my way home. Promise." He gave her a reassuring wave good-bye as he pedaled down the driveway and out into the street, his overloaded backpack giving him the appearance of a precariously balanced turtle.

Karen had time for a quick cup of coffee and bagel before taking Ethan to nursery school. Lucas fell asleep in the car on the way home, so once she had him settled in his crib, she gathered her maps and directions, the quilt block and pattern, and a copy of her portfolio. She packed all the papers into her briefcase and put everything in the car, just in case Nate came home later than anticipated and she had to rush out the door at the last minute. Lucas thoughtfully slept longer than usual, so she had time to iron her suit and find a pair of nylons without any runs. She rehearsed the interview in her mind, posing questions to herself and answering them aloud.

Lucas woke as soon as she lay down on her bed to rest so she would be fresh for the interview. Sometimes she suspected a device hidden in her bedsprings triggered an alarm in the children's rooms, because somehow they always knew as soon as her head touched the pillow. She took Lucas from his crib and tried to persuade him to nurse lying beside her on the bed so she could grab a few minutes of rest, but he fussed and complained until she took him to the rocking chair.

Afterward, Karen and Lucas played with blocks and stuffed animals until it was time to pick up Ethan from school. Although she had warned him they would need to leave right away, Ethan begged to stay and play with his friends, and since Lucas was squirming in her arms and gesturing desperately toward the playground, she agreed. She chatted with the other parents and kept careful track of the time, remembering to give the boys a ten-minute warning, and then five, and then two. Somehow Ethan still managed to be astonished when she told him that it was five minutes past noon and they needed to leave. Lucas did not want to leave, either, but he was still small enough to be carried against his will—unlike Ethan, who retreated to the farthest corner of the climbing structure and refused to budge. Mindful of the teachers and the other parents observing her, Karen projected loving sympathy as she reasoned, coaxed, and finally begged him to come down, all to no avail. After ten minutes, another mother offered to hold Lucas while she climbed the ladder, pried Ethan's fingers from the monkey bars, and took him down the slide on her lap, since she knew there was no way she could wrestle him down the ladder.

"Say good-bye to your teachers," she said cheerily when his feet finally touched pea gravel. She took Lucas back from the helpful mother and reached for Ethan's hand. Instead of taking hold, Ethan burst into tears and reached for her with both arms.

"Someone's tired," remarked the other mother. Karen replied with a tight smile and a nod. She bent down and hefted Ethan onto her right hip, and, balancing Lucas on her left, she managed to shuffle across the playground and out the gate.

Once out of sight of the playground, she abruptly set Ethan on the sidewalk. "Okay, that's enough. I need lots of cooperation today."

Tearfully, he sniffled, "Please pick me up."

"Honey, I know you're tired, but I can't carry both of you all the way to the car." She took his hand, and he reluctantly held hers. He dragged his feet, but he came. Suddenly she felt overwhelmingly weary. They went through this at least twice a week. Almost every other child in Ethan's class spotted their mother at the gate, cried out "Mommy!" and went running for a hug. Only Ethan acted as if a stranger had come to drag him off to the deepest circle of hell. Karen could only imagine what the teachers and other parents thought went on in the Wise home to evoke such a reaction.

As soon as she buckled Ethan into his car seat, he brightened and began chattering about his day at school as if nothing had happened. His mood could turn on a dime, leaving her dazed in the wake of his emotions. Lucas fell asleep again, which surprised her considering how long his morning nap had lasted, but he woke as soon as they pulled into the garage. She had hoped to find Nate waiting for her, but had not really expected him to be able to leave so early.

She fixed the boys their lunch—peanut butter and jelly sandwiches and sliced bananas—and stood at the counter while they ate, too nervous to swallow a bite herself. She had not been on a job interview in eight years. She had not had a sustained conversation with any adult other than Nate, Janice, or her mother in more than four. What if she had forgotten how to talk about anything but her children?

At a quarter to one, she began glancing out the window, watching for Nate on his bike. Ethan finished eating and went into the living room to play, but Lucas pushed the pieces of his sandwich around on his plate and mashed his bananas into a sticky paste. At ten minutes to one, she phoned Nate's office. He did not answer, so she left a message on his voice mail and decided to take his absence as a good sign; he must already be on his way home. She did not try his cell, knowing that he could not answer it while riding his bike.

"Sweetie, are you going to eat your lunch?" she asked Lucas absently, standing at the window. In response, Lucas picked up a peanut butter and jelly triangle and dropped it disdainfully on the floor.

Sighing, she unbuckled him from his booster seat and washed his face and hands. When he toddled off to join his brother, she cleared the table and wiped up the mess on the floor, keeping one eye on the clock. It was one o'clock. If he had left campus at twelve-thirty, the latest he promised her he would leave, he should have arrived home already. Even in bad weather, he never needed more than a half hour to bike home from the office.

She called his office again, and then tried the cell. After five rings, he answered in a low voice. "Hello?"

"Where are you?"

"I'm stuck in this meeting," he griped in an undertone.

"You mean you haven't even left campus yet?"

"Honey, I can't talk right now. I'll call you back as soon as I can."

"But—"

"I'm sorry, but I have to hang up. Bye."

She fumed as the line went dead. She hung up the phone and began pacing. At a quarter past, Lucas ran back into the kitchen and reached for her with his head tilted to one side, his sign that he wanted to nurse. She carried him back to the living room, settled on the recliner, and nursed him, glancing at the clock on the mantel and starting a slow burn.

At half past she knew she could not wait any longer. "I'm going upstairs to get dressed," she told Ethan, and carried Lucas, still nursing, to her bedroom. Lucas stomped his feet and wailed in protest when she set him down on the floor, and he would not be consoled with cheerful talk and smiles as she hastily showered, blew her hair dry, and squeezed into her suit. He clung to her legs as she put on her makeup, so she picked him up and fixed her hair as best she could with only one hand. At one-thirty she returned downstairs. Nate was nowhere to be seen.

"I can't believe this," she muttered, setting Lucas down on the kitchen floor. Instead of searching out his brother, he opened the pantry door and began taking out the boxes and cans on the bottom shelf and lining them up on the floor. She called Nate's cell phone again, hanging up with a bang when he did not answer. Maybe he was on his way. He had said he would call first, but maybe he had run for his bike as soon as the meeting ended rather than wasting time on the phone.

He was more than an hour late. He had better be on his way.

"Mama?" Lucas held up the familiar yellow box hopefully. "Chee-woes?"

"I already made you a yummy sandwich and you threw it on the floor," she snapped. She took a deep breath and reminded herself that she was not angry with *him*. "Sorry, honey. Of course you can have some cereal."

She buckled him into his booster seat and handed him a spoon so he could bang away happily on the table while she poured cereal and milk. "Ethan, how are you doing in there?" she called when it occurred to her she had not heard from him in some time.

"Fine," he called back, and something in his tone made her go to the doorway and look. He had turned on the television and was staring at a cartoon in which a vile-looking slime monster made deep-voiced threats to a shapely blonde girl wearing a cut-off shirt and military cargo pants. An indeterminate rodentlike creature was gnawing through the ropes that tied the girl to a metal barrel marked "Toxic Waste."

"What is this?" cried Karen, quickly switching off the television. "That is not PBS Kids."

"PBS Kids had Mr. Rogers. I don't like Mr. Rogers."

"You mean you don't like his show. Mr. Rogers was a very nice man." Karen shook her head. That wasn't the point. "You know you're not supposed to watch TV without asking."

Ethan's eyes were fixed on the dark television screen. "Can I watch TV?"

"No. Read a book."

"I can't read!"

"*Look* at a book." She returned to the kitchen where Lucas, still strapped into his booster seat, strained to reach his bowl of Cheerios on the counter. "Sorry, sweetheart." She snatched up the bowl and set it before him.

He peered into the bowl warily and looked up at her with a face full of doubt.

"It's Cheerios, honey, just like you wanted." She picked up his spoon and began feeding him. He took two bites before clamping his mouth shut and turning away. "Not hungry after all?" She rose and picked up his bowl. He let out a howl of protest that nearly made her drop it. "Okay, okay. Here it is." She set it down again and placed the spoon in his hand. He smiled angelically and began to eat.

She checked the clock. Ten minutes until two.

She blinked back tears of frustration and practiced her Lamaze breathing. She pulled the phone closer, sat down beside Lucas, and tried Nate's numbers one last time. It rang so long she was sure his voice mail would pick up, but instead Nate answered.

"Please tell me you're on your way home," she said.

"I'm not, honey. I'm still in the meeting. I can't talk—"

"Don't you hang up again. You'd better talk to me."

"Hold on." She heard muffled voices, a moment of quiet in which she feared he had hung up on her, and then Nate's voice at a normal volume. "Okay. I'm in the hall."

"Are you coming home?"

"No, Karen. I have to go back into the meeting."

"But I have to get to my interview. You promised you'd be home by twelve-thirty."

"I know. I know. I'm sorry. I had no idea this was going to run so long. We haven't even taken a break for lunch."

"Oh, poor you."

"Karen—"

"You're supposed to be here, right now, with the boys. I should already be on the road."

"I'm sorry. How many times can I say it? Can you call the quilters and reschedule?"

"Are you kidding me? This is a job interview. What kind of impression will that make?"

"Well . . ." Nate sighed. "Let's just hope they'll be reasonable and accommodate a working parent."

And if they didn't? So much for her dreams of becoming an Elm Creek Quilter. "Nate, if you come home now, I might still make it on time."

"I can't walk out of this meeting. It's too important."

"More important than a job interview?" cried Karen. "It's a meeting. You have a dozen meetings every week. They won't care if you miss the last twenty minutes of one meeting."

"It might run longer than that, and they will care. My whole tenure committee is here. I couldn't leave even if I wanted to."

"Surely they'll understand that you have a family emergency."

"This isn't an emergency and you know it."

"But it's just one meeting!"

"It's more than that. They'll consider it indicative of my commitment to the department."

"What about your commitment to me?"

"That's not fair."

"Not fair? I asked for one day. Not even a whole day. Just one afternoon for something I care about. And you promised."

"It's a job interview, Karen. Be realistic. What's the worst that could happen if you don't go to that interview today? And what's the worst that could happen if I don't get tenure? I'll lose my job, I'll have to find something else as if that won't be next to impossible as a failed assistant professor, we'll have to sell the house and uproot the kids and move God knows where. Listen. I'm sorry I've let you down, but this is my job and I can't leave just because you want me to."

"Nate—"

"I don't have a choice."

"You do have a choice."

"You're right. I do. And I've made it. I'm sorry."

She said nothing, stunned.

"Look," said Nate. "Call the quilters and see if you can reschedule for Friday or Saturday. If they won't, call someone else—Janice or one of the other moms. Someone will help you out. But I've got to go."

He hung up.

After a moment, Karen pressed the button on the receiver, waited for the dial tone, and called Janice.

"Hello?"

The voice was girlish, too young for Janice and too old for her daughters. "Um, hi. Is Janice there?"

"I'm sorry, she's not available at the moment. Would you like to leave a message?"

Then Karen recalled that Janice had mentioned hiring a baby-sitter to watch the kids while she and her husband went for an ultrasound. "No, thank you," she said, and hung up.

She called every other parent in the playgroup. Half were not home; the other half were either on their way out, or the background noise in their homes radiated so much chaos and confusion that Karen could not bring herself to ask them to take on two more children. She clutched the phone, racing through her mental list of baby-sitters and friends and people who owed her favors. She heard Ethan turn on the television and watched as Lucas began to fling soggy Cheerios out of his bowl using his spoon as a catapult. One sailed past her ear and stuck to the window; another landed on her sleeve. Immediately she brushed it off and snatched up a napkin to press the milk out of her clothes. Fortunately it was a dark suit. The spot would dry on the way to Waterford.

Sick to her stomach, she turned to the clock. It was a quarter past two.

Swiftly she unbuckled Lucas from his booster seat and snatched him up. "Ethan, honey, please go potty," she shouted toward the living room as she raced upstairs to change Lucas and put him in more presentable clothes.

"Why?"

"We're going for a ride."

She changed Lucas's diaper at a record pace and dug around in the laundry basket for a clean pair of overalls and onesie. All the while she strained her ears, praying that she would hear the door open and Nate calling out apologies.

"Mom?"

Karen glanced over her shoulder to find Ethan lingering in the doorway. One look told her she would have to change his clothes, too, since he had apparently used his shirt for a napkin after eating his peanut butter and jelly. "Did you go potty, honey?"

"I don't have to go."

"You should try to go. We're going to be in the car a long time."

"I don't have to pee. When I have to pee I feel a tickle in my penis and I don't feel one right now."

"I would like you to try. Just try. If you try and no pee comes out, that's fine."

Reluctantly, Ethan dragged himself from the doorway. She heard the sound of the toilet seat banging against the tank, and, a moment later, the boy who did not have to go potty doing exactly that.

"Okay, sweetie, you're done," she said, pulling on Lucas's socks. She coached Ethan through washing his hands and rushed him into a clean pair of jeans and a polo shirt. He complained about the collar and buttons, which he despised, but Karen insisted. She brushed their teeth and hair and ushered them downstairs to the foyer and into their shoes. She checked the diaper bag for supplies, tossed in a few snacks and drinks, and snatched up her purse and car keys.

"Where are we going?" asked Ethan as she rushed them outside to the car.

A reasonable question. "To my job interview."

Ethan climbed into his car seat glumly. "I don't want to go."

"Believe me, honey, this is not my first choice either." She gave him a sympathetic smile and a quick kiss.

He peered at her. "Mom—"

"What is it?" she said, struggling for patience. "We're in a very big hurry."

Whatever it was, he thought better of it. "Never mind. I love you."

Stabbed by guilt, she silently vowed to make it up to them. Later. She closed Ethan's door and hurried around to the other side of the car, but as she leaned over to place Lucas inside, she caught a whiff of his bottom. Muffling a groan, she told Ethan she would be right back and raced inside to change Lucas's diaper again.

They set out a full half hour later than Karen had originally intended. She might still make it, she thought grimly as she drove down Easterly Parkway toward 322, only slightly faster than the law permitted. She had no idea what she would do with the boys when she got there, but she would try to figure it out on the way.

"Muk," said Lucas. "Mama, muk."

"He wants milk," translated Ethan.

"Hold on." Keeping one hand on the wheel, she dug into the diaper bag on the front passenger seat and grasped his sippy cup. Straining to reach behind her, she asked Ethan to take the cup and hand it to his brother. She heard Ethan take a sip, and then something struck the back of her chair.

"No!" shouted Lucas. "Muk!"

"He wants *your* milk," Ethan clarified. "And I'd like some music, please. Wasn't that nice of me to say please?"

"Yes, honey. Very nice." She turned on the CD player, struck by a sudden and alarming vision of her sweet elder son becoming the most notorious, ingratiating teacher's pet in the history of elementary education.

"Muk!"

She really should have weaned Lucas a long time ago. "I'm sorry, sweetie, but I can't nurse you while I'm driving."

Lucas wailed.

"No, sweetie. Don't cry," she begged. "Come on. Sing with Mama. 'The wheels on the bus go round and round, round and round, round and round.' Ethan, help me."

Ethan joined in. "The wheels on the bus go round and round, all through the town!"

To Karen's relief, Lucas quieted down. As long as she kept singing, he was content, but if she paused to check the directions or change lanes, he broke into tears again. Even the break between songs was enough to make him whimper.

Twenty minutes later, Ethan had turned his attention to a picture book, she had become a hoarse solo act, and a glance in the rear view mirror revealed that Lucas's eyelids were starting to droop. She began singing louder, desperate to keep him awake. She knew her only chance at Elm Creek Manor would be if he slept through the interview, but he had already napped twice that morning and a third nap would guarantee active wakefulness for the rest of the day.

The motion of the car proved irresistible, and ten minutes later, Lucas was asleep. Karen switched off the CD player and wished she had thought to bring a bottle of water for herself. The singing had left her dry-mouthed and thirsty. She dug around in the diaper bag for a juice box and managed to puncture the foil with the straw without driving the car into a ditch or pouring apple juice down the front of her skirt.

"Mommy?" asked Ethan from the back seat. "What does 'tuck you' mean?"

"You mean like 'tuck you into bed'?" asked Karen. Ethan was always asking her to define words that he used every day, words whose meanings were, to Karen, so self-evident that she struggled to explain them without using the word itself in the definition. The other day he had asked her, "What is a bird?" She listed the standard details about feathers, nests, and eggs, to which he had replied, "No, Mommy. What *is* a bird?" Either he was a budding Zen master or he was trying to drive her insane.

"Mommy?"

"I'm thinking. Well, it means to snuggle your blankets and quilts around you so that you're warm and cozy in bed."

"What does it mean when there's no bed?"

"No bed?"

"What does it mean when you're mad at someone? Does it mean they should go to bed right now?"

Karen paused. "Honey, I don't understand."

"Like when someone takes your animal crackers at snack time and you hit them and they yell, 'Tuck you!' Does that mean they think you're naughty and you have to go to bed even though it's still daytime?"

"One of the kids at school said that?" gasped Karen. "Who?"

Ethan was silent.

"Who, Ethan? Who said that?"

"Well . . ." said Ethan slowly. "It definitely wasn't Graham. And he definitely didn't say it to Owen."

Ah. Graham. She should have guessed. Ethan had come home with several interesting Graham stories over the past school year. "That's a naughty thing some people say when they're angry. I don't want to hear you saying that, okay?"

"Okay," said Ethan, disappointed.

"Muk," murmured Lucas in his sleep.

Karen put in another CD.

She did not know whether to be grateful or alarmed when Ethan, too, drifted off to sleep. She was glad for the peace and quiet in which to collect her scattered thoughts, but she knew any chance that the boys would sleep peacefully in the tandem stroller while she chatted with the Elm Creek Quilters was long gone. If nothing else, they at least ought to be well rested and cheerful.

Both boys woke about fifteen miles from Waterford. She had made good time and wanted to press on, but Ethan's announcement that he had to go potty abruptly altered her priorities. Out of options, she pulled into the parking lot of McDonald's, and Ethan cheered in joyful disbelief at the sight of the golden arches. "Do *not* tell your father we came here," she instructed Ethan as she rushed the boys inside to the bathroom. She waited outside the stall trying to prevent Lucas from tipping over the garbage can while Ethan sat, asked for knock-knock jokes, told her another hair-raising Graham story, asked for fries and a shake, and did everything but go to the bathroom.

He looked up at her, swinging his feet, and his smile turned quizzical. "Mommy?"

"Honey, please, are you going to go or aren't you?" She checked her watch. "We are in a humongous hurry."

"Ooh-kay," he said, drawing out the word. "I guess I'm done."

"You may have fries but no ketchup," she said, wiping his bottom and quickly washing both boys' hands and her own. She made good on her promise, but the stop had cost them precious minutes. She would need a minor miracle to make it on time.

If she had not been to Elm Creek Manor before, she might have missed the turn completely, but she hit the brakes hard, turned the steering wheel sharply, and drove into a dense forest. The boys complained as the little car bounced over the gravel road. "Look! See? There's the creek," she said brightly as the water sparkled into view through the trees. She could not afford to put them in a bad humor now. "Just wait until you see the manor. It looks like a castle."

"Really?"

"Fwy!" shouted Lucas. A french fry whizzed past Karen's shoulder and landed on the dashboard. He had a remarkable arm for a toddler.

At a fork in the road, Karen took to the right. The left fork led to the parking lot behind the manor, but she would save time by parking closer to the front entrance.

They passed over Elm Creek on a narrow bridge, and soon afterward, they emerged from the midday twilight of the forest into sunshine. The gravel road gave way to a smooth, paved drive that gently curved across a broad, gently sloping green lawn. At last, just ahead, Karen caught sight of the three-story, gray stone manor graced by tall white columns. It was such a welcome, comforting sight that she let out a sigh of relief and forgot the clock for a moment.

The road ended in a circular driveway directly in front of the manor. "Look at the horse," exclaimed Ethan, pointing as they drove around a fountain of a rearing stallion in the center of the drive.

"Hort!" cried Lucas.

Karen pulled up to the curb as close to the manor as she dared. She didn't see any signs marking it as a fire lane, but with her luck, her car would get towed. "Yes, it's lovely, isn't it?"

"It *is* a castle," declared Ethan. "You were right, Mommy." Lucas babbled something that might have been agreement.

Karen turned off the car and glanced at her watch. She had exactly one minute before her interview was scheduled to begin. "Okay, boys. Lots of cooperation, remember?" She bounded from the car, briefcase and diaper bag in hand, and took the stroller from the trunk. Ethan stood by patiently as she tried to pry Lucas out of her arms and into the stroller, but he had had quite enough of sitting for one day and not nearly enough nursing, and he clung to her like a barnacle on a whale. She compromised by holding him and using the stroller to trundle the briefcase and diaper bag to the nearest of the two semicircular staircases leading from the driveway to a broad veranda. Too late, she remembered the wheelchair ramp at the rear entrance.

She managed to dislodge herself from Lucas, who stood at

the bottom of the stairs wailing as she hefted the stroller up the stairs. Just then, one of the tall double doors opened and a tall, slender woman exited the manor. She wore a blue blazer and tan slacks, and her light brown hair hung in gentle waves to her shoulders. Her large brown eyes looked startled, and perhaps even annoyed. Karen guessed that she was probably somewhere in her late thirties.

Their eyes met, and for a moment, Karen thought the woman was going to offer to help. Instead she said, "Watch out for the blonde," and hurried past. Surprised, Karen turned to watch her go, but the boys and the stroller needed her attention. What blonde? Lucas? She *was* watching out for him, although from the sound he was making, an outsider might think he was neglected. Why did everyone feel obliged to comment on her parenting?

On the veranda, she set down the stroller and dashed back downstairs for the boys. Carrying Lucas, holding Ethan's hand, and propelling the stroller along with her hip, she crossed the veranda and paused at the entrance. "Okay, boys," she said, catching her breath. "This is very important to Mommy. I need you to be on your absolute best behavior. Understand?"

Lucas didn't, of course, but Ethan nodded solemnly. Karen took a deep breath to steady herself and pulled a funny face to make Ethan grin. Then she pushed the door open and went inside.

She had remembered the grand foyer, with its ceiling open to the third story and the balconies adorned with quilts, but she had forgotten the steps dividing the black marble floor into the entranceway and the foyer proper. This was as far as the stroller would go. She nudged it out of the way against the wall at the bottom of the stairs, released Ethan's hand, and picked up her briefcase and the diaper bag. Ethan seized as much of her hand as he could reclaim, clinging to her fingertips and shoving the handle of the briefcase over her knuckles.

"Do you need a hand?" a woman called.

Karen wished that she had been able to find a moment to freshen up first, wished that she had been able to make a more graceful entrance, but it was too late now. She fixed a confident smile in place and turned to find a white-haired woman in pink-tinted glasses gazing down at her from the top of the stairs. She held a sewing basket in one hand and a small bundle of fabric in the other.

"Hi. I'm Karen Wise. I'm here for an interview." Karen studied the woman, certain she had seen her before. "You're one of the Elm Creek Quilters, aren't you?"

The woman let out a tinkle of a laugh. "Oh, aren't we all Elm Creek Quilters at heart? Camp's in session, you know. I'm just on my way outside to work on my quilt block in the fresh air." She nodded to a row of chairs lining the wall just outside the hallway leading to the west wing of the manor. "I saw Sylvia Compson and some of the others go into that parlor just around the corner. I believe if you wait outside in one of those chairs, someone will come out for you soon."

"The thing is . . . I'm a little late."

The woman shrugged cheerfully. "Seems to me they are, too, or someone would be standing here waiting for you." She came down the stairs and smiled at the boys on her way to the door. "Adorable."

"Thank you," said Karen. She hoped the Elm Creek Quilters agreed.

"Mommy?" asked Ethan after the white-haired woman went outside. "Can we go home now?"

"Not yet, honey. We just got here." She took the boys up the marble stairs and stood for a moment in the center of the foyer. Through the doors in front of her, she heard the murmur of voices and sewing machines coming from the ballroom turned classroom. She seemed to recall that the administrative office was in the second floor library, but the thought of hauling the boys, diaper bag, and briefcase up that grand oak staircase was too daunting. "Let's wait over here," she said to the boys instead, hoping for the best, and she led them to the chairs the woman had indicated.

Ethan had no interest in sitting after the long drive, but Lucas cuddled in her lap while his older brother invented a game involving jumping from one marble square to another in a pattern only he could discern. "Muk," said Lucas insistently, wriggling into position. Karen unbuttoned the three lowest buttons on her suit jacket, untucked her blouse from her skirt, and felt him latch on.

Ethan stopped leaping from square to square to observe them. "Aww. He's so cute. He looks just like a little caterpillar."

Curious, Karen asked, "How so?"

"You know. Because he's nursing."

"Caterpillars are insects, honey. They don't drink milk."

"Oh." Ethan reconsidered. "I mean, he's just like a little baby calf, and you're the big mommy cow!"

"That's exactly right." She managed a wan smile. "Thanks for that, honey."

Perplexed, he regarded her for a moment before the sound of an opening door drew their attention. A woman in a tan pantsuit entered the manor and glanced around before climbing the marble stairs. She carried a quilted tote bag on her shoulder and a plastic container in her other hand. She looked to be a year or two older than Karen, a few inches shorter, and more than a few pounds heavier. Her dark brown hair was gathered into a thick French braid that hung to the middle of her back.

"Hi," Ethan called out enthusiastically.

"Hello," the woman said, sounding equally delighted. She glanced questioningly at Karen. "I'm here for the job interview?"

"I think this is the line," Karen said, gesturing to the chairs beside her.

"Oh." The woman flashed an apologetic smile. "I guess I'm early."

"And I'm late," said Karen ruefully, realizing too late that it might not have been wise to acknowledge that point to the competition.

The woman seated herself two chairs down from Karen, set her bag at her feet, and politely averted her eyes from Lucas as he enjoyed his snack. "Baby-sitter cancel?"

"Husband had other priorities."

The woman tsked and shook her head. "Men."

Karen nodded emphatically. Lucas chose that moment to pop off the breast and beam at the newcomer. Milk spurted on his face and on Karen's skirt.

"Oh, no," she exclaimed. She would have brushed off the droplets before they soaked in, but her arms were full of Lucas. When she tried to set him down, he drew his knees up to his chest and refused to put his feet on the floor.

"Here. Let me take the little guy." The woman reached for Lucas, and Karen, red-faced with embarrassment, automatically handed him over. She restored bra, blouse, and jacket, then found a cloth diaper in the diaper bag and began blotting the dark spots on her skirt.

Just then, the door to the ballroom opened and a stout woman with long, gray-streaked auburn hair rushed past. "Sorry, sorry, it's my fault," she told them, then disappeared into the parlor with a bang of the door.

"Who was that whirlwind?" the woman asked Lucas in the musical, cheerful voice adults use when they address children but are really speaking to the other adults in the room.

"She's Gwen Sullivan, one of the teachers here. I took one of her classes a few years ago." Karen stood and tried to smooth out the wrinkles in her skirt with her hands. Why did she bother? She was a mess. She never should have come.

Lucas reached for her, and when she took him, he regarded her solemnly and patted her cheeks. "Mama. Sor-sor, Mama."

"It's all right, honey." She kissed him and closed her eyes as he rested his head on her shoulder. She was the one who should apologize. She never should have applied for this job. She was underqualified and overextended. The boys would miss her and she would worry about them. If she left now, the Elm Creek Quilters would forget about her canceled interview and by next summer she could face them again—as a camper.

"Would you like a cookie?"

Karen's eyes flew open. "Beg your pardon?"

"Would you like a cookie?" The woman opened the plastic container to reveal three dozen beautifully frosted sugar cookies, decorated to resemble quilt blocks. "I made more than enough. If you don't take some I'll eat them all myself, and I really can't afford to."

"I'll help," Ethan piped up.

The woman smiled at him. "Ask your mommy first."

Karen agreed, reminding him to say thank you. The woman insisted she take two cookies for each of them, so Karen did, tucking the extras into the diaper bag for the ride home, or for bribes during the interview should bribes become necessary. Her own cookie, a Double Nine-Patch, was the best sugar cookie she had ever tasted.

If she had any sense, she would take the boys and leave right then. She was no match for a woman who arrived early and brought homemade cookies.

The door to the parlor swung open. A woman who looked to be in her midthirties smiled at them, her eyebrows rising slightly at the sight of the children. "Hi," she greeted the two women. "I'm Sarah McClure. Thanks for coming. Sorry for the delay." She glanced down at the file folder in her hand and back to Karen. "Karen Wise?"

"That's me." Karen rose, surreptitiously brushing crumbs from her lap, and gathered up baby, diaper bag, and briefcase. "Ethan?"

He ended his game with one last, emphatic leap and joined her at the parlor door. "Hi," he said, beaming up at Sarah. "I'm Efan and this is my baby brother Lucas and this is my mommy Karen."

Sarah's smile widened. "Yes, we spoke on the phone. It's nice to meet you in person, Efan."

"Not Efan. E-Fan."

"I'm so sorry about this," Karen interjected. "My husband was supposed to come home in time to care for them—I promise this would never happen on a regular work day, but—"

Sarah guided them into the parlor. "Don't worry about it. Stranger things than this happen around here all the time. Trust me."

Karen managed a smile as Sarah shut the door behind them and indicated a high-backed, upholstered chair facing six women seated on sofas and chairs on the other side of a low coffee table. With its sharp corners and gleaming polished surface, it was naturally a magnet for the boys. With a quick, apologetic shrug for the Elm Creek Quilters, Karen settled her sons in a corner, pulled out soft toys, crackers, and sippy cups from the diaper bag, and quietly begged Ethan to keep Lucas amused while Mommy talked to the nice ladies. Then she took her seat as Sarah McClure made introductions. Most of the women looked at least vaguely familiar from her week at quilt camp. The silver-haired woman seated in an armchair much like her own was unmistakable—Sylvia Compson, award-winning Master Quilter, teacher, and member of the Quilters' Hall of Fame.

Sylvia peered at Karen over her glasses, and she was not smiling. "Well. What's this?"

"Karen had some child-care issues this morning," said Sarah. The woman on one end of the sofa—Judy—caught her eye and nodded understandingly.

"They're wonderful boys and they won't be any distraction," Karen promised.

"I can see that," said Sylvia dryly as Lucas toddled over to Karen and rested his head on her knee.

Karen smiled weakly and stroked his hair. "I know these are unusual circumstances for an interview, but I'm delighted to be here. It's an honor just to be considered for this position."

"I wonder . . ." Sylvia's gaze was piercing. "Did you feed your children directly before coming here?"

"Well . . ." Did she look like the kind of mother who forgot to feed her children? Forget to leave them at home, yes, but forget to feed them? Never. "They've eaten, thanks. If they get hungry, I brought snacks."

"Anything good?" asked Gwen, peering at the diaper bag. Karen, grateful for the levity, smiled at her.

"Your résumé is very strong," remarked Sarah. "You have impressive marketing and teaching experience."

"Have you ever actually taught *quilting,* though?" asked an attractive woman with blonde curls.

Karen considered her failed attempt to teach Janice and decided not to mention it. "No, but I'm confident my teaching skills will serve me well with any curriculum. Once you've taught required core courses to reluctant college freshmen, you can thrive in any classroom."

To her relief, most of the women smiled, but not Diane, and not Sylvia Compson. Karen felt her courage falter. She had admired Sylvia as long as she had been a quilter. Karen had been too shy to introduce herself during her week at quilt camp, but she had observed Sylvia at mealtimes and during the evening programs. Why was she frowning? And what was with that odd, impatient gesture she kept making, as if she were brushing loose strands of hair off her forehead?

Lucas struggled to climb onto her lap. Automatically Karen reached for him as the youngest of the women, Gwen Sullivan's beautiful auburn-haired daughter, asked her how she began quilting.

"I began here," Karen said. As she told them how she had longed to learn to make a baby quilt, Lucas tugged at her lapels and struggled with the buttons of her suit. Then Sarah McClure posed a question to her, and one from Gwen followed. All the while Lucas peppered the conversation with demands for "Muk!" ever increasing in volume and insistence.

At last she gave up and pleaded, "Lucas, honey, wouldn't you like some milk in a cup?"

"I think he wants milk in a shirt."

She started to hear Ethan's voice at her elbow, the last to discover he had crept silently closer rather than be the only one left out of the interview. "Honey, would you please go look at your book until I'm done?"

"Lucas is over here with you."

"Oh, just go ahead and let him nurse," said Gwen good-naturedly. "We're all friends here."

The blonde woman shot her a look. "Don't be ridiculous. Look at how big he is. He doesn't want to nurse. He's just fidgety." She turned to Karen. "Right?"

"Well," Karen managed to say, wrestling with her toddler, "actually—"

"He nurses all the time," said Ethan. "That's all he does. Nurse, nurse, nurse. And go poop in his diaper. He doesn't talk much. But he's very cute."

"How old is he?" asked the blonde woman, appalled.

"Eighteen months," said Karen. Lucas whooped with delight as he managed to unfasten a button.

The blonde woman shook her head in disbelief. "When they can walk over and ask for it, it's time to cut them off."

"Oh, Diane, please." Gwen rolled her eyes. "Breastmilk is the best, most natural food in the world. In some cultures, children nurse until they're four years old. It's only in western societies that we've so sexualized the female breast that we've forgotten what they're really there for. Breastmilk is full of antibodies and proteins that simply can't be reproduced in formula, no matter what the corporate manufacturers claim."

"Did you know that a child's IQ increases by five points for every month he or she nurses?" added Sarah.

The Elm Creek Quilters stared at her. "And why have you been studying up on breastfeeding?" inquired Gwen's daughter.

Sarah turned beet red. "No reason."

"I nursed Summer for almost three years," said Gwen with pride.

"I could tell," said Diane.

"How? Because she's so intelligent? So healthy?"

"No. Because that's exactly the sort of thing you would do. I'm just surprised you haven't bragged about it earlier." Diane fixed her attention on Karen, though it was obvious she was trying not to see Lucas, now happily suckling away. "So tell us. What makes you think you're qualified for this job, aside from your obvious ability to multitask?"

"Well, I'm a quilter, of course," said Karen. "I enjoy designing my own quilts, and I've mastered many of the techniques you listed in your ad." She probably could have put together a more cogent answer if she didn't have a baby at the breast. "I also have a sense of humor, and being a mother has definitely taught me how to deal with occasional minor disasters."

"And a few major ones," remarked Gwen, "if your experience is anything like mine. No offense, kiddo."

"Of course not, Mom," said Summer, as if she had heard it all before.

"I have another question," said Diane. "What kind of mother are you?"

Karen blinked at her. "What kind? Well, I suppose I'm attentive, loving, patient—most of the time—a bit of a worrier, creative—"

"That's not what I meant," Diane broke in. "I mean, what kind of mother *are* you, to even contemplate taking on a job outside the home when your children obviously need you?"

"I don't think this line of questioning is appropriate," said Sarah.

"I don't think it was even a real question," said Judy.

"It's a legitimate concern," said Diane. "For her and for us. She and her boys clearly have a strong attachment. If we hire her, we are forcing her to stick those two precious children in a day care center. How can we be a party to that?"

"I went to day care when I was a child," said Summer. "I turned out all right."

Diane waved that off. "That's different. Gwen's a single mother. She didn't have a choice."

"Ms. Wise's child-care arrangements are her concern, not ours," said Sylvia.

"They will be our concern if she cancels classes because she can't get a baby-sitter."

Karen was about to assure them that she would never cancel class, but she hesitated. She could not be sure that she would never miss a day because of the boys. What if Lucas had an ear infection? What if Ethan had a day off school?

"I think it's against the law to discriminate against a job applicant because she has children," said the dark-haired woman named Bonnie. "If it isn't, it should be."

Sylvia raised a hand. "Let's get this conversation back on track. I believe Sarah has several more questions on her list, and we don't want to keep Ms. Wise and her sons any longer than necessary."

"Just one." Sarah looked up from her copy of Karen's portfolio and smiled. "I wondered if you would read to us from the cover letter you submitted with your application. I have it here if you need it."

"That's okay. I brought one." Karen withdrew the letter from her briefcase, wondering what Sarah had in mind. Didn't each Elm Creek Quilter have her own copy, and wouldn't they have read it already?

"Start with the third paragraph from the top," said Sarah.

Karen nodded and read aloud:

"Please note that the nearly five-year gap in my employment record is voluntary, as I left my last position to raise my children. In all honesty, I had no intention of returning to the work force so soon, but when I saw your ad, I immediately reconsidered. I enjoy staying home with my children, but I could not pass up this opportunity to become an Elm Creek Quilter. I think every former camper considers herself an Elm Creek Quilter to some extent, but I feel that to deserve that title, and to deserve the privilege of joining the staff of Elm Creek Quilt Camp, a person must possess more than excellent technical skills and teaching abilities. In my time as a camper, I discovered teachers who passed along knowledge but also were willing to learn from their students, who honored the traditions handed down through the generations but were not afraid to push the art beyond its traditional boundaries. I encountered women committed to creating a supportive environment where quilters of all levels of experience could challenge themselves artistically without fear of ridicule or failure, because every risk honestly and courageously attempted is looked upon as a success. I learned about valuing the process as well as the product, and about honoring every piece's contribution to the beauty of the whole. Elm Creek Quilt Camp celebrates and honors the artist inside every woman, and I would consider it a great privilege and honor to join your circle of quilters."

Karen was almost afraid to meet the Elm Creek Quilters' eyes after she finished reading. Too much information, she decided. They probably thought she was a font of ingratiating rhetoric, spouting praise in order to win herself an interview. What they could not know was that she meant every word of it. That letter had been the easiest part of her application to complete because she had written from the heart.

"Thank you," said Sarah. "Does anyone else have anything to ask Karen?"

Karen took a deep breath to steady her nerves as Gwen continued the interview. She answered the remaining questions with Lucas on her lap and Ethan by her side. Occasionally Ethan piped up with responses of his own, which were invariably more insightful and wittier than her own. Lucas took a liking to Gwen's daughter and initiated a game of peek-a-boo, burying his face in his mother's shoulder, peeking out to catch Summer's eye, laughing, and hiding his face again. At Sylvia's prompting, Karen showed them her Elm Creek Quilts pattern and quilt block, which they added to her portfolio. She felt a glimmer of pride when they praised the artistry of her design and the ingenuity of the foundation paper piecing construction, but she doubted that that small demonstration of competence would be enough to win them over.

They shook hands all around at the end of the interview, but Karen did not bother to ask when she might hear from them. She packed the diaper bag and led the boys from the parlor to a bathroom a few doors down, in the west wing, where she changed Lucas's diaper and asked Ethan to try, just try, to go potty before they returned to the car.

As she washed her hands, she looked at herself in the mirror over the sink to see if she looked as hopeless and miserable as she felt. That was when she saw the Cheerio clinging to her bangs, slightly off-center above her forehead.

She gasped and brushed it out of her hair. How long had it been there? Immediately she guessed it: since Lucas's lunch. She had sat there on the phone trying to reach Nate, paying no attention as Lucas flung cereal across the room.

That explained Sylvia Compson's odd question about whether she had fed her children and her inexplicable gestures at the start of the interview.

"Why didn't anyone tell me?" she wailed. Sylvia's all too subtle gestures aside, everyone she had seen since lunchtime had allowed her to walk around with cereal clinging to her bangs.

"Tell you what?" asked Ethan, drying his hands on a paper towel.

"That I had a Cheerio in my hair! You must have seen it. Why didn't you tell me?"

"I tried to."

"When?"

"When you buckled me in the car and when I was on the potty at McDonald's. You seemed busy and mad so I didn't want to talk."

Karen closed her eyes and sighed, remembering. "Honey, I know I was impatient then, but I really, really wish you would have told me."

"I thought maybe you wanted it there."

"Why would I have wanted a Cheerio in my hair?"

He shrugged. "It looked pretty."

Karen could not think of any possible response to that, so she shook her head in disbelief and led the boys from the bathroom. When they passed the friendly woman in the tan suit on their way to the front doors to the manor, the woman said, "I hope your interview went well."

"I hope yours goes better," Karen replied wearily. The woman peered at her inquisitively and seemed on the verge of speaking, but just then the parlor door started to open. Karen quickly scooted the boys outside rather than face any of the Elm Creek Quilters again, pausing only long enough to fetch the stroller.

"Mommy, can we play in the water?" Without waiting for an answer, Ethan raced across the veranda and down the stairs toward the fountain in the center of the circular driveway.

"Look both ways before you cross," Karen called after him, although the driveway was lightly traveled compared to the road leading to the parking lot behind the manor. Her car was the only one parked in the circle. The other applicant, whom Karen could not help thinking of as the Cookie Lady, must have parked in the rear lot as Karen was supposed to have done. The Cookie Lady was probably at that moment making a wonderful impression on the Elm Creek Quilters. She would never know how Karen had set the stage for her, how she had made herself the ideal act to follow.

She set down Lucas and struggled to collapse the tandem stroller so that it would be easier to carry downstairs.

"Oh, dear."

At the sound of the voice, Karen glanced down the veranda and spotted the white-haired woman who had greeted them when they first arrived at Elm Creek Manor. She was seated in an Adirondack chair a few yards away, a quilt block in one hand, a threaded needle in the other.

"Is something wrong?" asked Karen as she carried the stroller to the grass below.

"I can't for the life of me figure out what I'm doing wrong," the white-haired woman said, holding up the quilt block and shaking her head in consternation.

Karen checked on Ethan, who was happily throwing leaves into the fountain and following their progress through the whorls of water. Assured that he was occupied, she scooped up Lucas and went to see what was the matter. "Maybe I can help."

"Oh, would you try, dear?" The woman smiled gratefully before gesturing to the center of the block. "I can't get this edge to lie smooth no matter what I try."

Karen pulled up a chair beside her, set down Lucas, and leaned over for a closer look. "I'm not that great at hand appliqué," she said apologetically, studying the Rose of Sharon block. Despite the woman's frustration, the block seemed nearly halfway completed. "I'm more of a fusible-webbing, machine-zigzag stitch kind of appliquér. But maybe . . ." She reached for the block. "May I?"

"Of course." The woman handed it to her.

Karen flipped it over and examined the stitches on the back. They were tiny, neat, and even. "I don't think the problem is your needlework. Your stitches are excellent. Maybe it's the appliqué. Did you baste the edges of the circle in place before you began sewing?"

"Of course."

"As I said, I'm no expert, but whenever I appliqué circles, I always cut a template out of cardstock, and then cut a circle from my fabric an eighth to a quarter of an inch larger. Then I place the template on the wrong side of the fabric, thread my needle, and take small running stitches in the fabric circle all the way around the edge, leaving longer tails at the beginning and the end." Karen demonstrated the movements with an imaginary needle and the woman's cloth. "Then I pull gently on the thread tails, drawing the fabric circle around my template. That makes a circle with perfectly smooth edges."

"What an ingenious idea," exclaimed the woman.

"I can't take credit for it. I read it in a book or a magazine somewhere. After I have my circle, I press it flat with a hot iron and use my sewing machine to baste the edges in place until I appliqué the circle to the background fabric."

"Do you sew right through the cardstock with your machine when you baste?"

Karen shrugged and returned to the quilt block. "I might not if I had a top of the line machine, but mine is secondhand and tough—built to withstand just about anything, but without all the fancy computerized stitches. There's not much I can do to hurt it."

"Well, thank you very much." The woman patted the quilt block as if to reassure it all would be well. "I will have to try that."

Rising, Karen nodded to the front doors of the manor. "I'm sure one of the Elm Creek Quilters could show you how."

"I've no doubt one of them could. Have a safe trip home, dear."

"Thanks." Karen scooped up Lucas and carried him on her hip as she went to join Ethan at the fountain, pushing the stroller along before her. Why had she bothered to bring it? It was one more bead on a string of bad decisions. Her sense of failure and impending rejection, which had ebbed as she chatted with the white-haired woman, suddenly returned in a torrent. Discouraged, she allowed the boys to play near the fountain for a few minutes longer, concealing her disappointment and weariness behind smiles and encouragement for their game. Then she coaxed them back into their car seats and drove home.

The boys had slept too much that day to fall under the spell of the car's motion another time, so although Karen longed to be alone with her thoughts, she gave in to Ethan's requests for stories and sang along with the CD as they wished. She owed them after dragging them through that debacle. She also owed them supper, and she was not in any hurry to get home.

When they reached the outskirts of State College, she pulled over at an Eat 'N Park and treated all of them to buttermilk pancakes. The boys bounced happily on the padded vinyl seats of their booth and made sticky messes of themselves with the maple syrup, but they charmed the waitress as well as several nearby diners and Karen's heart lifted each time they made her laugh. She even ordered a Dutch apple pie to go before remembering that Nate did not deserve his favorite treat, not that day and possibly not for the rest of their marriage. But she was not bold enough to ask the waitress to remove the charge, so she paid the bill, cleaned the boys with wet wipes, and took them home.

Nate was waiting for them on the front stoop. As she drove past him into the garage, she glimpsed his expression, somehow both wary and resolute. He met her at the car door before she turned off the engine.

"How did it go?" he asked, backing away from the door as she opened it.

"How did it go?" She could not even look at him. She opened Lucas's door and unbuckled him from his car seat. "I had to take two small children on a job interview. How do you think it went?"

Nate went around to the other side of the car for Ethan. "If I could have gotten out of that meeting—"

"You could have." Carrying Lucas, she reached into the front seat for the pie. She brushed past Nate and went into the house. "Like you said, you made your choice."

"I put an existing full-time job ahead of a potential part-time job. I'm sorry, but from where I stand, that looks like the only logical choice."

She slammed the pie box on the kitchen counter and glared at him. He carried the diaper bag and her briefcase, which he set on the floor. He reached for Lucas but she would not hand him over.

Ethan followed a pace behind his father. "We were good, Mommy. Even Lucas. Except for the Cheerio. You said."

His words abruptly drained the force of her anger. "Yes. You were both as good as I could have expected. You did what I asked and you used good manners. Thank you."

Ethan beamed and ran off to the living room. A second later, she heard PBS Kids on the television. Lucas squirmed until she set him down, and he toddled off after his brother.

"Karen, I said I was sorry."

"If you don't want me to work, why not just say so?"

A muscle in his jaw tightened and relaxed. "I did not deliberately sabotage you and you know it."

"One day, Nate. I asked for one day."

"And I had every intention of giving it to you, but I couldn't. Honey—"

He reached for her, but she avoided his touch and fled downstairs to the basement, where she sat on the folding chair in front of her sewing machine and covered her face with her hands so the boys would not hear her cry.

Chapter Three
Anna

live oil, roasted red pepper, rosemary, basil, sea salt, a pinch of white pepper, and—and what? What had she forgotten? With no time to rummage through her notes, Anna closed her eyes and willed the recipe to emerge from her subconscious. It wasn't her fault she was unprepared. This was supposed to have been her night off, but when her boss called and asked if she would be willing to take over the provost's dinner for several important college donors, she told him she would be there in ten minutes. For months she had begged him to entrust her with a special event like this one. She had assisted senior chefs for years and was eager to try her hand at the head chef position. As she raced from her apartment to the kitchen of the banquet room of Nelson Hall, where the guests were due to arrive in less than two hours, she ran through the menu given to her over the phone. It was not difficult, and she was confident she could handle it even on such short notice. Then she arrived at the kitchen to discover that two of her work-study students had failed to show and the fresh vegetables her predecessor had requested from the College Food Service's prep room in South Dining Hall

had arrived frozen. By the time she sorted out that mess, she was a half hour behind schedule. Ordinarily she thrived on improvising in the face of unexpected complications, but today, the additional stress made her head ache.

Ideally, she should set the sauce aside for a half hour to allow the flavors to blend, but she had run out of time and would have to serve it as is—if she managed to finish it at all. "What did I forget?" asked Anna, thinking aloud, not really expecting an answer.

"Thyme," replied her favorite work-study student, almost at her elbow. "You added thyme when you made this for Junior Parents' Weekend."

"Of course. Thyme." Anna measured the last of the herbs into the processor and punched the blend button. "Thank you, Callie."

"Whatever," said Callie, trying unsuccessfully to conceal a grin of pleasure. Unlike the rest of the crew on duty that night, Callie had a passion for food and was not simply putting in hours to earn textbook and beer money. She watched everything Anna did and asked admiring questions, making Anna feel almost as if she had a protégé. Sometimes Anna was tempted to encourage Callie to enroll in a culinary institute after graduation, but she worried that Callie might be insulted. Just because Anna had no idea what anyone would do with a degree in American Studies did not mean that it was not useful. What would she know about it? She had known she wanted to be a chef since the seventh grade and had never explored other options. According to her boyfriend, Anna had a disgraceful tendency to be skeptical of any education that was not immediately practical, but she was working on it.

"The provost set down his salad fork," remarked another student, peering through the round window in the kitchen door instead of stirring the chocolate sauce for the raspberry tarts even though Anna had already asked him twice. He was a business major and considered such mundane tasks beneath him because he believed he was destined to become the CEO of a major international corporation before reaching his thirties. He didn't need to learn how to cook; he needed to observe the wealthy donors dining with the college provost because one day he would be among them.

Make yourself useful, Anna silently ordered him, but she said, "Do they look like they're ready for the main course?"

"I . . . think so."

"Okay. Just a minute." Anna took the pitcher of herb sauce and hurried to the gleaming stainless-steel counter where her assistants were spooning wild rice pilaf and sautéed vegetables onto warmed plates, assembly line fashion. "Where are the salmon fillets?"

"Here," said Callie, removing the first of several trays from the broiler.

Anna gestured to Callie and the laconic observer by the door. "Callie and Rob. Get the salmon on the plates." Something in her tone made even Rob promptly obey. As soon as each fillet was in position, Anna dressed it with sauce. "Okay. Servers, come and get 'em. And take care of the head table first this time, please?"

She had little time to talk except to issue instructions or urge a server to hurry. She had scarcely enough time to monitor the progress of the meal in the banquet room on the other side of the door, but she found moments where she could. Her position in Waterford College's College Food Services could rise or fall depending upon the diners' response to her entrée.

Occasionally Rob returned to the window in the door to describe the progress of the meal. "The provost just tried the fish. He's smiling. So is the guy next to him."

"On which side?"

"Um, his right. Our left."

Anna closed her eyes and breathed a deep sigh of relief. That "guy" was the college's most generous donor. If he was happy with the meal, she could consider it a successful evening even if the kitchen caught on fire.

She couldn't relax until after dessert was served, when all she had to worry about was keeping the servers circulating with coffee and making sure they refilled the cream pitchers and sugar bowls and didn't confuse regular with decaf. Despite its inauspicious beginning, the banquet appeared to be a success.

Afterward, the provost came into the kitchen to congratulate Anna on a job well done. "Glad to help," she said, and she was pleased when he continued on through the kitchen, where her student workers were busy cleaning up, to thank them as well. It was common knowledge on the Waterford College campus that working for food services was the lowest of the low as far as work-study jobs were concerned—minimum wage for menial tasks and, except on special occasions such as this, the indignity of cleaning up after their more fortunate classmates in the dining halls. A word of thanks and a handshake from the provost was a nice perk, and Anna was so relieved to have survived the evening that she intended to provide her students with another: all of the extra desserts they could carry back to the dorms.

Before leaving, the provost paused at the door, scrutinized Anna, and said, "Are you new here? I don't think you've been in charge of any of my dinners before."

"This is my sixth year at Waterford College," said Anna. "I've worked some of your other events, but always as an assistant."

"This is your first banquet as head chef?"

Anna nodded. "The head chef assigned to your event called in sick. I guess I'm the understudy."

"Understudy or not, you've done an exemplary job," the provost said. "I wasn't even aware of any emergency. Your dishes were intriguing, and your response to the situation is the very definition of grace under pressure."

Anna glowed. She knew that a successful banquet with delicious food and excellent service could mean that next year's faculty salary increases would be paid for by donations rather than tuition increases. "Thank you."

"What's your name again?"

"Anna. Anna Del Maso."

"Well, Anna Del Maso, I'll be asking for you again." He nodded a good-bye and left the kitchen.

As she walked home after the banquet, Anna wished she could share her triumph with Gordon. She wasn't sure if she should call him. When she called off their dinner plans, they'd had—not a fight, exactly—more like a heated disagreement. "Can't they get someone else?" he had griped when she called from her cell phone, already hurrying down the stairs of her apartment building on her way to the job.

"They could, but I don't want them to," she said.

"Don't you all use the same recipes? Can't they call that woman you work with—Sandra? Mandy? She's worked there almost as long as you."

"Andrea," corrected Anna. "She started here two years after I did and I don't think she wants the responsibility. I do. This is for the provost. This could be my big break."

"Oh, come on. Big break? In College Food Services?"

Anna paused to wait for the crosswalk, annoyed by the sneer in his voice. "If I prove myself, I could finally get promoted to head chef."

He was silent so long she thought the connection had broken. "Is that what you really want?"

It wasn't her ultimate career goal, no, but it was a significant step in the right direction. The light changed and she hurried across the street. "Of course."

"Do you really think it's a good idea for you to be working more banquets? All those heavy sauces, the rich desserts—"

"I'll renew my gym membership."

"Don't be so defensive. I'm just saying it would be easier to eat healthy if you're working the dining halls."

And easier still if she left the profession altogether. Gordon had made that point before. "I'm almost there, Gordon, I've got to go." She hung up without waiting for a good-bye and immediately regretted it. Gordon was easily offended and never accepted an apology unaccompanied by a humbling show of atonement. She would have to make it up to him tomorrow night with a dinner as impressive as the provost's.

The central, bewildering puzzle about Gordon was that although he liked delicious food as much as the next person, he did not want his girlfriend to be a chef. Or maybe it was not such a puzzle—if she were thin, her choice of profession might not bother him at all, especially if she also had a Ph.D. to hang on her wall to impress his friends. Like Gordon, they were liberal arts graduate students and aspiring intellectuals with whom Anna had very little in common. Anna would never admit it to Gordon, but his friends intimidated her, and she was relieved that he rarely suggested they go out with them.

Anna had never dated anyone who wasn't thrilled that she enjoyed cooking, not until Gordon came along. She thought Gordon ought to appreciate her job, if not for all the delicious, home-cooked, gourmet meals, then for the fact that her work had brought them together. They had met the previous year at a dinner given by the English department to honor a retiring professor. It was the first week of the semester and they had not yet hired enough work-study students, so Anna had to help carry serving trays to the buffet table. A bearded, stocky man not much taller than she had followed her into the kitchen to compliment her on the marinated mushrooms and had stuck around to chat. She was flattered by the attention of someone so well spoken and knowledgeable about world affairs, especially since most academics ignored her, so she accepted his invitation to go out for coffee the following afternoon. His topics of conversation differed so drastically from what she and her friends talked about that she feared she would bore him, but he did not seem to mind that she mostly listened, asking occasional, carefully constructed questions to reveal as little of her ignorance as possible.

Apparently she had made a good impression because that date led to another, and soon they were seeing each other steadily. He was often too busy with his teaching and research to take her out, but several times a week he managed to stop by her apartment on his way home from the library for a late supper. It wasn't an ideal arrangement, but he promised her things would improve once he had his degree and no longer had to hit the books sixteen hours a day. She was pleased by this hint that he thought they had a future together because he usually brushed off her hesitant attempts to discuss the direction of their relationship. Most often, he said that he hoped she agreed that modern relationships needed to throw off their patriarchal tendencies and allow all parties room to be. To be *what,* she wasn't sure, and in this case she didn't want to reveal her naïveté by asking.

She paused to shift her purse; the strap kept slipping off her shoulder and bumping into the paper grocery bag she carried, heavy with carefully wrapped containers of salmon in fresh herb sauce, grilled vegetables, and raspberry tart with chocolate glaze. College Food Services officially discouraged employees from taking leftovers home, but to discourage was not to forbid, and Anna hated to see all that food go to waste. It pained her to throw away good food when she had to monitor her own grocery budget so carefully. If she splurged on luxuries now, she might never have enough money saved to open her own restaurant.

She had the place all picked out—Chuck's, a diner across the street from the main gate of campus. Its excellent location guaranteed it a steady business, even though the current owner was nearing retirement and lately had put only a halfhearted effort into running the place. He had sent his two children to Waterford College in hopes that they would take over the business, but they left Waterford for good as soon as they received their degrees.

Anna hoped he would hold off his retirement for a few more years, just long enough for her to have amassed a down payment. She had an excellent credit rating and ought to be able to get a small business loan to cover the rest. And then she would say good-bye to the dining hall and hello to her own menus and the freedom to work with ingredients that did not have to be purchased in bulk quantities.

The short walk from campus to her three-story red brick walk-up on the eastern end of Main Street always seemed longer at the end of a grueling shift in the kitchen, and hauling the grocery bag up three flights left her winded. She set the bag on the floor outside her apartment door and dug in her purse for her keys.

A door opened behind her. "Oh, hey, Anna. Just getting off work?"

Anna glanced up. "Hi, Jeremy. Just going out?"

Jeremy shook his head, scrubbing a hand through his dark, wildly curly hair. "Not to do anything fun, if that's what you mean. I have an exciting night planned with my dissertation. I'm going down to Uni-Mart for a snack and something caffeinated. Want me to bring you anything back?"

"Don't waste your money on junk food," protested Anna, reaching into the grocery bag. It was a wonder he had any taste buds left. "Here. I brought home extras from the provost's party."

"Any meat?" he asked, his eyes hopeful behind round, wire-rimmed glasses.

"Does fish count?"

"Fish always counts. Just please don't tell Summer."

Anna laughed and agreed, amused by his guilty expression. Jeremy's girlfriend was a vegetarian, and although she didn't insist that Jeremy also avoid meat, he did so when dining with her to spare her feelings. "Take this," she said, loading his arms with College Food Services containers. "Salmon, veggies, plus dessert."

"Chocolate?"

"There's chocolate sauce for the raspberry tart."

"You are the best neighbor in the world," he said fervently, peeking in the container holding his dessert. "Thank you for this. Once again. I swear I wasn't waiting by the door for you to come home."

Anna smiled and found her keys. "You do seem to have a strange way of knowing which nights I work a banquet and when I'm just at the dining hall."

"Can I at least get you a cup of coffee?"

"No, thanks, I'm fine." She unlocked her apartment and carried her bags inside. "See you later."

Anna had hoped Gordon would be waiting for her, but she was not surprised to find the apartment dark and quiet. She was disappointed, but not surprised. Graduate students kept long hours, and she had not yet called him to apologize. Besides, she had already given away his share of the leftovers.

She flipped on the light with her elbow and placed her burdens on the kitchen counter beside the answering machine, whose light was definitely not blinking to notify her of a message. The kitchenette was wholly inappropriate for a chef—no bigger than a walk-in closet with a small refrigerator, a single sink, a two-burner electric stovetop, and an oven too small to accommodate her jelly-roll pan. "Someday," she said aloud. Someday when she had her own restaurant, she wouldn't care what her kitchen at home looked like. Someday, when Gordon finished his degree, they could move in to a wonderful new home with a state-of-the-art kitchen where she would cook him romantic dinners and serve him marvelous breakfasts in bed.

"Someday," she said again, setting the table for one.

After supper, she washed the dishes, checked the phone for a dial tone to make sure it was working, and decided to unwind before bed by quilting for a little while. After taking her sewing machine from the closet to the kitchen table and retrieving her cutting board from beneath the day bed, she laid the quilt top in progress on the floor and pondered it from atop a chair. "Somehow everything in my life ends up being about food," she murmured, frowning thoughtfully at the blue circles appliquéd on a background of white and brown. There was no escaping it. What she had intended as an abstract arrangement of circles of varying sizes and hues set against two contrasting forms in brown and white now resembled nothing so much as a cascade of ripe blueberries falling from an overturned bucket into a pool of rich cream. At least it would complement her strawberry pie quilt, her eggs Benedict quilt, and her chocolate soufflé quilt. If anyone asked, she would say that the resemblance was intentional. She could claim the quilts were a series: Quilts from the Kitchen.

Not that anyone would ask, since it was unlikely that anyone would ever see them. Anna had shown her quilts to Jeremy and his girlfriend once, but since Summer moved out of his apartment and into Elm Creek Manor, Anna rarely saw her anymore.

She wouldn't show her quilts to Gordon, either. Gordon knew she quilted but wasn't interested—although it might be more accurate to say that her quilting perplexed him. After he told her that she was too intelligent to spend her time stitching away pointlessly, she had learned to conceal her quilting projects as soon as she heard his key in the lock. When he had quoted some eighteenth-century woman's essay denouncing women who had nothing better to do than sit around "stitching upon samplers," Anna had felt wounded. The wound had stung even more when Gordon had added that Theresa taught that insulting essay in her creative nonfiction class.

Gordon's roommate Theresa had been a part of their relationship from the beginning. Even on that first night as Anna and Gordon talked in the kitchen while the rest of the English department enjoyed dessert in the other room, Gordon found ways to bring Theresa into the conversation. When he did it again on their first official date at the coffee shop, Anna asked him if he and Theresa were dating or if they had broken up. He laughed and said that he and Theresa were "special friends," but they had never had a romantic interest in each other. "Romantic love is mere biochemistry, anyway," he said, waving a hand dismissively. Anna nodded to indicate that she understood, though she wasn't sure she did. It seemed a rather cynical attitude for a first date.

More than fourteen months had passed since then, and Anna had yet to meet the mystery woman. She felt certain she would recognize Theresa if she saw her, though. She must be brilliant and alluring; nothing else could explain Gordon's preoccupation. Anna envisioned a tall, willowy, raven-haired woman with artistic hands and haunting eyes. Since she was a poet, she probably dressed all in black, or maybe she draped herself in yards of wildly colored ethnic print fabric. Theresa definitely wouldn't be twenty pounds on the wrong side of plump, like Anna, and she would never fear that her boyfriend was ashamed of her job or her lack of a graduate degree or her double-digit dress size. No, Theresa's mind would be focused on loftier affairs.

"But she probably can't even boil water," Anna said aloud.

She waited until it was too late for Gordon to call. Only then did she put away her quilting, turn out the lights, and go to bed.

When she woke the next morning, Anna decided to take her day off seriously and eat a meal prepared by someone else for a change. She considered going to the Bistro, a favorite spot for breakfast and lunch for local residents and college faculty, a popular student hangout in the evenings when the bar opened. She would probably run into some friends there, so she would not have to dine alone. L'Arc du Ciel was another possibility; although the most exclusive restaurant in town far exceeded her usual budget for dining out, their Sunday brunches were sublime and she could pick up a few ideas.

She quickly settled upon a far less gastronomically pleasing option, but one that had become her favorite dining spot nonetheless: Chuck's. She tucked a tablet of graph paper and a pencil into her purse and walked a few blocks down the street to the restaurant that would hopefully one day be hers.

She ordered a chocolate cappuccino and a blueberry muffin, seated herself at an inconspicuous corner table, and, while she waited for her breakfast, drew a floor plan of the restaurant on the graph paper. Since she had never been in the kitchen and could see very little of it through the window where the cooks placed orders for the servers to pick up, she left that part of the drawing blank. By the time her breakfast arrived, she had sketched a rough blueprint of the dining areas and entryway. As she ate, she studied her drawing and compared it to her surroundings, drawing new lines and erasing others. She would remove the counter and the seven stools to make room for more tables. Where the order-up window was now, she would install a brick oven, as much for atmosphere as for cooking. She would replace the wood paneling with off-white stucco to brighten the room and make it more inviting. The entry should be extended to create a small foyer between the outside door and the door to the dining room. Currently there was only one door, and it led directly outside. That wasn't a problem now, in midsummer, but she recalled from previous visits that in less temperate weather, every new customer brought in the cold and sometimes even drifts of snow. In January she had seen customers leave rather than take a table near the door.

A merry jingle reminded her of another change she would make—lose the bell over the door. It was fine for a diner, but not for the intimate but friendly, elegant yet casual restaurant she intended to create. She added a quick note to her drawing, then glanced up in time to see the couple who had entered. As the man smiled at the woman and gestured to an empty booth, Anna went motionless from surprise. He was Gordon.

Instinctively, she put her graph paper on the floor beside her chair and set her purse on top of it. She held still as the couple approached, and when Gordon's expression didn't change, she realized that he had not noticed her.

"Hi, Gordon," she said when they had almost passed her table.

Gordon stopped short. "Anna? Well, hello. What a surprise."

"Yes. It is." Anna tried not to stare at his companion. This couldn't be Theresa, the mysterious, glamorous Theresa. This woman was shorter than Anna and not much thinner, and wore thick glasses with black plastic rims. Her frizzy brown hair hung almost to her waist and was held away from her face with an elastic band. A bit of white fuzz clung to her left eyebrow.

Gordon turned to the woman. "Theresa, this is my friend, Anna. Anna, this is my roommate, Theresa."

"Nice to meet you." Theresa leaned forward and extended her hand.

Awkwardly, Anna shook it. "Nice to meet you, too, finally. Won't you join me?"

Gordon glanced over his shoulder. "Actually, we were just—" He broke off when he saw that Theresa was already pulling out a chair and sitting down. He shrugged and took the seat beside her.

"I've heard a lot about you, Theresa," Anna said. "All good, of course."

Theresa's thick eyebrows shot up. "Really? From whom?"

Anna paused. "From Gordon, of course."

"Oh." Theresa flashed him a quick grin before returning her attention to Anna. "How do you and Gordon know each other?"

Anna looked from Gordon to Theresa and back, puzzled. "Well, I'm sure Gordon's already told you how we met at an English department function, and since then we've been seeing each other—"

"All over campus," interrupted Gordon. "Just like this morning. That's what happens at a smaller college. Wherever you go, you see people you know. Right?"

"Right," echoed Anna, uncertain.

Theresa rested her elbows on the table and scrutinized her. "So, which department are you in? Are you a grad student or on the faculty?"

"Neither. I'm a chef for College Food Services."

"Anna graduated from Elizabethtown College," added Gordon quickly. "You've probably heard of it. It's highly regarded for an undergraduate liberal arts education. Anna hasn't decided upon a graduate school yet."

Anna looked at him, speechless. She had already completed all the post-baccalaureate study she needed at the Culinary Institute of New York.

"It's often best to take time off before returning for a graduate degree." Theresa sat back, a fond smile playing on her lips. "For three years after I earned my A.B. in English Language and Literature from the University of Chicago—"

"Summa cum laude," interjected Gordon.

Theresa rolled her eyes. "If you must. Summa cum laude from the University of Chicago, I wandered the continent with some of my more hedonistic friends. It was a wonderful opportunity to explore my own depths, gather grist for the mill. But now it's back to work. What degree are you going for, Ann?"

"It's Anna. Actually, I don't really need a graduate degree for my work."

Theresa pondered that briefly. "I suppose I don't, either, technically. You either are a poet or you aren't; no amount of training can modify the soul. If I want to teach at the university, however, I have to have my MFA. That's the system. That's the price we all pay."

"An MBA would be useful, right, Anna?" Gordon persisted.

"I guess so," said Anna reluctantly. "Marketing, management—sure. An MBA would be helpful, I suppose." She looked at Gordon to see if she had said the right thing. He smiled his thanks, visibly relieved.

Somehow she managed to get through the rest of the encounter. Gordon and Theresa drank seemingly endless refills of coffee until they were wired from the caffeine. Anna sat quietly as they talked to each other, laughing at each other's jokes, gossiping about departmental politics, discussing writers she had never heard of whose works she had never read. Finally it ended, and she was able to walk home, alone and very annoyed.

It was after ten o'clock at night when Gordon finally called. "Anna, about today."

She broke in before he had the chance to make excuses. "Why haven't you told Theresa about me?"

"Why should I have told her?"

"Because we're involved, and she's your roommate and a friend. My friends know about you."

"That's different."

"How so?"

"I prefer to keep my personal life private."

Her throat tightened. "You're ashamed of me because I'm not in graduate school. Because I'm not going to be some tenured professor in an ivory tower some day."

"How could you say such a thing? That's ridiculous. I also might add that it's not fair of you to resort to cheap stereotypes about academics."

"Not fair? Do you really want to talk about not fair?"

"Anna—"

"Gordon, I'm proud of my career. I've worked and studied very hard to get where I am. What I do is just as creative as Theresa's poetry."

"I know. I know. I was an idiot. I was wrong. After breakfast I told Theresa all about us. She liked you. She thought you were great."

"Am I supposed to feel honored?"

"I said I was sorry. Can't you forgive me?" said Gordon. "How can you not forgive me after I admitted I was wrong?"

He persisted, and eventually she gave in. He wanted to come over and continue the apology in person, but she refused. She was too tired to make up in the way he meant, and she had to get up early the next morning.

Conflicting work schedules kept them apart for the next two days, but on Wednesday, Anna hurried home from her lunch shift at South Dining Hall and baked Gordon a seven-layer chocolate hazelnut torte as an apology for her outburst on the phone. She packed it carefully in a bakery box and walked to campus to catch the bus to the east side. Having never visited his apartment, she had needed to look up his address in the campus directory and check the bus schedule to see which route to take. His answering machine picked up when she called to let him know she was on her way, but she decided to go even though he was not there. He usually went home for supper, so he would probably arrive before she did.

As she rode the bus, her purse on the seat beside her and the cake box balanced on her lap, she began to have second thoughts. Uninvited and unexpected might not be the best way to make her first visit to Gordon's apartment. Whenever her friends expressed their bewilderment at his failure to invite her over after fourteen months of presumably exclusive dating, Anna had always managed to find a plausible excuse for him, but the encounter at the diner had left her rattled. Maybe she should leave the box outside his door. Or maybe she should get off at the next stop and take the first bus back toward campus. Surely Gordon would come to see her within a few days, while the torte was still reasonably fresh. She could wait until then to present it.

But she was his girlfriend. She pulled the wire to signal her approaching stop and got off the bus. They had been dating for more than a year. Surely a guy wouldn't complain if his girlfriend of almost fourteen months decided to stop by his apartment, especially to make up after an argument, especially bearing a seven-layer chocolate hazelnut torte.

She found his address and climbed the stairs to the second floor apartment. Theresa answered her knock.

"Hi," Anna said, forcing a smile. "Is Gordon home?"

"Not at the moment." Theresa glanced over her shoulder as if to make sure. "Do you need something?"

Anna kept the smile firmly in place. "I'm Anna. Gordon's girlfriend? We met Sunday at Chuck's Diner?"

"Oh, right, right." Theresa opened the door wider and waved her in. "Did you want to wait for him to get home? I think he has office hours until six."

"That's all right." Anna looked around the cluttered room. Books and newspapers were stacked on every horizontal surface. "I'll just leave this in the kitchen and go."

"Good enough." Theresa led her into the adjacent kitchen and cleared a space on the counter. "I would have cleaned up, but Gordon didn't mention you were coming."

Anna set down the box. "It's a surprise." She lifted the lid and let Theresa peek inside.

Theresa's eyes lit up. "Oh, I get it. Chocolate for love, right? That's great. Too bad it's not heart-shaped. Gordon loves the irony of bourgeois kitsch."

"It's not a quiche. It's a chocolate hazelnut torte."

Theresa burst into laughter. "Oh, Anna, you're priceless. I can see why Gordon likes you."

Anna's smile felt tight and strained. She had said something wrong, or funny, or both, but she wouldn't let Theresa know it was unintentional.

"Where did you get this?" Theresa asked, inhaling the delicious aroma. "That bakery on the west side?"

"No, I made it."

"Really?" She shook her head in regret. "You're so lucky. I wish I had time to bake. I haven't cooked in years. I'm always too busy."

"I'm a chef. It's what I do."

"Oh." Theresa nodded. "That's right. But you're really just, like, a lunch lady, right? Not a real 'chef' chef, as in a restaurant, right?"

Anna could not think of a reply that would suffice.

"Not that there's anything wrong with that," Theresa added. "Someone has to feed the students' bodies while we feed their minds, isn't that so?"

"There's a lot about what you said that isn't so," said Anna. "I'm not a server on the cafeteria line, if that's what you think. I develop recipes, direct the cooks, supervise my student workers—and that's just in the dining halls. I also prepare banquets and special events, sometimes for the provost himself."

"Of course you do," said Theresa encouragingly. "You absolutely should feel good about what you do. Never forget that every contribution to the academy is important, from the president to the lowliest custodian."

"I do feel good about what I do," said Anna. Something in Theresa's tone, in direct contradiction to her words, suggested that she should not.

"Absolutely," said Theresa again, nodding.

They stood there looking at each other in strained silence. Anna couldn't think of anything else to say, so she stammered something about having to catch the bus and left.

As she rode home, she felt tears of embarrassment and anger gathering. How dare that woman make her feel inferior? Theresa was "too busy" to bake; important people like her never had time to cook for themselves. Only insignificant people like Anna could afford to waste time over pots and pans. People with doctorates hired people like Anna to save themselves from such menial tasks.

"You're really like, just, like, a lunch lady, right?" Anna muttered, imitating Theresa. "Not a real, like, 'chef' chef, right?" For a poet, Theresa was amazingly inarticulate. She was also a snob, and Anna hated that she had been too surprised to defend herself properly. What was worse, though, was the sinking suspicion that if Gordon had been there, he would have agreed with every word Theresa had uttered.

They were perfect for each other.

Anna ought to face the facts: She and Gordon were a mistake. She had never doubted herself or her life choices before they got involved, but now she did little else. What precisely did he find so offensive about Anna's cooking and quilting? She was hardly a throwback to the Dark Ages just because she enjoyed traditionally female pursuits. She was not about to stop voting and driving and she defied anyone to try to stuff her into a corset. Admittedly, Gordon and Theresa knew much more about feminist theory than Anna ever would—their English department offered entire courses on the subject—but it hardly seemed very liberating to expect Anna to become ashamed of her talents just because they did not meet other people's expectations.

What on earth was wrong with being a chef?

Gordon had known what she did for a living from the very first. Why had he asked her out if he was ashamed of her? Unless those feelings had come along later, courtesy of Theresa's influence.

Anna walked home from the bus stop dejected and lost in thought. Jeremy, descending the apartment stairs in a rush, almost ran into her. "Sorry, Anna," he said cheerfully, but a second glance stopped him short. "Hey. What's wrong?"

Anna just shook her head.

"What did Gordon do now?"

How did he know? She never complained about Gordon to him. She had a sudden, frantic worry about the thickness of the building's walls. "It's nothing like that," she said. "I'm just—I don't know. I'm just tired."

"Uh huh." He leaned against the banister, studying her. "Maybe you're tired of Gordon."

"I'm not tired of him, but maybe I am tired of some of the things he does."

"What's the difference?"

She did not want to pursue this line of questioning, knowing where it would lead. "There must be a difference. What a person *is* is not the same as what they *do.*"

And that was precisely what Gordon would never understand.

Jeremy still looked concerned. "If you ever need to talk—"

"I know. You're right across the hall." She continued upstairs. "See you, Jeremy. Thanks."

Upstairs, she checked her answering machine—Gordon had not called—and washed her cake pans and batter bowls in the tiny sink. She had a sudden craving for a rich dessert and wished she had kept the torte for herself. Gordon would not appreciate it. He and Theresa would make it the subject of a research paper for an academic journal: "Tortes and the Chauvinistic Female in Contemporary American Society." They would probably win an award and Anna would end up assigned to the English Department's celebratory banquet.

Rather than make and devour an entire second torte, Anna brought out her sewing machine and worked on the blueberry quilt. Sending the fabric beneath the needle with the pedal all the way to the floor was as effective a form of therapy as eating, and much better for her.

A few hours later, she heard a pounding on the front door over the cheerful, industrious buzz of the sewing machine. She finished a seam and went to the door. Through the peephole, she saw Gordon standing in the hallway, his hands behind his back.

She resisted the instinct to rush around to conceal all evidence of her quilt. She opened the door. "Hi, Gordon."

"Hi," he said. "Thanks for the cake. Theresa and I tried it. It was delicious."

She stood in the doorway, her hand still upon the knob. "I'm glad you liked it." She could not care less what Theresa thought.

"May I come in?"

She let him enter, and after she closed the door behind him, he held out a bottle of wine and a ribbon-tied scroll. "For you. A token of thanks."

Wine she recognized, but she eyed the scroll warily. "What's this?"

He held out the scroll until she took it. "It's a poem. A sonnet. I wrote it for you."

"You wrote me a sonnet?" She untied the ribbon and carefully unrolled the paper. "That's sweet. No one ever wrote me a poem before."

"I hope you like it."

She read the lines, trying to make sense of them. "Come, Sleep; O Sleep! the certain knot of peace," it began, and became even less clear as it went on. Maybe it was the old-fashioned language he had used, but the poem didn't seem very romantic. It sounded more like someone complaining about insomnia.

Gordon must have sensed her doubt. "It's about a man who begs for sleep to overtake him so that he's no longer tortured by thoughts of the woman he cares for."

"Thoughts of me torture you?"

"No, no. What I mean is, thoughts of not being with you, not being able to have you. Thoughts that you might be angry at me." He gestured to the paper. "That's why in the poem I'm so eager to fall asleep, because then I can dream about you."

"Oh. 'Livelier than elsewhere, Anna's image see.' That's the dream."

"Exactly." He placed his hands on her shoulders and kissed her on one side of her face, close to her mouth. "I'm sorry I wasn't home when you came over. Theresa said you left in a huff."

"I did not," said Anna. "And even if I had, I had every reason to, after what Theresa said."

"What did she say?"

"She called me a lunch lady."

"Did she?" Gordon considered. "Don't you prepare lunch in the dining halls?"

"Yes, but my job title is not 'lunch lady.'"

"Did you tell Theresa your job title?"

"I . . ." Anna tried to remember. "I think I told her I was a chef. I can't remember."

"If you can't remember, how can you expect her to?" He kissed her other cheek, lingering. "Just forget it. Theresa loved the cake. I loved the cake. Let's not fight anymore." He kissed her on the lips.

She returned the kiss, and as she did, she reminded herself that she was annoyed with Theresa, not him. Gordon did love her, even if he never said it in those exact words.

Suddenly it occurred to her that she and Gordon both wanted the other to be something they weren't. If it was wrong for Gordon, it was wrong for her, too. She had to accept him as he was and hope he would learn to do the same.

But how could she get Gordon to appreciate *her* for who *she* was? Distracting his attention away from Theresa couldn't hurt. It was a pity Theresa didn't have a boyfriend of her own. If Gordon saw that Theresa was happily involved with someone else, he might lose interest.

Maybe that was the answer: find someone for Theresa. But whom? Theresa would probably want someone well educated and interested in the arts, but most of the men Anna knew who fit that description were confirmed bachelors nearing retirement age or already married.

Except for one. The perfect one.

After that flash of inspiration, Anna was so eager to get started with her plan that she could not get rid of Gordon fast enough. As she guided him to the door, he protested mildly until she reminded him about his upcoming candidacy exam, when he perked up and agreed that he ought to get to the library. She watched from the window as he strolled down the block and turned the corner; then she hurried across the hall and knocked on Jeremy's door. Jeremy was the ideal prospective boyfriend—cute, considerate, smart, funny. If Anna were not already attached, she might ask him out herself.

Anna gave him her brightest smile when he answered the door. "Hi, Jeremy. Listen. I have a huge favor to ask."

"Sure. What is it?"

"Would you go out on a double date with me, Gordon, and Gordon's roommate, Theresa?"

"Go where with whom?"

"I know it's a lot to ask. Double dates can be awkward if everyone doesn't know everyone else and blind double dates are even worse. But if you could do this for me, I would make it up to you, I swear. Chocolate desserts every night for a month."

"Seriously? Every night?" Then he shook his head. "Wait. Hold on. Anna, you know I have a girlfriend."

"But I thought . . ." Anna hesitated. "When Summer moved out, I thought you broke up. I thought she was going away to graduate school in a few months."

Jeremy shifted his weight and shrugged. "She did, we did, and she is, but we're back together and planning to stay that way. At least that's what I'm planning."

"Oh." Anna considered. "Well, do you think she would mind?"

"I think she might."

"What if all four of us agreed that we were just going out as friends?"

"Anna, you're making my head hurt."

"I'm sorry. I know this sounds strange, but Gordon has this—I don't know what to call it—this strange fixation on his roommate.

Fixation isn't the right word. He's letting her influence him too much. I think it would be healthier if she met some other guys, and, and, maybe—"

"Found her own boyfriend so she'd leave yours alone."

"Yes." Anna gave him a feeble grin. "That's it exactly."

He tried to hide a smile. "So, knowing I'm already seeing someone, you want to hook me up with someone you don't even like."

"I wouldn't have put it exactly that way."

Jeremy laughed. "Anna—"

"I know. I'm out of my mind. But is there any way you could do it? You're the most perfect guy I know."

"For Theresa?"

"For anyone. If they had a contest, you would win. But even if you don't become Theresa's boyfriend—"

"I won't. That's a promise."

"Even if you don't, you'll still show her that there are men other than Gordon in the world. You'll encourage her to start looking around."

He regarded her with amused patience. "Do you really expect me to believe anything you say after you call me the most perfect guy you know?"

He had to pick the most honest part of her request. "That's not mere flattery."

"So you say." He sighed and ran a hand through his unruly curls. "Okay. I'll do it. For you."

"And for the desserts."

"And for the desserts, sure. As long as there are no expectations beyond one night out."

"I promise to present it as a night out with friends. Just friends."

"All right." Jeremy looked as if he regretted it already. "I hope Gordon is worth all this."

"Of course he is," said Anna staunchly.

"Anyway, I'm glad you came over. I have something to tell you." He opened the door wider and beckoned her inside. His apartment, like all of those on his side of the building, was larger than hers, with two bedrooms and a substantially larger kitchen and living room. "Since Summer's going away, there's an opening for a quilt teacher at Elm Creek Quilts. Two openings, actually, since another teacher is leaving, too."

"Really?" Anna watched as he dug into his backpack and took a sheet of paper from a folder. "Are they looking for someone whose quilts are similar to Summer's? Because mine are sort of . . . different."

"They're unique," he agreed, handing her the page. One glance told her it was ad copy. "Here's what you need to know. I've already told Summer you might apply, so they'll be looking out for you. I know it's not the same as running your own restaurant, but it might be fun."

"I'm sure it would be. Thank you." She had told him once that she might look for a second job to help her build up her savings more rapidly, but she had not expected him to remember her offhand remark. Gordon did not even know of her plans, and Jeremy had already found her a promising lead.

Now she really owed him.

Back in her own apartment, she read the ad, carefully noting the job requirements. She never sewed anything by hand, but she could machine piece, appliqué, and quilt very well, at least in comparison to the quilts displayed at the Waterford Quilting Guild's annual show in the college library. She always drafted her own original patterns, and as for possessing the ability to tolerate quirky coworkers, emotional turmoil, and the occasional minor disaster, she had finely honed that skill thanks to her years in professional kitchens. Seasonal work with a flexible schedule was exactly what she needed from a second job.

Over the next week, she planned the double date and assembled her application for Elm Creek Quilts. Her old résumé was so outdated that she started over from the beginning, wishing that she had more quilting-related qualifications to mention. Although she had quilted for more than fifteen years and had worked part-time in her aunt's Pittsburgh quilt shop during high school, she had never taught quilting. She was not quite sure what to do about the ad's requirement for three letters of recommendations from former students. The ad didn't say they had to be *her* students. Maybe any former students of quilting would do.

Anna gave away almost all of her quilts as soon as she sewed on the bindings, but fortunately, she had taken photos of each to send to her aunt, who had retired to Arizona with her second husband after the overwhelming success of a local competitor, Quilts 'n Things, put her out of business. Anna found the negatives buried in a box at the back of her closet and had five-by-seven reprints made at a camera shop next door to Chuck's Diner. She did have to take new snapshots of her more recent, abstract "food" quilts, which she had not yet photographed since she did not really consider them complete. Still, she thought it only fair to show the Elm Creek Quilters the direction her quilts seemed to be taking, since they were so different from the traditional patterns with which she had begun. She also thought it wouldn't hurt to show as many quilts as possible, a little padding to compensate for the areas where her qualifications were a bit thin.

Arranging the double date proved to be more difficult. At first Gordon balked, claiming that he was uncomfortable socializing with people he did not know, but when she pointed out that he knew everyone but Jeremy and that she had attended that awful English department Holiday Gathering in December, where everyone brooded into their cocktails and hardly anyone spoke to her, he relented. Recalling that event, Anna wondered briefly if Gordon would have asked her to come had Theresa not stayed home with a bad cold that night. He had, after all, invited her at lunch on the same day, claiming that he had forgotten about it until a fellow student had mentioned it in the mailroom that morning. Everyone was supposed to bring an international hors d'oeuvre to share, but Gordon had told her not to trouble herself; he would heat up a couple of boxes of frozen egg rolls. He would have brought chips and salsa, but the student from the mailroom was bringing that. Appalled, Anna had insisted upon bringing her own Thai chicken peanut satays, which turned out to be the hit of the buffet table. For Anna, the diffident praise of her cooking was the only pleasant note of the entire discordant evening.

But this night out with just the two couples would be nothing like that. After several days of phone tag and trips across the hall to Jeremy's, Anna finally found an evening that accommodated everyone's schedules. The four would dine out at a popular chain restaurant two weeks from Friday.

In the meantime, Anna finished her application portfolio and sent it off to Elm Creek Manor. In lieu of the letters from former quilting students, Anna included three letters from supervisors at College Food Services and three additional letters from work-study students, including Callie, to give the interviewers a sense of her teaching abilities in the kitchen.

For the next few days, work kept her too busy to worry about Gordon or the job at Elm Creek Quilts. With the new school year approaching, College Food Services had begun preparing for the usual frenzy of welcome banquets and new faculty orientation luncheons. Anna had been assigned to the Freshman Orientation banquet—a stressful event requiring the college to reassure worried parents and impress their bored progeny, who always felt oriented enough by that time and would much prefer for their parents to be on the road home so they could sneak off for a little underage drinking at a fraternity party somewhere. She didn't see Gordon until the weekend, and that was only for a few short hours on Saturday night. He said both he and Theresa were looking forward to going out on the upcoming Friday.

Late Friday afternoon, after Anna rushed home from work to dress for the date, Summer Sullivan called from Elm Creek Quilts. She sounded so genuinely pleased that Anna had applied for the job that Anna was immediately seized by guilt and almost blurted out a confession. Fortunately she managed to restrain herself, as it was highly unlikely that Summer would have invited her to Elm Creek Manor the next week for a job interview if Anna told her of her plot to use Summer's boyfriend to distract another woman from her own boyfriend. The more Summer talked, the more Anna realized that her plan was actually a very bad idea. It was underhanded and unlikely to succeed. It was a wonder Jeremy had agreed to be any part of it.

But it was too late to back out now.

She finished the call, thanking Summer and promising to see her at Elm Creek Manor the following Wednesday. Then she quickly showered and dressed in a pink, short-sleeved mock turtleneck and an A-line denim jumper that fell just below the knee. It was not fancy, but it happened to be the most flattering item in her wardrobe. She considered putting her hair into the usual French braid, but decided to wear it down instead. The ends curled in a gentle wave where they brushed her shoulders, and although her chef's instinct was to tuck her hair out of sight beneath a tall white toque, she thought she looked surprisingly pretty. If only she didn't have those extra twenty pounds. Unfortunately, weight gain was an all-too-present occupational hazard. If she were any less careful, she could put on five pounds a year.

Jeremy knocked on her door about ten minutes before they were due at the restaurant. He wore a navy oxford shirt and light tan slacks, and although he did not seem his usual, easygoing self, he told her she looked beautiful and that he was looking forward to the evening. She thanked him with misgivings, suspecting that he was really looking forward to having the evening end.

"Summer called," Anna told him as they walked to the restaurant, and immediately regretted it when he shot her a look of guilty alarm. "To ask me to come for an interview at Elm Creek Manor, I mean. I'm also supposed to design an original quilt block, something to represent Elm Creek Quilt Camp."

"That's great. I'm sure you'll impress them."

"So you didn't tell Summer about tonight?"

"No." He paused. "Did you?"

"No."

"Good." Then he caught himself. "I don't mean that I'm concealing this from her, and I definitely don't mean that I'll ever ask Theresa out, but . . . some things just defy explanation. I thought the less I said, the better it would be."

Anna nodded, feeling terrible. She almost told him to forget the whole thing, that she would tell Gordon and Theresa that he had fallen ill and had to cancel, but they had come within half a block of the restaurant. Gordon and Theresa, waiting outside while Theresa finished a cigarette, had already spotted them.

"I didn't know she smoked," murmured Anna, knowing how Jeremy hated the smell. He often placed the assignments of his chain-smoking students in the apartment hallway to air out overnight before grading them.

"Don't worry about it," Jeremy replied, but his smile was strained. "It's just one dinner with friends."

They joined Gordon and Theresa, who wore black corduroys, a black turtleneck, and a black wool felt vest embellished with intersecting lines of white rickrack. Gordon, Anna was pleased to see, had dressed up in his one pair of navy dress slacks and a white shirt with a tie, an actual tie. She made introductions, everyone shook hands, and they entered the restaurant, where Anna was quick to request the nonsmoking section. They made small talk as they waited to be led to their table for four. It soon came out that each of them had eaten there before; in a town the size of Waterford, there were not many choices. Anna had chosen the restaurant because of its reputation as a nice place to take a date: pleasant atmosphere, moderate prices, typical American cuisine. If the quality of the food had been her primary concern, she would have cooked for them at home.

She was pleased to see that Jeremy and Theresa seemed to be getting along well. He talked about his research for the history department, Theresa talked about her poetry, Gordon talked about Theresa, and Anna said hardly anything. She didn't need to. The others were all liberal arts grad students and had plenty in common. Though Anna was the person who had brought them together, they didn't need her to guide the conversation.

Even the food was fairly tolerable, although even without tasting them Anna could list at least a dozen improvements she could make to each dish that was set before them. Her mind wandered as Gordon, with a couple of beers in him, began reciting Irish poetry and Theresa chimed in with explanations of the metaphors. Jeremy, to his credit, asked a few questions about the historical context of the poems, but Anna was not sure if he was genuinely interested or merely being polite. She supposed if she, who knew Jeremy was there under false pretenses, could not tell, Gordon and Theresa were unlikely to become suspicious.

The evening passed better than Anna could have anticipated until Theresa mentioned that Gordon would be taking his candidacy exam soon.

"I don't envy you," Jeremy said, grinning. "I'm glad that's behind me."

"Hear, hear," Theresa said. "No more exams for me, either."

"You still have to finish your dissertation and defend it," said Gordon. "You too, Jeremy."

As the others commiserated, Anna smiled and took a sip of water.

"We're all so overworked." Theresa sighed in mock despair. "I suppose the only one of us who has any leisure time is Anna."

For the first time that evening, everyone turned to look at her. It startled her so much that she almost choked on her water. She coughed and tried to speak, then set down the glass.

"I'm not exactly free," she said, managing a smile. "I'm gainfully employed, full-time. During our busy seasons, I might work up to sixty hours a week."

Jeremy nodded, but Theresa said, "That's a quantitative response to a comment that required a more qualitative analysis."

This time Gordon nodded. Annoyed, Anna said coolly, "If you speak to anyone who's dined at one of my banquets, I'm sure they'll tell you my work is of the highest quality."

"I said 'qualitative,' not 'quality.'" In an aside to Gordon, Theresa added, "A garbage man can work sixty hours a week, but it's still just tossing trash into the back of a truck no matter how well he does it. It's not exactly intellectually demanding."

"Working as a chef is intellectually demanding," said Jeremy. "Physically demanding, too. You're on your feet in a hot kitchen, directing cooks and servers, and racing to meet one deadline after another." The smile he offered Theresa was a pleasant mask. "If you have any doubts, you should try it yourself."

"Me?" She laughed. "I'm too busy. Who has time to cook anymore?"

"I have time to cook because it's my job," Anna pointed out. Again. For all her education, Theresa seemed unable to grasp the obvious.

"True," Theresa shot back. "But you can't seriously argue that you're as busy as a graduate student. I mean, come on. You have time for hobbies."

"Hobbies?"

"You know. That embroidery or whatever it is you do. Gordon says you've made some cute little crafts for your apartment." Theresa laughed. "You're going to make someone a great housewife someday."

She said housewife as if she considered it only a few steps above lunch lady on the rank of human endeavor. Anna refused to look at Gordon, which she supposed relieved him. He sat so stiff and wide-eyed in his chair it was as if he believed stillness would allow him to blend in to the background, camouflaged by his cowardice.

"Are you talking about Anna's quilts?" asked Jeremy.

"Quilts! That's what it was." Theresa rested her arms on the table and smiled indulgently at Anna. "You know, my grandmother made quilts."

Anna managed a tight-lipped nod. "Mine, too."

"Anna's quilts are true works of art," said Jeremy. "She won't brag about them, but she should."

Anna threw him a grateful look, but he might not have seen it because Theresa suddenly regarded him with new interest. "You know how to quilt? That's fascinating, a man pursuing the domestic arts."

Anna could not resist rolling her eyes. Suddenly, when practiced by a man, quilting was elevated from cute little craft to domestic art.

As Jeremy struggled to explain how he knew so much about quilting without mentioning that he was dating a founding member of Elm Creek Quilts, Anna fixed her gaze on Gordon. He simultaneously developed an urgent need for the waiter, or so his craning of the neck, shifting in his chair, and looking in every direction but Anna's suggested. Finally she caught his eye, but when she raised her eyebrows at him, he offered only a meek shrug. She picked up her wineglass and took a sip, shooting him a more pointed look over the rim, willing him to say something, anything, in her defense.

At last he caught the hint and spoke. "Anna's not planning to stay in the kitchen forever. She'll find out what busy really means when she goes back to grad school for her MBA."

An inch above the table, the glass slipped from her hand and hit the surface with a loud clunk. Somehow it stayed upright.

Puzzled, Jeremy said, "You're going to open your own restaurant *and* return to grad school?"

"Not all in the same week," Anna said, forcing a shaky laugh.

"This is an interesting turn of events." Theresa interlaced her fingers and rested them on the table. "So tell us the whole story. Where are you going? When do you start?"

Anna looked daggers at Gordon, who was studying his ribeye intently. "Let's just say I don't have any definite plans yet."

"Oh," Theresa said, drawing the word out, conveying in one syllable comprehension and pity, perhaps scorn. "And I suppose this plan to own your own restaurant is in a similar state of flux?"

"Those plans are actually a little further along." It would be difficult for them to be otherwise.

Jeremy looked from Anna to Gordon and back, but said nothing.

In his first helpful move all evening, Gordon brought up some gossip that had been spreading around campus, and soon he and Theresa were dissecting the latest developments with the rapid enthusiasm of soap opera fans during sweeps month. The topic of conversation did not return to Anna or her future plans, but the damage had been done. Theresa ignored her for the rest of the evening, and when Gordon spoke to her, his tone was hesitant and apologetic. At least he apparently realized that he had not provided the help she had needed, but it was no comfort.

Afterward, the couples parted outside the restaurant as they had arrived, although Gordon gave Anna a quick kiss and Theresa and Jeremy shook hands. Gordon and Theresa drove away in her car, and Jeremy and Anna walked back to their apartment building.

They climbed the stairs to the third floor and paused outside their doors. "When do you want your first dessert?" Anna asked Jeremy as she dug around in her purse for her keys.

He shook his head. "Forget about it. You don't have to."

"But the deal was a dessert every night for a month."

"I was just kidding. Who could eat that much dessert?"

Anna could, if she allowed herself. "So what did you think of Theresa?"

"She's nice when she's not being completely evil." He waited a moment before adding, "She and Gordon get along well."

Too well, Anna thought, and she knew that was Jeremy's point. "Do you think you'll ask her out sometime?"

He shrugged. "Maybe."

"And by 'maybe,' you mean 'no.'"

"Right."

Anna couldn't help smiling at the apologetic look on his face. "That's okay. I figured out a long time ago that this wouldn't work. Summer's a very lucky girl."

"Gordon's a very lucky guy, but he obviously doesn't realize it. You're beautiful, you're nice, and man, the way you cook—"

"Yeah, I'm nice and I'm a great cook," said Anna, suddenly depressed. "Too bad that's not enough. Gordon's afraid I'm going to blow up like a Thanksgiving Day parade balloon if I don't find myself a sugar-free, low-fat career."

"I wondered what was going on with that." Jeremy stepped forward and before she knew it he was wrapping her up in a bear hug. "Anna, you're good enough for anyone. Don't ever let Gordon make you feel otherwise. He is out of his mind not to realize how wonderful you are."

"Said the man dating a skinny girl."

Abruptly Jeremy released her. "What?"

"You call me beautiful to be polite and you say I'm good enough for anyone, but would you ever date someone who looked like me?" She heard the anger in her voice and knew she should stop. "What size is Summer? Four? Two?"

"I honestly don't know," said Jeremy. "I didn't fall in love with Summer because of her size."

"But if she had been my size, would you have been attracted to her? Would you have asked her out?"

Without pausing to consider it, he said, "If she had been the exact same person on the inside with twenty extra pounds on the outside? Yes."

"Oh, please."

"What?"

"You say that, but it's not true."

"How do you know it's not true?"

"Because fat girls don't get the cute guy."

He shook his head, incredulous. "I can't believe this. You're deluded. Fat girls get the cute guy every day."

"In what alternate reality?"

"In this reality. Okay. You want the truth? Yes, Summer is thin and pretty. Go ahead and call me shallow for noticing and appreciating that. But I didn't fall in love with her because of that. I fell in love with her for her warmth and her strength and her smile, her kindness and her confidence and the way she can find the humor in any situation. That's what makes her beautiful to me." He looked at Anna closely, exasperated. "It's kind of insulting that you don't get that. And that you don't think there's anything more to Summer than her looks."

Contrite, Anna said, "I've met Summer. I know she's a wonderful person."

"And so are you. And that's another thing I didn't say just to be polite."

Anna felt mean and guilty. Why had she vented at Jeremy, and after he had been so nice to her? "I'm sorry," she said. "The good news is you scolded the self-pity right out of me."

He frowned and shook his head. "If Gordon has said anything to make you feel this way about yourself—"

"Don't blame him," said Anna quickly. "This goes back long before I ever met him. He's a good person. Really. I guess we're just better by ourselves than with groups. Everything's fine when it's just the two of us."

"If you say so. You know him better than I do." Jeremy turned to unlock his door. "But don't forget what I said, promise?"

"Promise."

"Good."

They entered their separate apartments. Anna closed her door and watched through the peephole until he closed his.

On the morning of her interview, Anna woke filled with the same nervous energy that accompanied her throughout the day of an important banquet. She had taken the day off work, and with nothing to do until it was time to catch the bus out to Elm Creek Manor, she decided to bake cookies. She had to run down to Uni-Mart for a shockingly overpriced pound of butter, but the rest of the ingredients were already in her cupboard—Madagascar cinnamon, Penzey's pure vanilla extract, organic flour. She mixed the sugar cookie dough and let it chill while she ironed her tan suit and organized her interview materials. Back in the kitchen, she rolled out the dough and cut cookies in the shape of quilt blocks using the cutters her aunt had sent as a souvenir of her trip to the Road to California quilt show the previous January. She decorated them with pink, yellow, and lavender tinted frosting, which hardened while she dressed and braided her hair. She packed the cookies carefully in a plastic storage bin with a snap-on handle, put her papers and Elm Creek Quilts block in a tote bag, and met her bus at the stop on the corner.

Uncertain how long the bus ride to Elm Creek Manor would take, Anna left home two hours before her interview. Only three other passengers rode her bus, and they remained on board after Anna disembarked at a remote spot along the main highway where a gravel road led into a forest. The place looked exactly as

Summer had described it, but Anna still eyed the shadowed path worriedly before venturing forward. She picked her way through the loose stones, grateful she had worn her lowest heels but aware too late that she should have packed them in her tote and worn tennis shoes for the walk from the bus stop.

The road was narrow and winding, with no shoulder for her to scramble onto if a car came along. She passed a burbling creek, crossed a bridge, and was relieved when she finally emerged from the leafy wood onto a broad, green lawn divided by a paved road leading to the gray stone manor. If she did get the job and had to make this trip every day, she might finally get in shape.

She had seen pictures of Elm Creek Manor in the *Waterford Register,* but the real thing was far more impressive. It was easily larger and grander than the most impressive fraternity house near campus, although the comparison was probably not fair, considering that the quilters were not obligated to nail four-foot-tall Greek letters to the façade and adorn the veranda with spent kegs and beer cans.

Three women in workout clothes emerged through the tall double doors, descended the gray stone steps, and strode briskly along the front of the building, disappearing down a path through the trees. Another pair sat in Adirondack chairs on the veranda while a third woman held up a quilt block for them to admire. Anna considered going inside, but she was more than an hour early and did not want to annoy the Elm Creek Quilters by throwing off their schedule. She decided to explore the grounds on her own to get a feel for the place.

She wore a run in her nylon knee-highs from walking in the inappropriate shoes, but she enjoyed herself, stopping to chat now and then with some of the quilt campers, admiring the abundant fruit trees in the orchard, and relaxing for a while in a gazebo in a secluded garden. She followed a group of campers into the manor through the rear entrancc and couldn't resist peeking into the kitchen, which turned out to be larger than her own, but not at all what she expected to find in what was essentially an inn. How they managed to feed fifty-plus people three meals a day with that four-burner gas stove was a mystery. The pantry was well stocked, but she shook her head at the state of the cooking utensils. The whisk looked to be at least fifty years old, which she could have excused had it not been so bent out of shape. The hand mixer had rust, actual rust, on the handle. A sudden noise from an adjacent room startled her back out into the hallway before she could peek in the refrigerator. Realizing that it would probably not work in her favor if she were caught snooping, she quickly left through the back door, lost herself in a crowd of women crossing the parking lot, and walked around the manor to the front entrance.

On the stone staircase, she hesitated. She was still more than forty-five minutes early. Punctual was one thing; unable to tell time, quite another. If not for the blister developing on her heel and the sense that she ought to gather her thoughts before venturing inside for the interview, she would have made a second tour of the estate.

She glanced down the veranda. The group of three women had left, and now one white-haired woman sat alone, bent over a quilt block. As Anna watched, the woman shook her head and exclaimed to no one in particular, "I ought to just throw it in the scrap bag."

"What's wrong?" asked Anna. She sat down next to the woman, setting her tote bag and container of cookies on the floor. After all that walking, that Adirondack chair felt very good.

"I've been fussing with this silly block all day and haven't accomplished a thing." The woman flung the block onto her lap with an exasperated sigh. "I honestly don't know why I bother."

"It can't be that bad," said Anna. "Want me to take a look at it?"

The woman handed her the block, a traditional floral appliqué pattern Anna had seen before but whose name she could not remember. She examined the block, front and back, and tried to figure out what the woman was complaining about. Most of the quilters who had taken classes at her aunt's quilt shop would have been thrilled to master such tiny, even stitches. "I'm not quite sure what the problem is."

"This piece here," said the woman, indicating a small, leaf-shaped piece half attached to the background fabric. A small indentation marred the perfect smoothness of the curve, but not enough that anyone would notice it in a completed quilt.

"I think you're being too hard on yourself," said Anna cautiously, not wanting to offend. "Why don't you set this project aside and work on something else for a while? You can always come back to this when you're feeling less frustrated."

The woman regarded her with astonishment. "Of all the techniques you might have recommended, I never expected you to suggest I give up."

"That's not what I meant," said Anna. "Quilting is supposed to be fun. It's supposed to bring you joy. It shouldn't be such a struggle. If it's making you miserable, it's time to move on. Some quilts were born to be UFOs."

"UFOs?"

"You know. Unfinished Fabric Objects."

"Of course." The woman smiled. "I believe I've accumulated enough of those already. The trouble is, as much as I might like to try my hand at something else for a while, I must finish this block. It's for a guild exchange and I can't let the other ladies down."

"Oh. That's different." Anna took a second look at the block. Based upon what the woman had already sewn, Anna did not understand why she was struggling so much with that one particular, relatively easy piece. "I prefer to machine appliqué, but it wouldn't look very pretty if you switched in the middle of the block. Can I watch you sew for a few stitches?"

"Certainly, if you think it will help." The woman took a few labored, clockwise stitches around the curve of the leaf.

Anna watched and immediately spotted the potential problem. "Have you tried sewing in the other direction?" The woman peered at her inquisitively through her pink-tinted glasses. "You're right-handed, but you're sewing in a clockwise direction. It's a more natural movement for right-handers to sew counterclockwise."

"Why, I never thought of that." The woman rotated her block and turned her needle. "I think that might just do the trick once I get used to it. Thank you, my dear."

"In all honesty, you were doing just fine before I came along." Anna glanced at her watch, glad to see the conversation had used up another fifteen minutes. "Are you hungry? Would you like a cookie?"

"A cookie?"

Anna opened the container. "I baked three dozen. Help yourself."

"Oh, how charming. An Ohio Star." The woman took a cookie, her eyes alight with pleasure. "And a LeMoyne Star, too. These are far too pretty to eat."

"No, you have to eat them." Anna handed her a second cookie. "They taste even better than they look."

"If you insist, I will eat them, and I'll enjoy every bite." The woman smiled. "You are definitely going to make a wonderful impression. On whomever the lucky recipient of these cookies is, I mean."

"I didn't do it to make a good impression. When I'm nervous, I get this compulsion to bake, and it's either share the treats or eat them all myself. Not a good idea."

"I understand completely." The woman nibbled a point of the Ohio Star. "Delicious."

Anna thanked her for the compliment and bade her good-bye.

She returned the lid to the cookie container and entered the manor through the tall double doors. The foyer was grand and imposing, but Anna's attention was immediately captured by a young boy leaping from one black marble square to another, while a woman not much younger than herself nursed a toddler in a nearby metal folding chair.

The little boy looked up from his game and smiled at her. "Hi!"

"Hello," she answered, and glanced at his mother uncertainly. Campers wouldn't bring kids along, so she must be one of the Elm Creek Quilters. "I'm here for the job interview."

The woman gestured to the row of metal folding chairs next to a closed door. "I think this is the line."

"Oh," said Anna, embarrassed by her mistake. "I guess I'm early."

"And I'm late."

That seemed to be the least of the young mother's problems. The kids were cute, but it turned out the other woman had not intended to bring them along; when Anna asked if her baby-sitter had canceled, the mother implied that her husband had backed out at the last minute. Anna felt immediate sympathy. She tried to help, holding the baby when milk squirted all over his mother's clothes, making polite chat, and offering them all cookies. She avoided looking too directly at the other woman rather than have her curious glance be misinterpreted as a critical glare. It came as no surprise, though, when her efforts made little apparent difference to the young mother's stress level.

Anna wondered what the mother planned to do with her boys during her interview but was reluctant to ask. She considered offering to watch them, but they didn't know each other and the last thing this mother needed was some strange woman acting overly eager to watch her kids.

Not long after one of the Elm Creek Quilters dashed past them and disappeared inside the room, the door opened again and a woman around Anna's age peered out. "Hi. I'm Sarah McClure," she said. "Thanks for coming. Sorry for the delay." She glanced down at the file folder in her hand and looked at the mother. "Karen Wise?"

The mother rose, collected her belongings and children, and followed Sarah into the room. Anna leaned her head back and closed her eyes, her sigh echoing in the suddenly silent foyer. She wondered how many other quilters had applied for the job, and whether knowing Jeremy and Summer would give her an advantage. Perhaps their acquaintance had helped her land the interview, but she doubted it would mean much when the final selection process arrived. For all she knew, the Elm Creek Quilters had already eliminated her and had only agreed to see her as a courtesy to Jeremy.

Anna took a deep breath to settle her anxiety and rehearsed responses to potential questions. After less than an hour, the door opened and Karen ushered her boys down the hallway in the opposite direction. From the corner of her eye, Anna watched them go and wondered if they had gotten lost, but they soon reappeared and headed to the front door. The boys seemed happy enough, but Karen looked miserable and defeated.

"I hope your interview went well," said Anna, meaning it, but doubting it.

"I hope yours goes better," said Karen, leading the boys outside without waiting for a reply.

A few minutes later, Sarah McClure opened the door. "You must be Anna Del Maso."

"That's right." Anna rose and shook Sarah's hand before picking up her belongings. "Thank you so much for granting me this interview."

"It's our pleasure. I loved your quilts."

"Really?" Anna was pleased. "I know they've become a little unusual in recent years."

"They're brilliant. The photos you sent truly revealed your development as an artist."

An artist. Anna had never thought of herself as an artist. She wished Gordon and Theresa had been there to hear it. Of course, Gordon and Theresa's presence would have been so wildly unsettling that Anna surely would have made a mess of the interview.

Sarah escorted her into a parlor decorated in the Victorian style, but comfortable rather than fussy. Summer and five other women sat facing one lone armchair on the opposite side of a coffee table. Sarah invited Anna to sit there before taking her own place upon a loveseat closest to the door. Anna glanced at Summer and was heartened to see her smiling encouragingly.

Sarah introduced her fellow Elm Creek Quilters and began with a few questions about Anna's quilting history. Anna was glad to see a few nods when she mentioned that she had been quilting since her aunt had taught her at age fifteen. One dark-haired, ruddy-cheeked woman sighed wistfully as Anna spoke of her experiences working in her aunt's quilt shop, completing sample projects for her classes, assisting customers, and helping her aunt select new notions, books, and fabric lines at Quilt Market each fall in Houston.

"But lately you've been working in a different profession entirely," remarked Sylvia, studying her résumé.

"That's true. I have." Anna told them about her experience with College Food Services, and perhaps influenced by Theresa's derisive comments, she focused much more on her banquet work than on the daily tasks of the dining halls.

"I always wanted to be able to make a gourmet meal," said Sarah.

"Let me guess," said Anna. "You're too busy to cook."

"No, I just don't have the skills. Or the terminology. What's the difference between folding and braising and blending? When I see so many unfamiliar terms in a recipe, I panic and slam the cookbook shut." Sarah shook her head. "I wish I had a talent like yours. Ledgers I understand. Payroll taxes give me no trouble. Food? Forget it. It's a wonder I haven't starved to death or poisoned myself."

"You can't be that bad," said Anna.

"No, she really is," interjected the pretty blonde woman Sarah had called Diane.

"I could teach you a few things," said Anna, quickly adding, "I mean, if I get the job. Not that I wouldn't anyway, but if I get the job, I'll be around. Not that I would take time away from teaching quilting to cook."

Summer came to her rescue. "Did you bring your Elm Creek Quilts block to show us?"

Anna reached for her tote bag, and the sight of the plastic container reminded her of the cookies. "I brought these, too," she said, removing the lid. She handed the cookies to Sarah and placed the quilt block flat upon the coffee table. She told them about the evolution of her design as they passed the cookies around. Each Elm Creek Quilter took one, except for Gwen, who took two, and Diane, who handed off the container without looking inside to admire the cookies as the others had done. Anna did not take offense, guessing from Diane's trim figure that she had not allowed sweets to pass her lips in more than twenty years.

"These are elm leaves drifting on the breeze," continued Anna after describing her raw-edged appliqué method. "This is Elm Creek splashing over some pebbles, and this is the sun, or the warmth of sisterhood, or the light of illumination teachers pass on to their students. I thought I would leave that open to your interpretation."

Most of the Elm Creek Quilters chuckled, but Diane frowned and leaned closer for a better look. "It looks like a tossed salad."

"Diane," admonished Sylvia.

"You'll have to excuse her," said Gwen. "She has absolutely no appreciation for anything other than traditional blocks pieced by hand."

"I see the elm leaves," said Summer. "And that's definitely a creek."

"No, she's right," said Anna, suddenly seeing it. "It looks exactly like a tossed salad."

Diane gave Anna a sharp look, and Anna suddenly realized that the last thing Diane had expected was for her to agree.

"It's a lovely block," said the dark-haired woman who had seemed so engrossed by Anna's stories of her aunt's quilt shop.

Diane had composed herself as she paged through Anna's portfolio. "Looking through your material, I wondered . . . Have you ever taught quilting?"

Anna had been expecting the question. "No, I haven't."

"I see." Diane made a check mark on her notes. "You realize, of course, that all of the other applicants have taught at least a few classes."

"Not all of them," said Summer.

"I've never led a quilt class, but I have taught," said Anna. "In my current job, I've taught many student workers how to prepare food, how to follow safe kitchen practices, and other things. Years ago, I also assisted my aunt in classes at her quilt shop."

"But it's not the same, wouldn't you agree?" said Diane.

Anna hesitated. "It's not exactly the same, but I think it's relevant."

Diane's slight frown deepened. "I'm reluctant to suggest that the only reason you were granted this interview was because you're Summer's boyfriend's neighbor—"

"That is absolutely not true," said Summer.

"That's reassuring," said Diane. She studied Anna's résumé and shook her head. "I'm curious. When did you decide to become a quilting teacher? Based upon your education and employment history, I never would have guessed you were interested in quilting as a career."

"Well, actually . . ." Anna knew she would stumble if she wriggled out of the question with an evasive lie, so she decided to give Diane the truth. "Someday I want to own my own restaurant. That's why I'm looking for a second job, so I can save up the money faster."

"So this would be your second priority, not your first," said Diane, with a glance at Sylvia.

"I said second job, not second priority."

"There's nothing wrong with Anna taking on teaching responsibilities here as a second job," said Summer. "Our ad did mention that seasonal work and flexible hours were available. In fact, Anna's schedule could work to our advantage."

"We can discuss that later," said Sarah, meaning not in front of Anna. "Let's move along. Anna, I was intrigued by your lesson plan for the machine appliqué class. Would you tell us more about how you would run the class?"

Anna did, eager to switch to a safer topic. She answered the Elm Creek Quilters' other questions as best she could, but it was still a relief when Sarah rose and thanked her for coming.

"Thanks for the cookies, too," added Gwen.

"Yes, indeed," said Sylvia. "They were scrumptious."

"Here, have some more," said Anna, passing around the container again. "So I have fewer to carry home."

All but Diane gladly helped themselves to more cookies. Sarah offered to give her a tour of the grounds, but Anna assured her that she had already shown herself around.

The metal folding chairs were empty as Anna crossed the foyer, and the white-haired woman had left the veranda. Anna walked down the front drive toward the woods, going over the interview in her mind just as she always ran through the highlights and missteps of a banquet as she cleaned the kitchen afterward. She wished she had responded more articulately to Diane's queries. With just a few, pointed questions, Diane had dug out

Anna's weaknesses for the position, and Anna had not defended herself well. She should have said more about the teaching role she assumed with her student workers in the kitchen, her experience helping shoppers at her aunt's quilt shop, her creative inspiration. Thanks to Diane, the Elm Creek Quilters probably had no idea how badly Anna really wanted the job, not just as a source of revenue for her restaurant fund.

She made her way back down the gravel road to the main highway, arriving twenty minutes before the bus was due. She leaned against a small wooden sign and set her tote bag and cookie container on the ground at her feet, looking up every time a car passed. A blue midsized four-door car, so shiny it had to be nearly new, passed her once, disappeared around a bend, then returned and stopped on the shoulder, motor idling.

"Excuse me," the driver called. His dark hair and beard were sprinkled with gray, and he looked to be in his midforties, handsome except for a deep sadness in his eyes. He did not look like a salesman, at least not a prosperous one; his blue suit seemed a few years too old and his hair, though neatly trimmed, lacked the shiny, coiffed appearance Anna associated with salesmen. Likely he was one of the Elm Creek Quilters' husbands.

"I'm looking for the road to Elm Creek Manor," the man said, disproving her theory. "Do you know where it is?"

Guiltily, Anna jumped away from the sign and pointed into the woods. "It's that way. Sorry for blocking the sign."

The man smiled, and all trace of sadness disappeared. "It's not your fault. This isn't the first time I've missed it. Thanks."

He waved, turned onto the gravel road, and drove off into the woods. Anna watched his car disappear into the trees. *What a novelty,* she thought. *A man who asks for directions.*

◇◇◇

While she was gone, Gordon had left a message on her answering machine. Anna changed out of her suit and called him back.

"Where were you?" he asked. "I stopped by after my eleven o'clock class but you weren't home. You said you were taking the day off."

"I took the day off to go to a job interview."

"Oh. Right." He paused. "I walked all the way over there and had to settle for calling your answering machine on my cell."

Anna wanted to point out that he could have used that same cell phone to call before dropping by if the walk was too much for him, but when that petulant, spoiled child tone crept into his voice, she had to handle him carefully. "I'm sorry. I should have reminded you."

"Or left a note on the counter."

"Or that." She was suddenly uncomfortable at the thought of Gordon wandering about her apartment when she was not home. She had given him a key so he could let himself in when she was expecting him, and it had never occurred to her that he might use it at other times. But that was unfair; she had never told him the key came with restrictions. "I'm sorry," she repeated.

"I guess it's all right."

"My interview went well," she said, wishing he had asked. "Maybe we could do something to celebrate."

"Should we invite Theresa and Jeremy to join us? Theresa enjoyed meeting Jeremy. She's considering asking him out."

"That's nice," said Anna, wondering if she should warn him. "But I meant just the two of us."

"In that case, I can't make it tonight. What's your schedule like for the rest of the week?"

"Um, well, let me see." Anna took her pocket calendar from her purse and checked. "I have the usual weekday things, a dinner Saturday evening, and a brunch on Sunday."

"I'm busy every night next week. How about the next Saturday?"

"I'm free."

"Let's do something special a week from Saturday, then. Just the two of us."

"Great," she said, pleased. "What did you have in mind?"

"Oh, I don't know. You know I'm the spontaneous type. Surprise me."

"Oh." Her pleasure vanished. "Okay."

"So it's a date?"

"Sure. A week from Saturday."

Anna hung up the phone with a sigh. At least he wanted to have a special evening, just the two of them. It didn't matter who planned it.

By Tuesday evening she still had not decided how to spend their Saturday evening date. She was in the kitchen making a mug of cocoa and pondering her options when Jeremy knocked on the door. She was glad to see him, since they had hardly spoken since the double date. "I'm making some cocoa," she said, inviting him inside. "Want some?"

"Hot cocoa in summer?"

"People drink hot coffee in summer," she said, a little defensive. She shouldn't have to explain her chocolate addiction to someone who loved it almost as much as she did.

He shrugged. "Good point. Sure."

She cleared the kitchen table of her sewing machine and fabric while the kettle boiled, then fixed two mugs of cocoa and carried them to the table. "Have a seat."

"Thanks." Jeremy sat down and took a sip. "This is great. How did you make it?"

"Are you serious? It's the powdered mix from the grocery store."

"You don't put anything extra in it?"

"No."

"It never tastes this way when I make it." Jeremy took another drink, then set down his mug. "Have you heard anything from Elm Creek Quilts?"

"Not yet. Why? Should I have heard something by now? Did Summer mention something?"

"She hasn't said a word. That's why I'm curious." He took another sip, and she had the sudden impression that he was stalling for time. "I also wanted to see how things were going with you since the date with Theresa wasn't exactly a resounding success."

"Things are fine," said Anna, stirring her cocoa. "In fact, Gordon suggested we go out Saturday and celebrate my job interview."

"You mean the job interview you had last week?"

"He's been busy. And that's just as well because I'm having trouble thinking of where we should go."

"*You're* having trouble." He mulled it over. "If he wants to celebrate your successful job interview, why doesn't he just take you out? Why should you have to plan everything?"

"That's the way we like it," said Anna. "Gordon says it's sexist if he makes all the decisions."

"I see," said Jeremy. "When's the last time he made any decisions of this type?"

"Well—"

"When's the last time he did anything special for you?"

Anna took a sip, but the cocoa felt like chalk in her mouth. She set down the mug and met Jeremy's skeptical gaze evenly. "He wrote me a poem a few weeks ago. A sonnet."

"A sonnet?" echoed Jeremy. "I thought Theresa was the poet."

"She is," said Anna, hiding her sudden distress. "But Gordon knows a lot about poetry, too. Don't forget he's working on a Ph.D. in English literature. Anyway, why are you so upset about this? It's not any of your business."

"You're absolutely right." Jeremy stood up and pushed in his chair. "None of my business. But I still can't stand to watch him use you."

He left the apartment without another word.

Anna watched him go, heart constricting. Jeremy didn't know what he was talking about. He was completely out of line to insinuate that Gordon had not written the sonnet himself. Theresa *never* would have written a romantic poem for Gordon to give to Anna.

She knew it was a flimsy bit of evidence on which to place her trust.

Something about Jeremy's strange visit made her resolve to make her special date with Gordon a romantic evening at home. She would prepare for him the most elegant meal in her repertoire—at least, the most elegant meal that he would like, she could afford, and her minuscule kitchen could handle. She would adorn the table with fresh flowers and tall candles and play his favorite classical music in the background. Afterward they would go for a starlit stroll, observing the beauties of late summer on the campus grounds and sharing intimate conversation. When they returned they would curl up on the sofa with cappuccino and biscotti, and she would ask Gordon to tell her about his latest discoveries in the library and his progress on his thesis. He would love it.

She planned the menu and went well over her budget shopping at the organic market on Campus Drive. Hoping to appeal to Gordon's spontaneous side, she told him only that he should arrive around seven o'clock on Saturday.

All that day she worked, baking and preparing, cleaning and arranging, until she was satisfied. An hour before Gordon was due to arrive, she set the table and changed into her dressy black capris and a pink silk blouse. At seven, she lit the candles, turned on the CD player, and admired the scene. It was perfect. Gordon would be overwhelmed.

She jumped at a knock on the door, even though she had been

expecting Gordon and he was right on time. She hurried to answer, struck by a sudden wild fear that he had brought Theresa along, and a second fear that Jeremy would happen to step out into the hallway just in time to witness everything. She flung open the door, eager to usher Gordon inside before Jeremy saw them.

Gordon stood in the hallway, entirely alone and dressed in jeans and a sweatshirt from a Canadian Shakespeare festival he had attended five years before.

He looked her up and down. "You dressed up. I didn't think you wanted me to dress up."

"That's okay," Anna said, waving him inside. "It doesn't matter." She led him into the apartment and gestured to the beautiful table. "What do you think?"

He took in the flowers, the candles, the music, and the delicious aromas wafting from the kitchenette. "Anna, kitten, you did all this for me?"

"No, I called a caterer. Of course I did it."

Gordon shook his head. "You must have worked all afternoon on this."

She shrugged, smiling, and went to the oven. "Everything's about ready. Five more minutes for the entrée and then we can eat. Do you want to pour the wine?"

He followed her into the kitchenette and took her hands in his. "Anna, you shouldn't have done all this."

"Of course I should have." She freed one hand and touched his face, delighted with his reaction, which was even stronger than she had hoped. "We wanted to have a special date, right?"

He took her hand again and for the first time she noticed the regret and concern in his expression. "I know, but I feel tremendously uncomfortable about this."

"Uncomfortable?"

"Anna, I can't bear to think that you feel I'm shoving you into some traditional gender role. I don't want you to conform to a stereotype of womanhood out of some misguided belief that it's what I want for you."

"I just thought you might want a nice dinner."

"I do. But I don't think you should have to cook it."

"But I'm a chef. I don't understand what's wrong about me cooking for you. You're a literature student and you wrote me a poem."

"It's not the same thing." He steered her out of the kitchenette. "Let's go to my place. I'll cook for you."

"But—"

He raised her hands to his lips. "Please. Let me do this for you."

She thought about the days of planning and preparation, and about the delicious meal going to waste in the kitchen. She remembered Jeremy's criticism. What would he think now, with Gordon at last offering to do something special for her?

"Please?" he implored.

"All right," she said in a small voice. "Let me turn off the oven and clean up first. Will you wait for me outside?"

Gordon agreed and kissed her swiftly, grinning with relief. "Sure, okay. I'll be out front. Don't be long."

After he left, Anna stood fixed in place until the oven alarm roused her. She took the beef tenderloin en croûte from the oven, turned off the burners beneath the sautéed vegetables and the wild rice soup, and covered the chocolate mousse cake. She shouldered her purse, blew out the candles, and went across the hall to knock on Jeremy's door. Jeremy looked surprised to see her, but Anna didn't give him a chance to ask questions. "I made supper for me and Gordon, but we had a change of plans. We're going to his place. You should come over and eat so it doesn't go to waste. Or take it to your place and I'll get the dishes later. Maybe you can call Summer over, too. Wait—better not. It's beef."

"But—"

"Please lock up when you leave." Anna hurried down the stairs before she had to explain further.

Gordon was cheerful and talkative as they drove to his apartment. When they arrived, Theresa was sprawled out on the living room floor, wearing a gray sweatshirt and jeans frayed at the ankles. Anna felt prim and overdressed.

"Hey, Theresa," said Gordon. "We're going to make dinner. Are you hungry?"

"Sure." Theresa climbed to her feet. "What are we having?"

Gordon shrugged and turned toward the kitchen. "Beats me."

Anna followed, and as Gordon and Theresa pulled open cabinets and the refrigerator joking about how little food they had in the house, she leaned against the kitchen counter and watched them. Finally Gordon found a box of macaroni and cheese and held it up triumphantly. Theresa applauded and laughed, then dug up a dusty pot, rinsed it in the sink, and set water on to boil. As the pasta cooked, Gordon and Theresa bantered back and forth about department politics, but this time Anna made no attempt to follow the conversation. They had no colander to drain the macaroni, so Gordon tried to pour out the water in small trickles through a tea strainer, which sent Theresa into gales of laughter. Gordon and Theresa added margarine and milk and powdered orange cheese to the pasta, then stirred it all together and placed the pot in the center of the table with much ceremony. Anna found a diet soda in the refrigerator for herself and chose a seat at the end of the table. Gordon took the other end, and Theresa sat on his right.

Anna had not eaten since breakfast, but she found herself with no appetite. She took small bites of the rubbery pasta, forcing herself to smile and nod at appropriate intervals. Then suddenly, desperately, she wanted to leave the room.

"Will you excuse me?" she said. They broke off their conversation long enough to acknowledge her departure.

"Down the hall to the left," Theresa called after her. "You passed it on your way in."

Anna went to the bathroom and turned on the fan to drown out the noise from the dining room. She went to the sink to splash her face with water, and when she closed her eyes, she pictured the evening she had originally planned. She saw herself and Gordon gazing at each other over the wild rice soup, feeding each other bites of tenderloin en croûte, sighing with pleasure as the wineglasses reflected the candlelight.

She opened her eyes and caught a glimpse of herself in the mirror. The water had made her makeup run, and the towel racks were empty.

She sighed and blotted her face dry with tissues.

She left the bathroom, but instead of returning to the dining room, she turned in the opposite direction. She strolled down the hallway studying posters and photographs, touching a picture frame, fingering a plastic bowl of potpourri, allowing the laughter and talk to fade into the background. Each step took her farther from the dining room, and each step made it easier to continue. Then she was at the front door, which shut out the noise completely when she closed it behind her.

She descended the flight of stairs and left the building. She paused on the sidewalk to inhale deeply, and although the August evening was only pleasantly cool, she detected the scent of a wood-burning stove. The end of summer meant fewer salads and berry desserts, more meats and cream sauces. Harvest dishes—pumpkin soup, apple cobbler. Turkey with cranberry cornbread stuffing. Gnocchi in mushroom broth. When she opened her restaurant, she would design her menu around the four seasons, using locally grown organic produce and her own secret recipes, refined from years in the college's huge kitchens and her own tiny kitchenette.

Chuck's Diner was open until ten. Tonight she would take a

table for one, order a sandwich, and plan. One day that restaurant would be hers, and on the night of her grand opening, she would look back on this evening and marvel that she had ever allowed anyone to convince her to trade wild rice soup and beef tenderloin for powdered orange cheese pasta.

Chapter Four
Russell

Russell met Elaine at the Torchlight Run at Seafair. He had run the race every year since relocating from Indiana, but this was the first time he had signed up as part of a team from work. A coworker had talked him into it, insisting that Russ was the computer systems engineers' key to finally snatching victory from the marketing department's team, whose names had been engraved on the winners' bronze plaque in the employee lunchroom three years in a row. A techie team had never won, except for the year that an overly competitive manager in the software division had hired three college track stars as summer interns, which didn't count.

The self-appointed coach of Russ's team told him and their other two teammates that their best strategy was to stick together, shadowing the marketing guys until the last four hundred meters, when they could sprint ahead to the finish line. Rather than hold their faster runners back, Russ thought they each ought to strive for a personal best time and gamble that their average would beat the marketing guys', but he saw some merit in staying together so they could push one another. Then he spotted Elaine a few yards away in the pack, and all thoughts of the competition vanished. He instinctively slowed to get a better look.

"Move it, Russ," the coach called as he fell behind.

"Okay," he called back, weighing victory against getting a second look at a very attractive racer. He quickly decided bragging rights were just not that important and feigned a sore hamstring.

When his friends pulled too far ahead to witness his sudden recovery, Russ maneuvered through the pack toward the woman in the pink tank top, close enough to see the freckles on her pale shoulders. Her black hair was cut so short it barely moved in the breeze, but what struck him most was that of all the runners surrounding them, she was the only one smiling.

They crossed the finish line at nearly the same time, and he stayed close enough so that he did not lose her in the crowd at the postrace party. He squeezed into the buffet line behind her and handed her a plate as she gathered her napkin and plasticware. She thanked him, which gave him enough encouragement to speak to her. "You must love to run," he said, immediately regretting it. They had just finished a 10K race. Russell McIntyre, Master of the Obvious.

To his relief, instead of bursting into derisive laughter, she looked up at him, curious. "What makes you think so?"

"You were smiling exactly like that even at mile five."

She turned away to continue moving through the buffet line, but she seemed pleased. "I must have been thinking about how glad I was that the race was almost over. I really pushed myself today. I usually go at a slower pace."

"Were you after a personal best time?" Since they were technically in a conversation, Russ did not think she would mind if he accompanied her as she chose a table and sat down. "Or just this carbo-loading feast of pasta?"

"Definitely the carbs," she said. "No, I really just wanted to make sure I got here before my kids did, so they wouldn't worry that I had collapsed somewhere along the way."

"Your kids?"

"Yes, my kids. They're meeting me." A small, knowing smile played on her mouth. "They're legal in this state, you know. You don't even have to have a license."

Russ quickly recovered. "Are they with their baby-sitter? Or . . . your husband?"

"No husband, no baby-sitter. My daughter's sixteen, so she can drive when I'm sufficiently motivated to allow it. She dropped me off at the starting line and she and my son will pick me up later." She glanced at her watch. "In about an hour."

Sixteen? Russ was flabbergasted. Without thinking, he said, "How old were you when you had her, twelve?"

He was halfway through a hapless apology when he realized she was laughing.

Although he would catch grief from his coworkers on Monday for costing their department a bitter loss to those smug jocks from marketing, before Elaine left to meet her kids, Russ had her phone number and an invitation to call.

They met the next Friday evening for dinner at Elliott's Oyster House on Pier 56. They watched the ferryboats depart and arrive as the sun set behind the Olympic Mountains and shared their life stories. It turned out Elaine was twenty when she had Carly, twenty-two when she had her son, Alex, and twenty-eight when she and her husband divorced. Her ex, a chief financial officer for a dot-com, had decided he needed a new wife to go with his new lifestyle once his company's stock options made him a millionaire. Under California law, Elaine was entitled to half of his wealth, but she chose to accept a lower settlement in exchange for uncontested full custody of Carly and Alex. "I didn't want his money for myself anyway, not after what he did," she said breezily, dismissing his betrayal. "I'm so obstinate I wanted to refuse child support, too, but my lawyer talked me out of it. I'm glad he did. Do you know what college costs these days?"

Russ thought a better question was how any man could be deluded enough to believe any trophy wife could surpass Elaine. There was a moment when he was unsettled by their six-year age difference, but he quickly shrugged it off. She was so full of life and—and she just had a way about her that made her more attractive to him than most women his own age.

She worked in public relations for a local nonprofit, which meant that she spent her days trying to convince the wealthy and upper-middle class citizens of Seattle to write checks to support unwed, pregnant teenagers. "There's not a lot of money in that," she remarked once. "Orphaned babies? Sure. They're cute and innocent. You can always find someone willing to help cute little orphans. Teenagers, though, are not so cute, and if they're pregnant, conventional wisdom says they must not be so innocent. Some say these girls got what they deserved for their irresponsible behavior. If people only knew what these girls have been through, they might believe differently, but they don't know, and frankly, far too many of them don't want to know."

Her ex-husband's new wife had once been a spokesmodel for Toyota, but since her marriage, she had devoted herself full-time to promoting her husband's career and raising their baby boy. Elaine had met her successor only once; Carly and Alex saw her as the destroyer of their parents' marriage and rarely asked to visit their father at his new home. If they were frosty to their stepmother, they were fortunately only chilly to Russ, with promising warming trends as the months passed.

In December, Russ's best friends from college, Charlie and Christine, came down from Olympia to do some Christmas shopping and meet Elaine. Charlie was obviously relieved Russ was finally dating again after breaking up with his almost-fiancée, a fellow engineer he had left behind at his former employer when she decided she liked her job too much to follow him to the West Coast. Christine's opinion mattered more somehow, possibly because she was the more astute of the pair and also because Russ had once been half in love with her. They had met in history class the first semester of sophomore year, had shared notes, met for lunch, and studied for the midterm together. If Russ had not made the mistake of inviting her to the football tailgater where she met his roommate, she might have become his girlfriend instead of Charlie's. He had watched with dismay as she and Charlie hit it off better than he had expected, but he hid his feelings when she later asked him if he would be upset if she went out with Charlie.

What could Russ say? He didn't own her. He had never even kissed her. "Why would I mind?" he said. "Charlie's a great guy."

She beamed at him with such warmth and sweetness that he would have been filled with bliss had her happiness sprung from any other source but Charlie.

Still, Russ clung to a thin shard of hope: Charlie always moved on to a new girl every few weeks, leaving her bewildered, jilted predecessor with nothing but vague promises that he would call. Usually Russ felt sorry for the girls Charlie dumped, but this time he hoped that it *would* happen, and soon, because when it did he would be there to comfort Christine.

But even Charlie recognized what he had found in Christine. They dated exclusively for the rest of their college years, and eventually Russ resigned himself to their romance. It was impossible to avoid them—not that Russ tried very hard, because he liked Charlie, and his admiration for Christine increased as his infatuation diminished. Before long she, too, became a close friend. Still, Russ knew when he was welcome and when they wanted to be alone, which was probably why the three of them got along so well.

Christine tried to set him up with some of her friends, but although they were all friendly, smart, pretty girls, he never really clicked with any of them. Once, after an exam week all-nighter turned into a predawn breakfast off campus, the three friends' conversation turned from their sadistic professors to the dismal state of Russ's love life. That was when Christine delivered her devastating verdict: Russ was doomed because he was "too nice."

"Great," said Russ gloomily, loading his fork with pancakes. "So I should become a jerk?"

"That's not what I meant," said Christine.

"Are you saying that I'm not nice?" Charlie asked her, wounded. "I open doors for you. I remember birthdays. Your mother loves me."

"Of course you're nice, honey," said Christine, but when he wasn't looking, she rolled her eyes at Russ.

"Russ's problem is that he's waiting for the girl of his dreams," said Charlie. "Once he figures out that no such girl exists, he'll settle for a real girl."

Russ could tell from the pointed look Christine gave Charlie that she took in all that this implied and was not pleased, but she didn't rebuke him. Instead she turned to Russ and said, "Keep looking, Russ. You'll find her."

And in Elaine, he thought he had. She and Christine struck up a friendship immediately, and as soon as Charlie got him alone, he said, "Russ. Marry her. Marry her now. Don't give her the chance to get to know you better or she'll never have you."

"Very funny," said Russ, but he couldn't stop grinning. It meant the world to him that his best friends liked Elaine, because he was falling in love with her.

They married a year and a half after meeting in the road race. Charlie was the best man and Elaine's sister was the matron of honor. Carly and Alex, the only other attendants, tentatively approved of the marriage. They even consented to spend a week with their father so Russ and Elaine could honeymoon in the California wine country. They had mixed feelings about leaving their home to move into Russ's, but Elaine decided the sacrifice of next-door friends and a familiar school was worth it for a larger house in a better neighborhood on the other side of the city. Russ, eager for Elaine's children to feel welcome, offered to help them repaint their new rooms, choose new furniture—anything they wanted, anything that would make them feel at home. They thanked him politely and took him up on the offer, while a subtle nonchalance in their voices told him they would tolerate these new arrangements only because their mother loved him and they would be moving out soon anyway.

Elaine was thrilled with her new surroundings, not only because her kids would finish up high school in a much better district, but also because Russ agreed to let her turn the spare bedroom into a sewing room. Elaine was a quilter, and although Russ had known that about her, he had not entirely understood what that meant until moving day when she enlisted his help in carrying box after box of carefully folded fabric into her new sewing room.

"What's all this?" he asked, wondering how it would all fit and secretly concerned that she might ask to move their bed into the spare room so the master suite could become her sewing room.

"My stash, of course."

"Your stash?" It sounded vaguely illegal. "Do you think you'll have enough room?"

"I'll make it fit," she said cheerfully, and somehow she squeezed everything into the closet. Her sewing table took up the entire length of one wall, across the room from two bookcases stuffed full of books on quilt patterns and quilting history. She hung a large, flannel-covered board on another wall. As she designed a new quilt, she would press fabric shapes to it until they stuck, then stand back and study the arrangement, sometimes for twenty minutes at a time.

But helping Elaine set up her new sewing room, or "quilt studio," as she preferred to call it, was only the beginning of his initiation into the world of marriage to a quilter. The whirr of her sewing machine woke him in the morning, and she stitched by hand on the sofa beside him while they watched television at night. Before ironing his shirt and slacks every morning, he had to remove stacks of quilt squares from the ironing board. At least once a week, a quilt magazine turned up in their mailbox. Little bits of thread clung to everyone's clothing; fashion conscious Carly ran a lint brush over herself every morning before going to school at an age when most girls had probably never seen a lint brush. Elaine communicated via the Internet with other, similarly obsessed quilters from around the world; she peppered their dinner conversation with references to friends she had never seen in person, ladies who identified themselves by such names as "Quiltlady" and "Scrappbagg." He learned the hard way not to walk around in bare feet after she pin basted a quilt on the living room floor. Every vacation, every excursion to a new city turned into a quest to spend at least twenty dollars at every quilt shop within a ten-mile radius. He also discovered that one does not ask a hardcore quilter to sew on a loose button.

The first and only time he did so, Elaine stared at him in astonishment. "Would you ask Picasso to paint your living room?"

"I might," he said, "if he owned a three-thousand-dollar Bernina painting machine."

Elaine gave her sewing machine an affectionate pat. "It was only fifteen hundred, used, and worth every penny."

"I wouldn't have asked except you love to sew. You have enough fabric in here to outfit the entire Spanish Armada in full sail. What's one little button?"

She laughed, patted his cheek, and agreed to sew on the button. Unfortunately, she placed the shirt and the button on her worktable and promptly forgot about it. Eventually the shirt migrated to her stack of unfinished projects, and later he spotted it buried within her fabric stash. He knew any chance of having the shirt restored to its former usefulness had passed when his birthday came and she gave him a new shirt, identical in every way to the one trapped beneath an avalanche of cotton in her closet except that all of its buttons were intact.

Russ enjoyed teasing her about her quilting, partially because in this, he, Carly, and Alex shared common ground. Her quilting actually did not bother him at all. She never ignored him in favor of a quilt project, and quilting seemed therapeutic for her, helping her to relieve the stress of her emotionally demanding job. He loved her for the joy she took in making quilts for each of his nieces and nephews, and he loved coming home from work to find that she had hung a new quilt on a bare wall "because the wall looked cold." But it was when he overheard her on the phone with a friend from her quilting bee, marveling about how supportive he was of her quilting compared to her ex, that he vowed she would never hear a word of complaint from him about her quilting, no matter how many lost pins he found with the soles of his feet.

They wanted children, and as Elaine's thirty-ninth birthday approached, they decided not to wait any longer to start a family. "Continue the family," Elaine corrected. "We're already a family."

Russell agreed, for although Carly and Alex often seemed frustratingly indifferent to him, he loved them as if they were his own. He had shared more of the challenges and conflicts of their teenaged years than their own father had. After they had made the transition to college, the house seemed too big and quiet without a youngster around. Russ and Elaine understood they would face challenges as new parents at their ages, if they were fortunate enough to conceive at all, but they decided to try.

A year passed. Elaine halfheartedly suggested they see a fertility specialist, but they had long ago discussed whether they would be willing to take extraordinary measures to conceive and had decided they would not. They had begun to investigate adoption when Elaine surprised him one morning with the exciting news that she had missed her period. When a home pregnancy test came back negative, her face twisted with unshed tears, but she said that perhaps it was too early for the test to detect anything. When she failed a second test a week later but her symptoms persisted, she made an appointment with her ob-gyn, because she felt bloating and pressure in her abdomen, and she was certain the pregnancy tests were wrong.

When the diagnosis came back positive for ovarian cancer, Russ could not believe it. Elaine's mother and an aunt had died of breast cancer, and she was meticulous about her self-exams and annual mammograms. It was breast cancer that had been stalking them, breast cancer she had been keeping at bay. Russ was so certain that the diagnosis was wrong that he stormed from the doctor's office and went outside to sit on the curb until the dizzying blackness left his head. Before he was able to return, Elaine finished her appointment and joined him outside. He was ashamed that in her hour of horror and fear, *she* had had to comfort *him.* He knew he had failed his first real test as a husband.

The women of her quilting bee rallied around her as she underwent surgery and discovered that her cancer was already at stage II. At least three times a week, a quilter stopped by with a casserole ready to stick in the oven, with explicit cooking directions for Russ to follow. Her Internet quilting friends sent packages of fabric, quilt blocks, and chocolate. Everyone who knew and loved Elaine—and Russ was proud of how many, many people this included—prayed for her.

As she underwent chemotherapy, she began a new quilt. She took angry reds and sickening greens and blacks as deep as oblivion from her closet stash, cut jagged shapes, and pressed them to her design wall. She frowned at them from a chair, too weak to stand as long as she needed, a red polka-dot scarf covering her baldness, her eyes circled in dark shadows, her lips thin and pale.

"What are you making?" he asked her once, gently, wishing she would put this garish project aside in favor of the quilt she had been working on before her diagnosis, a pattern of golden stars and log cabin strips. The warm colors and familiar motions of sewing would cheer her up, he thought. Staring at the design wall seemed so bleak and despairing that he wished he could take her by the arm, lead her from the room, and shut the door on that quilt.

She rose from her chair with an effort, eyes fixed on the design wall. "This is my cancer quilt."

"This is what cancer looks like?"

"This is what cancer feels like." She shifted a red triangle to the right three inches. "This is what it feels like in me."

He held her at night when she cried. She exacted endless promises from him that he would take care of Carly and Alex, that he would show pictures of her to her future grandchildren, that he would not withdraw from the world after she had gone. He begged her not to ask him to plan for a life without her, but she insisted, and to placate her, he agreed to all that she asked.

Then, unexpectedly, she began to feel stronger. Her hair grew back; she bought new running shoes and began taking morning walks through the neighborhood. She left the cancer quilt undisturbed on the design wall and joined a round-robin quilt project with her Internet friends. She talked about getting a dog and returning to work, and she suggested they spend a long weekend in California's Napa Valley, enjoying some of the places they had discovered on their honeymoon. Most of all, she wanted the two of them to run in the Swedish SummeRun, a 10K race through Seattle and a fund-raiser for the Marsha Rivkin Center for Ovarian Cancer Research. It was a serendipitous event for Russ and Elaine, she said, since they had met in a road race and she definitely supported the research.

Russ was conflicted. He was thrilled that she felt well enough to begin running again and he was a fervent supporter of ovarian cancer research, but to run in a race with Elaine, especially for this cause, seemed to frame their relationship, putting a full stop at the end of their story. But if she meant to enter the race, he was determined to run beside her, to celebrate her triumph or to support her if she faltered.

A few days after they sent in their registration forms, Elaine told him that she wanted to reschedule her follow-up appointment with the oncologist to an earlier date. When he asked her why, she shrugged and said, "Just a feeling."

He had learned to trust her intuition, but he refused to believe that it was necessary to see the doctor sooner than planned. If they did not believe in her remission, trust in it entirely, it would cease to be. Then he was filled with a terrible fear that cancer cells might be even then growing and dividing within her, and that his superstitious delay might kill her. "Call," he urged her. "It's probably nothing, but call."

When tests confirmed that the cancer had resurfaced in her lymph nodes, Russ was flooded with feelings of rage and betrayal and despair so intense it made his head swim. Elaine, in contrast, seemed to have expected it. She grew still in the chair beside him as the doctor spoke about trying to join a clinical trial, nodding silently and stroking Russ's back to comfort him.

Even in the worst days of their mother's treatment, Carly and Alex had seemed certain that she would ultimately overcome the disease. Russ had marveled at their conviction and tried to follow their example once he saw how much their confidence heartened their mother. Now their certainty was shattered, and disbelief quickly shifted to despair. Carly, recently engaged, moved back home to help Russ care for Elaine. Alex drove down from his new job in Vancouver nearly every weekend. Even their father called once, near the end. Elaine wore a bemused expression as she listened on the phone, then laughed when he offered financial help and told him that if he really wanted to make a difference, he should give to Childhaven's Crisis Nursery instead. Russ never learned if he did.

The women of Elaine's quilting bee surrounded her with love. They brought food, laughter, and hope into the house and always seemed to appear right when Russ felt the most helpless and exhausted. He had taken a leave of absence from his job to care for Elaine, but he still felt as if there was never enough time, never enough that he could do for her.

Elaine's oncologist called in some favors and got her enrolled in a clinical trial. Russ convinced himself that this would cure her. Even as Elaine contacted Hospice and got her affairs in order, Russ clung to his faith in the power of her new meds. Then came the day when Elaine told him she had placed all of her important papers in the fireproof box in the closet so he would not need to worry about searching the whole house for them.

"I won't need to search for them because if we need them, you'll tell me where they are," he said firmly.

She looked at him with affectionate amusement. "I see. You're still in the denial stage."

"But the treatment," he said. "Your new medication. Why would they keep treating you if you weren't getting better?"

"Oh, sweetheart," she said, pressing her thin cheek to his. "Clinical trials aren't for the patients in them. You know that."

He knew it.

Elaine was determined to participate in the Swedish Summe-Run. Russ saw to it that she did. He pushed her the entire route in a wheelchair, but even this exhausted her. "All of this effort is going to pay off someday," she told him as they approached the finish line, smiling despite her fatigue. He nodded, unable to speak out of fear that he would start sobbing. It would pay off someday, but not soon enough to save Elaine. He remembered how full of life and happy she had looked running just ahead of him on the day they met. Now she was again moving ahead of him, away from him, but this time he could not follow.

Elaine died surrounded by Russ, her children, her sister, and her dearest friends. Her last words were for her children, gentle whispers for them alone that left them sobbing and smiling and choking out assurances. But before she turned to them, she asked Russ to hold her. "Thank you," she said. "I'm sorry."

"What do you mean?" he said. He meant, what in the world was she apologizing for? He was the one who was sorry, sorry that he could not save her, sorry that he had not been a better husband, sorry if he had ever disappointed her in any way for even a moment.

"Thank you for loving me," she answered. "Thank you for loving my children. They didn't always make it easy. They're going to need you. Their father will try to comfort them, but he'll just upset them."

Gently, his voice barely above a whisper, he asked, "Why did you say you're sorry?"

"I'm sorry I'm leaving you. I'm sorry we didn't have a baby together. I know how much that disappointed you."

"Oh, Elaine." He wanted to press her hard against him, but she was so delicate in his arms, like a broken bird. "You have never disappointed me. There's not a minute of any day since I've known you that I would change. Not one single minute."

He had so much more he wanted to say, but he was fighting back tears, trying not to let her see his anguish. She wanted him to be strong for Carly and Alex. He must let her think he could be, though he was convinced his grief would kill him.

It was not a relief when she finally passed. He had heard some families from the Hospice say that in the end it was a relief when their loved ones were finally released from their pain. For Russ, Carly, and Alex, nothing could be further from the truth.

Elaine had planned well. "That's Mom," said Carly when they discovered that she had planned her own funeral down to the last note of music and the suit she wanted Russ to wear. Somehow word got out on the Internet that she had died, and dozens of mourners introduced themselves to Russ and the children as friends from one quilting list or another. Even if they had not come, the church would have been full, as coworkers, residents of the Catholic Worker House where Elaine had once lived, and an astonishing number of young mothers with babies came to pay their respects.

"See how many lives your mother has touched," Russ said to Carly and Alex. They looked and saw through their tears, and they nodded.

After the Mass, Russ and the members of Elaine's quilting bee fulfilled her final request. They held up her quilts one by one as Bach cantatas played in the background, carried them down the aisles so that all could witness her artistry, then draped the quilts over the few empty pews until the back of the church was awash in color. Russ took in the quilts hungrily, seeing them as a reflection of Elaine's affectionate nature, her boundless humor, her compassion for the less fortunate—everything she was and had become over the span of more than twenty years the quilts had captured.

Afterward, Russ distributed the quilts as Elaine had instructed: one to a college roommate, another to her sister, one each to the members of her quilting bee. Her friends were grateful, and they hugged their quilts with eyes closed against tears or held them reverently as if cradling Elaine herself. Russ should have been comforted by their gratitude and appreciation, but each giving pained him as if pieces of Elaine were being carved from his memory.

The weeks passed, and somehow Russ endured them. His family leave ran out and he returned to work, where he went through the motions of his job and nodded numbly when people told him how sorry they were for his loss.

Carly had put her wedding plans on hold, but she decided to return to her own apartment so she could be closer to work and her fiancé. "You don't have to leave," Russ told her, dreading an empty house.

"I do have to," she told him. "If I don't move back in soon, my roommate will find a replacement for me. Besides, this is your house. It was never really ours."

That pained him. "Yes, it was. It was to me. I wanted you and Alex to feel at home here. I thought you did."

Carly looked away, and Russ recognized her indifferent shrug from her teenage years, the gesture with which she tried to disguise shame. "It was more of a home than our father's house ever was."

And Russ was grateful.

Before Carly moved out, she helped him go through her mother's belongings, sorting heirlooms and cherished keepsakes from items to be donated to one of Elaine's many causes. Carly took her mother's jewelry and a leather jacket Russ had given to her one Christmas. She divided family photographs into a set for herself and one for her brother. They folded her clothes carefully and placed them in paper sacks to deliver to the women's shelter. Russ had a sudden vision of himself walking in downtown Seattle and spotting a stranger standing in a doorway, carrying a bag of groceries, wearing Elaine's favorite sweater. He had to force himself to continue packing the clothes.

Last of all, they went to her quilt studio. When Russ opened the door, the sight of the cancer quilt staggered him. He could almost see Elaine there, arranging the red of blood, the green of disease, the black of oblivion. He couldn't bear it. He pulled the door shut and leaned against it as Carly stared at him.

"What is it?" she asked.

"No," he muttered.

"What's wrong?"

I can't, he thought, but said, "I'm too worn out to tackle that room today."

"Okay." She studied him, concerned. "But I'm leaving tomorrow. I don't know when I'll be able to come back to help."

"I'll take care of it on my own."

Carly followed him downstairs. "But there's so much to sort through. It's too much for one person."

"I said I'll take care of it," he said harshly. Carly raised her hands in a small gesture of surrender and shook her head as if to say it made no difference to her.

Carly returned two weeks later with a carload of boxes and garbage bags. Russ was pleased to see her and agreed that they should get started on the quilt studio, but he was actually just about to leave for Pike Place Farmer's Market. He would be glad for her company if she wanted to join him. Carly assented, and they spent the day seeing the sights and shopping for ingredients for their supper, which they prepared together. Russ asked her about work and her fiancé, and circumspectly asked if they had resumed planning their wedding. Although Russ had long privately considered Carly too young to get married, Elaine would not have wanted Carly to postpone her happiness for the year of mourning Carly seemed to believe was necessary. For his part, Russ saw no point in observing a symbolic year of mourning to suit social conventions. They would always mourn Elaine. One year or two years or ten years later, they would still mourn. To pretend that everything would be resolved on some arbitrary date was ridiculous.

"If you're postponing the wedding because you're having second thoughts, that's one thing," said Russ, after Carly gave a tearful account of her fiancé's bewildered unhappiness at her reluctance to set a new date. "You should take that time. But if you're doing it for your mother, I really think you ought to reconsider."

"I know I want to marry him," said Carly. "I just can't imagine getting married without Mom there. How can I celebrate when she's gone?"

"We'll have to figure out a way," said Russ quietly. "Your mother would be very annoyed if we never celebrated anything ever again just because she's not here to enjoy it."

Carly actually managed a laugh. "She'd be furious. Can you imagine what she'd say?"

"All too well."

They laughed together. Carly wiped her eyes and said she would call her fiancé as soon as she got home so they could choose a new wedding date.

They washed the dishes side by side. Afterward, Russ walked Carly to the door to say good-bye. Unexpectedly, she hugged him.

"I never thanked you for marrying my mother," she said, her voice muffled as she buried her face in his shoulder.

"Well . . ." Russ patted her on the back. "It's not something you need to thank me for. I was glad to do it. Thank you for letting *me* marry *her.*"

"It's not like I could have stopped her." Carly lifted her head so he could see that she was teasing. "I'm glad she was married to you when this happened. If she had still been married to my dad—well, he would have been totally useless. But you saw her through. You eased her way."

His throat constricting, Russ held Carly tightly.

When Carly opened the door to leave, she spied her car in the driveway and, through the windows, the boxes she had brought. She shot him a look that was mildly accusing. "We were so busy, we forgot about Mom's quilt studio."

"I guess we did. I'll get around to it. Maybe you could leave the boxes."

She did, and a few days later, she called to ask if he had sorted out the quilt studio yet. *Sorted it out?* Russ thought. He could not even open the door. "I haven't had a chance," he told her. "I've had a lot to do, catching up at work after the time off. You know."

"Yes, Dad," she said. "I know."

The last time she had called him Dad was at her high school graduation.

When he returned home from work the next day, he found a tentative, apologetic message on the answering machine. Elaine had been participating in a round robin quilt project with some friends from the Internet, the caller explained. When a member received another member's quilt block, she was supposed to add a border and mail it on to the next quilter in the circle. The person after Elaine had not received any packages in months, and three of the round robin quilts were missing. They had heard about the "recent tragedy," and hated to bother him about something so trivial, but they wondered if perhaps the quilt tops could be located among Elaine's belongings and sent on their way. The caller left an address.

Russ searched through the pile of unopened mail on the credenza in the foyer and found one large, padded envelope addressed to Elaine. Inside was a red, brown, green, and ivory quilt, partially completed, with a complicated star in the middle and two surrounding borders, one of squares, one of flowers and leaves. Russ tore open every envelope addressed to his dead wife, and although some contained fabric or quilt blocks, none but the first met the description the caller had left on the answering machine.

He climbed the stairs, touched the door to her quilt studio, and let his hand fall to his side. Then he went to his bedroom and dialed the phone.

"Hello?"

It was Christine, not Charlie. That made it easier. "Christine." He cleared his throat. "Christine, it's Russ. I need your help."

She arrived early the next morning, before he had eaten breakfast. That was his fault, not hers; he had sat at the table lost in thought without taking a bite for at least a half hour before her car pulled into the driveway. He scraped his clammy eggs and bacon into the trash and let her in.

Christine gave him one long, wordless hug, then held him at arm's length and gave him a searching look. "You stopped shaving?"

His hand flew to his jaw. "Yeah. Well. Sometimes I forget."

"You look like you're growing a beard." She smiled, wistful and sad. "It looks good on you."

He mumbled a thank you and led her upstairs. Christine pushed open the door to the quilt studio without giving him a chance to prepare himself, as if ignoring his need to steel himself would make the need vanish. "Should we find the round robin quilts first?" she asked, standing in the center of the room. Her gaze fell upon the design wall and lingered there.

"Sure," said Russ. He went to the stack of envelopes on the table beside Elaine's sewing machine. They held letters full of condolences and well-wishes and assurances of the senders' prayers. They turned Russ's stomach and he threw them in the trash.

Christine soon found the round robin projects neatly folded on Elaine's worktable. Russ set them aside to mail later and began assembling the collapsed cartons Carly had left. He opened the closet door, scooped up armfuls of folded fabric, and dropped them into an open carton. Christine did the same with the shelves of quilting books.

"What do you want to do with all this?" asked Christine when they had filled several cartons.

"Donate it. Give it away. Throw it away. I don't care."

He was conscious of Christine's silence, but at that moment he truly did not care what became of his wife's treasured accumulation of fabric and patterns. Now that he had finally broken through whatever had kept him from entering that room, he wanted to strip it bare of anything that reminded him of Elaine. She had called the quilt studio her haven, her sanctuary, but it had not saved her. She had not even been able to climb the stairs to reach it in the end.

He packed her sewing machine into a box and stuffed smaller pieces of fabric around it for protection. Sorting out her unfinished projects was harder, especially when he came upon the partially completed quilt with the log cabin blocks and the stars, the last quilt she had begun before her diagnosis. He recognized pieces from quilts he knew well—two for his nieces, one for Alex, one for their own bed—extra or imperfect blocks she had not been able to use but had been unwilling to discard. He found a stack of twenty small quilt blocks made up in old-fashioned looking material, each pattern different, from a class she had taken years before. Christine discovered a binder Elaine had kept of useful tips her Internet quilting friends had exchanged by email.

"Email," said Russ, suddenly remembering. He switched on the computer and checked her account. She had more than fourteen hundred email messages waiting. The last was a warning from her ISP that her account was full.

"I can't write back to all these people," he said.

"You don't have to," said Christine. She sat down and began typing. He hesitated, but returned to his own work, and before long Christine announced that she had sent one message to everyone in Elaine's address book letting them know that she had died. "There's no good way to deliver this kind of bad news," she said. "I hope this doesn't come as a shock to anyone."

"Most of them probably know already," said Russ, sealing a carton with heavy tape. "I think someone posted a link to her obituary on a message board."

The hours passed. They took a break for lunch; Russ made sandwiches and listened to Christine's news about Charlie and the kids. Christine seemed to want to tell him something else, but hesitated on the brink of speaking. He was getting used to that. Everyone wanted to comfort him, to find the right words that would bring him solace. He knew there were no such words.

It was harder to return upstairs than he had expected. He had thought the shock of pain would wear off from the sheer physical effort of putting away a life. Instead he had to force himself through the doorway of the room. And suddenly he understood why: The cancer quilt gaped like an open wound from the design wall.

Angrily, he snatched the fabric pieces one by one and stuffed them into a plastic bag.

"Careful," said Christine.

"Why?" He scraped the last pieces to the floor roughly. "What's the point? What was the point of any of it?"

"Oh, Russ. You don't mean that."

But he did. He wished he could articulate his anger, his demand for some divine justification for what had happened. Elaine's death was beyond unfair. God should not allow someone who had devoted her life to easing the suffering of others to die in pain. God should not have brought Russ and Elaine together just to shatter his heart by taking her away. All their dreams, all their plans, every word of tenderness, every gesture of affection, every kiss, every hope, every moment had been an empty promise, a tease, a waste.

Hollow and cold and helpless, he closed his eyes and let the bag of black and red and green fall to the floor.

Christine took it up. He watched as she gently picked up the remaining pieces of the quilt from the floor, brushed them off, and placed them carefully into the bag. She zipped the bag shut and put it in one of the last open boxes, where it quickly disappeared amid the abandoned quilting tools.

At last they finished. They packed up the last carton and sealed it, and as he straightened, Russ realized that he was exhausted, flooded with the kind of bone-aching weariness that usually followed a much more physically arduous day.

"What should we do with these?" asked Christine, gesturing to the cartons and boxes they had carried downstairs and stacked in the foyer. He wondered if she knew it was a different question than the one she had asked before.

Christine had driven her minivan, so he said, "If I help you load, will you take them?"

"Take them where?"

"Goodwill. St. Vincent de Paul's. Wherever."

"But Russ . . ." Christine looked around, then gestured to the box containing Elaine's sewing machine. "What about that? Don't you want to save that, at least?"

"What for?"

"I don't know. Mending? Maybe you should save it for Carly."

"Carly already took what she wanted to keep. If you want it, take it."

"I don't want it. I just thought . . ." She shook her head. "Quilting was such an important part of Elaine's life. I thought maybe you would want to keep something of that."

"I don't." He hefted the largest box in his arms and carried it out to her minivan.

He woke shortly after two A.M., shaking and sick at heart. The covers were soaked in sweat. He pushed them aside and stumbled downstairs to the kitchen, where he poured a glass of water and tried to stop shaking. He ached for Elaine.

Back in bed, he struggled for sleep. At seven the alarm clock roused him from a restless doze. He showered and dressed for work, but his heart seemed to be pounding unnaturally hard, as if he had sprinted up four flights of stairs. In the hallway, he paused by Elaine's quilt studio. The door was ajar; he pushed it open and took in the emptiness. Only the design wall remained, white flannel marked with a faint blue grid. A wave of grief swept over him and he pulled the door shut.

He needed to fill that space, he told himself as he drove to work. An exercise room. A home theater. Storage. All day he forced himself to consider alternatives rather than imagine the room without Elaine.

Two nights he wrestled with insomnia, fighting off memories of Elaine. On the third morning, he woke to the sounds of his own weeping. Ashamed, he snatched up the quilt and wrapped himself in it as he sat on the edge of the bed. He buried his face in the quilt and imagined he could still smell Elaine in it.

He picked up the phone and called Christine. The oldest boy answered; Russ asked for his mother with his teeth clenched to keep them from chattering. When she finally came to the phone, he said, "Where did you take them?"

"Russ?"

"Do you remember?" Three days had passed since Christine had driven off with the boxes. Elaine's possessions were surely scattered by now; he had no hope of gathering them together again. "The cartons. Her quilting things. Where did you take them?"

"Russ—"

"I need to find her cancer quilt. You put it in a green and white carton that used to hold copier paper. Did you donate it or throw it out or—"

"Russ," said Christine. "I have it."

She had kept everything for him, every box, a safeguard against future regret. Later that day, Charlie returned them. He helped Russ carry the boxes upstairs but left quickly, mercifully, before Russ began unpacking.

He searched for the cancer quilt first just to assure himself that it had not disappeared. He pressed each jagged piece to the design wall exactly as Elaine had arranged them, exactly as they had been indelibly seared into his memory.

He set up the sewing machine, found the manual, and read it cover to cover. The machine was capable of producing more stitches than he had known existed. He doubted he would need them all. As far as he could recall, Elaine had used only the one that went in a straight line and the one that zigzagged.

It took him four tries to thread the machine properly, but once he did, he proceeded slowly and methodically through a few practice seams. Elaine had always whizzed through everything, hacking off pieces that were too large or steaming them with the iron and stretching them if they were too small. That was her way in many things. Had been her way.

He hesitated before taking pieces of the cancer quilt from the design wall. How Elaine would have marveled at the sight of him. She probably would have smothered a laugh before diplomatically coaching him through his first few clumsy stitches.

He sewed a green triangle to a red, added a black pentagon, then stuck the assembled pieces to the design wall and stepped back to take a look. It didn't look like much. He took a few more pieces, sewed them together, and then a few more. He interrupted his work to set up the ironing board; he pressed all the sewn sections flat and discovered that they adhered to the design wall better. "What do you know," he said aloud, rearranging a few pieces, then immediately shifting them back to Elaine's original placement. It was her quilt, her last quilt. Nothing he did could improve upon it.

He sewed late into the night, and he worked on the quilt every weekend and every evening after work until the top was completed. Tentatively pleased, he stuck it to the design wall and studied it. The sight struck him like a punch in the gut. It was all sharp angles and angry colors; it was shattered glass and anguish. This is how Elaine had felt.

He had to leave the room.

When he returned to the quilt studio a few days later, he unpacked the boxes of books and returned them to the shelves. One title caught his attention: *All About Quilting from A to Z.* That sounded promising. He set it aside and referred to it later as he layered and basted the quilt top.

The book provided an entire section on machine quilting, but Elaine had never quilted any other way but by hand. Russ had often watched as she sat on the sofa beside him, quilt hoop on her lap, the rest of the quilt's layers bundled around her. The book said machine quilting could be sturdier and faster, but he decided to stick with what was most familiar.

He found Elaine's lap hoop in the largest of the cartons, put it around the center of the quilt, and tightened the screw until the three layers were secure and smooth. Carrying it downstairs so he could quilt during the Mariners game, he stepped on a corner of the quilt, tripped, and stumbled down several stairs before grabbing hold of the handrail. He swore softly, envisioning his skull cracked open upon the tile floor of the foyer. Untangling himself, he discovered that he had not torn the quilt, but had stepped on the hoop and broken one of the thin wooden circles.

The next day, he spent his lunch break at Elaine's favorite quilt shop, wandering the aisles in search of replacement parts for quilt hoops. He found new hoops and more gadgets for machine quilting than he would have imagined necessary, but no replacement parts. Occasionally an employee or another shopper, invariably female, would smile indulgently at him in passing. No one offered to help, but he suspected that was not because he looked like he knew what he was doing.

His lunch hour half over, Russ went to a large island in the middle of the room where a shop employee was cutting fabric.

She smiled at him as he approached, but she immediately returned her attention to her work.

"Excuse me," said Russ. "I'm trying to find some replacement hoops."

"Oh, I'm sorry." The woman set down her rotary cutter. "I just assumed you were the husband of one of our customers."

"No." Not quite.

"I'd be happy to help you. What did your wife send you in to buy?"

Inwardly, Russ winced. "She didn't send me. I broke the inner wooden circle of her quilting hoop and I was hoping to find a replacement."

"Before she finds out?" said the woman, amused.

"No," said Russ. "I need it to finish one of her quilts."

"Finish one of . . ." The woman's eyebrows rose. "Do you think that's a good idea? Maybe you should ask her first. I know if my husband started poking needles into my quilt, I'd really let him have it."

"If my husband did, I'd take away the scissors before he hurt himself," remarked a passing customer.

"Can you point me in the right direction?" asked Russ patiently.

"We don't sell replacement parts for quilting hoops," said the woman. "In fact, I don't know anyone who does. It probably wouldn't be very cost effective. You can buy a new hoop pretty cheap. Do you want me to show you where they are?"

"No, thanks. I remember." Annoyed and embarrassed, Russ purchased a hoop similar to the one he had broken and left the shop as quickly as possible.

He quilted in the evenings in front of the television, as Elaine used to do. Something about the repetitive motions of quilting allowed his mind to disconnect from himself, to float on a stratum out of reach of his anger and the slow, steady ache of loneliness. In those moments he could remember Elaine without pain.

Working on the cancer quilt became a way to fill the empty hours between work and sleep. The quilt became a tribute to her, a link to her. Sometimes he felt as if she were watching over his shoulder, encouraging him to persevere, shrugging off his mistakes. At first his stitches were huge, crooked, and scattered, as if someone had spilled a bag of long grain rice on the quilt. As the weeks passed, they became smaller and more precise, falling into a distinguishable pattern of loops and scrolls.

He finished the quilt a few weeks shy of the first anniversary of Elaine's death. Following the instructions in her books, he attached a hanging sleeve to the back of the quilt and hung it in the living room. It clashed with the rest of the furnishings, but he didn't care. In fact, he respected the disruption. He figured that was part of the message of the quilt.

On the night that marked one full year without Elaine, Christine and Charlie came into the city to distract him with dinner at his favorite restaurant. They didn't tell him that was the reason, of course, but he knew. When they came over to pick him up, they stopped short at the sight of the cancer quilt. Christine sucked in a breath; Charlie let out a low whistle.

"Interesting choice in . . . art, buddy," said Charlie dubiously.

"Elaine designed it," Christine warned in an undertone.

"I mean, it's great," said Charlie quickly. "It's . . . Wow. Elaine did good work."

"Elaine started it. I finished it."

Two pairs of eyes fixed on him. Then Charlie laughed. "You finished it?"

"That's right." Russ studied the quilt for a moment. "And I'm thinking about starting another."

"Why?"

Russ shrugged. "Something to do."

Charlie and Christine exchanged a look. Christine delicately changed the subject, and no one mentioned the quilt for the rest of the evening.

Elaine's books listed what must have been thousands of quilt patterns—stars and baskets and geometric designs with names like Shoo-Fly and Lone Star and Snail's Trail. Russ leafed through the pages and tried to pick one or two he wouldn't mind attempting, but cutting out precise pieces and sewing from point to point and making the same block over and over did not appeal to him. He liked the way Elaine's last quilt just fell together.

He needed something to fill the nights and weekends. Elaine had left an inexhaustible supply of fabric to experiment with, so he decided to improvise. It wasn't as if anyone else would see the quilt, unless he decided to hang it on the wall just to provoke another reaction from Charlie.

Russ had grudgingly admired Elaine's rotary cutter from the time he first saw her slicing through fabric, years before. It was sharp, fast, and metal—in short, it was a guy tool. After sorting her fabric stash by color, he took about a yard of green and a yard of blue, stacked them on top of the cutting mat, and, using Elaine's longest acrylic ruler as a guide, made four arbitrary slashes across the whole width of the fabric from left to right, varying the angle of the cut and the distance between them. He then turned the ruler and made four more slashes from top to bottom. He swapped every other green piece for blue and sewed the pieces together, checkerboard fashion. It was quick and satisfying, but the green and blue fabrics, so distinct and different when seen alone, blended into one mass when sewn together.

He tried again, this time choosing a deep green and a dull copper. Layering the fabrics as before, he cut more strips, some wide, some narrow. He swapped colors and sewed them together, for the first time racing along with something approaching Elaine's speed. When he put the quilt top on the design wall and stepped back to examine it, he let out a dry chuckle. Looking at the quilt was like looking out at a lush green field through the metal bars of a cage. Only one small opening at the bottom where the bars did not completely reach the edge allowed for an escape.

He returned to the quilt shop, ignoring the curious stares of the employees as he picked out batting and an iridescent quilting thread unlike anything in Elaine's sewing box just because it looked interesting. He came back a few days later after reading in one of Elaine's reference books that such thread was meant for machine quilting only. He intended to exchange the thread for something more suitable for hand quilting, but he left the shop with the spool of thread still in his pocket and a new sewing machine foot especially for free-motion machine quilting.

His first attempt was a disaster. The bobbin thread bunched and knotted on the back of the quilt, the stitch length on top of the quilt varied from minuscule to long enough to catch on the presser foot, and he could only sew a minute or two before the top thread stretched and snapped. He took a perverse pride in being responsible for what was probably the worst example of machine quilting ever produced. The only thing he did right was to practice on junk fabric first.

When he thought he had learned all he could from books and practice, he committed his quilt top to the needle. The results were mixed. The quilting stitches brought out an interesting depth and dimension to the flat surface of the quilt top that he liked, but the finished quilt had somehow become distorted from true square. Obviously he was doing something wrong, but he had no idea what or how to fix it.

Finally he called one of Elaine's quilting friends, Francine, a woman not quite his mother's age who had organized the delivery of casseroles and cookies in the weeks following Elaine's surgery and chemo. "You want help doing what?" she asked after he explained the purpose of his call.

"Free-motion machine quilting."

"Why?"

"Because I can't figure out what I'm doing wrong."

"You're trying to make a quilt?"

"Yes," he said, impatient. Why was it such a shock that he wanted to quilt? These quilters, who were so generous and encouraging to other women who wanted to learn to quilt, acted like he was demanding the right to use women's public restrooms.

"Why?"

Russ did not have a good answer for that. "Never mind. Thanks anyway."

"Wait!" commanded Francine. He returned the receiver to his ear. "Don't hang up. Our quilt guild has a machine quilting workshop coming up this weekend. There are still a few spots open. Ordinarily you have to be a guild member to sign up, but I think we can make an exception for you, as the husband of a longtime member."

"You mean, take a class with other people?"

"You're not afraid of us, are you?"

"No, but—" He doubted he would be any more welcome there than at the quilt shop. "I was hoping you could just give me a few pointers over the phone."

"It's much easier to learn by watching. We're meeting on Saturday at ten in the community center rec room, same place as always. Do you have a sewing machine?"

"There's Elaine's—"

"Don't forget to bring it. And some fabric to practice on. I'll sign you up and you can just pay at the door. See you then."

She hung up before he could refuse.

All week long he intended to call Francine back and cancel, but somehow, Saturday morning found him lugging Elaine's sewing machine into the community center. It appeared that all the other workshop participants had arrived early to set up their workspaces, but he found an unoccupied place near the back. Most of the women ignored him, but a few threw him curious stares as he searched for someplace to plug in Elaine's Bernina. After a while, a grandmotherly woman wearing her long gray hair in a bun helpfully pointed out the nearest power strip. He thanked her and sat down, already regretting that he had come.

But by the end of the afternoon, he had figured out where he had gone wrong with his first attempt at free-motion machine quilting; apparently, an uneven amount of quilting in different sections of the top could pull it out of shape. The instructor had also demonstrated a few techniques he had not seen in any of Elaine's books, and she talked about how different kinds of thread could produce different effects. Then he caught himself taking mental notes of ideas to share with Elaine when he got home, and all interest in the workshop drained from him like air from a punctured tire.

Francine approached him afterward and asked him how he had fared in the workshop.

"Not bad." He felt fairly confident about his machine quilting now, but none of the other quilters had talked to him during the breaks, and they all kept shooting him furtive, suspicious glances.

"You should join the guild."

"Me? Oh no. I don't think so. I wouldn't fit in."

Francine was a retired high school principal, and at this remark, she gave him a look that made him feel like a truant sophomore. "Why? Because you're a man?"

"To be honest, yes."

"Oh, please." She thrust a guild newsletter at him. "Don't be such a coward. You have a lot to learn, and a guild is the best place for that. You'll get a discount on future workshops, too. You're not the only man who quilts, you know."

He wasn't? Russ took the newsletter, gave it a quick look, and stuffed it in his pocket. "Maybe I can make a meeting now and then."

"Good. See you next Wednesday."

"I didn't say I'd come for sure."

"I know." She waggled her thick fingers at him over her shoulder as she departed.

He did go to the meeting, drawn by curiosity and hopeful that he would meet another male quilter. The lecture on Civil War era quilts was more interesting than he had expected, but the social break was a hassle, full of conversations that stopped as soon as he approached and more of those suspicious looks. It was a relief when Francine came over and, in her imposing way, asked if he was enjoying himself.

"Sure," he said. "But I was hoping to meet some of those other men quilters you mentioned."

"There aren't any men in our guild yet."

"But you said—"

"I said that male quilters exist, not that they are members of our guild. Of course, you could join and change all that."

Russ looked around at the other quilters, all women, all studiously ignoring his conversation with the guild president. "I don't think so."

He stuck around for the second half of the meeting, but left as soon as the motion to adjourn had been approved. Elaine had always enjoyed her monthly quilt guild meetings, so he had expected a warmer welcome, a friendlier crowd. Then again, Elaine always brought out the best in people. She could have warmed up even that chilly bunch. But a quilting guild was clearly no place for him.

Quilting was the first thing he learned to enjoy without Elaine, and for a long time, it was the only thing. Then he began to run again, to go out for a beer with some of the guys from work every so often, to take in an occasional Seahawks game with Charlie. But always he returned to quilting. He alternated between completing one of Elaine's unfinished quilts and one of his own designs. Trying to buy anything at the quilt shop, where he was alternately ignored and patronized, was such a demeaning experience that he started ordering his supplies through the Internet. One evening, web surfing after a purchase, he followed a shop's link to a quilt museum to a fabric designer to a quilt block archive, where he stumbled upon an online quilting guild.

Intrigued, he read the messages other members had posted. A neophyte would pose a timid question; a flurry of encouraging responses from more experienced quilters would follow. Someone would post a celebratory note announcing a quilt finished or blue ribbon won and the others would shower her with praise and congratulations. A frustrated quilter would ask for advice on a challenging seam or an impossible block arrangement and receive it. Here, at last, he had found that elusive quilting community Elaine had often spoken of—and he realized that, courtesy of the anonymity of the Internet, he could participate.

He signed on to the quilting list just to see what would happen. For the first few months, he was a "lurker," a member who read but never posted. Then he began to post brief replies, signing them with only his initials. No one knew he was a man and no one cared.

Then one day, as he checked his email after breakfast, he discovered a thread someone had started that just about knocked him out of his chair: "I just found this list and I'm wondering if there are any other men quilters out there? Not that I mind talking quilts with you ladies, but I was just wondering if I am the only guy—again." The message was signed, "Jeff in Nebraska."

The first response was from a woman who assured Jeff that there were several men in the group. The next four messages were from men announcing that they were proud to call themselves quilters and longtime members of the list. Another woman followed with a list of websites featuring the work of well-known male art quilters. A man from Australia wrote that he and his wife made all their quilts together. A man from Vermont wrote that he and his partner were male quilters and quilt shop owners. A woman who contributed at least one post to every discussion on the list chimed in, "Howdy, Jeff! We don't care if you're male, female, or a three-horned purple hermaphrodite from Saturn! You're welcome here as long as you quilt!"

Naturally, someone then wrote in claiming to be a three-horned purple hermaphrodite from Saturn who enjoyed quilting as well as embroidery, and the conversation deteriorated from there. But enough of the original thread remained to compel Russ to introduce himself.

"Hi," he wrote. "I guess it's about time I explained that RM stands for Russell McIntyre. I'm a man and a quilter. I started quilting when I wanted to complete one of my late wife's UFOs and I found out I enjoyed it. I've been quilting for almost three and a half years now and I've made nine quilts. (Four of my wife's, five of my own.) I don't know any men quilters in real life so it's great to finally meet some online."

For the first time he signed off using his full name.

He shut down the computer and went to work. By the time he got to his office and checked his email again, he had five personal messages welcoming him belatedly to the group. Three were from other men, two were from women, and each offered condolences on the death of his wife. They brought tears of renewed grief to his eyes, but he blinked them away, dashed off responses, and settled in to work.

Over the next few years, the five people who first responded to his introduction on the quilting list became close friends. They corresponded almost daily, swapped fabric and blocks through the mail, and met up at the Pacific International Quilt Festival each October. When one of the men started up a separate Internet group for men quilters, Russ signed on, but still retained close ties to the original group that had befriended him. To his surprise, he discovered that while some other men quilters had been ignored or patronized at quilt shops and guilds just as he had, others' experiences of the quilting world were quite different. Many admitted to enjoying preferential treatment in their guilds as the only man among a host of women, and others said they were treated no differently than any other quilter. Russ could only imagine what that would be like.

His style evolved in part because of inspiration from his online friends. He continued to layer, slash, and swap fabric, but he experimented with fabric dyed in gradients and curved cuts instead of straight lines. Through his Internet contacts, he was invited to submit a piece for an exhibit at the Rocky Mountain Quilt Museum featuring work by men quilters. Invitations to teach his unique style of quilting followed, as did requests to submit articles to quilting magazines.

On his fortieth birthday, he sat down with his financial advisor and discovered that he could retire early and live off his Athena Tech stock options quite comfortably for at least another forty years. Finally he would have enough time to work on that book proposal an editor had begged him to submit after observing his workshop at the American Quilter's Society show.

Soon after his book, *Russell McIntyre: A Man of the Cloth,* was published two years later, Russ had a solo exhibition in an eclectic art gallery in downtown Seattle. Carly and Alex came home a few days ahead of time so they could watch the exhibit being hung. Alex teased Russ at the gallery and at their celebratory dinner out afterward, calling Russ his stepdad, the great artiste, but the proud grin never left his face. On the morning before the exhibit debuted, Carly took Russ shopping and helped him pick out a new suit and tie. They both knew but did not acknowledge aloud that Elaine would have insisted upon it had she been there.

Even Charlie and Christine came down from Olympia, marking the first time they had seen his work in such an impressive setting. Christine was obviously thrilled for him, but Charlie seemed perplexed by all the fuss. "They're just quilts," Russ overheard him tell Christine. "They're nice, I guess, but they're not even big enough for a bed."

"Don't embarrass me," said Christine, exasperated. "This is art. They aren't supposed to fit a bed."

Russ was surprised to hear her snap at him, and he turned away so they would not know he had overheard. He stopped short at the sight of Francine, tilting her head as she examined a quilt. He made his way through the crowd to greet her. "Hello, Francine," he said, unable to conceal his surprise. "Thanks for coming." He had sent an announcement to the guild, but he had not expected anyone who remembered his fumbling attempts to join the guild to come.

"It's good to see you," she said. She had grown thin and her hair was grayer, but she had lost none of her imposing manner. "You've come a long way."

He shrugged. "I had a long way to go. You were right years ago when you said I had a lot to learn."

Francine eyed the quilts displayed on the gallery walls and indicated the many admirers with a nod. "Apparently you learned it. And to think I assumed you gave up quilting when you snubbed the guild."

"I snubbed the guild?" said Russ, incredulous. "You're kidding, right? They gave me the cold shoulder."

"You came to one meeting, and did you even bother to introduce yourself?" countered Francine. "Everyone adored Elaine. If they had known you were her husband, they would have made you feel at home."

"So that's what it takes for a man to be accepted in that guild."

"No one knew you were a serious quilter. Most of the members assumed you were there to meet women."

Russ almost choked. "That's a strange assumption, but it's not even the worst prejudice I've run into in the quilting world. You have no idea what it's like to go into a quilt shop or a quilt show and have everyone there assume I'm a blundering idiot who has to be watched carefully so he doesn't break something."

"Oh, I think I have a fairly good idea what that's like. I face it whenever I walk into an automobile repair shop."

His indignation promptly deflated. "Right. It's exactly like that."

She smiled. "Well. At any rate, I came to enjoy the show, but also to let you know that we would be thrilled if you would give the guild another try."

"Thanks. I'll think about it." He had no idea how he would find the time, but he would reconsider.

"I also feel compelled to mention that while I liked your book, I did not care for the title."

"It wasn't my choice," he said automatically, as he had done hundreds of times since the book came out. "The marketing department thought it was a clever play on words."

"Nonsense. It makes you sound like you've joined the clergy."

That was exactly what he had told his editor.

He and Francine parted ways. A few minutes later, he caught the arm of the gallery director and asked for a word. "Anything for you," she said, but her smile quickly faded when he asked her if she had considered his proposal to put on a retrospective of Elaine's work.

"Russ, darling," she said. "Your late wife's quilts are charming, and you are a dear to want to show her work. But I've gone over the schedule and I just don't think we can squeeze in another exhibit in the foreseeable future."

That was her euphemistic way of telling him she was not interested. "Thanks anyway."

"Oh, Russ." She gave his arm a squeeze. "Don't let this ruin your day. You've made three sales already and I overheard Bill Gates's representative asking you about a commissioned work for the corporate headquarters."

"For his house, actually," replied Russ, but his thoughts were of Elaine's quilts, hanging on the walls at home where hardly anyone ever saw them.

"Even better." She gave him a quick kiss on the cheek and moved off to greet an important patron who had just arrived. Beyond her he saw Charlie and Christine approaching. From their grins he knew they had seen the kiss.

"It doesn't mean anything," said Russ, rubbing his cheek with the back of his hand in case she had left traces of scarlet lipstick. "She does that to everyone."

"She got me twice already," admitted Charlie reluctantly. Russ knew he was dying to tease him, and Christine would have been thrilled to see him interested in someone new, even someone twenty years younger with multiple piercings and jet black hair dyed shocking pink at the tips. Almost seven years had passed since Elaine's death. He was forty-two, a year older than she had been when she died. Sometimes he could not believe that he had been her widower longer than her husband.

"Elaine would have loved this," said Christine. "She would have been so proud of you."

"Thanks," said Russ. He felt Elaine's presence so strongly then that he could not manage to say more.

Two weeks after the exhibit closed, Russ heard about an opening at Elm Creek Quilt Camp from a posting on the QuiltArt Internet list. Grace Daniels, a friend who was a museum curator in San Francisco, attended camp there every summer and gave it glowing reviews. He checked out their website and mulled it over for a few days before deciding to apply. He had all of the materials they wanted, so it was easy to assemble the application packet and send it off. A few weeks later when they called to invite him to Pennsylvania for an interview, he was away from home, teaching a series of workshops in Oregon and Idaho. He returned the message from the road; he and an Elm Creek Quilter named Sarah McClure quickly settled upon a date for the interview.

Sarah McClure also gave him an assignment: to design a quilt block pattern suitable as an emblem of Elm Creek Quilts. He didn't have the slightest idea how to begin. While he had many original designs saved on his computer, it would take a huge stretch of the imagination to believe any represented a quilters' retreat.

He went to Elaine's quilt studio and studied her fabric stash, hoping inspiration would strike. Elms meant leaves, bark, twigs—he pulled shades of green and brown from the shelves. A creek meant flowing water, whorls, eddies, pebbles on a creek bed—he selected blue, white, and gray. He tossed the folded fabric bundles onto the floor at random, taking in the colors and thinking.

The obvious answer was to put together some kind of pictorial appliqué block with elm trees, a creek, and a big stone manor like the one in the photograph on the website, but he had never tried that kind of appliqué and doubted a project so important should be his first attempt. Besides, the Elm Creek Quilters were probably familiar with his signature style and wanted to see how he could adapt it to their request and to the significantly smaller canvas. This was a test of his imagination and versatility, and he would lose points if he took an easier way out.

Since everyone else would probably appliqué elm leaves and creeks, he ought to focus on another aspect of Elm Creek Quilt Camp. Above all else, his Internet acquaintance who attended each year praised the camaraderie that developed among all the quilters, strangers as well as old friends. He knew something about that. It had not been easy to break into the traditional female world of quilting, but once he had, he had forged strong friendships there. Without them, he might never have survived the aching loneliness of life after Elaine.

After a few aborted attempts, he struck upon a design that represented, to him at least, the power of quilting to forge community. He chose shades of green, blue, and brown, layered them with white, and cut narrow strips on the diagonals. He swapped out fabrics and sewed the squares and rectangles together in a design that resembled banners of those four colors flowing from the corners of the block to the center, where they met and appeared to weave together. To him, the pattern symbolized the power of quilting to draw together people of disparate ages, races, nationalities, socioeconomic backgrounds, and genders, united by their passion for their art.

It occurred to him that his design might be too abstract for the Elm Creek Quilters' purpose; he could not imagine them actually using it as a symbol for the quilt camp. He had already failed the assignment in that respect. Still, it was an honest response to what the ideal of Elm Creek Quilt Camp meant to him, so he decided it was good enough.

A few weeks later, he flew into Pittsburgh, rented a car, and drove through the rolling, forested Appalachians into the valleys of central Pennsylvania. Though he had lectured in Lancaster twice, he had never been to this part of the state, and he now understood why Grace had warned him to allow plenty of time and to bring a map. Sarah's directions were fine until he left the interstate, but they fell apart not long after the Waterford city limits. He was supposed to look for a rural road through the woods marked by a small wooden sign for Elm Creek Manor. The turnoff had no name that Sarah knew of, so she had warned him to watch his odometer and go by the mileage rather than road signs.

When he arrived at the place where the gravel road was supposed to be, he found nothing but dense woods. He drove another mile, then turned around and backtracked until he started seeing signs for Waterford College again. Sighing in frustration, he turned the car around and drove back the other way, monitoring the odometer more carefully and driving more slowly as the mile approached. This time, a young woman stood on the grassy shoulder between the road and a narrow gravel driveway where the road to Elm Creek Manor ought to be, but he saw no sign.

"That can't be it," he muttered, driving on. Sarah had said that the road was not paved, but that strip of dirt and rocks couldn't possibly accommodate the kind of traffic a thriving business would generate. It must be the young woman's driveway, he thought, glancing at her in the rearview mirror. And if it was, he thought, turning the car around yet again, she ought to know the right way.

"Excuse me," he called to the young woman, slowing the car nearly to a stop. She was strikingly pretty, with big brown eyes and dark brown hair pulled back into a thick braid that hung to the middle of her back. She looked to be in her early thirties. "I'm looking for the road to Elm Creek Manor. Do you know where it is?"

The young woman bit her lip and stepped aside, revealing the missing sign. "It's that way," she said, gesturing to the narrow strip of gravel leading into the woods. "Sorry for blocking the sign."

"It's not your fault," said Russ, smiling. "This isn't the first time I've missed it. Thanks."

She nodded and gave an apologetic wave as he drove into the woods. The road wasn't as bad as it had looked from the highway, but it still was only barely passable. If an oncoming car suddenly appeared, one of them would have to pull off into the trees. He decided he would volunteer. His car was a rental.

The pretty girl standing by the sign . . . He wondered what she was doing there, waiting alone by the side of the road in the middle of nowhere. Was she a camper? He should have offered her a ride to the manor just in case. He felt a sudden surge of protectiveness for the girl. Something in her wary manner made him instinctively associate her with Carly, though they looked nothing alike. When he had first met Carly she had been so defensive, so purposefully aloof, so bruised by her father's abandonment. She had needed years to accept that Russ would not also leave her. Now she was a mother herself, and her little son called him Pop-pop, for grandpa.

He wished Elaine could have been there to hold her first grandchild within an hour of his birth, as Russ had.

The narrow road wound through the trees and opened into a clearing, an orchard to the west, a red barn built into the side of a hill on the right. Russ followed the road up the low slope and around the barn until it ended in a driveway at the rear of the manor. He parked the car, took his briefcase in hand, and climbed the back stairs to the rear door. It swung open before he could knock. A woman exiting the manor glanced at his raised hand and smiled. "Just go on in," she said. "Everyone does. You don't need to knock."

Russ took her advice and found himself in an empty hallway that dead-ended into another passage a few yards ahead. A frenzied buzz drew his attention to a doorway on his left, which turned out to be the entrance to the kitchen. A timer complained on the countertop, and the aroma of baked chicken filled the room. Next to a 1940s era stove, he saw a doorway leading to a brightly lit room.

"Hello?" he called. "Uh . . . your timer went off." When no one responded, he crossed the kitchen and peered inside a small, sunny sitting room. No one was within.

He turned off the buzzer and hesitated, wondering if he should take out whatever was inside the oven or at least turn down the heat. He might end up ruining the meal rather than salvaging it, though, so he left it alone and went to look for the missing cook.

He strode down the hallway and took a right at the intersection. He had almost reached an impressive front foyer when a door opened in front of him. A tall, silver-haired woman with just the slightest stoop to her shoulders stepped into the hallway, chatting with a much younger woman with glasses and long brown hair.

"Excuse me," said Russ.

The two women stopped so suddenly that someone else trying to leave the room crashed into them from behind. "Ouch," complained the woman Russ could not see.

"May I help you?" inquired the older woman.

Russ jerked a thumb over his shoulder. "I just passed by the kitchen. A timer was going off."

"My chicken," exclaimed the younger woman. She sprinted past Russ toward the kitchen.

The older woman sighed and turned to address someone behind her. "We can't manage like this much longer."

"We're pitiful," said a shorter, stockier woman as she emerged from the room. Her long red hair was streaked with gray. "It's only been a week and we're falling apart. Oh. Hello," she said, spotting Russ. "You must be Russ."

"How did you know?" he asked. He was sure he had never met her before.

"We don't get your kind around here much. And I recognize you from the photos in your book." She extended her hand. "I'm Gwen Sullivan, Elm Creek Quilter."

He shook her hand. "Russ McIntyre."

"Mr. McIntyre," said the older woman. "What a pleasure it is to meet you. Welcome to Elm Creek Manor. I'm Sylvia Compson."

"Thank you. Please, call me Russ."

The woman smiled graciously. "Russ it is, then. Allow me to introduce my colleagues." She introduced him to four other women as one by one they entered the hallway. Each shook his hand and greeted him in a friendly way, except for a pretty blonde who scowled and squeezed his hand too hard as if she had something to prove.

Great, he thought as he shook her hand and forced a cordial smile. Another woman quilter who resented men for invading her domain.

Sylvia Compson explained that they were taking a break after interviewing other applicants and that she would have just enough time to show him around the estate while the other Elm Creek Quilters returned to their classrooms. "Perhaps we should start there," she suggested, and led him across the three-story tall, marble-floored foyer into a large ballroom that had been subdivided into classrooms by movable partitions. When Grace had described the arrangement in her last email, he had had some concerns about noise levels and space. As he looked around, he observed students setting up workstations in some of the classrooms, talking and laughing together, clearly enjoying themselves. They didn't seem bothered by the lack of isolated classrooms; if anything, the arrangement seemed to foster a more collegial atmosphere.

Part of the ballroom had not been partitioned off. Beyond the classrooms, Sylvia showed Russ an open gathering space framed by tall windows and a raised dais along the far wall. A group of women had gathered there, and they sat listening attentively to a slight, gray-haired woman in a gray skirt and blue cardigan. One of the Elm Creek Quilters, Russ assumed, watching as the older woman gestured to a quilt the other women held outspread and talked about its design. He waited for Sylvia to introduce them, but when she just watched the woman, quietly thoughtful, he examined the quilt, a traditional block repeated in a traditional horizontal setting. If this was the kind of quilt Elm Creek Quilts expected from its teachers, he was out of luck.

The older woman glanced over her shoulder at them once, but

did not break off her conversation or otherwise acknowledge Sylvia except for a slightly guilty look she threw her before turning back to the campers. Russ thought that a bit odd, but Sylvia did not seem to mind. Instead she resumed the tour, taking him next to the dining room, where more than a dozen tables had already been set for dinner. "Sarah did invite you to stay for supper, didn't she?" she asked.

"She did, but I have to leave right after my interview to catch a flight home."

"You mean you won't even spend the night?"

Russ shrugged. "I wish I could, but I have a few speaking engagements in California beginning tomorrow."

"My goodness, you're popular. Not even a day off to rest between trips."

"I can rest on the plane. But that's part of the appeal of working here. I could let the students come to me for a change."

Sylvia nodded thoughtfully and continued the tour of the first floor, then led him up a carved oak staircase to show him an example of their guest rooms and the business office, a large library spanning the entire width of the south wing. Light spilled in through tall diamond-paned windows on the east, west, and south walls. Between the windows stood tall bookcases, shelves heavy with leather-bound volumes. A stone fireplace nearly as tall as Russ's shoulder dominated the south wall. Two armchairs and footstools sat before it, while more chairs and sofas were arranged in a square in the center of the room. Nearby, parallel to the western wall, was a broad oak desk cluttered with paperwork and computer peripherals, a tall leather chair pulled up to it.

The library, Sylvia told him, was where the Elm Creek Quilters conducted camp business, but it was primarily Sarah McClure's domain. She handled all their finances, marketing, and operations, allowing her co-director, Summer Sullivan, to concentrate on curriculum, faculty, and anything associated with the Internet.

"But Summer is leaving us for graduate school soon," said Sylvia with a sigh. "We will miss her dearly."

Russ nodded and made a mental note to mention his considerable Internet experience during the interview.

Next Sylvia showed him the estate grounds, which included the barn he had passed as he drove to the house, most of the woods, the orchard, and several gardens. He was amazed to learn that the estate was tended by only one caretaker and a few seasonal gardeners. *At last, other men,* he thought with relief as Sylvia introduced him to Matt McClure and his staff. It was probably too much to hope that one or two of them quilted.

Nearly a half hour passed before they returned inside for his formal interview. Sylvia escorted him to the room where they had first met, a fancy sitting room with too many doilies, throw pillows, tassels, and breakable knickknacks for him to feel entirely comfortable. When Sylvia said that the Elm Creek Quilters conducted camp business in the library, he had assumed his interview would take place there.

The other Elm Creek Quilters soon arrived and took seats across from him. The break between interviews had clearly not improved the mood of the blonde, Diane, who frowned as she took her place in an armchair. She opened up a folder, took out several pages of notes, and fixed him with a look of challenge.

He resigned himself to failure as far as winning her over was concerned. She had already made up her mind, and nothing he said would impress her. He would concentrate on the others.

Sarah McClure began the questioning by asking him how he became a quilter. He was glad to tell them how Elaine had inspired him, and not until he finished his response several minutes later did it occur to him that maybe he had gone on too long. "Sorry," he said with a self-deprecating smile. "I tend to ramble when talking about my late wife."

They smiled sympathetically—except for Diane. "Our students

generally don't like instructors who ramble," she said, checking off an item in her notes with a flick of her pencil.

"Russell, you're clearly an experienced teacher and you're apparently willing to go anywhere in the country to lead workshops," said Sylvia, without a glance at Diane. "Staying in one place from spring through autumn would be quite a change for you. Won't you miss the travel?"

He recognized a softball question when one was lofted his way; Sylvia had already gleaned an answer from their conversation during the tour. "Quite the opposite," he said. "Working for Elm Creek Quilts would allow me to teach more students more efficiently. Instead of traveling, I'll be able to develop new courses and make my own quilts. In the winter, when camp is out of session, I can resume my usual schedule of quilt guilds and conferences."

"So you aren't willing to make a year-round commitment to Elm Creek Quilts," said Diane.

"We don't need him for the full-year," said Summer, an edge to her voice. "That's why the ad said seasonal work available."

"If you need me year-round, I could do that," said Russ. "I didn't think it was an option."

"It isn't, yet," interjected Sarah as Diane prepared to speak. "Someday we may go to a full-year schedule, but not soon."

"We could do it soon if we weren't losing two founding members of our teaching staff," Diane shot back.

"Which brings us to the purpose of Mr. McIntyre's visit," said Sylvia. "Russ, would you please show us the Elm Creek Quilts block we asked you to design?"

He took it from his briefcase and explained his creative process as they passed it around the circle. "I know it's kind of abstract," he said.

"Kind of?" murmured Diane, her pretty features screwed up in bafflement as she examined his block, holding it right side up, upside down, at an angle. She finally gave up, shook her head, and passed the block on to Summer.

"I like it," said Summer. "It's different. And I, for one, can grasp the symbolism."

"Symbolism? Is that what it is?" said Diane. "I'm not so sure. I doubt anyone would look at this block and think 'Elm Creek Quilts.'"

Russ said nothing. If he were to be honest, he would have to agree.

"You would certainly bring a very different perspective to our faculty," remarked Sylvia, studying his résumé.

"I believe so," said Russ. "I think part of the reason my quilts have been received so well is that as a man, an outsider to the traditional quilting world, I don't feel as constrained by the accepted norms of what is and what isn't permitted in a quilt."

Sylvia allowed a brief flicker of a smile. "I was referring to your status as an acclaimed contemporary art quilter, but you're quite correct to say that your perspective as a man who quilts is also rare. And potentially valuable."

"Wait. Let's go back to something he just said," Diane broke in. "Do you mean to say that women quilters are constrained by accepted norms? We all just make the same quilts every other woman makes, like a mindless herd of cows?"

"That's not what he meant at all," protested Gwen. "Cows don't quilt."

"And they're not mindless," said Summer, with a pointed look for Sarah. "Which is why we should not eat them."

Bewildered, Russ tried to sort out the sudden shift in conversation until Diane caught his attention with a sigh of disappointment, as if she had hoped for so much more from him. "That's what I find so frustrating about men quilters. You come in at the last minute, jump on the quilting bandwagon, and assume that you can do it better than generations of traditional women quilters who have come before you simply because you have a penis."

"Diane," exclaimed Sylvia.

"I can't believe she said that," said Gwen in an aside to Summer. "She must be off her medication."

"I don't take medication," snapped Diane.

"Maybe you should start."

Sylvia shook her head. "Diane, I have no idea what has gotten into you today, but if you cannot control yourself, you will be banned from the remaining interviews."

Interesting, Russ thought. Apparently Diane hated everyone—or at least every applicant for the job she had seen that day.

With a stern look of warning for Diane, Sarah said, "Obviously, Russ, you don't have to respond to Diane's wholly inappropriate remark."

He thought for a moment. "I'll respond to a variation of it. First off, I don't think men are intrinsically better quilters than women, and I don't think I personally am better than traditional quilters simply because I'm a man. I said my perspective was different. Not better, not worse, just . . . different. Just like men and women are different."

"But equal," said Gwen.

"Of course, equal. Look, I'm not trying to make a big political statement here, but artists are shaped by their life experiences, and men and women have very different experiences in the world. I can be as empathetic as humanly possible, but there are some things about being a woman that I will never understand. Being a husband and father taught me that. And there are some things about being a man that women will never understand."

"What's to understand?" muttered Diane. "Beer. Football. Nascar. Duct tape. Fart jokes."

"Honestly, Diane," said Sylvia, exasperated. "Russ, I'm truly sorry."

But Russ had heard enough. "If that's the Elm Creek Quilts perception of male quilters, that could explain why none of the campers I've seen here today are men. That's an untapped and potentially lucrative market for you, but why should men come where they aren't welcome? From what I've seen today, men quilters could benefit a lot from a place like Elm Creek Quilt Camp, but you could learn a lot from them, too." He picked up his briefcase and stood. "But apparently only women can break into your circle of quilters. Thanks for inviting me. I know the way out."

"Nice going," said Gwen to Diane as he strode to the door.

Nice going, Russ told himself, disgusted, as he left the parlor and headed for the back door. *Brilliant strategy. Righteous indignation always wins over potential employers.*

Sarah followed him into the hallway. "Russ, please don't go. Diane—"

"It's not just her." Russ stopped and allowed Sarah to catch up. "But for what it's worth, I'm sorry I stormed out of there."

"You can come back. We can start over."

Russ shook his head. He knew nothing else he did or said would erase their negative impression of his outburst. "I don't think it will work out. If the faculty doesn't support a male colleague, why should your campers?"

"We would support you. You have an excellent reputation and we'd be fortunate to have you join our staff. I know men and women alike would sign up for camp just to meet you."

"Well . . ." Russ took one last long look around the manor. During Sylvia's tour, he had imagined himself living there, teaching there, creating, finding peace in surroundings that did not underscore Elaine's absence every time he passed from one room to the next. But thanks to Diane, he had blown his chance.

"Next time you're hiring," he said, "give me a call. Maybe the climate will be different."

Sarah nodded.

He made his way down the hall toward the back door. His hand was on the doorknob when he heard quick footsteps behind him. "Wait," a woman called. "Just a moment!"

Russ turned around to find a white-haired woman in pink-tinted glasses pursuing him, breathless. "Is something wrong?"

"I'm just . . ." She placed a hand on her hip and held up a finger as she caught her breath. Russ waited. "I'm having a little trouble with this quilt block."

"Uh huh." Baffled, he gestured down the hall toward the frilly parlor. "Back that way, there's a roomful of Elm Creek Quilters who would be glad to help you."

"Oh, I'm sure they're too busy." The elderly woman came closer and thrust a quilt block at him, panting. "You, on the other hand, seem to be free."

Studying her with increasing concern, he automatically took the block. "Maybe you should sit down."

"No, no, I'll be fine. But the quilt block. What do you think?"

He turned it over. It was a traditional, hand-appliquéd block, probably a Rose of Sharon variation. It looked fine to him. "Sorry. I don't do hand appliqué."

"But you're an experienced quilter. Surely you can recommend something."

"To be perfectly honest, I can't even spot the problem."

He held out the block, but she wouldn't take it back. "Oh, come now," she said. "You're just flattering me."

"No, really. It looks good to me." He glanced at his watch. "I'm on my way out. I have to catch a plane. Are you sure you don't want me to get you a chair, a glass of water, something?"

"No, thank you." Disappointed, she took her quilt block. "Thanks just the same."

Shaking his head in amazement, Russ left quickly before anyone else could stop him. He could not remember a stranger day spent in the company of quilters, and contrary to all stereotypes, they were not generally a sedate bunch.

He drove back to the Pittsburgh airport, dropped off the rental car, and added himself to the standby list for an earlier flight to Seattle. He spent an hour wandering idly through the stores on the concourse mall, passing most of that time testing gadgets at Sharper Image and wishing he had handled Diane's confrontational questioning better. When the announcement came that the earlier flight to Seattle was boarding, he went to the gate and received a seat assignment. "You're in luck," the ticket agent said as she issued him a new boarding pass. "It's wide open."

He took his seat on the aisle in the middle of coach, found a paperback in his carry-on, and settled in for the cross-country flight. Weary from the long, round-trip drive earlier that day, he dozed off and woke an hour later to find the plane at cruising altitude. He stretched, picked up his fallen book from the floor, and wished he had brought something more engrossing to read or that domestic flights still showed movies. Then, a few rows ahead, he glimpsed a woman working on a quilt block.

He watched as the fabric patches came together beneath her fingers. She had long, elegant hands and held the needle as if she were accustomed to it. The contrast between the contemporary batik fabric and the traditional appliqué pattern intrigued him. At least he assumed it was a traditional pattern, since she was sewing by hand; for all he knew, it was her own original design, but it did look familiar.

After a while, curious and with plenty of time on his hands, he put his book away and moved to the empty seat across the aisle from the woman. "Hi," he greeted her. "What are you working on?"

She seemed surprised by the question. "Oh. Nothing. It's just a block for a quilt."

"I can't place that pattern. Is it traditional?"

Her eyebrows rose. "Do you quilt?"

"Now and then," he said. "But I don't know much about appliqué. I do everything by machine."

She considered that, then gave a little shrug. She had long waves of light brown hair held back by a tortoiseshell barrette, and hazel eyes set into a soft oval face that suddenly reminded him of a sepia-toned photograph. "You could easily adapt this pattern to machine appliqué, but I prefer handwork. The process is more soothing, more contemplative."

"More portable," added Russ, indicating the cramped space of their coach-class seats.

"That, too." She smiled, and although he was certain she couldn't be more than four or five years younger than he, she suddenly seemed half her age, coltish, a girl. Maybe it was the sprinkling of freckles across her nose and cheeks, or the shy way she lowered her eyes back to her sewing after she spoke. Then she looked up at him again, her gaze open and friendly. "What kind of quilts do you like to make?"

If he had not left his carry-on back at his original seat, he would have shown her a copy of his book, impressed her, feigned nonchalance. If he ran back for it now, he would just look too eager to please. "They're more contemporary," he said instead. "I use a lot of color and contrast effects, rotary cutting, intersecting lines and so on. Mostly wall hangings."

She considered. "That sounds like the work of an art quilter I met at a conference once. He's very well known." She bit her lower lip, brow furrowed. "I have his book at home. What was his name again?"

Reluctantly, Russ said, "Michael James?" Everyone had heard of Michael James. Sometimes Russ thought he was the only male quilter anyone knew by name.

"No, but he's good, too. It's Ross—no, Russ. Russell McIntyre."

"We've met before?"

"You're Russ?"

He nodded.

"Really?" She studied him. "Your beard was longer then."

He rubbed his jaw absently. "I've been keeping it shorter for the past year or two. When did we meet?"

"We sat at the head table at the awards banquet at the AQS

show in Paducah. It was years ago, and there was this huge flower arrangement and a podium between us. I'm so sorry I didn't recognize you."

"That's okay. I didn't recognize you." He wrestled in vain with his memory. "You are . . . ?"

"Maggie Flynn." She held out her hand for him to shake. It was warm and smooth, except for a few quilting calluses on finger and thumb. "I did the Harriet Findley Birch book. The My Journey with Harriet quilts?"

She looked at him hopefully, and he was fervently grateful when his faulty memory suddenly kicked out the details. "Of course. Maggie Flynn." Now he realized why her appliqué pattern had looked familiar. Elaine had taken a My Journey with Harriet class at a weekend retreat with her quilt guild. Russ still had the twenty or so little blocks in reproduction fabrics she had made from Maggie's patterns. "You have a legion of followers. You're a genuine celebrity."

"Only in the quilting world," she said, but he could tell she was pleased.

"Are you teaching for a guild in Seattle?"

"No, I'm on my way home. I'll be in Seattle only long enough to catch a connecting flight to Sacramento. How about you?"

"Seattle's home for me. I'm just returning from a job interview." Instinctively, he shook his head to clear it of the memory.

Her eyes widened. "Job interview? Not at Elm Creek Quilt Camp?"

He paused. "You, too?"

She nodded.

"Oh."

"This is awkward."

"It shouldn't be," Russ quickly assured her. "I don't stand a chance. Believe me, I'm no longer in contention for the job."

"Your interview must have gone better than mine. There was this one woman—"

"Diane?"

"Yes! The blonde. What was her problem?"

"I have no idea. I thought she just hated men quilters."

"Don't worry; it's not that. She doesn't like women quilters, either." Maggie frowned and laid her quilt block on her tray table. "Or maybe just me."

Russ couldn't imagine how anyone could dislike Maggie. "Maybe it was a set up. Maybe she was there to be the devil's advocate." Which meant, of course, that he had fallen for it and failed the test entirely. "Are you a full-time instructor?"

"No, only part-time. I'm a geriatric care manager at Ocean View Hills—it's a senior citizens' home in Sacramento."

"It must be a very tall building to have an ocean view from Sacramento."

She smiled. "I've always thought the name was a bit silly. It won't matter for much longer, though. It's closing."

"That's too bad." Russ found himself hoping Maggie had made a better impression on the Elm Creek Quilters than she thought. "You'll probably get the Elm Creek job. I would think they'd be glad to have you on their staff. Your style is so versatile, and you could lecture on quilt history as well as teach quilting."

She gave him a rueful half-smile. "That's what I tried to tell them, but I think Diane was more persuasive."

"Trust me. After meeting me, Diane probably decided you could be her new best friend."

"I would put in a good word for you, but that would probably do you more harm than good."

Russ laughed.

Maggie stared at him, wide-eyed. "You have a nice laugh," she said softly, and quickly turned her gaze to her sewing, as if embarrassed by what she had said.

Russ was suddenly very glad that he had left Elm Creek Manor early.

He remained in his new seat for the rest of the flight. He and Maggie rejected the painful subject of their interviews and turned to their quilts, favorite quilt shops, industry gossip, quilting friends they had in common, their families. As the plane touched down they exchanged business cards and agreed to have lunch the next time they were scheduled at the same quilt show.

Russ intended to walk Maggie to her gate, but he lost her in the disembarking crowd after returning to his original seat for his carry-on. He was disappointed, but at least he had her card. He would email her from home.

He was almost to the security checkpoint when he turned around.

He found her flight on the monitor and raced to the departing gate. "Maggie," he called, finding her in the line to the jetway.

She looked his way, and her face lit up with surprise and, he hoped, pleasure. "Russ?"

"I'm coming through California this week on a teaching tour," he said. "Can we get together? Coffee, or dinner, or something?"

"I'd like that," she said. "Call me. Or email me. One or the other."

"I will."

She nodded and turned away to hand her boarding pass to the gate attendant. She glanced over her shoulder at him and waved, hesitating a moment before disappearing down the jetway.

"I'll see you next week," Russ called, but she was already gone.

Chapter Five
Gretchen

Gretchen rose carefully so she would not jostle her husband, still asleep on his side of the bed, supported with pillows to relieve pressure on his lower back. As she dressed, she paused to study his face, so dear to her even after forty-two years of marriage. Even in sleep Joe wore a slight grimace of pain. He was so handsome as a young man that all her friends had envied her. On their wedding day, she had considered herself the luckiest woman alive. She still considered herself blessed to have shared so many years with the man she loved, but she no longer believed in luck, good or bad. People made choices and lived with the consequences. Through the years she had discovered that some people had certain advantages that allowed them to escape the worst consequences of their bad decisions, but she wouldn't call that luck. If she did, she would have to wonder why good luck and bad had not been distributed more equitably, and dwelling upon that was the quickest route to bitterness.

By the time she started cooking breakfast, she heard Joe climbing out of bed—pushing himself to a seated position, swinging his legs to the side, grasping the back of the bedside chair, hauling himself to his feet. Morning was the worst time of the day for her husband, muscles stiff, medication yet to be taken. He hated for her to see him gritting his teeth and struggling to rise, so if he did wake first, he would feign sleep until she slipped downstairs. He didn't know she knew.

She set his eggs and sausage on the table as he entered the kitchen. "Morning, sweetheart," he said, kissing her. His cheeks were shaved smooth, his hair carefully combed. He looked as prepared for a day at work as any other husband on the street, even though his commute took him only as far as the garage.

"Morning to you, too." She poured his coffee and took her own seat to his left. It was a small table, just big enough for two plates, two cups, and a serving dish. Their dining room table sat four comfortably, six if they didn't mind getting a little cozy. When it was just the two of them, though, it was too much trouble to clear off her fabric and sewing machine three times a day.

"I forgot to tell you," said Joe, buttering a slice of toast. "Clyde came around yesterday to see if we wanted to meet him and Jan at the fish fry at the VFW tonight."

"I can't," said Gretchen. "Heidi's having a party. She wants me to come by and help out beforehand."

Joe frowned. "Will you still be on the clock or is this volunteer work?"

"Oh, Joe, don't start."

"All I'm saying is that she can afford to hire help. She doesn't need to draft you into service unless she's going to pay for it."

"I work for Heidi and you know it." Gretchen tried to sound reasonable, but it was exasperating that they still argued over this. "My family has always worked for hers. I don't think she could manage without me."

"Darn right she couldn't, which is why she should pay you what you're worth." He set down his coffee cup with a bang, a mulish look in his eye. "If I could work, you could quit your job and tell Heidi to stick it where—"

"I like my job," Gretchen reminded him. "I don't want to quit working. The quilt shop is like a second home to me."

"At least you could drop all the extra fetching and carrying and cleaning."

Gretchen bristled with annoyance—in part because she knew he was right. She liked Heidi, but it was often inconvenient to pick up Heidi's dry cleaning on her way in to work, or collect her mail and newspapers while her family was away on a Caribbean cruise, or to help the housekeeper clean Heidi's grand home in Sewickley for a party to which Gretchen would never be invited as a guest. "It's all part of the job," she said. "I prefer to think of it as helping out a friend."

Joe grunted, and Gretchen knew what he was thinking: In Heidi's eyes, Gretchen was closer to a servant than a friend.

Perhaps Heidi did not consider Gretchen a friend, but through the years, Gretchen had learned that a shared history was as important as affinity. Perhaps more so. As people who had known her since childhood grew scarcer, they became more precious, even if they were not the same people who made her laugh or whose company she most enjoyed. And if nothing else, Gretchen and Heidi shared a history, one that had begun before they were born.

When Gretchen's grandmother emigrated from Croatia, she lived with a cousin's family and found a job at a butcher's in the strip district in Pittsburgh. Because she was pretty, clean, and good with sums, she was occasionally told to ride on the wagon to make deliveries to the fine houses in Sewickley on the other side of the river. On one occasion she met Heidi's great-grandmother, who sized her up as a quiet, industrious sort of girl and hired her to replace her second housemaid, whom she had recently fired for theft. Gretchen's grandmother was almost let go herself when the lady of the house discovered she spoke only rudimentary

English, but she relented at the recommendation of the housekeeper, who appreciated a hardworking girl who would not talk back. Gretchen's grandmother was relieved to stay; the work was hard, but no more so than at the butcher's, and in the Albrechts' house, she had her own bed in a small, third-floor room she shared with the other housemaid.

Years later she married, but continued to live with and work for the Albrechts until well into her first pregnancy. When her own children were old enough, she returned to work as a housekeeper for her original employer's daughter, now married with a baby of her own. Gretchen's mother left school after the eighth grade to work alongside her mother, eventually taking over her position when her mother grew too old for the arduous labor. She married a steelworker and moved into a small house on a hill in Ambridge, where Gretchen was born a year later.

Gretchen was six when Heidi was born, and she remembered her mother leaving before dawn to catch the bus to Sewickley, where she bathed Heidi, fed her breakfast, and, in later years, escorted her to school. While Heidi was at school, Gretchen's mother tended the Albrecht home, hurrying to finish the work before it was time to walk Heidi home and prepare the family's supper. She returned home to her own family after dark, exhausted, but still eager to hear about her daughter's day. As soon as Gretchen was old enough, she learned to start supper early so her mother could put up her feet for a little while before Gretchen's father returned home from the steel mill.

Gretchen listened with amazement to the stories her mother told of little Heidi: the extravagant birthday parties, the closets full of dresses, the ridiculously inappropriate gifts Mr. and Mrs. Albrecht showered upon her. "A string of pearls for a four-year-old," she marveled one Christmas, "when all the poor little dear wants is their attention."

Gretchen did not think Heidi was a poor little dear. Heidi had everything—pretty clothes, a big house, and Gretchen's mother at her beck and call. If that wasn't enough for her, she was just being selfish.

Perhaps her mother sensed Gretchen's feelings, because when school ended for the summer the year she turned twelve, her mother received permission to bring Gretchen along with her to the Albrecht home. Mrs. Albrecht may have assumed Gretchen was there to begin learning the duties she would one day take over, but Gretchen knew her mother wanted to teach her only that Heidi's life was not one to covet. It was true that the Albrechts had come down in the world somewhat since Gretchen's grandmother's day, but they still lived in a large, luxurious house in one of Sewickley's most prestigious neighborhoods. Gretchen's mother as well as a cook, gardener, and driver waited upon them.

Six years Heidi's elder, Gretchen was more of a caregiver than a playmate to the younger girl, and she learned quickly to give in to Heidi's demands rather than try to teach her to share or to play nicely. The first time she told Heidi not to boss her around, Heidi burst into tears and fled to her mother, who was entertaining guests and was greatly annoyed by the interruption. It was Gretchen's mother she scolded, however, rendering Gretchen heartsick with shame. She did not make that mistake again, and eventually she convinced herself that Heidi could be a happy, charming girl if given her own way.

Since Gretchen was six years ahead of Heidi in school and an able student, she naturally slipped into the role of Heidi's tutor. It was then that Heidi's mother began to take more notice of her, complimenting a flattering change in hair style or suggesting she "smarten herself up a bit." "You're becoming a young lady," she said once. "Why don't you take some of your wages and buy yourself a pretty dress?" Relieved to have Heidi taken off her hands, she hurried off without waiting for a reply. Gretchen would have explained, if Mrs. Albrecht had let her, that the clothes her mother sewed for her suited her just fine, and she preferred to save her money for college. After discovering how much her tutoring had helped Heidi, she had contemplated becoming a teacher.

Gretchen made the mistake of confiding her plans to Heidi, who immediately decided that she wanted to be a teacher, too. Her declaration mystified Mrs. Albrecht, who could not fathom how such an idea would have entered her daughter's head. To her credit, Heidi did not reveal the source of her inspiration, not to spare Gretchen a reprimand but for the thrill of keeping a secret from her parents. Gretchen should have known better than to mention her private wish in Heidi's presence. Whenever she invented a game or made a joke, Heidi claimed it as her own, embellishing it for her parents, who praised her for her cleverness. If Gretchen happened to admire a dress in a storefront window, within days she saw Heidi wearing a younger girl's version of it to school. Gretchen's mother told her she ought to be flattered that Heidi admired her so, but Gretchen quietly resented Heidi's mimicry. Heidi honestly seemed to believe that the ideas and tastes she picked up from Gretchen originated in her own mind, or worse, that Gretchen's ideas naturally belonged to Heidi, just as Gretchen's family belonged to the Albrechts.

At eighteen, Gretchen graduated from high school and won a partial scholarship to college, where she intended to major in elementary education. This news astounded Mrs. Albrecht, who sat her mother down for a serious chat about Gretchen's future. In a conversation Gretchen overheard from another room, she explained how Gretchen's parents would be far wiser to direct her down a more practical path than to indulge an imprudent dream. "You want to be kind, I understand that," said Mrs. Albrecht sympathetically. "But you must think of how much more hurtful it will be later, when she discovers that one cannot rise above one's station in life."

Gretchen's mother thanked Mrs. Albrecht for the advice, and

on the bus home that evening, she tentatively suggested that Gretchen reconsider. Gretchen adamantly refused, but over the next few days, her mother's worried expressions and tearful arguments wore her down. She agreed to compromise: She would major in elementary education and home economics. Her mother's thankful relief at this promise filled her with a cold, angry helplessness that worsened when Mrs. Albrecht congratulated her for making such a sensible decision.

Two years into her program, she still would not admit aloud that her home economics courses were among her favorites. She learned to sew and design garments even better than her mother, and she especially enjoyed the creative outlet her quilting class provided. The instructor, a graduate of the college's art education program named Sylvia Compson, spiced her lectures about patterns and stitches with stories of the etymology of quilt block names, the role of the quilting bee in the lives of early American women, and commemorative quilts that promoted justice and social change. Gretchen took to quilting as if she had learned at her grandmother's knee, as most of the other students in the class had done. The small class size fostered the creation of deep friendships, strengthened by the teasing they endured from their fellow coeds who thought both home economics and quilting trivial subjects, pursuits in which no woman who wanted to be taken seriously would engage.

Perhaps that was why Gretchen rarely spoke of her inspirational teacher or home economics program to anyone but Joe, the handsome young man she had met at church and the one person with whom she felt she could be completely honest and free with her opinions. He was a wonderful dancer, a machinist at one of the steel mills, polite and respectful to her parents. He wanted to marry her right away but agreed to wait until she had taught for a few years, although sometimes after a date, when they had to tear themselves away from each other, breathless and dizzy from fervent kisses in the shadows of the pine trees obscuring her parents' view from the house, Gretchen considered abandoning her education and marrying him soon, tomorrow, that very night, because the wait seemed unbearable when he held her in his arms.

Even in those days, Joe did not like the Albrechts. He called Heidi's parents rich snobs who took advantage of Gretchen's mother, and his mouth turned in a skeptical frown whenever Gretchen had to cancel a weekend date to help Heidi with one crisis or another. He said nothing when Heidi went off to an exclusive New England college with plans to earn a teaching degree. His raised eyebrows and knowing look conveyed his meaning with perfect clarity, as it had when Mrs. Albrecht remarked that she and her husband could not be prouder of their daughter, for didn't it reveal Heidi's tremendous strength of character that she was so passionate about educating the less fortunate?

Joe had plenty to say, however, a few years after he and Gretchen married. As Heidi's own wedding approached, she asked Gretchen to make her a nearly identical gown, but of silk instead of cotton brocade and with lovely seed pearl accents. When Gretchen stayed up past midnight for the third night in a row in order to finish the gown in time, he folded his newspaper, flung it on the table, and said, "You be sure to keep track of your hours and charge her a living wage. No more favors for Princess Heidi." Then he stormed upstairs to bed.

Joe was not a temperamental man. Gretchen knew he wished the beautiful silk gown was for her, and that he could have afforded to buy it for her.

He hated that she needed to pick up occasional work from the Albrechts to supplement his wages from the plant and the small salary she received for teaching at a Catholic primary school. He did not want her to have to work, period, but he knew she enjoyed teaching, even on days when her more outspoken girls rolled their eyes when she assigned a sewing project and declared that they ought to be allowed to take metal shop with the boys instead. He took as much overtime as he could, but every time they saved up a promising sum, the car broke down or the furnace went out or the roof needed to be repaired. But they were frugal and found their happiness within each other, and as they slowly built up a nest egg, they were hopeful that more prosperous times would come their way.

Then came the dark morning when the principal came to Gretchen's classroom and in a hushed voice informed her that the plant foreman had called. Joe had been taken to Allegheny General Hospital after a support beam fell and pinned him to the floor. His back was broken and he was not expected to live.

When he survived that first night and regained consciousness the next morning, Gretchen seized that faint glimmer of hope and would not allow the doctors' grim predictions to dispel it. Stubborn to a fault and determined to prove his doctors wrong, Joe lived when they said he would die and fought to learn to walk again after they concluded he never would. They urged Gretchen to convince him to accept their diagnosis, to encourage him to let go of false hope, but Gretchen refused. Let the rest of the world condemn him to a wheelchair; someone had to believe in him. Joe needed her to believe in him.

Bedridden for months and in almost constant pain, Joe struggled to regain use of his legs—and to accept that for the time being, he must allow his wife to do things for him that a grown man ought to do for himself. Gretchen quit her job to care for him. Their modest savings quickly disappeared, but Gretchen made ends meet on a small monthly stipend from Joe's union. When that proved insufficient, she paid a call on Heidi and asked for work. Heidi grandly offered her a job cleaning her house on Saturday mornings, when Gretchen could arrange for a neighbor to check in on Joe.

She knew from his silence that he hated to see her going hat in hand to the Albrecht family, but he did not lash out at her as some husbands might have done. He redoubled his efforts to recuperate, and within months he could sit up in bed unassisted. Soon he could move from the bed to the chair on his own, and within a year, he could stand. From the kitchen below she would hear him attempting slow, shuffling steps across the bedroom floor, but she resisted the temptation to dash upstairs to watch, knowing his pride would suffer. For Joe, it was bad enough that she had to work to support them, a fact of their married life they both accepted but did not discuss. If he did not want her to watch him struggle to walk, she would leave him alone until he was ready.

There were no more Saturday night dances or Sunday matinees with friends. Instead, they entertained themselves in the evenings by listening to the radio or reading aloud to each other. Most often, Joe would read aloud while Gretchen quilted. His voice, as strong and deep as before the accident, comforted her, and the piecework drew her attention from the shabby furniture, her made-over dresses, the diminishment of their expectations, the loneliness and isolation of their lives. Gretchen's scrap quilts brought warmth and beauty into their home, allowing them to turn the thermostat a little lower or to conceal a sagging mattress and threadbare sofa cushions. Gretchen knew Joe appreciated the softness and bright colors, since he rarely left the house except to go to church.

Gretchen was glad that Joe admired her quilts, for it seemed that no one else did. No one she knew quilted anymore. Her women friends were taking on jobs outside the home, enrolling in community college, competing in local elections, and declaring that women could do anything men could do. Gretchen had known that for a long time, but it was quite another thing to watch from the sidelines as other women her age and younger broke into realms from which they had traditionally been excluded. Even Heidi, who had given up teaching after one unfortunate semester, had worked her way onto boards and committees that a generation ago would have pleasantly but firmly steered her toward a woman's auxiliary instead of allowing her to be a part of the decision making. Gretchen watched with awe and admiration as other women's lives became busier and fuller, and she nodded vigorously when former coworkers talked about equal pay for equal work and valuing woman's contributions. It took her time to realize that they were not referring to many of the contributions she valued most.

Other women had abandoned quilting, but not because they were too busy. Quilts had become old-fashioned, the craft of the poor and the unsophisticated, an unwelcome reminder of the limitations of their mothers' and grandmothers' lives. Quilting, with its inherent association with the domestic sphere and the traditional "woman's work" of housekeeping and family tending, was something for women to avoid tripping over as they strode into the male world of work that mattered.

Gretchen refused to apologize for her love of quilting, but she decided to stop discussing it one Saturday morning at Heidi's house. Heidi had set Gretchen to work clearing out some old cartons from the basement, where she stumbled across a box of old fabric scraps, half-sewn patchwork blocks, and an envelope stuffed full of brittle, yellowed quilt patterns clipped from the newspaper. The envelope bore Heidi's great-grandmother's name and the address of their older, grander house. Gretchen immediately hurried off to report the find to Heidi, who regarded her with bewildered skepticism as she described the treasure trove downstairs.

"Do you think it's worth anything?" asked Heidi when Gretchen had finished.

"As a memento of your grandmother, of course," said Gretchen, taken aback. "I don't think it's something you could sell. I suppose a historical society might be interested in the donation . . ."

"I doubt it. Just toss it out."

"But—" Gretchen hesitated. "The fabric is still usable, and the blocks are charming."

"What would I do with them? Sew them together? Make a quilt?"

"That's what I would do."

Heidi laughed. "You're still quilting? Honestly, Gretchen, I don't see how you of all people can afford to waste your time that way. Think of how much you charge an hour and how many hours it takes to make a quilt. You could buy the best comforter at Gimbel's or Kaufmann's for less that that. It's a bad return on your investment."

"Quilting is not just about saving money."

"You are so right. It's also about what we consider truly important. We aren't chained to the kitchen anymore, and we can't let anyone forget it. If we women don't insist upon spending our time as thoughtfully as we spend our money, we'll never be considered equal to men."

Stung, Gretchen nevertheless nodded. "What should I do with the box, then?"

Heidi shrugged dismissively. "If you want it so badly, you take it."

Gretchen did exactly that, but as she pieced a dozen pastel Dresden Plate blocks into a lap quilt, she brooded over Heidi's words, an echo of a more prevailing message that Gretchen was out of step with her times. She did not understand why. In an era where the work of women was expanding and being recognized and earning greater respect than ever before, why was "women's work" so denigrated? Gretchen did not want quilting and cooking and caring for children to be respected *despite* the fact that they were tasks traditionally accomplished by women, but *because* of it.

But she knew no one else who shared her opinion, so she kept her quilting to herself. She quilted to add beauty to her life, to give purpose to her hours, to distract her from the unfairness of fate.

Her longtime prayers were answered when Joe began to walk

again; tears came to her eyes whenever she recalled his proud demonstration of his new, halting gait across the kitchen. He had hoped to return to work, but he never fully recovered his old strength, and an accidental jolt could leave him gasping from pain. His dream of returning to his former occupation faded, and with it, his hope.

It broke Gretchen's heart to see him turning in upon himself, giving up, growing old before his time. Before long, she realized that it was beyond her powers to cheer him up, but she resolved not to sink into despair with him. She found a new job as a substitute teacher, and while it was not steady work, it did help pay off some outstanding debts and it gave her a chance to get out of the house. In the evenings after a day away, she found she could be more cheerful with Joe, and she had more interesting stories to tell him.

Gradually he returned from his melancholy. He resumed seeing old friends, even though they thoughtlessly ribbed him about loafing and living off his wife's earnings. He planted a garden in the small patch of land behind their house and learned how to preserve the harvest. Then one evening, he paused in the middle of the chapter he was reading aloud and said, "You sure seem to get a lot of pleasure out of your sewing."

She smiled. "We've been married six years and you only just noticed?"

"What is it you like so much? It's not just having a pretty quilt at the end, is it?"

"I suppose I just like working with my hands. Keeping busy."

Joe was quiet for a moment. "Maybe I should try that."

"You want to quilt?"

"No, no, not quilting. Something else."

The next day he went on his usual slow walk around the neighborhood and returned accompanied by a boy pushing a white wooden rocking chair in a wheelbarrow. It looked to be at least fifty years old, with a split armrest and a few missing spindles on the back. Gretchen watched from the window as the boy unloaded the chair on the sidewalk. Joe gave the boy a coin from his pocket, sent him on his way, and dragged the chair out of sight into the garage.

She gave him fifteen minutes, then went outside to find out what was going on. She discovered him on one knee beside the chair, vigorously rubbing off the peeling white paint with sandpaper.

"Where did you find that old thing?" she asked.

"On the Gruebers' curb. They threw it out."

Gretchen could see why. "What are you doing?"

He turned stiffly to face her, straining the limit of his back's flexibility. "Fixing it."

"It needs a lot of fixing." She folded her arms over her chest. "And when you're done?"

"I'm going to sell it, unless I get so attached that I can't part with it."

"I see." She watched as he returned to sanding the chair. "Tomato soup and grilled cheese sandwiches for lunch sound all right to you?"

"Suits me fine."

"I'll call you when it's ready." She left him to his work.

True to his word, Joe repaired and finished the chair beautifully and sold it for twenty dollars. He took on a bureau and matching chest next, and sold both to a shop in Sewickley for fifty dollars. Within months, neighbors and strangers alike were stopping by the garage at all hours of the day to browse through the finished pieces on display or to schedule an appointment to drop off worn or damaged furniture for him to refurbish. Joe made a sign and hung it above the entrance to the garage: "Joseph Hartley: Fine Furniture Repaired and Restored." He worked when he felt able, rested when the strain on his back and legs became too much. He checked out library books on cabinet making and woodworking, and soon he began designing and building his own original pieces. An antique shop in downtown Sewickley began carrying his work. After the *Pittsburgh Post* ran a half-page article on him, customers from as far away as Harrisburg commissioned custom-made pieces.

Two years after bringing home that old rocking chair, Joe surprised Gretchen with the gift of a new sewing machine. "Joe," she exclaimed, running her hand over the gleaming new Singer. "What's the occasion?"

"Don't you like it?"

"Of course I like it, but—" Then she saw how proudly he beamed, how he could barely contain his delight, and she caught herself before asking if they could afford it. "I love it. Thank you."

He put his arms around her. "I saw it on the store shelf and it occurred to me that good things come from your quilting. You ought to have the right tools for the job."

The sewing machine was well broken in a year later when two teenage girls knocked on the door. Gretchen did not recognize them, but she guessed they were sisters. Both wore their straight blonde hair long and parted down the middle, denim jeans that flared at the ankle, and loose peasant blouses. The elder of the two had appliquéd a black-and-white peace emblem over her heart with such large, uneven stitches that Gretchen had to hide a wince.

"What can I do for you girls?" she asked, smiling at the two youngsters on her doorstep. "Are you looking for the furniture man?"

"No, we're looking for you," said the older girl. "Mrs. Johnson lives next door to us and she says you know how to make patchwork quilts."

"Why, yes, I do." Gretchen had made a baby quilt for Trudie

Johnson's son, now six years old or thereabouts. She was pleased Trudie remembered.

"Could you teach us?" asked the younger sister.

"Teach you how to quilt?"

The girls nodded. "Yes, please," said the older girl.

"Does your mother know you're here?"

They nodded again, and the younger girl added, "She says it's all right with her as long as we aren't a nuisance."

"Why do you want to learn?" asked Gretchen. "Is this for Girl Scouts?"

"No," said the elder girl. "We just want to know how."

Gretchen hesitated, considering. Their request sounded very odd to her, two girls she had never seen before coming around the house seeking quilting lessons. The girls must have interpreted her puzzlement as reluctance, because they exchanged a worried look. The elder girl quickly blurted, "We could trade you. We could help you around the house and you could give us lessons."

"That's an intriguing thought." They certainly seemed sincere in their interest. Kids these days seemed to do as they pleased, with few responsibilities and an endless supply of amusements. Anyone from their generation willing to do chores in exchange for something must truly want it.

Gretchen opened the door wider. "Very well," she said, welcoming them inside. "You can start with the dishes."

The Hellerman sisters came for their lessons every Saturday morning and Wednesday afternoon after school. Gretchen usually saved them a token amount of housework, but they were such a pleasure to have around that she would have taught them regardless. They were eager to learn, so cheerful and inquisitive, that Gretchen enjoyed instructing them in the making of templates, the matching of colors in calicos and solids, the small and precise motions of the running stitch. She was astonished to learn from them that traditional handicrafts fascinated all of their friends, who were learning quilting, knitting, weaving, candle making, soap making, preserving, and a whole host of other domestic skills that had almost entirely skipped their mothers' generation. When Holly and Megan had finished their sampler quilts, Gretchen agreed to teach a few of their friends. She was asked to teach a Saturday workshop for a group of Girl Scouts, and a few weeks later, a high school class studying the pioneers invited her as a guest speaker.

One afternoon, Gretchen ran into one of her quilting pupils at the grocery store with her mother. The mother thanked Gretchen for sharing her talents and said, "Susan makes quilting seem like so much fun. Do you think someday you might teach a class for adults?"

"I honestly hadn't considered it," said Gretchen. "I don't think there would be enough interest."

"I think you're wrong," the woman declared. "If you ever do start up an adult class, please let me know."

A week later, the woman called to tell Gretchen that she had a list of six friends who would gladly pay Gretchen to teach them how to quilt. Surprised and flattered, Gretchen agreed. She reserved the public meeting room at the Ambridge library for each Wednesday evening at seven and dug out her old lesson plans from her home economics teaching days. On the first day of class, she distributed a list of supplies her students needed to purchase for the following week. They would each make a six-block sampler quilt, choosing the blocks they liked best from a collection of thirty patterns. The blocks were interchangeable, and by adding sashing and borders, the quilts would be large enough for a twin bed. In this way, each new quilter could create her own unique project without departing too much from the standard curriculum. Gretchen was thrilled to be in front of a classroom again, so when her students asked if they could bring friends along, she consented. Before long, her class doubled in size.

Some of the women owned sewing machines and had made their own clothes once upon a time; others barely knew how to thread a needle. Together they learned to choose patterns and fabric, to draft patterns and make templates, to sew a running stitch and set in pieces. They shared confidences as they quilted, as Gretchen imagined women had at quilting bees a hundred years ago and more. She was so grateful for the company of other quilters that when they finished their sampler quilt classes, she suggested they continue their weekly meetings as friends.

At one meeting of the Wednesday Night Stitchers, as they called themselves, a member hurried into the room digging into her tote. "You'll never believe what my sister-in-law sent me from Colorado," she announced. "A magazine about quilts!"

Everyone crowded around to see. Gretchen, who had envisioned something on the order of *Life* magazine with a photo of a brilliantly colored quilt on the cover, was somewhat let down by the few pieces of paper stapled together with the words *Quilter's Newsletter Magazine* on the masthead. But when it was her turn to leaf through the pages, she felt a stirring of excitement and belonging that she had not felt since that long-ago home economics education course in college, with the admired instructor who was as passionate about precise piecing as she was about the storied heritage of American quilting. For so many years she had felt that her love for quilting isolated her until at last she discovered a small group of like-minded friends. Now she realized that they were not alone, that they were part of a larger community, a circle of quilters that had kept quilting alive and were passing along their skill and wisdom as generations of women had before them.

Over the years, Gretchen observed that interest in quilting was slowly and steadily growing. *Quilter's Newsletter Magazine* began running full-color photographs and acquired some competitors. Fabric manufacturers began creating a wider variety of prints than the traditional floral calicos. Quilting guilds like the

Wednesday Night Stitchers began cropping up in cities and towns across the nation. Then, in 1976, this interest blossomed into a veritable quilt revival. The Bicentennial created a surge of renewed interest in American history, inspiring people to search for family heirlooms in their attics and closets and under their beds. Suddenly, quilts were spoken of as if they were more than just bed coverings; they were art to be displayed on walls, historical artifacts to be studied, time capsules reflecting the social, political, and aesthetic milieu of their makers—just as Sylvia Compson had asserted in the classroom so many years before.

Gretchen knew quilting was back to stay when Heidi phoned, suggesting she come in to work early the next Saturday morning so she could show Heidi how to quilt. "I thought I'd make a quilt out of flannel," she said. "Warm and cozy, to use at the cabin. What do you think?"

Gretchen did not want to come in to work any earlier than usual, nor had she ever heard of piecing a quilt from flannel, but she did not want to discourage Heidi. "How about if I stay later, instead?"

"I can't. I have a fund-raising luncheon at the Sewickley Academy."

Gretchen thought for a moment, and then, with misgivings, said, "Do you want to come to my quilt club meeting on Wednesday? We all pitch in to help newcomers."

"I was really hoping for private lessons . . . but I suppose that would be fine."

"All right," said Gretchen, already regretting her offer. She waited until Heidi found a pen before dictating the time, date, and directions.

"I'll see you there," said Heidi. Suddenly she laughed. "You sure were clever all those years ago when you talked me out of my great-grandmother's quilting materials, weren't you? If I had only known how much they were worth."

She hung up before Gretchen could reply.

When Gretchen went to the garage to repeat Heidi's comment to Joe, he looked up from staining a sleigh bed and shook his head. "You never should have asked her to join you and your friends."

"I know." But it was too late now. "I can always hope that she'll have a miserable time and never come back."

Joe laughed shortly. "Not Heidi. If it's yours, she wants it, and she'll try to take it. That's the way she's always been."

"Heidi has everything," said Gretchen, trying to make a joke of it. "She doesn't need my little bit."

"Who said anything about need? I said want, and Heidi has a way of getting what she wants."

Joe turned out to be all too prescient. Heidi never mentioned her great-grandmother's quilting again, but instead set about learning to quilt with more diligence than Gretchen had known she possessed. She charmed the other women with her enthusiasm and infectious humor, and if she referred to Gretchen once too often as her cleaning lady, no one seemed to think less of either of them for it. Besides, Gretchen *was* Heidi's cleaning lady, and there was no sense in being too proud to acknowledge it.

Heidi absorbed everything the other women taught—everything but their rules. She mixed plaids and stripes. She shunned small-scale floral calicos. Instead of selecting a multicolored focus fabric and choosing other fabrics to match, she enthused about color wheels, complementary colors, and split-complementary color schemes, jargon she had picked up in a painting class. She combined cottons with polyesters and wools. She refused to prewash. And although Gretchen secretly predicted—and perhaps even hoped—that Heidi's reckless ways would result in disastrous quilts, somehow her collisions of incongruous methods worked, earning the grudging admiration of the Stitchers' most conservative traditionalists.

It was Heidi who suggested that the Wednesday Night Stitchers write up bylaws and officially declare themselves a quilt guild. It was Heidi who was selected as the first president. And as the other members celebrated their transformation from a group of friends to a recognized nonprofit organization, Gretchen smiled and agreed that these changes certainly were remarkable, while silently she mourned the passing of an era.

Not all of the changes Heidi inspired made her long for the old days. One of her first acts as guild president was to organize a directory of quilting guilds in Pennsylvania, West Virginia, and Ohio. The guilds shared information about quilt shows, guild activities, and teachers willing to travel. When Heidi defied alphabetical order and placed Gretchen's name at the top of the teachers' list, she received more invitations for speaking engagements than her schedule could accommodate. She felt obliged to thank Heidi, since the money she saved from her speaking fees enabled her to buy a new color television for the living room. Her gratitude evaporated when, in front of three other Wednesday Night Stitchers, Heidi replied, "It was my pleasure. I just hope the fame doesn't go to your head or my toilets will never be clean again!"

Gretchen could have died when the other women laughed.

"You shouldn't take that from her," said Joe when she told him about it. "After all you've done for her, she still acts like a spoiled brat. She'll never grow up, and you shouldn't put up with it."

"What am I supposed to do?" said Gretchen. "If I talk back, she could fire me."

"So? Let her fire you. I'm making decent money now. You have your quilt teaching. We'll get by."

But Gretchen, who balanced the family checkbook, knew that the wages she received from Heidi often made the difference between ending the week in the black or in the red.

◇◇◇

Gretchen celebrated her fiftieth birthday by splurging on an airline ticket to Houston to attend the International Quilt Festival. She had never seen so many glorious quilts in one setting—and even more thrilling was the sense of being surrounded by other women as passionate about quilts and quilting as she was. She took classes with some of the brightest stars in the quilting world, attended lectures, struggled to stick to her budget in the merchants' mall, and enjoyed many spontaneous conversations with quilt lovers from around the country.

One seminar in particular, "From Quilt Lover to Quilt Shop Owner," resonated so strongly with her that she reread her notes every evening after she returned to her hotel room, footsore and exhausted but brimming with inspiration for new quilts. Joe was the only person who knew that the prospect of attending this seminar was what had convinced her to come to Houston. For the past year they had examined their finances, studied their budget, investigated local average rents, and planned, and hoped. Joe wanted her to find an alternative to working for Heidi; Gretchen longed to fulfill a fond wish to earn a living doing what she loved best.

On Gretchen's first night home, she and Joe stayed up late into the night discussing their options, papers covered in notes and figures spread across the kitchen table. Shortly after one in the morning they concluded that they could do it. Gretchen could run a quilt shop, and considering how many quilters lived on their side of the river, how many new quilters joined their ranks every year, and how under served their area was, it could be a very successful quilt shop.

One significant obstacle stood in the way: the enormous up-front expenses necessary just to open the shop doors. She could purchase some inventory on credit, but she would still have to pay for remodeling, advertising, wages, insurance—the list went on much too long for their savings. Gretchen would have to apply for a business loan.

"It should be a piece of cake," Joe assured her. They had no outstanding debts except for their mortgage, but their monthly payments were reasonable and they would have it paid off in another eight years.

Gretchen first applied at the bank where she and Joe had held accounts since they married. They had been very good clients, never bounced a check, rarely dipped below the minimum balance, so Gretchen was crushed and bewildered when the bank turned down her application. "I don't understand," she said to the loan officer. "We have good credit."

"You have satisfactory credit," the younger man said, nodding, though he had not really agreed with her. "But you don't have a business credit record. Once you have that established, we will gladly reconsider your case."

Gretchen thanked him and left without explaining that until she opened her quilt shop, she would not be able to establish a business credit record. Until she had the loan, she could not open her quilt shop. Joe had never sought a loan for his woodworking, so she doubted he had much business credit, either, so he could not take out the loan on her behalf.

She applied elsewhere, was rejected and tried again, until every bank in Ambridge, Sewickley, and Coraopolis had turned her away. When her last application met with refusal, she tearfully broke the bad news to Joe. He tried to comfort her as she finally admitted defeat. "It was a foolish dream," she said. "I never should have allowed myself to get my hopes up."

"What kind of talk is that?" protested Joe. "What happened to the housekeeper's daughter who paid her way through college to become a teacher? What happened to the girl who told a husband with a broken back that he could walk again if he didn't quit?"

She grew up, Gretchen thought. She grew up and wised up and learned that life doesn't always reward persistence. But she hated to disappoint Joe. "I suppose I could apply to a bank in Pittsburgh," she said, though she had assumed a smaller, hometown bank would be more amenable.

"We could take a second mortgage."

"No, Joe," said Gretchen. "Absolutely not. I won't do it. I won't risk our home, not even for this. No matter how well I've planned, the shop might fail. There's always that chance."

He knew better than to argue when she got that tone in her voice, but his brow furrowed and he regarded her with fond sympathy. "If that's what you told the loan officers, no wonder they turned you down."

Joe's encouragement strengthened Gretchen's resolve, but she knew she would run headlong into the same problem at any other bank she tried. If she were ever to make her dream a reality, she had to swallow her pride and seek help from the one person to whom she did not want to become further indebted.

The following Saturday, she lingered after collecting her paycheck and asked Heidi if she had a moment. Seated in the parlor she had dusted so many times, Gretchen outlined her plans for opening a quilt shop in Ambridge. She gave Heidi a copy of her business plan and explained the problems she had encountered trying to secure a small business loan.

"I just don't know, Gretchen," said Heidi. "I agree this could be a marvelous business opportunity—and a potentially lucrative investment—but I'm leery about lending such a large sum to a friend. Money quarrels can destroy a friendship."

"We won't have any reason to quarrel," Gretchen assured her. "We'll have everything in writing, in a contract just as if the loan was made through a bank. I'll pay the going interest rate, of course."

"Of course," echoed Heidi. "I'll need to think about it and talk to my husband. Do you need an answer right away?"

"No," said Gretchen, although she had hoped for one. "Take whatever time you need."

They shook on it, and Gretchen left feeling hopeful and just the tiniest bit anxious. Heidi's husband was tightfisted and suspicious. He was likely to complain even though the money for the loan would come from Heidi's trust fund, a bequest from her grandmother that was, according to Heidi, none of his concern.

A few days later at the meeting of the Wednesday Night Stitchers, Heidi behaved normally, as if unaware that Gretchen's future happiness rested on her decision. Gretchen waited all evening for her to mention the loan, unwilling to seem like a nag by bringing it up herself. On Saturday morning, she could wait no longer and had barely closed the back door behind her when she asked Heidi if she had discussed the loan with her husband.

"He's still looking over a few details," replied Heidi. "I'll have some news for you in a few days."

Her smile meant to encourage, but Gretchen felt faint with nervousness. It was unlike Heidi to need an entire week to convince Chad to agree to something she was determined to do. Was he balking at a flaw in her business plan? Was Heidi herself uncertain if she should help Gretchen? The waiting and the worry troubled her sleep and made her short-tempered with Joe, until she almost wished she had consulted every last bank in Pennsylvania before approaching Heidi.

At last, on Wednesday evening, Heidi began the new business portion of the guild meeting by declaring that she was about to make a very important announcement. Although she only glanced at Gretchen, seated in the back, Gretchen knew at once that the answer to her request was forthcoming. Not even Heidi would decline a friend's request for a loan so publicly, so Gretchen straightened in her chair, heart pounding as if it would burst with happiness. In the moment Heidi paused to allow the murmurs of expectation to build, Gretchen envisioned the Stitchers' response to the good news: their exclamations of delight, their congratulatory embraces, their promises to become her shop's best customers. She was still lost in a joyful reverie when Heidi announced that she intended to open a quilt shop in downtown Sewickley by summer and hoped they would all turn out for the grand opening.

Gretchen sat stunned in her chair while her friends showered Heidi with applause and the exact good wishes she had imagined for herself. Heidi needed a good five minutes to quiet them so she could proceed with the meeting. Not once did she look Gretchen's way.

Gretchen left the meeting at the social break without speaking to anyone.

Joe was furious. "She stole your business plan," he thundered. "She took all your ideas, all our research, and kept them for herself. She can't be allowed to get away with this."

But Gretchen did not know what to do. Had Heidi broken any laws? Without a doubt, what she had done was sneaky and underhanded—unethical, yes, but illegal? Heartsick, Gretchen could not even begin to pursue that question. She hardly saw the point. Even if she obtained a loan elsewhere, she could not open a quilt shop in Ambridge with Heidi's shop practically next door in Sewickley, not if she expected it to succeed. And Heidi would have known that.

Gretchen dreaded Saturday morning. For the first time in her life, she deliberately arrived late to work, hoping Heidi would have already left for a tennis lesson or board meeting or garden society brunch. Unfortunately, Heidi was waiting for her just inside the back door. "We should talk," she said before Gretchen was out of her coat.

"All right." Gretchen set down her purse and regarded Heidi evenly. She felt strangely calm. "Let's talk about how you pretended to consider my request for a loan to distract me while you stole my idea."

"How could you say such a thing?" exclaimed Heidi. "That's not what happened."

Gretchen stared at her, amazed. Did Heidi really believe she could bluff her way out of it? "I showed you my business plan and the next thing I know, you're opening a quilt shop."

"That's not fair. I didn't follow your plan. For one thing, my quilt shop will be in Sewickley, not Ambridge. I admit the timing is unfortunate, but I've been planning this for a long time. You don't really think I could have set everything in motion in one week, do you?"

It had been a week and a half between Gretchen's request and the announcement at the guild meeting, a more than sufficient amount of time for someone with Heidi's connections. "I hardly know what to believe. If you were already planning to open a quilt shop, why didn't you tell me when I asked for the loan?"

"I can explain." Heidi sank into a chair at the kitchen table and gestured for Gretchen to sit. "I've wanted to run my own company for years. You know that. You've heard me talk about it."

Gretchen shrugged and sat down, reluctantly. Heidi had mentioned an interior decorating service, a wedding planning service, and a myriad of other businesses throughout the years, but she had never seemed serious about any of them.

"When I first mentioned a quilt shop to Chad, he dismissed it just as he had all my other ideas." A frown of annoyance briefly cut Heidi's face and disappeared. "Worse, he thought it was silly and frivolous, a waste of my time. So when you asked for the loan, I did seriously consider it. I thought that if I couldn't have a shop of my own, investing in yours would be the next best thing. You did write up an excellent plan. It was very professional."

"Joe helped a lot," said Gretchen quietly.

"A lot of credit goes to you both, then, because when I showed Chad everything you had presented to me, he realized that there was much more to 'this quilting thing' than he had thought. All I wanted was for him to agree to the loan, but instead he told me I should go ahead with my original plan to open my own shop."

Gretchen studied her for a moment. Heidi's expression was so open and guileless, her clear blue eyes pleading for understanding and forgiveness. "You never mentioned wanting to run a quilt shop."

"Of course not! No one pays any attention to my career plans anymore. Who can blame them? I've thrown out so many ideas and haven't stuck with any of them."

Gretchen wondered why Heidi seemed so convinced that this time would be any different. She did not know what to say. How could she convey to Heidi her disappointment, her sense of loss? Could she persuade Heidi to step aside, forget her own shop and grant the loan for Gretchen's dream instead?

Heidi broke the silence. "You know, you could still get a bank loan and open your own quilt shop."

Gretchen knew Heidi was wrong on at least two counts, but she was too frustrated and defeated to argue. She shook her head.

"I'm sorry," said Heidi, reaching for her hand. "But in a way, I'm glad you won't be setting up a competing shop. I had hoped you would come and work for me."

Gretchen yanked her hand free. "You have a lot of nerve."

"Gretchen—"

Standing, Gretchen waved her to silence. "Don't. I can't talk about this anymore. I have work to do."

She left the kitchen with Heidi staring after her in astonishment.

Quilts 'n Things opened three months later. Lingering doubts about the truth of Heidi's explanation kept Gretchen away for the first two weeks, but eventually her curiosity overcame her resistance. Heidi greeted her excitedly, bounding over to her from behind the cash register and giving her an impulsive and entirely unexpected hug. "I'm so glad you came," she said. "I wanted your opinion so many times, but—" She shrugged. "You know."

Gretchen nodded, taking in the scene. "Congratulations," she said, more impressed than she cared to admit. The former shoe store had been decorated to resemble a country farmhouse, with bolts of brightly colored fabric arranged in antique armoires and pie cupboards. In the center of the room, an old kitchen table had been transformed into a cutting table. A partial wall that resembled the entrance to a one-room schoolhouse separated the back of the room from the main sales floor; through the doorway, Gretchen spied several rows of wooden desks and a blackboard hanging on the wall. Everywhere she looked, Gretchen found enticing displays of the latest fabrics, notions, patterns, and products to satisfy any quilter's heart's desire.

Heidi regarded her expectantly. "What do you think?"

"It's wonderful," said Gretchen. Even when she had envisioned her own quilt shop, she had not imagined anything so warm and enchanting. It was the kind of shop in which she could gladly spend an entire day and half a paycheck. "I'm sure it will be an enormous success."

"I'm so glad you feel that way." Heidi took her hand and led her to a small office tucked away in a back room, all but invisible from the shop floor. "I'm sure you noticed my classroom space. I would like you to be my first teacher."

"I don't know . . ."

"Not just a teacher. A partner." Heidi indicated a sprawl of paperwork on the desk. "I haven't forgotten your business plan. I know you have some capital. You asked me to invest in your shop, and now I'm asking you to invest in mine."

Gretchen felt a small glimmering of hope. "I would be a partner?"

"A junior partner, but still, part owner. We would run this place together." Heidi squared her shoulders as if to summon up an inner reservoir of resolve. "All right. You're forcing me to do something I know I'm going to regret. You're fired."

"What?"

"You're fired. As my cleaning lady. Now that you're unemployed, I'd like to rehire you as my quilting instructor and junior partner." Heidi placed a sheaf of papers in Gretchen's hands. "Here's a contract. You'll have two weeks of vacation each year and a health care plan. Including dental."

Through Chad's insurance company, no doubt, with a high deductible. But still . . . "Why?" she asked. Heidi knew many other perfectly capable quilting instructors. Was this her admission of guilt? Her apology? Nothing Heidi did could compensate for stealing Gretchen's dream, intentional or not.

"I need you," said Heidi in a small voice.

Gretchen was about to retort that nothing she had seen that day gave her that impression, but something in the younger woman's expression stopped her short. It was the look of the little girl she had tutored, the one who wanted to dress like her and be a teacher like her, the little girl who had wanted so badly to be loved and admired.

"You don't need me," said Gretchen. Heidi didn't, not really. "But . . . I think I would like to work here."

Heidi beamed.

Over the years, as the junior partner of Quilts 'n Things, Gretchen was able to accomplish everything she had hoped to as owner of her own shop. She loved every part of her day, from opening the cozy shop in the morning to selecting stock, helping customers, making sample quilts to display on the walls above the fabric bolts, and teaching, especially when she introduced new quilters to the craft. She still cleaned up Heidi's messes, but she would rather sweep up thread and put away fabric bolts than scrub bathrooms. She had come to appreciate Heidi's creative imagination, which not only manifested itself in her quilt designs, but also in the way she ran the shop. She would hold spontaneous one-day sales that had the store packed with shoppers from the time they unlocked the doors in the morning until long after their usual closing hour. She would throw parties based upon the silliest themes—"Three Months Until Christmas Day" or "Fabric Appreciation Week"—to the delight of their customers, who willingly seized upon any excuse to buy more fabric. She held an annual quilt show in the store where customers could vote for the Ugliest Quilt of All Time. Gretchen was appalled when Heidi first announced the contest, and she could not believe that anyone would humiliate herself by putting her name to any quilt entitled to that dubious honor. But ten brave souls entered that first year, and the winner was crowned while wearing a paper bag over her head. She had to be led by the hand to the front of the store to receive her prize, a basket of fat quarters and a gift certificate to one session of classes at the shop. Every year the contest grew, the entries becoming ever more abominable, until Heidi had to put her foot down and exclude any quilts that were deliberately made badly, so that only the truly and unintentionally awful would be considered for the grand prize.

Most winners used their gift certificates to enroll in a Quilting for Beginners course, and most made dramatic improvements. They all bought fabric, books, and notions at Quilts 'n Things, and many signed up for more advanced classes. Gretchen never would have thought to increase class enrollments by demonstrating to potential customers how sorely they needed the help.

"I wonder if this is how Ami Simms attracts new students," Gretchen remarked once.

Heidi did not look up from the rack of quilt patterns she was arranging—not in alphabetical order as Gretchen would have done, but according to season. "Who?" she asked absently.

"Ami Simms. I said, I wonder if she uses her contest to get more students to enroll in classes, but I was only joking. She probably has so many students she has to turn some away."

Heidi glanced over her shoulder at Gretchen, puzzled. "What contest?"

"The Worst Quilt in the World contest. She's been running one for years. I assumed that's where you got the idea."

Heidi shook her head and shrugged, turning back to her work. "I've never heard of her, or her contest. Maybe she took the idea from us."

"Never heard of Ami Simms?" repeated Gretchen, dubious. "Of course you have. We carry her books. We met her at Paducah three years ago."

Heidi made a helpless, apologetic gesture as she filed patterns. Gretchen watched her in disbelief. Why on earth would Heidi pretend she had never heard of Ami Simms? Was she that unwilling to admit she had taken inspiration from Ami's contest rather than invent it herself?

Gretchen already knew the answer to that one.

Although she and Heidi did not always agree, Gretchen liked to think they complemented each other: Heidi brought the imagination and spark to the business, while Gretchen understood how to turn her partner's outlandish ideas into workable plans. Heidi was energetic and inventive; Gretchen, steady and practical. They were two halves of an excellent management team, and neither could have succeeded as well without the other. Gretchen often thought, however, that although they were both essential to the success of Quilts 'n Things, Heidi seemed to have most of the fun.

As the years passed, the quilt shop thrived, riding the surging wave of the quilting revival. Gretchen wasn't sure whether Heidi was a trendsetter, putting forth styles and products she liked best and taking a chance that others would share her tastes, or if she was simply quick to perceive the sways and swells of popular opinion and could adapt quickly to match them. Either way, Quilts 'n Things earned a reputation for being the place to shop for everything new and innovative in the quilting world. Heidi advocated rotary cutter techniques and establishing a presence on the Internet when Gretchen was still worrying about how to best provide templates for their block-of-the-month kits. Heidi invested in a longarm quilting machine and charged customers by the hour to use it at a time when Gretchen and her friends were still wrestling with the question of whether a machine-quilted top could be considered a true quilt. Before long, Gretchen began to notice a clear division within their clientele: the younger, newer quilters brought their questions to Heidi and ignored Gretchen, while the older, longtime quilters sought Gretchen's advice and assumed Heidi was her less experienced assistant. Gretchen, to her secret shame, never clarified the reality of their arrangement.

Sometimes Heidi went too far. Gretchen was shocked and angered when she returned from her day off to discover that her partner had replaced all the shelves of her beloved floral calicos with brightly colored, exotic batiks. "Our customers will love these," Heidi protested, bewildered by Gretchen's reaction.

"Our customers love the calicos," insisted Gretchen.

"They can still have them," Heidi hastened to reassure her, and compromised by relocating the remaining bolts to the back shelves where they stored clearance merchandise. But hardly anyone bothered to look for them because they had usually reached their spending limits by the time they made it that far into the store. Taking inventory at the end of the month, Heidi remarked that only about five yards of the calicos had sold, and that she had been right to move them to make room for the highly popular batiks. When Gretchen pointed out that Heidi's decision had become a self-fulfilling prophecy, Heidi merely shrugged. She did not need to perpetuate the argument; she had had her own way and she was selling fabric. For the sake of workplace harmony, Gretchen masked her annoyance and contented herself with making sure her fellow calico lovers knew exactly where to find the bolts and by placing baskets full of floral calico fat quarters at the checkout line to encourage impulse purchases.

Their educational philosophies differed even more than their tastes in fabric. Gretchen instructed aspiring quilters as she had been taught, learning the fundamentals of quiltmaking while making simple blocks and moving on to more difficult patterns and new skills when the basics were mastered. Heidi believed that contemporary women did not have time to quilt as their grandmothers had. If they were going to spend an entire Saturday at a quilting workshop, they wanted to have a finished top at the end. Her classes emphasized rotary cutting, quick piecing, working with prepared patterns, and machine sewing every stitch. "Look at how many of my students finish their workshop quilts, bring them back to show us, and sign up for another class," said Heidi when they were planning the next session of courses and were trying to efficiently divide up the classroom time.

"That's true," said Gretchen. It was easier to win over Heidi if she agreed with her first. "But at the end of the semester, my students can look at any quilt block, figure out how it's constructed, design their own quilts, and draft their own patterns. Your students can make that one quilt. They make it quickly and well, but they can only make that one quilt. They might vary the colors or size, but it's always the same."

"That's what they like," countered Heidi. "They want certainty. They enjoy the feeling of accomplishment. They like having finished quilts to put on beds or give to grandchildren for Christmas. Their friends see the quilts and sign up for the next class. Maybe your students can decipher any pattern, but they also have closets stuffed full of UFOs."

Gretchen knew her students did finish quilts—perhaps not as many as Heidi's, but the quilts they did complete were unique, each one an original creative expression of its maker. The mass production of Heidi's students could not compete. Of course, she would never say so aloud. Heidi's students were lovely women and they enjoyed quilting as much as Gretchen's favorite pupils did. But their sole focus on reproducing other quilters' patterns underscored another important difference between the two partners: Gretchen was most concerned with process, Heidi with product.

For many years, their partnership weathered minor disagreements and occasional full-blown arguments. They always reconciled, in part because Gretchen never failed to appease Heidi when she became tearful and melodramatic, but mostly because Quilts 'n Things was too important to them both to sacrifice its success to petty squabbling.

Just in time for its tenth anniversary, Quilts 'n Things was selected to appear in a special issue of *Contemporary Quiltmaker* magazine titled "The Best Quilt Shops of the Millennium." Privately, Gretchen and Joe agreed that the title smacked of hyperbole and really ought to be amended to "The Best American Quilt Shops Currently in Operation That Carry Our Magazine," but neither would have suggested they decline to participate. For all her self-deprecating jokes, Gretchen was honored to be included, and Heidi was thrilled with the prospect of so much free publicity.

The three days the team from the magazine spent in Sewickley was as close to stardom as Gretchen figured she was ever likely to get. Their stylist helped her select an outfit and did her hair and makeup for the photo shoot at the store. A reporter interviewed her at length, twice on her own and once more with Heidi and their two part-time employees. As he inquired about her vision for the shop, the inspiration for her quilts, and her history as a quiltmaker, Gretchen was struck by the realization that no one had ever asked her these questions before. She had quilted most of her life, and now, finally, someone cared enough to ask. Best of all, the reporter represented tens of thousands of readers who also cared.

A few months later, the magazine arrived from the printer's and was arranged with much fanfare on the new book display at the front of the quilt shop. Gretchen knew that the reporter had interviewed

Heidi just as thoroughly as her, and yet she was stunned when she turned to the article and discovered a full-page photo of Heidi beaming out at her. A caption identified her as "Heidi Mueller, owner, creative inspiration, and driving force behind the finest quilt shop in western Pennsylvania." Scattered among the photos of customers browsing through the shop were some of Heidi smiling over a cup of coffee in her kitchen, lecturing to an adoring class in the schoolhouse, wearing a look of thoughtful introspection as she arranged bolts of fabric—and one small group photo of Heidi standing with her arms folded in the foreground as Gretchen and the two other employees smiled admiringly at her from behind the checkout counter. Amid the paragraphs about how Heidi launched the shop and kept it running with the help of her "able assistants" was one quote from the lengthy interviews Gretchen had given the reporter. "Our customers tell us every day how much the shop reflects Heidi's creativity," Gretchen had told him. "She has a true gift for inspiring new quilters to take up the needle."

If not for that quote and the small staff picture, Gretchen would have not appeared in the article at all. No one who read the magazine would suspect her true role at Quilts 'n Things.

Heidi was throwing a Publication Day Party, so Gretchen could not slip on her sweater and walk home to sort things out on her own. Dazed, she moved through the celebrating crowd, accepting their congratulations, autographing the small group picture, helping customers with their purchases, and keeping up appearances. The cash register rarely paused in ringing up sales. The magazine had indeed brought out the quilters, which ultimately was the most important thing. The success of the shop, she reminded herself when she was finally able to escape home, was more important than personal recognition.

Joe did not entirely agree.

He read the article and might have stormed off to the shop to give Heidi a piece of his mind if his old injury had not been acting up, forcing him to lie prone on the sofa and restrict his movements. "How did she do it?" he asked, eyes glittering with barely suppressed rage. "How did she pull this off? You talked to that reporter for hours."

Gretchen felt dull and tired. "I suppose I didn't sing my own praises enough."

"And Heidi exaggerated hers." He winced as he shifted to his side. "You ought to call that magazine and set them straight."

"What good would that do?"

"They might print a retraction."

"And again, what good would that do?" The quilting world ran largely on goodwill. Anything she said against Heidi would make Gretchen seem small and spiteful, and Quilts 'n Things would suffer for it.

"It would set the record straight. Heidi's taken all the credit."

"She can have it," said Gretchen wearily. "I'm still a partner, no matter what the rest of the world thinks."

But she soon discovered that Heidi was all too willing to believe her own press. In the shop, her requests took on the air of commands. She ignored Gretchen's recommendations when it came time to order new fabric. She adjusted their schedules so that Gretchen worked every weekend instead of alternating with her as they had always done before. She slipped so naturally into the role of manager that it was difficult to disagree with her without seeming petty. Their other employees did not seem to object to the shift in power, if they even noticed it. Gretchen was struck by the alarming possibility that from their perspective, perhaps nothing had changed. Perhaps this was the way it had always been, and Gretchen was just the last to know.

Gretchen's love for the quilt shop endured, but she was no longer content. Enjoying her work took more effort, but she put a smile on her face and reminded herself how much better off she was now than she had been as an itinerant quilting instructor and Heidi's housecleaner.

But she was well aware that Heidi deliberately failed to reorder bolts of Gretchen's favorite floral calicos unless a customer made a specific request. She also altered the teaching schedule, assigning more classes to herself and fewer to Gretchen. Gretchen found it difficult to criticize the changes. From an economic standpoint they made perfect sense, as an increasing number of their customers preferred Heidi's methods. And yet she missed the old days, when she felt more useful, more relevant.

When Heidi began self-publishing a line of original patterns under the Quilts 'n Things name, Gretchen welcomed the new direction for their partnership, hoping that it would renew her creative spark as well as her interest in the job. She missed that sense of anticipation that something unexpected and delightful would be waiting for her when she went into work each day. But when she approached Heidi with two designs that she wanted to publish, Heidi balked. "These are nice quilts," said Heidi, returning the drawings with an apologetic shrug, "but they don't really have the right look for the line."

"What do you mean?" asked Gretchen, hurt.

"Well, they're kind of old-fashioned, don't you think? The first three Quilts 'n Things patterns were for brightly colored, fun, modern quilts. Yours are more . . . retro. You're locked into this blocky-blocky sampler style, and most quilters have moved beyond that." Heidi spoke gently, but that took none of the sting from her words. "Why don't you try to make a more contemporary design, and maybe we can consider publishing that?"

Gretchen tried to convince Heidi that many quilters still enjoyed making samplers, as evidence pointing to the brisk sales within their own shop of books like *Dear Jane, Quilted Diamonds,* and *My Journey with Harriet.* Their customers' requests that they stock more reproduction fabrics indicated that the "retro" look appealed to quilters as much as contemporary designs did.

When Heidi continued to refuse, Gretchen grew indignant. "I am as much a part of Quilts 'n Things as you are," she declared.

"A pattern line using the Quilts 'n Things name should represent my style as well as yours."

Heidi turned away, shaking her head. She busied herself with paperwork on the desk and muttered under her breath.

A word caught Gretchen's ear. "What did you say?" The office door was open and passing customers might hear, but she did not care.

"I said that you're the *junior* partner," said Heidi. "You apparently need the reminder. I can't put my store's name to anything I'm not proud of. If you don't like it, my daughter would be happy to buy out your share, or you can be a silent partner and not come into the shop anymore."

Shocked, Gretchen could not reply. Heidi studied her for a moment, took her silence as submission, and left Gretchen alone in the office.

Gretchen went home without a word for anyone. She called in sick the next morning and was relieved when one of the part-time employees answered so she did not have to speak to Heidi. Heidi would consider her excuse a lie, but it was not. Gretchen *was* sick—sick at heart, sick and tired. Worst of all was the sinking suspicion that Heidi's decision was justified. Gretchen's quilts *were* old-fashioned. She had branched out from her beloved floral calicos in recent years to tone-on-tones and graphic prints, but her quilts were still composed of traditional blocks in traditional layouts. They were beautifully and exquisitely made, if she did say so herself, with perfect points and graceful curves, each tiny piece in its precise and perfect place. But in an age of raw edge appliqué and fusible webbing, none of that seemed to matter anymore.

It was time she faced facts: The quilting world had passed her by. She felt like a mother who had nurtured a child from the utter dependence of infancy through the awkward teenage years only to watch her child suddenly blossom into a Phi Beta Kappa cardiologist or Supreme Court justice or rocket scientist too busy and too important to call home anymore. She had loved quilting at a time when few others did, but it had grown away from her, and she could not change to keep up with it. A woman like her was fortunate to have any connection at all to the wider quilting world beyond her own sewing machine and lap hoop. She would be a fool to throw that away.

And she had Joe to think about. The years had not been kind to his old injury, and there were days when his back was so stiff and painful that he could not manage his tools. For years he had spoken wistfully of retiring to the country, where he could enjoy his woodworking without the pressure to complete pieces for clients. Gretchen longed to grant him that wish, but they knew they had to remain in the city so Gretchen could work. Retirement was a long time off for both of them. It might never come.

When Gretchen returned to the quilt shop, chastened and resigned, she and Heidi continued on as if their confrontation in the office had never occurred. Perhaps as a conciliatory gesture, from that day forward Heidi worked on the Quilts 'n Things patterns away from the shop, on her own time, and never asked Gretchen to hang the pattern packs on the display rack or to fill Internet orders. Occasionally, Heidi would admire a quilt Gretchen had made and agree to consider it for the Quilts 'n Things pattern line; she must have thought she was being supportive and encouraging, but the sketches and instructions always ended up in Gretchen's employee mailbox with a brief note of rejection providing only the vaguest of explanations why they were not suitable. Gretchen found Heidi's ongoing interest painful to bear. It would have been a relief had Heidi stopped asking for submissions they both knew she would eventually reject.

It would have been a greater relief if Heidi had limited their contact to the hours they spent within the store, but apparently that was not to be. Gretchen had worked for Heidi for so long that she could hardly refuse to help when asked, not without putting greater strain on an already troubled relationship. And if Heidi more frequently asked her to do unpaid favors outside of the quilt shop, Gretchen never acknowledged that she complied because she was the junior partner, or because Heidi's daughter was waiting in the wings to buy out her share.

On the afternoon of Heidi's party, Gretchen left one of the part-time employees in charge of closing the shop and ran Heidi's errands at the dry cleaner's, the bakery, and the florist. Then it was off to the Muellers' large home in an arboreal neighborhood of Sewickley, where she found a caterer's truck in the driveway behind a van bearing the logo of a professional housecleaning service. A bit put out, Gretchen went around to the back of the house to her usual entrance, wondering why Heidi had asked her to come over when she apparently already had sufficient help.

Heidi was in the kitchen instructing the two caterers. "Gretchen, finally," she greeted her, taking the dry cleaning. "I'll run these clothes up to the master suite so you can get started."

"What do you need me to do?" asked Gretchen. "You seem to have everything covered."

"You're right. I'm probably fine, but you know how stressed out I get over Chad's business parties. It's easy to throw a get-together for friends, but when the purpose is to impress potential clients . . ." Heidi ran a beautifully manicured hand through her dark brown pixie cut and sighed. "I still have to shower, and dress, and—well, since you're here anyway, would you mind taking a walk through the house to make sure everything is spotless? You never know how hired help is going to perform. My mother always said they do worse on important occasions out of spite."

Gretchen winced, but the caterers and the middle-aged woman scrubbing Heidi's tile floor did nothing to indicate they had overheard, although they could not have avoided it. "Of course," she agreed. Heidi thanked her and hurried off, the recently pressed dress and suit slung over one shoulder, their thin plastic sheathes rustling crisply.

Feeling foolish, Gretchen strolled through the house going through the motions of inspecting the cleaners' work. Heidi could easily handle the task herself, but perhaps she sought Gretchen's professional opinion. She found only two problems so minor that they hardly qualified as problems: The shortest of the four cleaners had neglected to dust a high shelf that Gretchen, too, had occasionally missed back in the day, and an old copy of *Quilter's Newsletter Magazine* had slipped beneath a sofa cushion in the family room.

On a closer look, Gretchen discovered that it was not an old issue, after all, but the most recent. The address label indicated that it was the store copy, from the subscription Heidi had ordered for Quilts 'n Things so the four employees would leave the copies for sale in pristine condition on the racks. They had a longstanding agreement that no one could take the store copy home until everyone else had read it, but Gretchen had never seen this issue. Apparently the rule was flexible where Heidi was concerned.

"Oh, you didn't need to be that thorough," said Heidi, entering the room and finding her replacing the cushion. "I can't imagine our guests will peek under there."

"Do you mind if I borrow this?" asked Gretchen, holding up the magazine. "The cover quilt is exquisite."

Heidi's eyebrows rose in muted incredulity. "It's a little beyond you, don't you think?" She gestured for the magazine. "I'm in the middle of an article. I'll let you have it when I'm finished."

Gretchen reluctantly handed it over. "The other girls might wonder why it's not in the break room."

"Only if you tell them." Then Heidi smiled. "Oh, come on. I'm not the first to bend the rules a little. I promise I'll bring it back as soon as I'm done. There's a quilt I might want to teach next session. I need to study it for a while and make a sample top."

"You could just photocopy those pages."

"Gretchen! I'm surprised at you. That's a violation of copyright law."

Gretchen thought the situation was covered under the Fair Use provision, but she did not want to make a fuss that would delay her return home to Joe. She dropped the subject, told Heidi that the cleaners were progressing nicely, and left before Heidi could assign her another errand.

On Monday morning, she opened the store alone and put on a pot of coffee for early bird shoppers. Heidi's weekends off had extended into Mondays, but Gretchen did not mind. She rather looked forward to days when Heidi was unlikely to stop by. The shipment of *Quilter's Newsletter Magazine* arrived midmorning, so Gretchen unpacked the boxes and stocked the shelves, admiring the cover quilt anew. She wondered how long Heidi would hold on to the store's copy and thought of how they always had one or two of the previous month's issues left over when the new edition arrived.

Surely they could spare one copy, just this once.

At lunchtime, Gretchen left the shop in the care of the part-time helpers, discreetly took a copy of the magazine from the rack, and retired to the break room with her ham sandwich, apple, and pint carton of skim milk. The cover quilt was indeed beyond Gretchen's abilities, as Heidi had rightly noted; the Grand Prize winner of the Tokyo International Great Quilt Festival had taken its maker nearly eight years to complete. Gretchen would have to content herself with admiring the photograph of the original.

She spent a half hour pleasantly browsing through the magazine, lingering over the classified section, where she often picked up ideas from other shops or found a bargain. A quarter-page ad immediately caught her attention, and she held her breath as she read that Sylvia Compson's Elm Creek Quilt Camp was seeking two new teachers.

Elm Creek Quilt Camp. What a lovely, enchanted place it had seemed to Gretchen five years earlier when she and Heidi had visited. Fortunately, Heidi had declared it a research trip and deducted their tuition and fees from the Quilts 'n Things account or Gretchen would not have been able to afford to go. Heidi had heard about the marvelous success of the Elm Creek Quilters and was exploring the possibility of creating a similar quilters' retreat closer to home. Gretchen had had a wonderful time, but was not surprised when Heidi concluded that they could not possibly reproduce what Sylvia Compson and her associates had created. "If I had inherited an enormous mansion in the middle of the countryside, I could do it, too," she grumbled as they drove home. Gretchen refrained from pointing out that Heidi had inherited something very much like it, along with an impressive trust fund. What Heidi lacked was a group of close quilting friends she could rely upon to help run the business as Sylvia had in the Elm Creek Quilters. For all the people who admired Heidi and enjoyed her company, Gretchen was the only person she consistently relied upon.

How wonderful it would be to become a teacher at Elm Creek Quilt Camp, to work side-by-side with the marvelous woman who had inspired her in college so many years before. She envied the lucky women who would be invited to join that remarkable circle of quilters.

Then she thought some more. Well, why not? Why couldn't she be one of those lucky quilters? In fact, this job, coming along at precisely the right time, could be an answer to her prayers. She could make a break from Heidi and yet remain within the quilting world. The ad said a live-in arrangement was possible; living at Elm Creek Manor would fulfill Joe's dream of retiring to the country. The estate was large enough that they could surely find a place for him to set up a woodworking shop—perhaps in that red barn the caretaker used.

Gretchen pulled hard on the reins of her wildly galloping imagination. She had not even applied and she was already packing the moving van. It would not be easy to move from the home she and Joe had shared throughout their married life, and at their ages, it would be challenging to put down roots someplace new. When it came right down to it, Joe might not want to try. She would speak to him before allowing her hopes to rise.

But she already knew that she would gladly take the least desirable classes at the worst times of the day for the opportunity to become an Elm Creek Quilter.

At the end of the workday, she bought the magazine and hurried home to show it to Joe. "Huh," he said, scanning the ad. "What do you know."

"Is that all you're going to say?"

"Well . . ." He searched her expression for the right answer. "Looks like they're hiring in Waterford. Too bad it's hundreds of miles away. That's a long commute."

"We could move."

He shrugged. "I suppose we could."

"Joe, I want to apply for this job."

He studied her, and she knew he could tell she was serious. "Well, all right then. Give it your best shot. They'd be lucky to have you."

The best thing about Joe was that he sincerely believed that.

Gretchen had not typed a résumé in more than twenty years. She no longer even owned a working typewriter. When Joe agreed that neatly printing her application materials by hand looked unprofessional, she went in early to Quilts 'n Things every day for a week to use the store's computer unnoticed, though she suffered pangs of guilt for using company resources to obtain another job. She had many lesson plans from which to choose, while three of her favorite students wrote letters of recommendation and promised not to divulge her plans to anyone. Joe was an able photographer and had taken pictures of all Gretchen's quilts throughout the years. She wished he had not insisted that she pose with them. Compared to the glossy, perfectly lit photos in the quilt magazines, hers always looked like amateur snapshots—which, she supposed, they were. An amateur photographic record of how her quilts had remained timeless while she had aged.

She sent off her application with a hope and a prayer.

Six weeks later, just as she was beginning to wonder if her package had been lost in the mail, a young woman from Elm Creek Quilt Camp phoned to invite her for an interview. She also asked Gretchen to design an original quilt block to represent Elm Creek Quilts. Gretchen planned her design as she made supper that evening: She would take the traditional Oak Leaf block, alter it to resemble elm leaves, and place a Little Red Schoolhouse block in the center. It was so literal and obvious she worried that other applicants might come up with the same idea. She would have to rely upon her precise handiwork to give her the edge.

It was far more difficult to summon up the courage to ask for the time off so she could travel to Waterford. Gretchen did not know what to tell Heidi.

"That's easy," said Joe. "Lie."

"I couldn't do that," said Gretchen, surprised that he would suggest it. "I don't want to and I can't do it convincingly anyway."

"If you tell her you're going for a job interview, she'll either fire you or make you so miserable that you'll wish she would."

Gretchen knew that, too. She could not risk the job she had for the one she wanted. Together she and Joe worked out a solution: Gretchen would say she needed the time off for professional development to improve her teaching opportunities. That was true. Misleading and incomplete, but true.

"Professional development?" asked Heidi dubiously a few days later when Gretchen asked for the time off.

Gretchen nodded. The phrase was a holdover from her substitute teaching days, the reason many teachers had given for needing her services.

"You never needed 'professional development' before."

"I needed it," Gretchen clarified. "I just never asked for time off for it."

Heidi shrugged and granted her the days off, perhaps hoping that Gretchen would return prepared to embrace the way of quick-pieced, rotary-cut, one-day quilts.

On the day of the interview, Joe offered to drive her to Elm Creek Manor. As much as Gretchen longed for his company and moral support, she knew three hours in the car would leave his back in painful knots. He stowed her overnight bag in the trunk, kissed her, and held her for a long time.

"Do you have your maps?" he asked, after her gentle reminder that she had a schedule to keep.

"Yes, honey, but I remember the way." She gave him one last hug and climbed into the car.

"Do you have your triple A card?"

"Yes, and my AARP card and my charge card." She buckled her seat belt. "And my driver's license and registration."

"Do you have change in case you need to call me?"

"I have four quarters in my purse," she assured him. "Don't worry so much. I'll be fine."

She blew him a kiss as she pulled out of the driveway. He followed the car to the sidewalk and was still standing there when other houses and street signs blocked her sight of him in the rearview mirror.

Gretchen had not taken such a long car trip alone in many years, not since she gave up traveling to teach at other quilting guilds. A book on tape she had checked out from the library kept her company as the car wound through the familiar, forested hills of western and central Pennsylvania until she reached Elm Creek Manor, nearly two hours before her interview. She parked in the lot behind the manor and listened to the tape until the end of the chapter, then shut it down and wondered how to fill the time. She decided to stroll through Elm Creek Manor and see if anything had changed since her visit.

Entering through the back door, Gretchen passed by the kitchen and stopped short at the sight. It was in a state of utter disarray, with cupboard doors hanging ajar, dirty pots and pans loaded into the sink, and dishes cluttering every countertop. It was nothing like the warm, busy, cozy place she remembered, and she could not imagine Sylvia Compson standing for it. She hoped the rest of the camp had not experienced a similar decline.

To her relief, the rest of the manor seemed to be in perfect order. Smiling campers passed her in the halls, chatting with one another or lost in thought as they contemplated the day's classes. A peek into the banquet hall revealed four young men clearing away the lunch dishes. One dark-haired young man seemed to be in charge, but the others seemed to follow his direction only grudgingly. If they were the new kitchen staff, that would certainly account for the state of the kitchen.

Gretchen moved on to the ballroom, her favorite place in the manor and where she had spent most of her time during her week at camp. The room bustled with activity, and every glance into a classroom revealed quilters working busily as their instructors demonstrated techniques or strolled past tables checking their students' progress. A murmur of nostalgia and longing tugged at her. *If only,* she thought. If only she could get the job, she would belong here. This was where she was meant to be. She could not bear to spend the rest of her days dissatisfied and unappreciated at Quilts 'n Things, or worse yet, set adrift with only the purchase price of her share in the store to sustain her.

She had lingered long enough in a doorway for the instructor to glance up and catch her eye. "Would you like to come in?" the dark-haired, ruddy-cheeked woman invited.

Gretchen shook her head in apology and moved on. She left the partitioned section of the ballroom for the dais where, she remembered, a few quilters would often gather to work on their projects when they were not scheduled to be in class. If she could engage them in conversation, she might be able to glean some information about the state of the camp that might help her in her interview.

Five women had pulled up chairs in a half circle and worked on projects of their own as they offered advice to a younger woman hand piecing a nine-patch block. Gretchen quickened her step; sharing some of her hand-piecing secrets would allow her to join the conversation. But as she drew closer, the quilt draped over another woman's lap drew her attention.

"That's a lovely quilt," she said, wondering why it looked so familiar.

The five women looked her way. "Thank you," said the woman Gretchen had addressed, adjusting her lap hoop to offer a better look. The sense that she was looking upon something she knew well increased, but at first Gretchen could not explain why. Of course she recognized the traditional Dogtooth Violet block, because four years earlier, she had made her own Dogtooth Violet quilt and taught it as a class for advanced quilters. Her fingers had memorized the shape of every triangle, the thickness of the folded seam allowances where they met in the middle of each edge, the precise way to hold the central star when attaching the corner triangles so that the bias edges would not stretch and distort the block.

But it was more than just the familiar block. Gretchen stifled a gasp. The plum, green, gold, and black batiks that the other woman had used were much more vivid than the muted florals Gretchen had chosen for her version, but otherwise it was the same quilt. Gretchen quickly scrutinized the other woman's features and dismissed the obvious explanation that she was a former student.

Gretchen had taught the class only once; after the first time, Heidi had banned it from the schedule with the excuse that such small classes barely paid for themselves. Gretchen would have remembered if this woman had been one of her eight students.

But how was it possible that someone she had never met had duplicated her quilt so precisely, down to the size and number of the blocks and the outer border of isosceles triangles alternating in height to echo the Dogtooth Violet shapes? They were traditional patterns; she had not invented them. It was possible that someone else could have made a quilt similar to hers—but identical in every detail except for the fabric?

The woman misinterpreted her stunned silence. "It's not as difficult as it looks," the woman assured her. "The quilt pictured with the pattern was hand pieced, but I machine pieced mine."

"Pattern?" echoed Gretchen.

The woman nodded. "A friend of mine took a class at a quilt shop a few years ago. I kept calling to see if I could sign up for the next session, but they never taught that class again. The quilt shop owner said her teacher wasn't interested."

"She said that?"

The woman nodded. "So my friend gave me her pattern. I could make a copy and mail it to you if you like."

"Thank you, but that's not necessary," said Gretchen. "I designed it."

The other quilters regarded her with new interest, but the woman who had made the Dogtooth Violet quilt looked worried. "I hope you don't mind that we copied your pattern without permission."

Other quilters might, but Gretchen thought one copy was negligible—and the woman had certainly tried to enroll in her class. "I don't mind at all. In fact, I'm pleased that you liked the pattern so much. Your fabric selections are so different from my own that at first I didn't even recognize it as my design."

"Do you have a book?" asked one of the other quilters. "I'd buy it for more patterns like this one. This is exactly the kind of quilt I like: traditional, but versatile enough that I can spice it up with the fabrics I like best."

The others nodded in agreement. "I'm afraid not," said Gretchen.

"You should really think about doing one."

Gretchen smiled. If it were that easy, she wouldn't have been so discouraged by Heidi's refusal to publish her patterns under the Quilts 'n Things line. "Maybe someday."

"Tell us about your quilt," urged another of the women. "What inspired you? How did you get the points so perfect? Did you use foundation paper piecing?"

"I hand pieced mine," Gretchen told them, and she went on to explain how she had made her quilt, from the selection of the block, which she had first seen in a collection of antique patterns, to the choice of the perfect floral calicos and solids, to the layout and piecing of the top. She felt as if she were back in the classroom again, using the new Dogtooth Violet quilt as a visual aid to help explain her process. Midway through her impromptu presentation, the women looked past her as if momentarily distracted. Without breaking the thread of conversation, Gretchen glanced over her shoulder and spotted an elderly woman and a younger, bearded man pausing to watch as they crossed the ballroom a few yards away. She recognized Sylvia Compson at once, but since Heidi had insisted they keep a low profile during their week at Elm Creek manner—and since Gretchen had felt too guilty about their spy mission to introduce herself to Sylvia as a former student—Gretchen doubted Sylvia recognized her. With a pang of worry, she considered ending her talk rather than look like a show-off, but she could not be so abrupt to her new acquaintances. She took a breath and persevered, hoping Sylvia would not think Gretchen had made herself too comfortable at Elm Creek Manor, that she presumed too much.

After she heard Sylvia and her companion continue on their way, Gretchen wrapped up her little talk and bade the quilters good-bye. She left the manor, returned to her car, and sat in the driver's seat watching campers pass in and out of the back door, reflecting upon the chance encounter with a beautiful quilt she had, in a sense, helped create. But how different it appeared from her own quilt and from those of her eight Dogtooth Violet students! She had encouraged them to use floral calicoes and solids in class, and her most daring student had only ventured as far as a geometric, tone-on-tone palette. As a result, her students' quilts resembled differently hued versions of her own rather than an entirely new expression of their individual creativity. What might they have created if she had not steered them toward her own preferences? What might she have learned from them?

Had her resentment of Heidi's rejection of her favorite traditional fabrics blinded her to an entire world of artistic possibilities?

For years, she had clung stubbornly to her favorite blocks and fabrics as if she had to fight Heidi for the right to use them. Would they have remained her favorites if not for that? Would Gretchen's tastes have evolved naturally over time if she had not felt obligated to defend her first choices?

Had her refusal to capitulate to Heidi allowed her to stagnate as an artist?

It was an uncomfortable thought, but she forced herself to face it. For years, she had defined her quilts in opposition to Heidi's instead of striking out on her own independent path. Her designs were fine; the chance encounter in the manor had proven that. But what might her quilts be today if not for her relationship with Heidi? In the very act of struggling to avoid Heidi's influence, she had allowed Heidi's tastes to define her own.

With still more than an hour to go before her interview, Gretchen ate the sandwich and apple she had packed for lunch, wishing she had remembered to bring along something to drink and that she had not left home so early. With too much time to fill, her thoughts bounded from her new uncertainty about her growth as a quilter to the heightened importance of her forthcoming interview until her stomach was in knots.

A continued tour of the manor seemed out of the question, not that Gretchen really believed she was likely to run into anything else as disconcerting as she had already experienced that day. Still, she could not remain in the car working herself into a state of nerves or she would be in no condition to meet the Elm Creek Quilters. She left the car, shutting the door firmly behind her, and strode briskly away from the manor, across the bridge over the creek, past the red banked barn, and into the orchard, where already fruit was ripening. The fragrance of the apples and the sound of birdsong restored her sense of calm, and she resolved to put forth her best effort in the interview.

She prepared for their questions as she wandered among the rows of Red Delicious and Jonathan apple trees, rehearsing possible answers and points she intended to raise if the interviewers did not. With still more than a half hour to go, she returned to the manor in time to witness the back door open with a bang and the bearded man from the ballroom emerge, briefcase in hand. He strode across the parking lot and climbed into a newer model blue car, shaking his head in either disgust or disbelief. She instinctively turned aside as he drove past, but he did not appear to even notice her, much less recognize her as the presumptuous woman making herself too much at home at the front of an impromptu Elm Creek Quilt Camp class.

With any luck, Sylvia would have the same reaction. Gretchen stopped by her car for her purse and the accordion file containing her Elm Creek Quilts block, steeled herself, and returned to the manor. When she passed the kitchen, she glimpsed two of the young men from the banquet hall scrubbing pots halfheartedly while another swept the floor. Her fingers itched to take the broom and demonstrate the proper technique, but she left him to it.

Assuming that one of the Elm Creek Quilters would expect to

meet her at the front door, she headed toward the front foyer, but just before she reached it, she heard voices coming from a room on her left. She glanced through the open doorway and discovered the Elm Creek Quilters gathered within a charming Victorian parlor. She paused and rapped twice on the open door.

"Hello," she greeted them, smiling as they looked up from an intense conversation. "I'm Gretchen Hartley. I've come for an interview. I realize I'm a bit early. Should I wait outside?"

"No, come right in," said a brunette in her thirties, whom Gretchen recognized as Sarah McClure, one of the founders of Elm Creek Quilts. "Our last interview ended early."

She said the last with a disapproving frown for an attractive blonde woman at least ten years her senior, who responded with a pout of injured innocence.

"Please sit down," said Sylvia Compson, gesturing to an armchair on the other side of a coffee table from the Elm Creek Quilters. Gretchen nodded and took her seat. She waited nervously during the few moments the Elm Creek Quilters took to rearrange papers and files. Before long, Sarah looked around the group, noted that everyone was ready to begin, and turned to Gretchen with a smile and a request to describe her quilting experience.

At sixty-six, Gretchen had a lot of history to share. She told them about the old days, when she felt as if she was the only woman who quilted anymore, and how the quilting revival had brought her new opportunities to teach and lecture. She described the founding of Quilts 'n Things, carefully selecting details to avoid any appearance of conflict with Heidi. She reflected upon how she had traveled to quilt guilds, conferences, and trade shows—to teach and to learn, to observe shifting trends in the modern quilting world, and to pass on the traditions that previous generations had bequeathed her. This wealth of experience made her uniquely qualified to become an Elm Creek Quilter.

Or at least that was what she tried to tell them. Joe had made her promise to promote herself as if she were praising her best friend, but Gretchen had been brought up to believe that no one liked a woman who bragged, that confidence was often mistaken for arrogance, and that it was always best to err on the side of modesty and allow others to sing her praises on her behalf. She struggled to articulate how much she had to offer Elm Creek Quilts, but to her own ears her voice sounded meek and humble, as if she felt undeserving of the honor of their presence, as if she knew she were only Heidi Mueller's cleaning lady suffering delusions of grandeur. For the first time since childhood, she wished she were more like Heidi, who never allowed anyone to see her disturbed by a moment of self-doubt.

"I'm familiar with the Quilts 'n Things pattern line," said Sarah. "Have you published any of your designs?"

"No." Compelled to be completely honest, Gretchen added, "I have submitted designs to my business partner, who makes the selections, but she didn't believe my quilts fit in with the rest of the line."

"And yet your patterns are being distributed by your former students and enjoyed by others," remarked Sylvia. "Or so I overheard earlier today. I'm surprised you didn't mention it."

Gretchen shrugged. "I didn't think that counted. And—I didn't want to brag."

Several Elm Creek Quilters exchanged smiles of amusement. "This is an occasion when bragging is perfectly acceptable," Sarah told her.

"I understand," said Gretchen. "But bragging isn't something that comes naturally to me."

"That much is apparent," said Sylvia, the corners of her mouth turning in the barest hint of a smile. "In fact, you must be the most inappropriately unassuming quilter I've ever met. You talk about how the quilting revival gave you so many opportunities, and yet never once do you point out that without quilters such as yourself nurturing and passing on the traditions of quilting, that revival never would have come to be. Elm Creek Quilt Camp itself likely never would have existed without quilters like you."

For a moment, the praise from her former teacher left Gretchen speechless. "And quilters like you," she said to Sylvia when she had recovered.

Sylvia nodded her thanks, and a look of understanding passed between them.

"That's all well and good," said the pretty woman with the blond curls, "but let's not overstate things."

"By all means, let's hear it," declared Gwen, whom Gretchen recalled as an outspoken woman inclined to make innovative, artsy quilts of the sort Heidi preferred. "You certainly haven't minced words with any of our other applicants. Why start now?"

"Because she made our last applicant flee for his life," said Judy, gesturing toward the door.

Diane raised her hands in appeasement. "I admit I've challenged our applicants. We should. We're Elm Creek Quilts. We ought to have the most rigorous hiring procedure around."

Sylvia regarded Diane sternly over the rims of her glasses. "Thorough questioning is important, dear, but so are respect and diplomacy."

"Of course," said Diane, a faint flush appearing on her cheeks as she studied a copy of Gretchen's résumé. "I agree that you deserve some credit for keeping quilting alive through a long dry spell, Gretchen, but isn't it true that your style never really left the late seventies?"

Gwen shook her head and sighed.

"Diane," warned Sarah. "Tread carefully."

Gretchen forced herself to remain perfectly still in her chair, against her better instincts that were shouting at her to follow the previous applicant's example and flee for the door. "If you're suggesting my quilts are traditional, I accept that. Willingly. But I must add that my traditional quilts and traditional ways appeal to many quilters. My students' achievements and my full lecture schedule are proof of that."

"You say traditional," said Diane. "I say old-fashioned. If I had not been warned to use tact, I might have said dowdy or frumpy instead. I definitely would have said boring."

"That is quite enough," said Sylvia. "Do I have to ask you to leave?"

"I won't leave before asking her about this." Diane pulled a sheet of paper from the file on her lap. Gretchen could not read what was printed upon it, but it brought uncertainty to the Elm Creek Quilters' expressions. "You might not like my tactics, but you have to admit this raises doubts about her qualifications to teach for us—and her truthfulness."

Gretchen could not imagine what she was talking about. Every detail of her résumé was true, if understated. Her students' letters of recommendation praised her so highly that she had almost been too embarrassed to include them in her packet.

"Even if you don't care for my quilts," said Gretchen, breaking into the sudden silence, "I hope you can agree that my artistic style and my teaching ability are two very different things. My skills are sound whether or not you like what I do with them. I have taught for a very long time, and I've taught many different types of students successfully."

"Not everyone thinks so."

Gretchen stared at Diane in confusion. What on earth could she mean?

"Allow me to share a few excerpts from an employer evaluation." Diane frowned at the page in her hand. "'Mrs. Hartley runs her classes in a strict, didactic fashion and is impatient with questions. . . . She is short-tempered and sarcastic with anyone who suggests modernizing her patterns or techniques. . . . Her classes are the least popular of those offered at our shop and the drop-off in attendance each week is significant.' Shall I go on?"

Gretchen felt tears welling up in her eyes. The letter had said "our shop." *Heidi* had written those hateful things about her. "You called Quilts 'n Things?" she managed to say. "You told them I'm applying for this job?"

Diane regarded her incredulously, and Gretchen realized that the first words from her lips should have been an emphatic denial. Now it appeared that she agreed with the evaluation and was distressed only because the Elm Creek Quilters had discovered the truth.

"Of course we called the shop," said Diane. "We had to check your references. You only had two, and everyone from your era retired from the Ambridge School District a long time ago."

Gretchen blinked back the tears and cleared her throat. "I have no idea why my employer said those things, unless she's angry that I'm looking for another job. All I can tell you is that those—those things are simply not true."

"Indeed," said Sylvia dryly. "One wonders why she has kept you on so many years if you are so dreadful a teacher."

"One wonders something else," said Sarah, studying Diane. "Why would you of all people want to undermine Gretchen's chances for this job? You're an old-school quilter yourself. For years you've been telling us to offer more hand-piecing classes, more hand-quilting workshops. I've heard you say that only quilts made entirely by hand are true quilts. And here we have an applicant who is everything you say you want. Why aren't you begging us to offer her the job?"

"That's right," said Summer, her expression taking on a new light of understanding. "You're not only nasty to the quilters you don't want to hire. You're nasty to everyone."

Warily, Diane looked around the circle of suspicious quilters. "I'm just a nasty person."

"True," cried Gwen. "You heard her admit it. I didn't say it this time. She said it herself."

Sylvia sighed, rose from her chair, and sat beside Diane. "The jig is up, my dear," she said gently, taking Diane's hand. "Why don't you tell us what this has been all about?"

Diane maintained her expression of wide-eyed innocence for only a moment before it crumpled into distress. "I don't want to hire anyone."

"Of course, dear." Sylvia patted Diane's hand. "I understand."

Gretchen didn't, and by the look of things, neither did the other Elm Creek Quilters, who seemed to have forgotten her. She was so relieved that the subject had shifted from Heidi's malicious letter that she sat motionless in her chair rather than remind them of her presence.

Diane ran her index finger below her eyelids to prevent her mascara from smearing. "It was working," she told Sylvia defensively.

Sylvia shook her head, smiling in amused sympathy. "No, dear, I don't believe it was."

"I get it," said Summer. "You thought that if we couldn't hire any replacement instructors, Judy and I wouldn't leave."

"You wouldn't," retorted Diane. "You'd never leave knowing how much we still need you. I've told you both a hundred times that you can't be replaced, and you won't be replaced, if I have anything to do with it."

"I'm sorry," said Judy to Diane. "I've accepted another job. I'll miss all of you very much, but I'm still going."

"And I start school next semester," said Summer. "I couldn't postpone my enrollment, not after they accepted my application past the usual deadline."

"Brilliant strategy," remarked Gwen. "Too bad it was doomed to fail on the grounds of sheer silliness. You do realize you've left us worse off than before, right?"

"What could be worse than Summer and Judy leaving us?" said Diane.

The dark-haired teacher who had invited Gretchen into her

classroom sighed. "Judy and Diane leaving us with two openings on our staff that can't be filled because you've insulted and intimidated every applicant."

"I'm still interested in the job," said Gretchen.

All eyes fixed on her.

She shifted uncomfortably in her chair. "If . . . if I'm still in the running. I know my employer gave me a terrible review, but—"

"Oh, please," said Diane. "Anyone can see she's just resentful that you were invited for an interview and she wasn't. How stupid does she think we are?"

Gretchen stared at her. "Heidi applied for the job?"

"We really shouldn't discuss the other applicants," Sarah broke in quickly. "I think we've covered everything, don't you?" The other Elm Creek Quilters nodded. Diane sniffed miserably, accepting the box of tissues Gwen passed her. "Is there anything you'd like to add, Gretchen?"

"Well, there's my block—"

"Of course. Please, show us."

Gretchen quickly brought out the Elm Creek Quilts block she had created and handed it to Sarah. They passed it around the circle, nodding and murmuring in appreciation—even Diane, who had abandoned her show of disapproval. When the block had traveled all the way around the circle, Sarah asked if anyone had any more questions.

"I have one," said Sylvia. "You remind me of one of my star pupils from very early in my career. She was also named Gretchen, but her last name was not Hartley. You wouldn't be her, by any chance, would you?"

Gretchen glowed. Sylvia had called her a star pupil. "Hartley is my married name. I was in your home economics course in college."

Summer stared at Sylvia. "You taught home ec?"

"Only because they wouldn't hire me to teach quilting in the art department." Sylvia fixed her gaze on Gretchen. "Why didn't you mention that you're one of my former students?"

Gretchen fidgeted and gestured to the copy of her résumé in Sylvia's hand. "I described my educational background in some detail."

"Yes," said Gwen, amused, "and you somehow managed to omit that one important fact."

"I honestly didn't think Sylvia would remember me," confessed Gretchen. "I didn't want to seem as if I was taking advantage of an earlier acquaintance, especially since it was so long ago. It didn't seem fair to the other applicants."

"All's fair in love, war, and job interviews," said Sylvia, smiling faintly. "In the future, I hope you won't be so reluctant to sing your own praises."

Gretchen smiled back, her spirits rising. "I'll remember that."

After that the interview wrapped up quickly. Sarah waited while Gretchen retrieved her overnight bag from the car and then led her upstairs to a comfortable suite on the second floor where she would spend the night.

After unpacking her things and hanging up her change of clothes in the wardrobe, Gretchen returned downstairs to call Joe from the campers' phone in the converted ballroom. She passed a white-haired woman perhaps not quite ten years older than herself sewing in an armchair in the foyer.

Suddenly the woman set down her work. "I'm going to flunk out of quilt camp. I just know it."

Gretchen paused. "I don't think you need to worry about that," she said. "The teachers here don't grade your work. All they ask is that you try."

"That's the problem. They'll think I haven't been trying very hard when they see this Rose of Sharon block. They'll think I've been sleeping in class."

"Nonsense. They'll think no such thing." The woman looked unconvinced, so Gretchen added, "Do you want some help?"

"Yes, please. If you have time."

Gretchen didn't, not really. She wanted to call Joe right away so she would have time to properly prepare for dinner with the Elm Creek Quilters, where they would surely continue to evaluate her even though the official interview had ended. It was too bad she had not run into this woman before her interview, when she had so much time to fill. "I'm in no hurry," she said, crossing the foyer.

The woman handed her the Rose of Sharon block, and Gretchen quickly spotted what had so frustrated her: a slight bulge in the side of an appliqué leaf where a perfectly smooth curve should have been. "Your stitches are excellent," remarked Gretchen, inspecting the underside of the block. "The problem must be in the preparation of the appliqué. From the feel of it, I'm guessing you used freezer paper. Did you place it wax-side up on the wrong side of the fabric and iron the seam allowance down so it stuck to the wax?"

The woman nodded. "That's right."

"You might want to try placing it wax-side down instead and ironing it so the whole appliqué sticks to the wrong side of the fabric."

"Wax-side down?" echoed the woman, puzzled.

"That's right. Then take a little glue stick and glue the seam allowance to the smooth side of the freezer paper. Your edges will be smoother and they'll stay put until your appliqué is sewn in place on the background fabric. When you want to remove the paper, just cut through the back as you ordinarily would, and press the block with a damp cloth between the block and your iron to loosen up the glue. The paper will come right off."

Gretchen returned the block to the woman, who was staring at her. "That's very clever."

"I've found it to be a very useful technique."

"I have honestly never heard of that method, not in all my years of quilting."

"I didn't invent it," said Gretchen, startled by a curious look in the woman's eye. "I just picked it up along the way."

"Even so," said the woman, rising. "Even so. Thank you very much, Gretchen."

Gretchen nodded a good-bye and watched as the white-haired woman disappeared into the parlor where the Elm Creek Quilters were still conferring, or perhaps comforting Diane. Only then did Gretchen realize that she had not told the woman her name. She was almost completely certain she had not.

Curious, she almost knocked on the parlor door on the way to the ballroom but decided against it. As she hurried off to tell Joe about her day, she thought of Diane and her desperate, misguided, and rather poorly conceived plan to prevent her friends from leaving. How wonderful it must be to work with friends who loved you enough to risk utter foolishness to keep you close.

The place where one worked and the work one did was not enough. Without the company of good friends, even the most interesting job could become drudgery, something to be endured rather than enjoyed. No wonder Gretchen had been dissatisfied with Quilts 'n Things, a place that most quilters regarded as the mortal world's closest equivalent to heaven.

Whatever else happened, Gretchen knew she could not go back to work for Heidi. Their partnership had fractured beyond repair, and it was long past time for Gretchen to move on. She had made her decision and nothing would change her mind. She did not need to talk it over with Joe, who had been encouraging her to quit for years. She did not need to rehearse her departure speech, or spend hours writing and rewriting a letter of resignation, or worry about what other people would think of her or how Heidi would explain things to their customers after she was gone.

Tomorrow she would stop by Quilts 'n Things on her way home and break the news to Heidi.

Whatever the Elm Creek Quilters decided, Gretchen's days at Quilts 'n Things were over.

Chapter Six

The Elm Creek Quilters

Perhaps to convince Diane that nothing could prevent them from leaving, Summer and Judy wanted to begin discussing the candidates right away, but Sylvia thought they needed some time alone to reflect—and in some cases, to allow their tempers to cool. She announced that they would meet in the parlor the following day between supper and the campers' evening program to deliberate.

Before dismissing them, Sylvia instructed the Elm Creek Quilters to evaluate the applicants based upon everything they had presented since the selection process began, and not only upon the applicants' performances in the interview. It was fair to say that, thanks to Diane, the applicants would have fared better in a classroom with only the questions and problems of real students to confront them.

"We must consider all of the applicants' qualities," said Sylvia. "Not only how many years they've quilted, or how much teaching experience they have, or how many awards and accolades their quilts have won, but all of those things, and more. Why do they want to work here? What will they bring to our circle of quilters, beyond their technical expertise? How will they fit in with us, and how will they complement one another? What will their presence here mean for the future of Elm Creek Quilt Camp? Our choice will say as much about us and what we want for Elm Creek Quilts as it says about those we decide to hire."

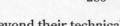

"Can't we just draw straws?" grumbled Diane.

Sylvia smiled. "No, dear. I'm afraid there's too much at stake."

Heidi's eyes went wide. "You can't mean that."

"I do," said Gretchen. Already the office felt like a stranger's. "Please ask your daughter to contact me about purchasing my share of the business. If she isn't interested, I'll find someone else."

"But—but what about the shop? Who will cover for you?"

"I'm sure one of our part-timers would be glad to go full-time."

Heidi's expression was both lost and trapped. "But we've been together so long."

"Perhaps too long." Gretchen shouldered her purse and rose from her chair. "Good-bye, Heidi."

She turned and left the office with her head held high, prouder of herself than she had been in many years.

But she could not deny the small ache of regret that a longtime friendship was over, and that something that had begun with so much promise had ended in disappointment.

The morning after her disastrous interview, Karen woke to a soft rapping on the door to find sunlight streaming in through the window. She sat up with a gasp and frantically searched the bed beside her for the baby. Lucas was not there, nor could she remember getting up in the night to nurse him.

"Good morning, honey." The door eased open and Nate entered, carrying a tray. She caught the aroma of coffee.

"Where's Lucas?"

"Downstairs in the kitchen."

"Alone?" She threw back the covers.

"No, honey, stay in bed. He's not alone. Ethan is keeping an eye on him."

"Our four-year-old is keeping an eye on the baby?"

"Just for a minute. They're eating oatmeal. They're fine."

"When did Lucas wake up?"

"Around four, four-fifteen."

"I didn't hear him. He was in his crib crying for"—she glanced at the clock—"four hours, and I didn't hear him?"

Nate shook his head. "He wasn't crying. I got up with him and gave him a sippy cup. He fell asleep and I put him back in his crib. He slept until about a half hour ago."

"You're telling me he willingly went back to sleep without nursing?"

"And now he's downstairs having breakfast with his brother. I think you're up to date now, just in time for your own breakfast." He unfolded the legs of the tray and set it across her lap. "I made waffles."

"Breakfast in bed." She sat up as Nate placed a pillow behind her back. "Looks like the sufferings of a guilty conscience."

"You could just say thank you."

"Thank you," she said, after a moment. "But you know this doesn't make everything all right."

"I know." He sat down on the edge of the bed. "What will?"

She studied the tray he had prepared for her—waffles in maple syrup, coffee with soymilk, veggie faux sausage, and orange juice. "I don't know."

"I'm sorry I ruined your shot at the job."

She shrugged and picked up her fork. "They haven't said no yet." But she knew it was only a matter of time.

"Daddy!" came Ethan's shout from downstairs.

"Da-Da!" echoed Lucas.

"I think you're being summoned."

Nate nodded and turned to go, but already they heard footsteps scampering on the stairs. Nate snatched up the tray and moved it to the dresser just in time to avoid the two little boys who ran into the room and hurled themselves at Karen. "Mama," cried Lucas, delighted, as he and his brother tumbled over her, burying her in hugs and kisses.

"Hello, Lucas. Good morning, Ethan," she said, hugging Lucas and tousling Ethan's hair. "Did you have a good night?"

"Pretty good. Are you still mad at Daddy?"

She glanced up at Nate, who looked back at her anxiously. "Not so much. And how about you, pumpkin?" She kissed Lucas on his soft cheek. "You were such a good boy, going back to sleep for Daddy so nicely."

"Good," agreed Lucas, snuggling closer for another kiss. He patted her chest. "Muk."

"Oh, muk, is it?" she growled, tickling the boys, who shrieked in delight and tried to get away. "That's all I am to you people: milk in a shirt!"

Nate stood outside the play, closed off from them, watching, but Karen did not draw him in.

Mrs. Stonebridge kept her promise to stay at Ocean View Hills as long as at least one friend remained, but two days after Mrs. Blum left, her son arrived to take her to a new residence near his home in Santa Cruz.

Mrs. Stonebridge was in her eighties now. She had acquired a walker and white hair and aches and pains in her hands that made quilting a challenge, but to Maggie she was the same admirable, diplomatic leader, sorting out differences and disagreements with grace and humor. She had comforted her departing friends and had organized a round-robin quilt project among the Courtyard Quilters. In the days leading up to their separation, each quilter sewed a sixteen-inch block in her favorite pattern. Before the first of many departures, they exchanged blocks. Each quilter would add a border of her own favorite blocks to the center she had received, and on the last day of the month, she would mail the growing quilt top to the next quilter in the circle. After each quilter had added a concentric border to every other quilter's center block, the tops would be returned to their owners in their new residences, a keepsake of dear friends.

In this way their circle of quilters would endure even though they could no longer gather every morning in their favorite chairs by the windows with the view of the courtyard garden.

When it was time for Mrs. Stonebridge to go, Maggie escorted her outside and waited while her son loaded her belongings in the car. "I'll miss you," she said, hugging the older woman. She was startled by how thin and fragile Mrs. Stonebridge felt in her arms.

Mrs. Stonebridge patted her on the cheek. "You take care of yourself, my dear."

Maggie nodded and blinked back tears as Mrs. Stonebridge's son helped her into the front seat. Just as her son started the car, Mrs. Stonebridge rolled down the window. "I forgot to tell you," she called over the noise of the engine. "Guess who's going to be down the hall from me?"

"I don't know," Maggie replied. "Who?"

"Lenore Hicks."

The car pulled away from the curb. "Don't get between her and pie," Maggie shouted.

Mrs. Stonebridge laughed and waved to her through the window until the car turned onto the main avenue and drove out of sight.

Anna did not hear from Gordon for almost a week after the macaroni and cheese dinner at his apartment. She wondered if he had been waiting for her to apologize or if it had simply taken him that long to discover she had left.

She had her answer when she returned home from working as the lead chef at a banquet for the provost, who had requested her by name. Gordon's voice on the answering machine was clipped and irritable. "You were inexcusably rude to sneak out like that without even telling us you were going. Theresa's feelings were hurt. We may not be able to cook like you, but we did our best. Call me if you want to apologize."

Anna didn't. She erased the message and went across the hall to share the banquet leftovers with Jeremy. She hoped Summer had told him whether the Elm Creek Quilters had made their decision, but he had not heard anything.

Two days later, she discovered another answering machine message: "Anna, kitten. I'm not mad anymore. Give me a call and let's talk."

Once again she hit the erase button and did not return his message. She was growing accustomed to his absence and found she did not mind it.

As the days passed, his messages became more worried, more forlorn. "I miss you," he said once, and, "I'm sorry." He did not elaborate, and she suspected he did not know exactly why he ought to be sorry, just that saying so might bring her back.

Maybe it would. He seemed genuinely remorseful, if not for the right reasons. But how would she know for certain unless she gave him another chance?

One afternoon, she came home from work to discover that Gordon had visited her apartment in her absence. He had left a dozen roses in a vase on the kitchen table and a heartfelt note asking her to call and let him know she was all right. In the postscript, he added the last lines of the sonnet he had written her: "Thou shalt in me, livelier than elsewhere, Anna's image see." The memory of a happier occasion pained her.

The sight of the roses had startled her so much that she had left the apartment door ajar, and as she stood gazing at the note and wondering what to do, Jeremy peered in from the hallway. "Nice flowers."

Quickly Anna returned the card to the envelope. "No one's ever given me a dozen red roses before."

"Very romantic."

"You don't have to be sarcastic. He's trying."

"Have you called to thank him?"

"Not yet."

"Are you going to?"

"I don't know." Anna tossed the note onto the table and touched a rose petal. "He hasn't paid so much attention to me in months."

"Take my advice and don't call. That bouquet doesn't mean anything. Anyone can buy flowers. I could buy you flowers."

"It's not just the flowers," Anna insisted. "Gordon cares about me. He gave me a gift—a gift from the heart. He wrote me a sonnet. How many guys do you know who write their girlfriends a sonnet?"

"None," said Jeremy flatly. "And I say that having met Gordon. Let me see this alleged sonnet. I bet it came out of a greeting card."

"I don't have it on me," said Anna, flustered. "Anyway, it's private."

He gestured for her to hand it over. "Come on."

She hesitated, but he was resolute, and she wanted to prove to him that Gordon had written her a poem. Unless Theresa had written it—but she squelched that thought and went to her bedroom for the poem. Reluctantly, she gave it to Jeremy, who unfolded the page and read the words with a deepening frown.

"It's not from a greeting card," she told him.

"I know," he said, and he looked as if he were sorry he had asked. "It's by Sir Philip Sidney, a sixteenth-century English poet. Gordon just changed the woman's name from Stella to Anna. Every undergraduate English major knows this poem."

Anna felt faint. She had been seconds away from calling Gordon to apologize and forgive him everything.

The Elm Creek Quilters were so divided in their opinions about the applicants that the evening of deliberation Sylvia had arranged quickly proved to be insufficient. If they could have chosen by a simple majority vote, they could have selected their two finalists within a day, but Sylvia insisted their decision be unanimous. It would not do to admit someone into their circle of quilters unless everyone could give the newcomer an unqualified welcome.

"But that doesn't mean Summer and I aren't leaving if we can't agree," said Judy.

"I know that," said Diane so quickly that they all knew Judy had interrupted her in the midst of plotting an interminable filibuster.

Within four days they reached their first decision: Karen Wise would not be one of the two finalists. Diane thought that anyone incapable of finding a baby-sitter for a job interview was not resourceful enough to handle the various crises Elm Creek Quilters faced every day. The others considered this view too harsh, but they agreed that although Karen was a fine quilter, she was less experienced than the other applicants. Elm Creek Quilt Camp students expected a great deal from their classes and workshops, and it might be unfair to them—and to Karen—to give them a novice teacher.

"She's never taught quilting, not even at a quilt shop," said Diane, echoing an earlier concern. "I'm not sure why we invited her to an interview."

Because of her letter, Sylvia explained. No other applicant had so perfectly articulated the spirit of Elm Creek Quilts. Sylvia had thought Karen deserved to make her case for that reason alone. If she had taught even a single class at a quilt shop, Sylvia might be willing to take a chance on her, but her teaching experience was too different from what she would face at quilt camp. Karen was simply not ready.

"In a few years, perhaps, but not now," said Sylvia, and with some regret, placed Karen's portfolio on the pile with the other eliminated applicants.

Everyone loved Anna, and not only for the delicious cookies. "I ranked her first out of all the applicants," said Bonnie. "If we ever open a quilt shop here in the manor, her experience at her aunt's store will be invaluable."

"Her aunt's store went out of business," reminded Diane.

"I'm sure that wasn't Anna's fault."

"Gretchen has more relevant quilt shop experience than Anna," said Sarah, who privately was not convinced that the manor ought to include a retail store. "But our most immediate need is for teachers. Anna has taught quilting, but not recently."

"Anna has other talents," remarked Sylvia.

The Elm Creek Quilters exchanged questioning looks. Then Sarah caught on. "Oh, yes. Please. Hire her today."

Summer looked uncertain. "But she applied for a teaching position. Would she be insulted if we asked her to take a different job?"

"It won't hurt to ask," said Gwen.

"Indeed," said Sylvia. "She can always refuse."

She set Anna's portfolio aside.

The Elm Creek Quilters needed another week to decide the fates of the remaining three candidates, who were so well-qualified in different ways that it was difficult to choose. All three had years of teaching experience, each had designed original quilt patterns, each had developed a following that might help boost camp enrollment. Each possessed qualities that made the Elm Creek Quilters eager to welcome them into their circle of quilters, and each raised questions about how they would fit in.

For all Maggie's skill and depth of knowledge of quilt history, she was not very versatile in her style. Would she be willing and able to teach other classes if their campers were not interested in reproducing the Harriet Findley Birch quilt?

"She has taught other classes," said Sarah, reading from Maggie's résumé. "Machine and hand appliqué. Machine and hand piecing. Hand quilting. The list goes on."

"So does her list of upcoming speaking engagements," said Diane. "How committed to us can she be if she's going to be traveling all the time? Are we ever going to get to know her if she just shows up to teach her camp classes and then heads out to a quilt guild as soon as camp is over?"

"I didn't get the impression that she intended to continue her exhausting travel schedule," said Sylvia. "I believe that's why working for us appeals to her so much."

"Anyway, Russell McIntyre has the same problem," said Sarah.

Everyone acknowledged that this was true, and the debate turned to him. All agreed that Russell was an accomplished art quilter who had developed his own style and techniques. As a man in a predominantly women's field, he would indeed bring a new and valuable perspective to Elm Creek Quilts. But he seemed to know very little about quilting history and traditions, and out of all the applicants, he had been the only one to fail Agnes's test.

"It wasn't a fair test in his case," reasoned Gwen, who had placed Russell at the top of her list. "He doesn't do hand appliqué. We knew that."

"He didn't fail the test by not knowing how to help me," said Agnes, removing her pink-tinted glasses and rubbing her eyes wearily. "He failed by not wanting to help."

"But he was on his way out, and he wanted to leave as quickly as possible," said Gwen. "Diane had insulted him."

"Diane insulted everyone," Judy pointed out. "Russell was the only one to leave before the interview was over. He was the only one who refused to help Agnes."

"But . . ." said Gwen, then shrugged. "Never mind. You're right."

Gretchen, on the other hand, had soared through Agnes's test. Not only had she been willing to take the time to help a stranger, she had offered a solution Agnes had never heard of before. "We should hire her at once," said Agnes. "She has so much to offer our students."

"But for how long?" asked Diane. "I like that she's a traditionalist. No one loves quilting by hand more than I do. But isn't Gretchen getting a little close to retirement to make such a drastic career change?"

"It's not that drastic," said Judy. "She's been quilting and teaching for decades."

"Maybe too many decades," said Diane, sparing a furtive glance for the elder Elm Creek Quilters.

"We can't discriminate on the basis of age," said Sarah.

Diane held up her hands. "I'm just saying we need to think of how long the people we choose are likely to stay with us."

Agnes regarded her coolly. "I'm older than Gretchen. Is my job in jeopardy?"

"Of course not," said Diane. "Forget I mentioned it."

But they could not forget, and as the intermittent discussion wore on, the Elm Creek Quilters pieced together a solution with as much care as if it were a quilt they hoped would become a cherished heirloom.

Their first unanimous vote came in favor of Maggie, whose strengths as a quilter, teacher, designer, and historian set her slightly ahead of the other two. After that, their second choice became clear. Most of Gretchen's strengths overlapped with Maggie's, but Russell possessed other skills and experiences Maggie did not. As a pair they complemented each other well, better than Maggie and Gretchen did.

The second unanimous vote came nearly three weeks after the interviews. Once Sylvia was assured all were at peace with their decision, she instructed Sarah to call the applicants.

When the phone rang, Maggie eagerly picked up, hoping the caller was Russell. Since his visit the previous weekend, he had called almost every evening from the road. His quilt guild tour was winding down and he was supposed to return home that afternoon. She had not expected him to call until later, but she was glad he had. She wanted to tell him that she had decided to accept his invitation to visit him in Seattle the following week. She was not sure why she had hesitated, prompting him to add that she should think about it and let him know. No hard feelings if she couldn't come. The guest room would be ready either way.

But the voice on the line belonged to a woman. "Maggie?"

"Yes?"

"This is Sarah McClure from Elm Creek Quilts."

"Oh, of course." Here it came: the moment of rejection she had dreaded. "How are you?"

"Fine, thanks. I'm calling with good news. On behalf of all the Elm Creek Quilters, I'd like to offer you the teaching position. We would be delighted if you would join our faculty."

"I—" Maggie sat down. "Really? You're really offering me the job? But I did so badly in the interview. Are you sure?"

Sarah laughed. "Are you trying to talk me out of it? Of course we're sure. You won't need to begin teaching until the new camp season in March, but we'd like to have you out here no later than January. Does that sound all right?"

"That sounds fine. Better than fine. It sounds wonderful." Then Maggie thought of Russell, and suddenly relocating to Pennsylvania lost its appeal. "I don't suppose you could tell me who the other new teacher is?"

"I really shouldn't, not until I've notified the other applicants."

Maggie felt a thrill of delight. She was the first new teacher Elm Creek Quilts had called.

She hesitated only a moment, a moment in which she considered Russell's qualifications for the job and decided that if the Elm Creek Quilters had chosen her, they surely also intended to make an offer to someone like Russell. Even if they did not, she could not afford to throw away the job offer of a lifetime all because of one marvelous weekend and a dozen phone calls with a man she had only just met. No matter how wonderful he seemed. No matter how much she already liked him. No matter how readily he laughed.

She thanked Sarah and told her she would begin planning her move to Pennsylvania. Sarah promised to be in touch.

As soon as Maggie hung up, she dialed Russell's number. The line was busy.

Maggie smiled as she replaced the receiver. Very likely, he was on the line with Sarah McClure at that very moment.

Russell heard the phone ringing as he unlocked the front door. Dropping his bags on the porch, he bounded inside and snatched up the phone just as the answering machine clicked on.

"Hold on a moment," he called over the outgoing message, fumbling for the off switch. "Okay, sorry about that. Hello?"

"Hello, Russell McIntyre?"

A woman, but not Maggie. "Yes?" he said, disappointed. He should have let the machine get it.

"This is Sarah McClure from Elm Creek Quilts."

"Oh, hi." He had never expected to hear from them after storming out of the interview. The memory of it still embarrassed him.

"I'm calling with good news. After considering all the candidates, we've decided to offer you one of the teaching positions. You won't be expected to teach until the new camp season begins in March, but we'll need you here by January so we can prepare. How does that sound?"

"Uh—" Russell's thoughts flew to Maggie, to her warming

smile, the feel of her hand in his, and knew he could not move so far away from her. "I'm curious. Who else did you hire?"

"I'm afraid I can't say. Not all of the applicants have been notified."

"Oh. Right." Russell considered. Maggie was convinced that she had failed miserably in the interview. She had told him she was certain that she would not be offered the job. He decided to believe her. "I'm afraid my plans have changed. I'm no longer able to accept the job."

"You don't want the job?"

She sounded incredulous, and with good reason. "I'm truly very sorry it didn't work out."

"Is this because of a certain overzealous interviewer?" asked Sarah. "I assure you, our decision to choose you was unanimous, and she's eager to make amends."

"It's not that," said Russell, although he was satisfied to hear it. "I've decided that I want to stay on the West Coast, that's all."

"All right, then," said Sarah, still sounding as if she did not believe he was turning her down. "Would you consider joining us as a visiting instructor on occasion? I still believe we have a lot to offer each other."

"Thanks. I'll consider it," said Russell. "I'm sure we can work something out."

But he was impatient to get off the line. He would rather work out travel arrangements for Maggie's visit to Seattle than for some future, hypothetical visit to Elm Creek Quilt Camp.

"I can't believe it," said Sarah, hanging up. "After all that, he doesn't want the job."

Sylvia shrugged. "After what Diane put him through, I suppose we can't be too surprised."

"I'm surprised," said Sarah. "We aren't the least bit turndownable. Now what are we supposed to do? Call an emergency meeting and have another vote? Deliberate another two weeks? That's just enough time for all of our applicants to find other work or to become so irritated at us for taking so long that they'll brush off our offer just like Russell did."

"I don't think that's necessary," said Sylvia. "There's really only one other choice, don't you agree?"

After two weeks with no word from Elm Creek Quilts, Gretchen was tempted to call and ask how the selection process was going and if she was still in the running. She refrained, in part because she did not want to nag, in part because she was too busy working out the final details of her separation from Quilts 'n Things. Heidi's daughter, submitting to pressure from her mother to decline Gretchen's offer to sell her share of the store, had come around only after other potential buyers surfaced. Rather than allow control of the store to leave the family, Heidi relented, and her daughter eagerly made Gretchen a fair market bid. Now all that was left was the paperwork.

Naturally, all the local quilters were astonished when the news broke that Gretchen was leaving Quilts 'n Things on unpleasant terms. A frenzy of gossip circulated through the quilting bees, spurred on, no doubt, by Heidi's embellished version of recent events. Gretchen refused to demean herself by carrying on her disagreement with Heidi through the rumor mill. When mutual acquaintances asked her what had happened, she told them, simply and without acrimony. Then she left them to make up their own minds. It was too soon to tell which friends would stand by her, which would abandon her out of loyalty to Heidi, and which would try to balance precariously between them, in hopes that one day they might make amends and everything might go back to the way it was before.

Gretchen knew that would never happen. She also knew—and

this was a nagging worry—that she would have to find some work to occupy her time and pay the bills. The sale of her share of Quilts 'n Things would carry her and Joe a little ways, but it would not last forever.

When Sarah McClure finally called, Gretchen's heart leaped and she eased herself into a chair, holding her voice carefully neutral. She could not tell from the young woman's greeting if she intended to deliver good news or bad.

Thankfully, Sarah got right to the point. When she asked Gretchen if she could be available by January, Gretchen said, "I could be available next week if you like. If you need a substitute teacher, I'd be delighted to fill in anytime. Just say the word."

How fortuitous that she had already cleared her calendar by resigning from the quilt shop.

Joe waited nearby until Gretchen hung up. "Well?" he asked.

She flung her arms around him. "How soon can you pack up your workshop? We're moving to Elm Creek Manor!"

Karen was in the kitchen fixing the boys a snack of soynut butter and strawberry jam sandwiches when the phone rang. Sylvia Compson was kind and regretful as she delivered the bad news Karen had expected since leaving Elm Creek Manor.

"I'm very sorry," Sylvia said.

"That's all right." Or it would be, if Karen thrived on disappointment and rejection. "I expected as much when I couldn't find a baby-sitter and the interview turned into a debate on the merits of extended breastfeeding."

"That wasn't the reason at all," said Sylvia. "We appreciate a rousing discussion as much as anyone. We simply found that some of our other candidates had more teaching experience. Perhaps if you teach at your local quilt shop, the next time we hire, you'll be among the most qualified."

"Thank you for the suggestion," said Karen, although she doubted there would be a next time.

When she hung up, she found Nate listening in from the doorway. "Who was that?"

"Sylvia Compson from Elm Creek Quilts."

"And?"

Karen shook her head.

"I'm sorry, honey." Nate wrapped her in a hug, and she rested her head on his chest. "I know you really wanted that job."

"It's all right," said Karen, and she meant it. In a way, it was even a relief. She had no idea how she would have managed working outside the home and raising the boys without driving herself to the brink of exhaustion.

"But I know how much it meant to you." Nate hesitated. "I know you want a paying job so that you can feel like you're doing something important."

"That's not it." Karen pulled away and picked up the knife, slicing Lucas's sandwich into squares and Ethan's into triangles, the way they preferred. "I think that what I do now is important. Not making sandwiches, but all of it. What could be more important than raising my two children to be self-confident, compassionate, moral adults? I just wish other people respected what I do. I know I shouldn't care what other people think, but I wish other people thought that what I do is important."

"And by 'other people,'" said Nate, "you mean me."

She set the knife in the sink and tightened the lid on the strawberry jam jar. "Yes, Nate. I mean you."

"I get it," he said. "I get it."

She doubted he did. If he did get it, if he really understood how she felt—but how could she expect him to understand when she herself could barely sort out her conflicted feelings? She loved her children dearly. They were more precious to her than any job could ever be. But one moment she felt utterly fulfilled by motherhood, and the next as if she were trapped, spent, finished. Old and ugly, tired and used up. She missed feeling special. She missed that sense of anticipation that everything lay ahead of her, anything was possible, that she could do anything, be anything, be admired and cherished and beloved. She missed feeling wanted for herself, for the woman she was and not merely the housekeeping chores she performed. At the same time, she knew that taking care of her children was her duty and her calling and whatever she did or failed to do in the boys' early years would affect them so profoundly that nothing else she ever did would leave such a mark on the world. She was angry that no one appreciated the importance of the task appointed to her and ashamed that she wished she could escape its drudgery. She felt both taken for granted and selfish. She was ashamed that she could not simply enjoy her beautiful sons, children any parent would be grateful to have, and that what seemed to come so naturally to other women was a continuous uphill struggle for her. She felt like a failure, hopelessly inadequate to a task that was far too important to entrust to anyone else.

If she could have joined the circle of quilters at Elm Creek Manor—that would have made her special again. She knew how foolish it was to feel that way, but she could not help it. If Nate only knew how fortunate they both were that she had sought fulfillment from a new job rather than another man. But it didn't matter now.

"I'm sure you honestly believe you do understand," she told Nate, and called the boys for lunch.

Nate said nothing. He left the kitchen frowning, but not in anger. He frowned as he did when wrestling with an especially difficult piece of computer code.

Later, while the boys napped, Nate found her in the basement where she worked on the last block for her Pickle Dish quilt. "I made a spreadsheet," he announced.

"That's great, honey," she said, not really listening. It was hardly a revelation. He made spreadsheets all day long.

"No, I mean I made one for us." He turned her chair and placed a thin stack of papers in her hands. She glanced at them, curious. "It's a schedule. A new, revised family schedule."

"Can something be both new and revised?" she asked dubiously, paging through the sheets. She paused at the sight of a block of time labeled in blue. "What's this?"

"That's 'Mom Time.'"

She could read; she just didn't know what it meant. "That's when I do my mom work? Because there's no way I can fit everything into two and a half hours after supper."

"No, that's when you're *not* allowed to do any mom work. See? I'll come home at five-thirty every night. No exceptions. We'll have supper, and then from six until eight-thirty, you do whatever you like. Read a book, talk on the phone with your mom, take a long bath—"

"Speaking of baths, if I'm reading or talking, who—"

"*I'll* give the boys their baths. I'll get them their snacks, play with them, brush their teeth, read stories, all the things you usually do so you can have time for yourself." He shrugged. "Maybe you could even use that time to teach a class at the quilt shop so you can get the experience the Elm Creek Quilters are looking for."

"But you've always needed the evenings to work. Won't you go through laptop withdrawal?"

"If I can't get my work done during the day, I can finish after the boys go to bed."

She shook her head, skeptical. "Taking care of the boys doesn't mean parking them in front of the TV, you know."

"I know that. Karen, I want to help, but you have to let me."

He had a point; she knew it. Now that he had finally offered to share more of the parenting load, she couldn't refuse because he would not do everything as well as she did. She'd had years of practice. He would need time to catch up, to learn how to care for the boys his own way, because her way was not the only right way.

Perhaps she would look into teaching a class at her favorite quilt shop.

Perhaps someday she would have a second chance to join the circle of quilters at Elm Creek Quilts.

Maggie called Russell twice more before reaching a ring instead of a busy signal. When he answered, she breathlessly said, "Was that Elm Creek Quilts on the line?"

"Maggie?"

"Yes, it's me. Hi! How was your trip? You had a busy signal. Were you speaking with Sarah McClure?"

"How did you know?"

"Because they called me, too, right before you. I knew they'd offer you the job. I knew it! You couldn't possibly have done as badly in the interview as you said."

"You mean they offered you the other teaching position?"

"Yes! Won't it be fun to work together?"

Russell let out a heavy sigh.

"What's the matter?" asked Maggie. "Didn't Sarah call to offer you the other job?"

"Yes. She did."

"Then what's wrong?" Suddenly Maggie had a horrible thought. He did not want to work with her. Or see her again. She had completely misinterpreted his signals. It wouldn't be the first time. "If you're worried that I might—you know, expect to see you all the time, I wouldn't. I just thought—"

"Maggie, that's not it. I turned down the job."

"Why?"

"Because I didn't want to move so far away from you."

His words warmed her heart—for a moment. "You didn't think I'd get the job?"

"*I* thought you would, but *you* said you didn't stand a chance."

"And you believed me?"

"Yes! Yes, I did. I have a terrible problem with that. When people tell me something, I tend to believe them."

Maggie burst into helpless laughter. It would have been flattering if he had assumed she would be offered the job, but it was even more revealing that he had turned down his offer in order to be closer to her. "What do we do now?"

She held her breath, fearful that he would suggest she reject her offer, too. She couldn't. She couldn't afford to even if she wanted to.

"I'll call Sarah back," said Russell. "Maybe it's not too late. I'll tell her I changed my mind."

"Call me right back and let me know what she says."

"I will. I promise. I have to hang up now."

"I know."

"I'll call you right back."

"Okay."

"You hang up first. I can't hang up on you."

"Russell, you're being silly." But she was tickled. "Okay. I'll hang up first."

And she did.

Cursing himself, Russell raced to his office, dug his notes on Elm Creek Manor from his files, and punched in the phone number. Another young woman answered, and he asked for Sarah. He paced impatiently around the room as far as the phone cord would allow while he waited for her to pick up the extension.

Finally she answered. "Russell? Sorry for the wait. What can I do for you?"

"I've reconsidered and I'd be happy to accept your offer," blurted Russell. "I can start whenever you like."

"I'm sorry," said Sarah. "I've already given the job to someone else."

In less than thirty minutes? "Then I'm too late?"

"I'm afraid so. The other applicant has already accepted the job." Sarah sounded sincerely regretful. "I know it's not the same, but we would still like to have you as a visiting instructor."

"Yes," said Russell quickly. "Anytime. For as long as you like."

"We won't have our schedule ready until late winter. I'm not sure what we'll have available. It might not be more than two or three weeks throughout the whole camp season."

"I'll take any openings you have. All of them."

"Sure," said Sarah. He knew she was wondering what had inspired his new enthusiasm. "We'd be glad to have you."

He hoped so. He intended to become Elm Creek Quilt Camp's most frequent visiting instructor.

On Saturday afternoon, the Elm Creek Quilters bade their campers good-bye and settled back to enjoy their one evening off before the next group of quilters began to arrive on Sunday. They completed their last chores of the week together, relieved to have reached the end of their search for new teachers, full of anticipation for what the newcomers would bring, and saddened by the approaching departure of two dear friends. They would not have many more days like this one, when all of the original Elm Creek Quilters were together, celebrating the end of another successful week.

When the work was finished, they lingered on the veranda rather than returning to their own homes and families right away. They chuckled about the week's mishaps, made plans for the next session of camp, and mulled over Russell McIntyre's inexplicable change of heart.

"I hope we made the right choice," said Diane.

"Time will tell," said Sylvia. With a sigh, she rose stiffly from her chair and rubbed her hands together. She noted ruefully that they seemed to have become permanently waterlogged. "In the meantime, I have a sink full of dirty dishes awaiting me."

"I'll help," said Summer, rising. "I'll be glad when Anna can start."

Sarah gasped.

All eyes turned to her.

"You did call her, didn't you?" asked Gwen.

Sarah shook her head. "I was so thrown by Russell's refusal that I forgot."

"Never mind," said Sylvia. "I'll take care of it."

"I'm sorry," said Anna. She never should have answered the phone. "But I can't."

"Please," begged Gordon. "Just give me another chance."

"What good would it do?" asked Anna. Why didn't he see it? They were unsuited for each other. They did not make each other happy. If she took him back, nothing would change. Forcing themselves back into couplehood would not resolve their differences. She would always worry that he considered her inferior; he would always nag her about her weight and her lack of interest in Derrida. She would always wonder if he preferred Theresa; he would forever hope in vain that she would take an office job in a building without a kitchen, a lunchroom, or even so much as a vending machine.

"It won't work," she told him firmly. "We don't work."

"I can change. Tell me how and I will."

She didn't want him to change for her any more than she wanted to change herself for him. "Good-bye, Gordon."

"Wait," he cried as she began to hang up. "'Come, Sleep; O Sleep! the certain knot of—'"

"Stop right there," said Anna. "I can't stand all that silly unrequited courtly love stuff. It's so annoying. You're not Sir Philip Sidney and I'm not Stella. Don't dream about me, don't plagiarize poems for me, and, whatever else you do, don't call me."

She hung up the phone with a crash. Almost immediately, it rang again. Irritated, Anna snatched up the receiver. "I mean it. If you don't stop calling, I'm going to block your number."

"I beg your pardon?"

"Sylvia?" gasped Anna. "I'm so sorry. I thought you were someone else."

"I certainly hope so. I can't imagine what I might have done to warrant that greeting."

"I really do apologize." Anna groped for an explanation. "Boyfriend trouble."

"Of course. It usually is. Well, whatever the young man has done, I believe I have some news that might cheer you up."

"Really?"

"When you visited the manor, you may have noticed the state of our kitchen."

How did they know? "I did sort of sneak a peek in passing."

"Our chef recently retired, and his replacement quit after only a week. We've been at loose ends ever since trying to take care of all the cooking in addition to teaching and managing the camp. In your interview you mentioned that you hope someday to own your own restaurant. The position I can offer you is not quite the same, but you would be in charge of all of our food service—planning the menus, preparing meals, purchasing supplies, and so forth."

Anna sat down so suddenly that she landed hard on the arm of her chair. "I would be in charge? I would be the head chef?"

"Why, yes. In fact, you would be our only chef."

Anna's thoughts whirled. Working for Elm Creek Quilt Camp would be very much like running her own restaurant. No more cafeteria lines, no more indifferent student employees to prod along, no more lunch lady jokes. She would be the head chef of—of a hotel. A resort. And she already knew she would like her coworkers.

"We offer room and board in addition to your salary, if you wish," said Sylvia, adding dryly, "and we could arrange for caller ID on your phone extension."

“I’d love to be your chef,” said Anna. “On two conditions. First, I’ll need to hire a few assistants.”

“Our previous chef had assistants. I would not expect you to do without. What is your second condition?”

“We remodel your kitchen,” said Anna. “At the very least, you’ll need a six-burner stove and a double oven. Your pantry is fine, but you need more counter space and a much larger refrigerator. I don’t know how you’ve managed, considering all the people you feed.”

“You seem to have given this a great deal of thought for someone who took only a quick peek into the kitchen in passing,” remarked Sylvia.

“It might have been more than a peek. You really do need to expand. How often do you use that little room off the kitchen?”

“My sitting room?” asked Sylvia. “Well, not as much as I used to, I suppose.”

“If we knocked out that wall . . .”

“Oh, my. I had no idea you had such extensive changes in mind.” Sylvia considered. “However, I must admit you’re right. We are long overdue for an upgrade. Our last chef was miserable with the state of the kitchen, but he was less determined than you to ask for what he needed.”

Anna smiled and did not mention that this was a rather recent upgrade of her own.

Cradling the phone between her shoulder and ear, she dug in her tote bag for her pad of graph paper and a pencil. She flipped past the floor plan of Chuck’s Diner and began a new sketch, planning the kitchen of her dreams with her new boss.

Anna couldn’t wait to show that circle of quilters—*her* circle of quilters—all she could do.